ZANE GREY

THE DESERT OF WHEAT

HarperPaperbacks
A Division of HarperCollins*Publishers*

HarperPaperbacks   *A Division of* HarperCollins*Publishers*
10 East 53rd Street, New York, N.Y. 10022

Cover photo courtesy of Culver Pictures

First HarperPaperbacks printing: April 1991

Printed in the United States of America

HarperPaperbacks and colophon are trademarks of
HarperCollins*Publishers*

10 9 8 7 6 5 4 3 2 1

The Plotters

Kurt's poor father was being misled and robbed. At the sight of Glidden's hungry eyes and working face and clutching hands Kurt pulled his hat far down, drew his revolver, and leaped forward with a yell, "Hands up!"

He discharged the revolver right in the faces of the stunned plotters, and, snatching up the bundle of money, he leaped over the light, knocking one of the men down, and was gone into the darkness.

Wheeling round the end of the freight-car, he darted back, risking a hard fall in the darkness, and ran along the several cars to the first one, where he grasped his rifle and kept on. He heard his father's roar, like that of a mad bull, and shrill yells from the other men. Kurt laughed grimly. They would never catch him in the dark. While he ran he stuffed the money into his inside coat pockets. Beyond the railroad station he slowed down to catch his breath. His breast was heaving, his pulse hammering, and his skin was streaming.

"Now—what shall—I do?"

HarperPaperbacks
by Zane Grey

*L*ATE in June the vast northwestern desert of wheat began to take on a tinge of gold, lending an austere beauty to that endless, rolling, smooth world of treeless hills, where miles of fallow ground and miles of waving grain sloped up to the far-separated homes of the heroic men who had conquered over sage and sand.

These simple homes of farmers seemed lost on an immensity of soft gray and golden billows of land, insignificant dots here and there on distant hills, so far apart that nature only seemed accountable for those broad squares of alternate golden and brown, extending on and on to the waving horizon-line. A lonely, hard, heroic country, where flowers and fruit were not, nor birds and brooks, nor green pastures. Whirling strings of dust looped up over fallow ground, the short, dry wheat lay back from the wind, the haze in the distance was drab and smoky, heavy with substance.

A thousand hills lay bare to the sky, and half of every hill was wheat and half was fallow ground; and all of them, with the shallow valleys between, seemed big and strange and isolated. The beauty of them was austere, as if the hand of man had been held back from making green his home site, as if the immensity of the task had left no time for youth and freshness. Years, long years, were there in the round-hilled, many-furrowed gray old earth. And the wheat looked a century old. Here and there a straight, dusty road stretched from hill to hill, becoming a thin white line, to disappear in the distance. The sun shone hot, the wind blew hard; and over the boundless undulating expanse hovered a shadow that was neither hood of dust nor hue of gold. It was not physical, but lonely, waiting, prophetic, and weird. No wild desert of wastelands, once the home of other races of man, and now gone to decay and death, could have shown so barren an acreage. Half of this wandering patchwork of squares was earth, brown and gray, curried and disked, and rolled and combed and harrowed, with not a tiny leaf of green in all the miles. The other half had only a faint golden promise of mellow harvest; and at long distance it seemed to shimmer and retreat under the hot sun. A singularly beautiful effect of harmony lay in the long, slowly rising slopes, in the rounded hills, in the endless curving lines on all sides. The scene was heroic because of the labor of horny hands; it was sublime because not a hundred harvests, nor three generations of toiling men, could ever rob nature of its limitless space and scorching sun and sweeping dust, of its resistless age-long creep back toward the desert that it had been.

*   *   *

Here was grown the most bounteous, the richest and finest wheat in all the world. Strange and unfathomable that so much of the bread of man, the staff of life, the hope of civilization in this tragic year 1917, should come from a vast, treeless, waterless, dreary desert!

This wonderful place was an immense valley of considerable altitude called the Columbia Basin, surrounded by the Cascade Mountains on the west, the Coeur d'Alene and Bitter Root Mountains on the east, the Okanozan range to the north, and the Blue Mountains to the south. The valley floor was basalt, from the lava flow of volcanoes in ages past. The rainfall was slight except in the foothills of the mountains. The Columbia River, making a prodigious and meandering curve, bordered on three sides what was known as the Bend country. South of this vast area, across the range, began the fertile, many-watered region that extended on down into verdant Oregon. Among the desert hills of this Bend country, near the center of the Basin, where the best wheat was raised, lay widely separated little towns, the names of which gave evidence of the mixed population. It was, of course, an exceedingly prosperous country, a fact manifest in the substantial little towns, if not in the crude and unpretentious homes of the farmers. The acreage of farms ran from a section, six hundred and forty acres, up into the thousands.

Upon a morning in early July, exactly three months after the United States had declared war upon Germany, a sturdy young farmer strode with darkly troubled face from the presence of his father. At the end of a stormy scene he had promised his father that he would abandon his desire to enlist in the army.

Kurt Dorn walked away from the gray old clapboard house, out to the fence, where he leaned on the gate. He could see for miles in every direction, and to the southward, away on a long yellow slope, rose a stream of dust from a motorcar.

"Must be Anderson—coming to dun Father," muttered young Dorn.

This was the day, he remembered, when the wealthy rancher of Ruxton was to look over old Chris Dorn's wheat fields. Dorn owed thirty thousand dollars and the interest for years, mostly to Anderson. Kurt hated the debt and resented the visit, but he could not help acknowledging that the rancher had been lenient and kind. Long since Kurt had sorrowfully realized that his father was illiterate, hard, grasping, and growing worse with the burden of years.

"If we had rain now—or soon—that section of Bluestem would square Father," soliloquized young Dorn, as with keen eyes he surveyed a vast field of wheat, short, smooth, yellowing in the sun. But the cloudless sky, the haze of heat rather betokened a continued drought.

There were reasons, indeed, for Dorn to wear a dark and troubled face as he watched the motorcar speed along ahead of its stream of dust, pass out of sight under the hill, and soon reappear, to turn off the main road and come toward the house. It was a big, closed car, covered with dust. The driver stopped it at the gate and got out.

"Is this Chris Dorn's farm?" he asked.

"Yes," replied Kurt.

Whereupon the door of the car opened and out stepped a short, broad man in a long linen coat.

"Come out, Lenore, an' shake off the dust," he said, and he assisted a young woman to step out. She also wore a long linen coat, and a veil besides. The man removed his coat and threw it into the car. Then he took off his sombrero to beat the dust off of that.

"Phew! The Golden Valley never seen dust like this in a million years!...I'm chokin' for water. An' listen to the car. She's boilin'!"

Then, as he stepped toward Kurt, the rancher showed himself to be a well-preserved man of perhaps fifty-five, of powerful form beginning to sag in the broad shoulders, his face bronzed by long exposure to wind and sun. He had keen gray eyes, and their look was that of a man used to dealing with his kind and well disposed toward them.

"Hello! Are you young Dorn?" he asked.

"Yes, sir," replied Kurt, stepping out.

"I'm Anderson, from Ruxton, come to see your dad. This is my girl Lenore."

Kurt acknowledged the slight bow from the veiled young woman, and then, hesitating, he added, "Won't you come in?"

"No, not yet. I'm chokin' for air an' water. Bring us a drink," replied Anderson.

Kurt hurried away to get a bucket and a tin cup. As he drew water from the well he was thinking rather vaguely that it was somehow embarrassing—the fact of Mr. Anderson being accompanied by his daughter. Kurt was afraid of his father. But then, what did it matter? When he returned to the yard he found the rancher sitting in the shade of one of the few apple trees, and the young lady was standing near, in the act of removing bonnet and veil. She had thrown the linen coat over the seat of an old wagon bed that lay near.

"Good water is scarce here, but I'm glad we have some," said Kurt; then as he set down the bucket and offered a brimming cupful to the girl he saw her face, and his eyes met hers. He dropped the cup and stared. Then hurriedly, with flushing face, he bent over to recover and refill it.

"Ex-excuse me. I'm—clumsy," he managed to say, and as he handed the cup to her he averted his gaze. For more than a year the memory of this very girl had haunted him. He had seen her twice—the first time at the close of his one year of college at the University of California, and the second time on the street in Spokane. In a glance he had recognized the strong, lithe figure, the sunny hair, the rare golden tint of her complexion, the blue eyes, warm and direct. And he had sustained a shock which momentarily confused him.

"Good water, hey?" dissented Anderson, after drinking a second cup. "Boy that's wet, but it ain't water to drink. Come down in the foothills an' I'll show you. My ranch's called 'Many Waters,' an' you can't keep your feet dry."

"I wish we had some of it here," replied Kurt, wistfully, and he waved a hand at the broad, swelling slopes. The warm breath that blew in from the wheatlands felt dry and smelled dry.

"You're in for a dry spell?" inquired Anderson, with interest that was keen, and kindly as well.

"Father says so. And I fear it, too—for he never makes a mistake in weather or crops."

"A hot, dry spell! ... This summer? ... Hum! ... Boy,

do you know that wheat is the most important thing in the world today?"

"You mean on account of the war," replied Kurt. "Yes, I know. But father doesn't see that. All he sees is—if we have rain we'll have bumper crops. That big field there would be a record—at war prices . . . And he wouldn't be ruined!"

"Ruined? . . . Oh, he means I'd close on him. . . . Hum! . . . Say, what do you see in a big wheat yield—if it rains?"

"Mr. Anderson, I'd like to see our debt paid, but I'm thinking most of wheat for starving peoples. I—I've studied this wheat question. It's the biggest question in this war."

Kurt had forgotten the girl and was unaware of her eyes bent steadily upon him. Anderson had roused to the interest of wheat, and to a deeper study of the young man.

"Say, Dorn, how old are you?" he asked.

"Twenty-four. And Kurt's my first name," was the reply.

"Will this farm fall to you?"

"Yes, if my father does not lose it."

"Hum! . . . Old Dorn won't lose it, never fear. He raises the best wheat in this section."

"But father never owned the land. We have had three bad years. If the wheat fails this summer—we lose the land, that's all."

"Are you an—American?" queried Anderson, slowly, as if treading on dangerous ground.

"I am," snapped Kurt. "My mother was American. She's dead. Father is German. He's old. He's rabid since the President declared war. He'll never change."

"That's hell. What're you goin' to do if your country calls you?"

"Go!" replied Kurt, with flashing eyes. "I wanted to enlist. Father and I quarreled over that until I had to give in. He's hard—he's impossible.... I'll wait for the draft and hope I'm called."

"Boy, it's that spirit Germany's roused, an' the best I can say is, God help her!... Have you a brother?"

"No. I'm all father has."

"Well, it makes a tough place for him, an' you, too. Humor him. He's old. An' when you're called—go an' fight. You'll come back."

"If I only knew that—it wouldn't be so hard."

"Hard? It sure is hard. But it'll be the makin' of a great country. It'll weed out the riffraff.... See here, Kurt, I'm goin' to give you a hunch. Have you had any dealin's with the I. W. W.?"

"Yes, last harvest we had trouble, but nothing serious. When I was in Spokane last month I heard a good deal. Strangers have approached us here, too—mostly aliens. I have no use for them, but they always get father's ear. And now!... To tell the truth, I'm worried."

"Boy, you need to be," replied Anderson, earnestly. "We're all worried. I'm goin' to let you read over the laws of that I. W. W. organization. You're to keep mum now, mind you. I belong to the Chamber of Commerce in Spokane. Somebody got hold of these by-laws of this so-called labor union. We've had copies made, an' every honest farmer in the Northwest is goin' to read them. But carryin' one around is dangerous, I reckon, these days. Here."

Anderson hesitated a moment, peered cautiously around, and then, slipping folded sheets of paper from his inside coat pocket, he evidently made ready to hand them to Kurt.

"Lenore, where's the driver?" he asked.

"He's under the car," replied the girl.

Kurt thrilled at the soft sound of her voice. It was something to have been haunted by a girl's face for a year and then suddenly hear her voice.

"He's new to me—that driver—an' I ain't trustin' any new men these days," went on Anderson. "Here now, Dorn. Read that. An' if you don't get red-headed—"

Without finishing his last muttered remark, he opened the sheets of manuscript and spread them out to the young man.

Curiously, and with a little rush of excitement, Kurt began to read. The very first rule of the I. W. W. aimed to abolish capital. Kurt read on with slowly growing amaze, consternation, and anger. When he had finished, his look, without speech, was a question Anderson hastened to answer.

"It's straight goods," he declared. "Them's the sure-enough rules of that gang. We made certain before we acted. Now how do they strike you?"

"Why, that's no labor union!" replied Kurt, hotly. "They're outlaws, thieves, blackmailers, pirates. I—I don't know what!"

"Dorn, we're up against a bad outfit an' the North-west will see hell this summer. There's trouble in Montana and Idaho. Strangers are driftin' into Washington from all over. We must organize to meet them—to prevent them gettin' a hold out here. It's a labor union, mostly aliens, with dishonest an' unscrupulous leaders, some of them Americans. They aim to take advantage of the war situation. In the newspapers they rave about shorter hours, more pay, acknowledgement of the union. But any fool would see, if he read them laws I showed you, that this I. W. W. is not straight."

"Mr. Anderson, what steps have you taken down in your country?" queried Kurt.

"So far all I've done was to hire my hands for a year, give them high wages, an' caution them when strangers come round to feed them an' be civil an' send them on."

"But we can't do that up here in the Bend," said Dorn, seriously. "We need, say, a hundred thousand men in harvesttime, and not ten thousand all the rest of the year."

"Sure you can't. But you'll have to organize somethin'. Up here in this desert you could have a heap of trouble if that outfit got here strong enough. You'd better tell every farmer you can trust about this I. W. W."

"I've only one American neighbor, and he lives six miles from here," replied Dorn. "Olsen over there is a Swede, and not a naturalized citizen, but I believe he's for the U.S. And there's—"

"Dad," interrupted the girl, "I believe our driver is listening to your very uninteresting conversation."

She spoke demurely, with laughter in her low voice. It made Dorn dare to look at her, and he met a blue blaze that was instantly averted.

Anderson growled, evidently some very hard names, under his breath; his look just then was full of characteristic Western spirit. Then he got up.

"Lenore, I reckon your talk'll be more interesting than mine," he said, dryly. "I'll go see Dorn an' get this business over."

"I'd rather go with you," hurriedly replied Kurt; and then, as though realizing a seeming discourtesy in his words, his face flamed, and he stammered: "I—I don't mean that. But father is in bad mood. We just quarreled. —I told you—about the war. And—Mr. Anderson, I'm— I'm a little afraid he'll—"

"Well, son, I'm not afraid," interrupted the rancher. "I'll beard the old lion in his den. You talk to Lenore."

"Please don't speak of the war," said Kurt, appealingly.

"Not a word unless he starts roarin' at Uncle Sam," declared Anderson, with a twinkle in his eyes, and turned toward the house.

"He'll roar, all right," said Kurt, almost with a groan. He knew what an ordeal awaited the rancher, and he hated the fact that it could not be avoided. Then Kurt was confused, astounded, infuriated with himself over a situation he had not brought about and could scarcely realize. He became conscious of pride and shame, and something as black and hopeless as despair.

"Haven't I seen you—before?" asked the girl.

The query surprised and thrilled Kurt out of his self-centered thought.

"I don't know. Have you? Where?" he answered, facing her. It was a relief to find that she still averted her face.

"At Berkeley, in California, the first time, and the second at Spokane, in front of the Davenport," she replied.

"First—and—second? . . . You—you remembered both times!" he burst out, incredulously.

"Yes. I don't see how I could have helped remembering." Her laugh was low, musical, a little hurried, yet cool.

Dorn was not familiar with girls. He had worked hard all his life, there among those desert hills, and during the few years his father had allowed him for education. He knew wheat, but nothing of the eternal feminine. So it was impossible for him to grasp that this girl was not wholly at her ease. Her words and the cool little laugh suddenly brought home to Kurt the immeasurable distance between him and a daughter of one of the richest ranchers in Washington.

"You mean I—I was impertinent," he began, struggling between shame and pride. "I—I stared at you. . . . Oh, I must have been rude. . . . But, Miss Anderson, I—I didn't mean to be. I didn't think you saw me—at all. I don't know what made me do that. It never happened before. I beg your pardon."

A subtle indefinable change, perceptible to Dorn, even in his confused state, came over the girl.

"I did not say you were impertinent," she returned. "I remembered seeing you—notice me, that is all."

Self-possessed, aloof, and kind, Miss Anderson now became an impenetrable mystery to Dorn. But that only accentuated the distance she had intimated lay between them. Her kindness stung him to recover his composure. He wished she had not been kind. What a singular chance that had brought her here to his home—the daughter of a man who came to demand a long-unpaid debt! What a dispelling of the vague thing that had been only a dream! Dorn gazed away across the yellowing hills to the dim blue of the mountains where rolled the Oregon. Despite the color, it was gray—like his future.

"I heard you tell father you had studied wheat,"

said the girl, presently, evidently trying to make conversation.

"Yes, all my life," replied Kurt. "My study has mostly been under my father. Look at my hands." He held out big, strong hands, scarred and knotted, with horny palms uppermost, and he laughed. "I can be proud of them, Miss Anderson.... But I had a splendid year in California at the university and I graduated from the Washington State Agricultural College."

"You love wheat—the raising of it, I mean?" she inquired.

"It must be that I do, though I never had such a thought. Wheat is so wonderful. No one can guess who does not know it!... The clean, plump grain, the sowing on fallow ground, the long wait, the first tender green, and the change day by day to the deep waving fields of gold—then the harvest, hot, noisy, smoky, full of dust and chaff, and the great combine-harvesters with thirty-four horses. Oh! I guess I do love it all.... I worked in a Spokane flour mill, too, just to learn how flour is made. There is nothing in the world so white, so clean, so pure as flour made from the wheat of these hills!"

"Next you'll be telling me that you can bake bread," she rejoined, and her laugh was low and sweet. Her eyes shone with soft blue gleams.

"Indeed I can! I bake all the bread we use," he said, stoutly. "And I flatter myself I can beat any girl you know."

"You can beat mine, I'm sure. Before I went to college I did pretty well. But I learned too much there. Now my mother and sisters, and brother Jim, all the family except Dad, make fun of my bread."

"You have a brother? How old is he?"

"One brother—Jim, we call him. He—he is just past twenty-one." She faltered the last few words.

Kurt felt on common ground with her then. The sudden break in her voice, the change in her face, the shadowing of the blue eyes—these were eloquent.

"Oh, it's horrible—this need of war!" she exclaimed.

"Yes," he replied, simply. "But maybe your brother will not be called."

"Called! Why, he refused to wait for the draft! He went and enlisted. Dad patted him on the back.... If anything happens to him it'll kill my mother. Jim is her idol. It'd break my heart.... Oh, I hate the very name of Germans!"

"My father is German," said Kurt. "He's been fifty years in America—eighteen years here on this farm. He always hated England. Now he's bitter against America. ...I can see a side you can't see. But I don't blame you— for what you said."

"Forgive me. I can't conceive of meaning that against anyone who's lived here so long.... Oh, it must be hard for you."

"I'll let my father think I'm forced to join the army. But I'm going to fight against his people. We are a house divided against itself."

"Oh, what a pity!" The girl sighed and her eyes were dark with brooding sorrow.

A step sounded behind them Mr. Anderson appeared, sombrero off, mopping a very red face. His eyes gleamed, with angry glints; his mouth and chin were working. He flopped down with a great, explosive breath.

"Kurt, your old man is a—a—son of a gun!" he

exclaimed, vociferously; manifestly, liberation of speech was a relief.

The young man nodded seriously and knowingly. "I hope, sir—he—he—"

"He did—you just bet your life! He called me a lot in German, but I know cuss words when I hear them. I tried to reason with him—told him I wanted my money—was here to help him get that money off the farm, some way or other. An' he swore I was a capitalist—an enemy to labor an' the Northwest—that I an' my kind had caused the war."

Kurt gazed gravely into the disturbed face of the rancher. Miss Anderson had wide-open eyes of wonder.

"Sure I could have stood all that," went on Anderson, fuming. "But he ordered me out of the house. I got mad an' wouldn't go. Then—by George! he pulled my nose an' called me a bloody Englishman!"

Kurt groaned in the disgrace of the moment. But, amazingly, Miss Anderson burst into a silvery peal of laughter.

"Oh, Dad! . . . that's—just too—good for—anything! You met your—match at last. . . . You know you always—boasted of your drop of English blood. . . . And you're sensitive—about your big nose!"

"He must be over seventy," growled Anderson, as if seeking for some excuse to palliate his restraint. "I'm mad—but it was funny." The working of his face finally set in the huge wrinkles of a laugh.

Young Dorn struggled to repress his own mirth, but unguardedly he happened to meet the dancing blue eyes of the girl, merry, provocative, full of youth and fun, and that was too much for him. He laughed with them.

"The joke's on me," said Anderson. "An' I can take

one....Now, young man, I think I gathered from your amiable dad that if the crop of wheat was full I'd get my money. Otherwise I could take over the land. For my part, I'd never do that, but the others interested might do it, even for the little money involved. I tried to buy them out so I'd have the whole mortgage. They would not sell."

"Mr. Anderson, you're a square man, and I'll do—" declared Kurt.

"Come out an' show me the wheat," interrupted Anderson. "Lenore, do you want to go with us?"

"I do," replied the daughter, and she took up her hat to put it on.

Kurt led them through the yard, out past the old barn, to the edge of the open slope where the wheat stretched away, down and up, as far as the eye could see.

2

"WE'VE got over sixteen hundred acres in fallow ground, a half section in rye, another half in wheat—Turkey Red—and this section you see, six hundred and forty acres, in Bluestem," said Kurt.

Anderson's keen eyes swept from near at hand to far away, down the gentle, billowy slope and up the far hillside. The wheat was two feet high, beginning to be thick and heavy at the heads, as if struggling to burst. A fragrant, dry, wheaty smell, mingled with dust, came on the soft summer breeze, and a faint silken rustle. The greenish, almost blue color near at hand gradually in the distance grew lighter, and then yellow, and finally took on a tinge of gold. There was a living spirit in that vast wheat field.

"Dorn, it's the finest wheat I've seen!" exclaimed Anderson, with the admiration of the farmer who aspired high. "In fact, it's the only fine field of wheat I've seen since we left the foothills. How is that?"

"Late spring and dry weather," replied Dorn. "Most of the farmers' reports are poor. If we get rain over the Bend country we'll have only an average yield this year. If we don't get rain—then a flat failure."

Miss Anderson evinced an interest in the subject and she wanted to know why this particular field, identical with all the others for miles around, should have a promise of a magnificent crop when the others had no promise at all.

"This section lay fallow a long time," replied Dorn. "Snow lasted here on this north slope quite a while. My father used a method of soil cultivation intended to conserve moisture. The seed wheat was especially selected. And if we have rain during the next ten days this section of Bluestem will yield fifty bushels to the acre."

"Fifty bushels!" ejaculated Anderson.

"Bluestem? Why do you call it that when it's green and yellow?" queried the girl.

"It's a name. There are many varieties of wheat. Bluestem is best here in this desert country because it resists drought, it produces large yield, it does not break, and the flour mills rate it very high. Bluestem is not good in wet soils."

Anderson tramped along the edge of the field, peering down, here and there pulling a shaft of wheat and examining it. The girl gazed with dreamy eyes across the undulating sea. And Dorn watched her.

"We have a ranch—thousands of acres—but not like this," she said.

"What's the difference?" asked Dorn.

She appeared pensive and in doubt.

"I hardly know. What would you call this—this scene?"

"Why, I call it the desert of wheat! But no one else does," he replied.

"I named father's ranch 'Many Waters.' I think those names tell the difference."

"Isn't my desert beautiful?"

"No. It has a sameness—a monotony that would drive me mad. It looks as if the whole world had gone to wheat. It makes me think—oppresses me. All this means that we live by wheat alone. These bare hills! They're too open to wind and sun and snow. They look like the toil of ages."

"Miss Anderson, there is such a thing as love for the earth—the bare brown earth. You know we came from dust, and to dust we return! These fields are human to my father. And they have come to speak to me—a language I don't understand yet. But I mean—what you see—the growing wheat here, the field of clods over there, the wind and dust and glare and heat, the eternal sameness of the open space—these are the things around which my life has centered, and when I go away from them I am not content."

Anderson came back to the young couple, carrying some heads of wheat in his hand.

"Smut!" he exclaimed, showing both diseased and healthy specimens of wheat. "Had to hunt hard to find that. Smut is the bane of all wheat growers. I never saw so little of it as there is here. In fact, we know scarcely nothin' about smut an' its cure, if there is any. You farmers who raise only grain have got the work down to a science. This Bluestem is not bearded wheat, like Turkey Red. Has that beard anythin' to do with smut?"

"I think not. The parasite, or fungus, lives inside the wheat."

"Never heard that before. No wonder smut is the worst trouble for wheat raisers in the Northwest. I've fields literally full of smut. An' we never are rid of it. One farmer has one idea, an' some one else another. What could be of greater importance to a farmer? We're at war. The men who claim to know say that wheat will win the war. An' we lose millions of bushels from this smut. That's to say it's a terrible fact to face. I'd like to get your ideas."

Dorn, happening to glance again at Miss Anderson, an act that seemed to be growing habitual, read curiosity and interest, and something more, in her direct blue eyes. The circumstance embarrassed him, though it tugged at the flood gates of his knowledge. He could talk about wheat, and he did like to. Yet here was a girl who might be supposed to be bored. Still, she did not appear to be. That warm glance was not politeness.

"Yes, I'd like to hear every word you can say about wheat," she said, with an encouraging little nod.

"Sure she would," added Anderson, with an affectionate hand on her shoulder. "She's a farmer's daughter. She'll be a farmer's wife."

He laughed at this last sally. The girl blushed. Dorn smiled and shook his head doubtfully.

"I imagine that good fortune will never befall a farmer," he said.

"Well, if it should," she replied, archly, "just consider how I might surprise him with my knowledge of wheat.... Indeed, Mr. Dorn, I am interested. I've never been in the Bend before—in your desert of wheat. I never before felt the greatness of loving the soil—or caring for it—of growing things from seed. Yet the Bible teaches that, and I read my Bible. Please tell us. The more you say the more I'll like it."

Dorn was not proof against this eloquence. And he quoted two of his authorities, Heald and Woolman, of the State Agricultural Experiment Station, where he had studied for two years.

"Bunt, or stinking smut, is caused by two different species of microscopic fungi which live as parasites in the wheat plant. Both are essentially similar in their effects and their life history. *Tilletia tritici*, or the rough-spored variety, is the common stinking smut of the Pacific regions, while *Tilletia foetans*, or the smooth-spored species, is the one generally found in the eastern United States.

"The smut 'berries,' or 'balls,' from an infected head contain millions of minute bodies, the spores or 'seeds' of the smut fungus. These reproduce the smut in some-what the same way that a true seed develops into a new plant. A single smut ball of average size contains a sufficient number of spores to give one for each grain of wheat in five or six bushels. It takes eight smut spores to equal the diameter of a human hair. Normal wheat grains from an infected field may have so many spores lodged on their surface as to give them a dark color, but other grains which show no difference in color to the naked eye may still contain a sufficient number of spores to produce a smutty crop if seed treatment is not practiced.

"When living smut spores are introduced into the soil with the seed wheat, or exist in the soil in which smut-free wheat is sown, a certain percentage of the wheat plants are likely to become infected. The smut spore germinates and produces first a stage of the smut plant in the soil. This first stage never infects a young seedling direct, but gives rise to secondary spores, or sporida, from which infection threads may arise and penetrate the shoot of a young seedling and reach the growing point. Here the fungus threads keep pace with the growth of the plant and reach maturity at or slightly before harvesttime.

"Since this disease is caused by an internal parasite, it is natural to expect certain responses to its presence. It should be noted first that the smut fungus is living at the expense of its host plant, the wheat, and its effect on the host may be summarized as follows: The consumption of food, the destruction of food in the sporulating process, and the stimulating or retarding effect on normal physiological processes.

"Badly smutted plants remain in many cases undersize and produce fewer and smaller heads. In the Fife and Bluestem varieties the infected heads previous to maturity exhibit a darker green color, and remain green longer than the normal heads. In some varieties the infected heads stand erect, when normal ones begin to droop as a result of the increasing weight of the ripening grain.

"A crop may become infected with smut in a number of different ways. Smut was originally introduced with the seed, and many farmers are still planting it every season with their seed wheat. Wheat taken from a smutty crop will have countless numbers of loose spores adhering to the grains, also a certain number of unbroken smut balls. These are always a source of danger, even when the seed is treated with fungicides before sowing.

"There are also chances for the infection of a crop if absolutely smut-free seed is employed. First, soil infection from a previous smutty crop; second, soil infection from wind-blown spores. Experiments have shown that separated spores from crushed smut balls lose their effective power in from two to three months, provided the soil is moist and loose, and in no case do they survive a winter.

"It does not seem probable that wheat smut will be controlled by any single practice, but rather by the combined use of various methods: crop rotation; the use of clean seed; seed treatment with fungicides; cultural practices and breeding; and selection of varieties.

"Failure to practice crop rotation is undoubtedly one of the main explanations for the general prevalence of smut in the wheat fields of eastern Washington. Even with an intervening summer fallow, the smut from a previous crop may be a source of infection. Experience shows that a fall stubble crop is less liable to smut infection than a crop following summer fallow. The apparent explanation for this condition is the fact that the summer fallow becomes infected with wind-blown spores, while in a stubble crop the wind-blown spores, as well as those originating from the previous crop, are buried in plowing.

"If clean seed or properly treated seed had been used by all farmers we should never have had a smut problem. High percents of smut indicate either soil infection or imperfect treatment. The principle of the chemical treatment is to use a poison which will kill the superficial spores of the smut and not materially injure the germinating power of the seed. The hot-water treatment is only recommended when one of the chemical 'steeps' is not effective.

"Certain cultural practices are beneficial in reducing the amount of smut in all cases, while the value of others depends to some extent upon the source of the smut spores. The factors which always influence the amount of smut are the temperature of the soil during the germinating period, the amount of soil moisture, and the depth of seeding. Where seed-borne spores are the only sources of infection, attention to the three factors mentioned will give the only cultural practices for reducing the amount of smut.

"Early seeding has been practiced by various farmers, and they report a marked reduction in smut.

"The replowing of the summer fallow after the first fall rains is generally effective in reducing the amount of smut.

"Very late planting—that is, four or five weeks after the first good fall rains—is also an effective practice. Fall tillage of summer fallow, other than plowing, seems to be beneficial.

"No smut-immune varieties of wheat are known, but the standard varieties show varying degrees of resistance. Spring wheats generally suffer less from smut than winter varieties. This is not due to any superior resistance, but rather to the fact that they escape infection. If only spring wheats were grown our smut problem would largely disappear; but a return to this practice is not suggested, since the winter wheats are much more desirable. It seems probable that the conditions which prevail during the growing season may have considerable influence on the percent. of smut in any given variety."

When Dorn finished his discourse, to receive the thanks of his listeners, they walked back through the yard toward the road. Mr. Anderson, who led the way, halted rather abruptly.

"Hum! Who're those men talkin' to my driver?" he queried.

Dorn then saw a couple of strangers standing near the motorcar, engaged in apparently close conversation with the chauffeur. Upon the moment they glanced up to see Mr. Anderson approaching, and they rather hurriedly departed. Dorn had noted a good many strangers lately—men whose garb was not that of farmers, whose faces seemed foreign, whose actions were suspicious.

"I'll bet a hundred they're I. W. W.'s," declared Anderson. "Take my hunch, Dorn."

The strangers passed on down the road without looking back.

"Wonder where they'll sleep tonight?" muttered Dorn.

Anderson rather sharply asked his driver what the two men wanted. And the reply he got was that they were inquiring about work.

"Did they speak English?" went on the rancher.

"Well enough to make themselves understood," replied the driver.

Dorn did not get a good impression from the shifty eyes and air of taciturnity of Mr. Anderson's man, and it was evident that the blunt rancher restrained himself. He helped his daughter into the car, and then put on his long coat. Next he shook hands with Dorn.

"Young man, I've enjoyed meetin' you, an' have sure profited from same," he said. "Which makes up for your dad! I'll run over here again to see you—around harvesttime. An' I'll be wishin' for that rain."

"Thank you. If it does rain I'll be happy to see you," replied Dorn, with a smile.

"Well, if it doesn't rain I won't come. I'll put it off another year, an' cuss them other fellers into holdin' off, too."

"You're very kind. I don't know how I'd—we'd ever repay you in that case."

"Don't mention it. Say, how far did you say it was to Palmer? We'll have lunch there."

"It's fifteen miles—that way," answered Dorn. "If it wasn't for—for Father I'd like you to stay—and break some of my bread."

Dorn was looking at the girl as he spoke. Her steady gaze had been on him ever since she entered the car, and in the shade of her hat and the veil she was adjusting her eyes seemed very dark and sweet and thoughtful. She brightly nodded her thanks as she held the veil aside with both hands.

"I wish you luck. Good-bye," she said, and closed the veil. Still, Dorn could see her eyes through it, and now they were sweeter, more mysterious, more provocative of haunting thoughts. It flashed over him with dread certainty that he had fallen in love with her. The shock struck him mute. He had no reply for the rancher's hearty farewell. Then the car lurched away and dust rose in a cloud.

CHAPTER

3

WITH a strange knocking of his heart, high up toward his throat, Kurt Dorn stood stock-still, watching the moving cloud of dust until it disappeared over the hill.

No doubt entered his mind. The truth, the fact, was a year old—a long-familiar and dreamy state—but its meaning had not been revealed to him until just a moment past. Everything had changed when she looked out with that sweet, steady gaze through the parted veil and then slowly closed it. She had changed. There was something intangible about her that last moment, baffling, haunting. He leaned against a crooked old gatepost that as a boy he had climbed, and the thought came to him that this spot would all his life be vivid and poignant in his memory. The first sight of a blue-eyed, sunny-haired girl, a year and more before, had struck deep into his unconscious heart; a second sight had made her an unforgettable reality: and a third had been the realization of love.

It was sad, regrettable, incomprehensible, and yet somehow his inner being swelled and throbbed. Her name was Lenore Anderson. Her father was one of the richest men in the state of Washington. She had one brother, Jim, who would not wait for the army draft. Kurt trembled and a hot rush of tears dimmed his eyes. All at once his lot seemed unbearable. An immeasurable barrier had arisen between him and his old father—a hideous thing of blood, of years, of ineradicable difference; the broad acres of wheatland so dear to him were to be taken from him; love had overcome him with headlong rush, a love that could never be returned; and cruelest of all, there was the war calling him to give up his home, his father, his future, and to go out to kill and to be killed.

It came to him while he leaned there, that, remembering the light of Lenore Anderson's eyes, he could not give up to bitterness and hatred, whatever his misfortunes and his fate. She would never be anything to him, but he and her brother Jim and many other young Americans must be incalculable all to her. That thought saved Kurt Dorn. There were other things besides his own career, his happiness; and the way he was placed, however unfortunate from a selfish point of view, must not breed a morbid self-pity.

The moment of his resolution brought a flash, a revelation of what he owed himself. The work and the thought and the feeling of his last few weeks there at home must be intensified. He must do much and live greatly in little time. This was the moment of his renunciation, and he imagined that many a young man who had decided to go to war had experienced a strange spiritual division of self. He wondered also if that moment was not for many of them a letdown, a throwing up of ideals, a helpless retrograding and surrender to the brutalizing spirit of war. But it could never be so for him. It might have been had not that girl come into his life.

The bell for the midday meal roused Kurt from his profound reverie, and he plodded back to the house. Down through the barnyard gate he saw the hired men coming, and a second glance discovered to him that two unknown men were with them. Watching for a moment, Kurt recognized the two strangers that had been talking to Mr. Anderson's driver. They seemed to be talking earnestly now. Kurt saw Jerry, a trusty and long-tried employee, rather unceremoniously break away from these strangers. But they followed him, headed him off, and with vehement nods and gesticulations appeared to be arguing with him. The other hired men pushed closer, evidently listening. Finally Jerry impatiently broke away and tramped toward the house. These strangers sent sharp words after him—words that Kurt could not distinguish, though he caught the tone of scorn. Then the two individuals addressed themselves to the other men; and in close contact the whole party passed out of sight behind the barn.

Thoughtfully Kurt went into the house. He meant to speak to Jerry about the strangers, but he wanted to consider the matter first. He had misgivings. His father was not in the sitting room, nor in the kitchen. Dinner was ready on the table, and the one servant, an old woman who had served the Dorns for years, appeared impatient at the lack of promptness in the men. Both father and son, except on Sundays, always ate with the hired help. Kurt stepped outside to find Jerry washing at the bench.

"Jerry, what's keeping the men?" queried Kurt.

"Wal, they're palaverin' out there with two I. W. W. fellers," replied Jerry.

Kurt reached for the rope of the farm bell, and rang it rather sharply. Then he went in to take his place at the table, and Jerry soon followed. Old man Dorn did not appear, which fact was not unusual. The other hired men did not enter until Jerry and Kurt were half done with the meal. They seemed excited and somewhat boisterous, Kurt thought, but once they settled down to eating, after the manner of hungry laborers, they had little to say. Kurt, soon finishing his dinner, went outdoors to wait for Jerry. That individual appeared to be long in coming, and loud voices in the kitchen attested to further argument. At last, however, he lounged out and began to fill a pipe.

"Jerry, I want to talk to you," said Kurt. "Let's get away from the house."

The hired man was a big, lumbering fellow, gnarled like an old oak tree. He had a good-natured face and honest eyes.

"I reckon you want to hear about them I. W. W. fellers?" he asked, as they walked away.

"Yes," replied Kurt.

"There's been a regular procession of them fellers, the last week or so, walkin' through the country," replied Jerry. "Today's the first time any of them got to me. But I've heerd talk. Sunday when I was in Palmer the air was full of rumors."

"Rumors of what?" queried Kurt.

"All kinds," answered Jerry, nonchalantly scratching his stubby beard. "There's an army of I. W. W.'s comin' in from eastward. Idaho an' Montana are gittin' a dose now. Short hours; double wages; join the union; sabotage, whatever thet is; capital an' labor fight; threats if you don't fall in line; an' Lord knows what all."

"What did those two fellows want of you?"

"Wanted us to join the I. W. W.," replied the laborer.

"Did they want a job?"

"Not as I heerd. Why, one of them had a wad of bills thet would choke a cow. He did most of the talkin'. The little feller with the beady eyes an' the pockmarks, he didn't say much. He's Austrian an' not long in this country. The big stiff—Glidden, he called himself— must be some shucks in thet I. W. W. He looked an' talked oily at first—very persuadin'; but when I says I wasn't goin' to join no union he got sassy an' bossy. Thet made me sore, so I told him to go to hell. Then he said the I. W. W. would run the whole Northwest this summer—wheat fields, lumberin', fruit harvestin', rail-roadin'—the whole kaboodle, an' thet any workman who wouldn't join would git his, all right."

"Well, Jerry, what do you think about this organization?" queried Kurt, anxiously.

"Not much. It ain't a square deal. I ain't got no belief in them. What I heerd of their threatenin' methods is like the way this Glidden talks. If I owned a farm I'd drive such fellers off with a whip. There's goin' to be bad doin's if they come driftin' strong into the Bend."

"Jerry, are you satisfied with your job?"

"Sure. I won't join the I. W. W. An' I'll talk ag'in' it. I reckon a few of us will hev to do all the harvestin'.

An', considerin' thet, I'll take a dollar a day more on my wages."

"If father does not agree to that, I will," said Kurt. "Now how about the other men?"

"Wal, they all air leanin' toward promises of little work an' lots of pay," answered Jerry, with a laugh. "Morgan's on the fence about joinin'. But Andrew agreed. He's Dutch an' pig-headed. Jansen's only too glad to make trouble fer his boss. They're goin' to lay off the rest of today an' talk with Glidden. They all agreed to meet down by the culvert. An' thet's what they was arguin' with me fer—wanted me to come."

"Where's this man Glidden?" demanded Kurt. "I'll give him a piece of my mind."

"I reckon he's hangin' round the farm—out of sight somewhere."

"All right, Jerry. Now you go back to work. You'll never lose anything by sticking to us, I promise you that. Keep your eyes and ears open."

Kurt strode back to the house, and his entrance to the kitchen evidently interrupted a colloquy of some kind. The hired men were still at table. They looked down at their plates and said nothing. Kurt left the sitting room door open, and, turning, he asked Martha if his father had been to dinner.

"No, an' what's more, when I called he takes to roarin' like a mad bull," replied the woman.

Kurt crossed the sitting room to knock upon his father's door. The reply forthcoming did justify the old woman's comparison. It certainly caused the hired men to evacuate the kitchen with alacrity. Old Chris Dorn's roar at his son was a German roar, which did not soothe the young man's rising temper. Of late the father had taken altogether to speaking German. He had never spoken English well. And Kurt was rapidly approaching the point where he would not speak German. A deadlock was in sight, and Kurt grimly prepared to meet it. He pounded on the locked door.

"The men are going to lay off," he called.

"Who runs this farm?" was the thundered reply.

"The I. W. W. is going to run it if you sulk indoors as you have done lately," yelled Kurt. He thought that would fetch his father stamping out, but he had reckoned falsely. There was no further sound. Leaving the room in high dudgeon, Kurt hurried out to catch the hired men near at hand and to order them back to work. They trudged off surlily toward the barn.

Then Kurt went on to search for the I. W. W. men, and after looking up and down the road, and all around, he at length found them behind an old straw stack. They were comfortably sitting down, backs to the straw, eating a substantial lunch. Kurt was angry and did not care. His appearance, however, did not feaze the strangers. One of them, an American, was a man of about thirty years, clean-shaven, square-jawed, with light, steely, secretive gray eyes, and a look of intelligence and assurance that did not harmonize with his motley garb. His companion was a foreigner, small of stature, with eyes like a ferret and deep pits in his sallow face.

"Do you know you're trespassing?" demanded Kurt.

"You grudge us a little shade, eh, even to eat a bite?" said the American. He wrapped a paper round his lunch and leisurely rose, to fasten penetrating eyes upon the young man. "That's what I heard about you rich farmers of the Bend."

"What business have you coming here?" queried

Kurt, with sharp heat. "You sneak out of sight of the farmers. You trespass to get at our men and with a lot of lies and guff you make them discontented with their jobs. I'll fire these men just for listening to you."

"Mister Dorn, we want you to fire them. That's my business out here," replied the American.

"Who are you, anyway?"

"That's my business, too,"

Kurt passed from hot to cold. He could not miss the antagonism of this man, a bold and menacing attitude.

"My foreman says your name's Glidden," went on Kurt, cooler this time, "and that you're talking I. W. W. as if you were one of its leaders; that you don't want a job; that you've got a wad of money; that you coax, then threaten; that you've intimidated three of our hands."

"Your Jerry's a marked man," said Glidden, shortly.

"You impudent scoundrel!" exclaimed Kurt. "Now you listen to this. You're the first I. W. W. man I've met. You look and talk like an American. But if you are American you're a traitor. We've a war to fight! War with a powerful country! Germany! And you come spreading discontent in the wheat fields . . . when wheat means life! . . . Get out of here before I—"

"We'll mark you, too, Mister Dorn, and your wheatfields," snapped Glidden.

With one swift lunge Kurt knocked the man flat and then leaped to stand over him, watching for a move to draw a weapon. The little foreigner slunk back out of reach.

"I'll start a little marking myself," grimly said Kurt. "Get up!"

Slowly Glidden moved from elbow to knees, and

then to his feet. His cheek was puffing out and his nose was bleeding. The light-gray eyes were lurid.

"That's for your I. W. W.!" declared Kurt. "The first rule of your I. W. W. is to abolish capital, hey?"

Kurt had not intended to say that. It slipped out in his fury. But the effect was striking. Glidden gave a violent start and his face turned white. Abruptly he hurried away. His companion shuffled after him. Kurt stared at them, thinking the while that if he had needed any proof of the crookedness of the I. W. W. he had seen it in Glidden's guilty face. The man had been suddenly frightened, and surprise, too, had been prominent in his countenance. Then Kurt remembered how Anderson had intimated that the secrets of the I. W. W. had been long hidden. Kurt, keen and quick in his sensibilities, divined that there was something powerful back of this Glidden's cunning and assurance. Could it be only the power of a new labor organization? That might well be great, but the idea did not convince Kurt. During a hurried and tremendous preparation by the government for war, any disorder such as menaced the country would be little short of a calamity. It might turn out a fatality. This so-called labor union intended to take advantage of a crisis to further its own ends. Yet even so, that fact did not wholly explain Glidden and his subtlety. Some nameless force loomed dark and sinister back of Glidden's meaning, and it was not peril to the wheatlands of the Northwest alone.

Like a huge dog Kurt shook himself and launched into action. There were sense and pleasure in muscular activity, and it lessened the habit of worry. Soon he ascertained that only Morgan had returned to work in the fields. Andrew and Jansen were nowhere to be seen.

Jansen had left four horses hitched to a harrow. Kurt went out to take up the work thus abandoned.

It was a long field, and if he had earned a dollar for every time he had traversed its length, during the last ten years, he would have been a rich man. He could have walked it blindfolded. It was fallow ground, already plowed, disked, rolled, and now the last stage was to harrow it, loosening the soil, conserving the moisture.

Morgan, far to the other side of this section, had the better of the job, for his harrow was a new machine and he could ride while driving the horses. But Kurt, using an old harrow, had to walk. The four big horses plodded at a gait that made Kurt step out to keep up with them. To keep up, to drive a straight line, to hold back on the reins, was labor for a man. It spoke well for Kurt that he had followed that old harrow hundreds of miles, that he could stand the strain, that he loved both the physical sense and the spiritual meaning of the toil.

Driving west, he faced a wind laden with dust as dry as powder. At every sheeted cloud, whipping back from the hooves of the horses and the steel spikes of the harrow, he had to bat his eyes to keep from being blinded. The smell of dust clogged his nostrils. As soon as he began to sweat under the hot sun the dust caked on his face, itching, stinging, burning. There was dust between his teeth.

Driving back east was a relief. The wind whipped the dust away from him. And he could catch the fragrance of the newly turned soil. How brown and clean and earthy it looked! Where the harrow had cut and ridged, the soil did not look thirsty and parched. But that which was unharrowed cried out for rain. No cloud in the hot sky, except the yellow clouds of dust!

On that trip east across the field, which faced the road, Dorn saw pedestrians in twos and threes passing by. Once he was hailed, but made no answer. He would not have been surprised to see a crowd, yet travelers were scarce in that region. The sight of these men, some of them carrying bags and satchels, was disturbing to the young farmer. Where were they going? All appeared outward bound toward the river. They came, of course, from the little towns, railroads, and the cities. At this season, with harvesttime near at hand, it had been in former years no unusual sight to see strings of laborers passing by. But this year they came earlier, and in greater numbers.

With the wind in his face, however, Dorn saw nothing but the horses and the brown line ahead, and half the time they were wholly obscured in yellow dust. He began thinking about Lenore Anderson, just pondering that strange, steady look of a girl's eyes; and then he did not mind the dust or heat or distance. Never could he be cheated of his thoughts. And those of her, even the painful ones, gave birth to a comfort that he knew must abide with him henceforth on lonely labors such as this, perhaps in the lonelier watches of a soldier's duty. She had been curious, aloof, then sympathetic; she had studied his face; she had been an eloquent-eyed listener to his discourse on wheat. But she had not guessed his secret. Not until her last look—strange, deep, potent—had he guessed that secret himself.

So, with mind both busy and absent, Kurt Dorn harrowed the fallow ground abandoned by his men; and when the day was done, with the sun setting hot and coppery beyond the dim, dark ranges, he guided the tired horses homeward and plodded back of them, weary and spent.

He was to learn from Morgan, at the stables, that the old man had discharged both Andrew and Jansen. And Jansen, liberating some newly assimilated poison, had threatened revenge. He would see that any hired men would learn a thing or two, so that they would not sign up with Chris Dorn. In a fury the old man had driven Jansen out into the road.

Sober and moody, Kurt put the horses away, and, washing the dust grime from sunburnt face and hands, he went to his little attic room, where he changed his damp and sweaty clothes. Then he went down to supper with mind made up to be lenient and silent with his old and sorely tried father.

Chris Dorn sat in the light of the kitchen lamps. He was a huge man with a great, round bullet-shaped head and a shock of gray hair and bristling, grizzled beard. His face was broad, heavy, and seemed sodden with dark, brooding thought. His eyes, under bushy brows, were pale gleams of fire. He looked immovable as to both bulk and will.

Never before had Kurt Dorn so acutely felt the fixed, contrary, ruthless nature of his parent. Never had the distance between them seemed so great. Kurt shivered and sighed at once. Then, hungry, he fell to eating in silence. Presently the old man shoved his plate back, and, wiping his face, he growled, in German:

"I discharged Andrew and Jansen."

"Yes, I know," replied Kurt. "It wasn't good judgment. What'll we do for hands?"

"I'll hire more. Men are coming for the harvest."

"But they all belong to the I. W. W.," protested Kurt.

"And what's that?"

In scarcely subdued wrath Kurt described in detail, and to the best of his knowledge, what the I. W. W. was, and he ended by declaring the organization treacherous to the United States.

"How's that?" asked old Dorn, gruffly.

Kurt was actually afraid to tell his father, who never read newspapers, who knew little of what was going on, that if the Allies were to win the war it was wheat that would be the greatest factor. Instead of that he said if the I.W.W. inaugurated strikes and disorder in the Northwest it would embarrass the government.

"Then I'll hire I.W.W. men," said old Dorn.

Kurt battled against a rising temper. This blind old man was his father.

"But I'll not have I.W.W. men on the farm," retorted Kurt. "I just punched one I.W.W. solicitor."

"I'll run this farm. If you don't like my way you can leave," darkly asserted the father.

Kurt fell back in his chair and stared at the turgid, bulging forehead and hard eyes before him. What could be behind them? Had the war brought out a twist in his father's brain? Why were Germans so impossible?

"My Heavens! Father, would you turn me out of my home because we disagree?" he asked, desperately.

"In my country sons obey their fathers or they go out for themselves."

"I've not been a disobedient son," declared Kurt. "And here in America sons have more freedom—more say."

"America has no sense of family life—no honest government. I hate the country."

A ball of fire seemed to burst in Kurt.

"That kind of talk infuriates me," he blazed. "I don't care if you are my father. Why in the hell did you come to America? Why did you stay? Why did you marry my mother—an American woman?...That's rot—just spiteful rot! I've heard you tell what life was in Europe when you were a boy. You ran off. You stayed in this country because it was a better country than yours.... Fifty years you've been in America—many years on this farm. And you love this land...My God! Father, can't you and men like you see the truth?"

"Aye, I can," gloomily replied the old man. "The truth is we'll lose the land. That greedy Anderson will drive me off."

"He will not. He's fine—generous," asserted Kurt, earnestly. "All he wanted was to see the prospects of the harvest, and perhaps to help you. Anderson has not had interest on his money for three years. I'll bet he's paid interest demanded by the other stockholders in that bank you borrowed from. Why, he's our friend!"

"Aye, and I see more," boomed the father. "He fetched his lass up here to make eyes at my son. I saw her—the sly wench!...Boy, you'll not marry her!"

Kurt choked back his mounting rage.

"Certainly I never will," he said, bitterly. "But I would if she'd have me."

"What!" thundered Dorn, his white locks standing up and shaking like the mane of a lion. "That wheat banker's daughter! Never! I forbid it. You shall not marry any American girl."

"Father, this is idle, foolish rant," cried Kurt, with a high warning note in his voice. "I've no idea of marrying...But if I had one—whom else could I marry except an American girl?"

"I'll sell the wheat—the land. We'll go back to Germany!"

That was maddening to Kurt. He sprang up, sending dishes to the floor with a crash. He bent over to pound the table with a fist. Violent speech choked him and he felt a cold, tight blanching of his face.

"Listen!" he rang out. "If I go to Germany it'll be as a soldier—to kill Germans!...I'm done—I'm through with the very name....Listen to the last words I'll ever speak to you in German—the last! *To hell with Germany!*"

Then Kurt plunged, blind in his passion, out of the door into the night. And as he went he heard his father cry out, brokenly:

"My son! Oh, my son!"

The night was dark and cool. A faint wind blew across the hills, and it was dry, redolent, sweet. The sky seemed an endless curving canopy of dark blue blazing with myriads of stars.

Kurt staggered out of the yard, down along the edge of a wheat field, to one of the strawstacks, and there he flung himself down in an agony.

"Oh, I'm ruined—ruined!" he moaned. "The break—has come!...Poor old dad!"

He leaned there against the straw, shaking and throbbing, with a cold perspiration bathing face and body. Even the palms of his hands were wet. A terrible fit of anger was beginning to loose its hold upon him. His breathing was labored in gasps and sobs. Unutterable stupidity of his father—horrible cruelty of his position! What had he ever done in all his life to suffer under such a curse? Yet almost he clung to his wrath, for it had been righteous. That thing, that infernal twist in the brain, that was what was wrong with his father. His father who had been fifty years in the United States! How simple, then, to understand what was wrong with Germany.

"By God! I am—American!" he panted, and it was as if he called to the grave of his mother, over there on the dark, windy hill.

That tremendous uprising of his passion had been a vortex, an end, a decision. And he realized that even to that hour there had been a drag in his blood. It was over now. The hell was done with. His soul was free. This weak, quaking body of his housed his tainted blood and the emotions of his heart, but it could not control his mind, his will. Beat by beat the helpless fury in him subsided, and then he fell back and lay still for a long time, eyes shut, relaxed and still.

A hound bayed mournfully; the insects chirped low, incessantly; the night wind rustled the silken heads of wheat.

After a while the young man sat up and looked at the heavens, at the twinkling white stars, and then away across the shadows of round hills in the dusk. How lonely, sad, intelligible, and yet mystic the night and the scene!

What came to him then was revealing, uplifting— a source of strength to go on. He was not to blame for what had happened; he could not change the future. He had a choice between playing the part of a man or that of a coward, and he had to choose the former. There seemed to be a spirit beside him—the spirit of his mother or of someone who loved him and who would have him be true to an ideal, and, if needful, die for it. No night in all his life before had been like this one.

The dreaming hills with their precious rustling wheat meant more than even a spirit could tell. Where had the wheat come from that had seeded these fields? Whence the first and original seeds, and where were the sowers? Back in the ages! The stars, the night, the dark blue of heaven hid the secret in their impenetrableness. Beyond them surely was the answer, and perhaps peace.

Material things—life, success—such as had inspired Kurt Dorn, on this calm night lost their significance and were seen clearly. They could not last. But the wheat there, the hills, the stars—they would go on with their task. Passion was the dominant side of a man declaring itself, and that was a matter of inheritance. But self-sacrifice, with its mercy, its succor, its seed like the wheat, was as infinite as the stars. He had long made up his mind, yet that had not given him absolute restraint. The world was full of little men, but he refused to stay little. This war that had come between him and his father had been bred of the fumes of self-centered minds, turned with an infantile fatality to greedy desires. His poor old blinded father could be excused and forgiven. There were other old men, sick, crippled, idle, who must suffer pain, but whose pain could be lightened. There were babies, children, women, who must suffer for the sins of men, but that suffering need no longer be, if men became honest and true.

His sudden up-flashing love had a few hours back seemed a calamity. But out there beside the whispering wheat, under the passionless stars, in the dreaming night, it had turned into a blessing. He asked nothing but to serve. To serve her, his country, the future! All at once he who had always yearned for something unattainable had greatness thrust upon him. His tragical situation had evoked a spirit from the gods.

To kiss that blue-eyed girl's sweet lips would be a sum of joy, earthly, all-satisfying, precious. The man in him trembled all over at the daring thought. He might revel in such dreams, and surrender to them, since she would never know, but the divinity he sensed there in the presence of those stars did not dwell on a woman's lips. Kisses were for the present, the all too fleeting present; and he had to concern himself with what he might do for one girl's future. It was exquisitely sad and sweet to put it that way, though Kurt knew that if he had never seen Lenore Anderson he would have gone to war just the same. He was not making an abstract sacrifice.

The wheat fields rolling before him, every clod of which had been pressed by his bare feet as a boy; the father whose changeless blood had sickened at the son of his loins; the life of hope, freedom, of action, of achievement, of wonderful possibility—these seemed lost to Kurt Dorn, a necessary renunciation when he yielded to the call of war.

But no loss, no sting of bullet or bayonet, no torturing victory of approaching death, could balance in the scale against the thought of a picture of one American girl—blue-eyed, red-lipped, golden-haired—as she stepped somewhere in the future, down a summer lane or through a blossoming orchard, on soil that was free.

CHAPTER

4

*T*OWARD the end of July eastern Washington sweltered under the most torrid spell of heat on record. It was a dry, high country, noted for an equable climate, with cool summers and mild winters. And this unprecedented wave would have been unbearable had not the atmosphere been free from humidity.

The haze of heat seemed like a pall of thin smoke from distant forest fires. The sun rose, a great, pale-red ball, hot at sunrise, and it soared blazing-white at noon, to burn slowly westward through a cloudless, coppery sky, at last to set sullen and crimson over the ranges.

Spokane, being the only center of iron, steel, brick, and masonry in this area, resembled a city of furnaces. Business was slack. The asphalt of the streets left clean imprints of a pedestrian's feet; bits of newspaper stuck fast to the hot tar. Down by the gorge, where the great green river made its magnificent plunges over the falls, people congregated, tarried, and were loath to leave, for here the blowing mist and the air set into motion by the falling water created a temperature that was relief.

Citizens talked of the protracted hot spell, of the blasted crops, of an almost sure disaster to the wheat fields, and of the activities of the I. W. W. Even the war, for the time being, gave place to the nearer calamities impending.

Montana had taken drastic measures against the invading I.W.W. The Governor of Idaho had sent word to the camps of the organization that they had five days to leave that state. Spokane was awakening to the menace of hordes of strange, idle men who came in on the westbound freight trains. The railroads had been unable to handle the situation. They were being hard put to it to run trains at all. The train crews that refused to join the I.W.W. had been threatened, beaten, shot at, and otherwise intimidated.

The Chamber of Commerce sent an imperative appeal to representative wheat raisers, ranchers, lumbermen, farmers, and bade them come to Spokane to discuss the situation. They met at the Hotel Davenport, where luncheon was served in one of the magnificently appointed dining halls of that most splendid hotel in the West.

The lion of this group of Spokane capitalists was Riesinberg, a man of German forebears, but all American in his sympathies, with a son already in the army. Riesinberg was president of a city bank and of the Chamber of Commerce. His first words to the large assembly of clean-cut, square-jawed, intent-eyed westerners were:

"Gentlemen, we are here to discuss the most threatening and unfortunate situation the Northwest was ever called upon to meet." His address was not long, but it was stirring. The Chamber of Commerce could provide unlimited means, could influence and control the state government; but it was from the visitors invited to this meeting, the men of the outlying districts which were threatened, that objective proofs must come and the best methods of procedure.

The first facts to come out were that many crops were ruined already, but, owing to the increased acreage that year, a fair yield was expected; that wheat in the Bend would be a failure, though some farmers here and there would harvest well; that the lumber districts were not operating, on account of the I. W. W.

Then it was that the organization of men who called themselves the Industrial Workers of the World drew the absorbed attention of the meeting. Depredations already committed stunned the members of the Chamber of Commerce.

President Riesinberg called upon Beardsley, a prominent and intelligent rancher of the southern wheat belt. Beardsley said:

"It is difficult to speak with any moderation of the outrageous eruption of the I. W. W. It is nothing less than rebellion, and the most effective means of suppressing rebellion is to apply a little of that 'direct action' which is the favorite diversion of the I. W. W.'s.

"The I. W. W. do not intend to accomplish their treacherous aims by anything so feeble as speech; they scorn the ballot box. They are against the war, and their method of making known their protest is by burning our grain, destroying our lumber, and blowing up freight trains. They seek to make converts not by argument, but by threats and intimidation.

"We read that western towns are seeking to deport these rebels. In the old days we can imagine more drastic measures would have been taken. The westerners were handy with the rope and the gun in those days. We are not counseling lynch law, but we think deportation is too mild a punishment.

"We are too 'civilized' to apply the old Roman law, 'Spare the conquered and extirpate the rebels,' but at least we could intern them. The British have found it practicable to put German prisoners to work at useful employment. Why couldn't we do the same with our rebel I. W. W.'s?"

Jones, a farmer from the Yakima Valley, told that businessmen, housewives, professional men, and high-school boys and girls would help to save the crop of Washington to the nation in case of labor trouble. Steps already had been taken to mobilize workers in stores, offices, and homes for work in the orchards and grain-fields, should the I.W.W. situation seriously threaten harvests.

Pledges to go into the hay or grain fields or the orchards, with a statement of the number of days they were willing to work, had been signed by virtually all the men in North Yakima.

Helmar, lumberman from the Blue Mountains, spoke feelingly; he said:

"My company is the owner of a considerable amount of timbered lands and timber purchased from the state and from individuals. We have been engaged in logging that land until our operations have been stopped and our business paralyzed by an organization which calls itself the Industrial Workers of the World, and by members of that organization, and other lawless persons acting in sympathy with them.

"Our employees have been threatened with physical violence and death.

"Our works are picketed by individuals who camp out in the forest and who intimidate and threaten our employees.

"Open threats have been made that our works, our logs, and our timber will all be burned.

"Sabotage is publicly preached in the meetings, and in the literature of the organization it is advised and upheld.

"The open boast is made that the lumbering industry, with all other industry, will be paralyzed by this organization, by the destruction of property used in industry and by the intimidation of laborers who are willing to work.

"A real and present danger to the property of my company exists. Unless protection is given to us it will probably be burned and destroyed. Our lawful operations cannot be conducted because laborers who are willing to work are fearful of their lives and are subject to abuse, threats, and violence. Our camps, when in operation, are visited by individuals belonging to the said organization, and the men peaceably engaged in them threatened with death if they do not cease work. All sorts of injury to property by the driving of spikes in logs, the destruction of logs, and other similar acts are encouraged and recommended.

"As I pointed out to the sheriff of our county, the season is a very dry one and the woods are and will be, unless rain comes, in danger of disastrous fires. The organization and its members have openly and repeatedly asserted that they will burn the logs in the woods and burn the forests of this company and other timberholders before they will permit logging operations to continue.

"Many individuals belonging to the organization are camped in the open in the timbered country, and their very presence is a fire menace. They are engaged in no business except to interfere with the industry and to interfere with the logging of this company and others who engaged in the logging business.

"We have done what we could in a lawful manner to continue our operations and to protect our employees. We are now helpless, and place the responsibility for the protection of our property and the protection of our employees upon the board of county commissioners and upon the officers of the county."

Next President Riesinberg called upon a young reporter to read paragraphs of an I. W. W. speech he had heard made to a crowd of three hundred workmen. It was significant that several members of the Chamber of Commerce called for a certain paragraph to be reread. It was this:

"If you workingmen could only stand together you could do in this country what has been done in Russia," declared the I. W. W. orator. "You know what the workingmen did there to the slimy curs, the gunmen, and the stool pigeons of the capitalistic class. They bumped them off. They sent them up to say, 'Good morning, Jesus.'"

After a moment of muttering and another silence the president again addressed the meeting:

"Gentlemen, we have Anderson of Golden Valley

with us today. If there are any of you present who do not know him, you surely have heard of him. His people were pioneers. He was born in Washington. He is a type of the men who have made the Northwest. He fought the Indians in early days and packed a gun for the outlaws—and today, gentlemen, he owns a farm as big as Spokane County. We want to hear from him."

When Anderson rose to reply it was seen that he was pale and somber. Slowly he gazed at the assembly of waiting men, bowed; then he began, impressively:

"Gentlemen an' friends, I wish I didn't have to throw a bomb into this here camp-fire talk. But I've got to. You're all talkin' I. W. W. Facts have been told showin' a strange an' sudden growth of this here four-flush labor union. We've had dealin's with them for several years. But this year it's different . . . All at once they've multiplied and strengthened. There's somethin' behind them. A big unseen hand is stackin' the deck . . . An', countrymen, that tremendous power is German gold!"

Anderson's deep voice rang like a bell. His hearers sat perfectly silent. No surprise showed, but faces grew set and hard. After a pause of suspense, in which his denunciation had time to sink in, Anderson resumed:

"A few weeks ago a young man, a stranger, came to me an' asked for a job. He could do anythin', he said, An' I hired him to drive my car. But he wasn't much of a driver. We went up in the Bend country one day, an' on that trip I got suspicious of him. I caught him talkin' to what I reckoned was I. W. W. men. An' then, back home again, I watched him an' kept my ears open. It didn't take long for me to find discontent among my farmhands. I hire about a hundred hands on my ranches durin' the long off-season, an' when harvest comes round a good many more. All I can get, in fact.... Well, I found my hands quittin' me, which was sure onusual. An' I laid it to that driver.

"One day not long ago I run across him hobnobbin' with the strange man I'd seen talkin' with him on the Bend trip. But my driver—Nash, he calls himself—didn't see me. That night I put a cowboy to watch him. An' what this cowboy heard, put together two an' two, was that Nash was assistant to an I. W. W. leader named Glidden. He had sent for Glidden to come to look over my ranch. Both these I. W. W. men had more money than they could well carry—lots of it gold! The way they talked of this money proved that they did not know the source, but the supply was unlimited.

"Next day Glidden could not be found. But my cowboy had learned enough to show his methods. If these proselyters could not coax or scare trusted men to join the I. W. W., they tried to corrupt them with money. An' in most cases they're successful. I've not yet sprung anythin' on my driver, Nash. But he can't get away, an' meanwhile I'll learn much by watchin' him. Maybe through Nash I can catch Glidden. An' so, gentlemen, here we have a plain case. An' the menace is enough to chill the heart of every loyal citizen. Any way you put it, if harvests can't be harvested, if wheat fields an' lumber forests are burned, if the state militia has to be called out—any way you put it our government will be hampered, our supplies kept from our allies—an' so the cause of Germany will be helped.

"The I. W. W. have back of them an organized power with a definite purpose. There can hardly be any doubt that that power is Germany. The agitators an' leaders throughout the country are well paid. Probably they, as individuals, do not know who pays them. Undoubtedly a little gang of men makes the deals, handles the money. We read that every U. S. attorney is investigating the I. W. W. The government has determined to close down on them. But lawyers an' law are slow to act. Meanwhile the danger to us is at hand.

"Gentlemen, to finish let me say that down in my country we're goin' to rustle the I. W. W. in the good old western way."

CHAPTER
5

G *OLDEN VALLEY* was the Garden of Eden of the Northwest. The southern slope rose to the Blue Mountains, whence flowed down the innumerable brooks that, uniting to form streams and rivers, abundantly watered the valley.

The black reaches of timber extended down to the grazing uplands, and these bordered on the sloping golden wheat fields, which in turn contrasted so vividly with the lower green alfalfa pastures; then came the orchards with their ruddy, mellow fruit, and lastly the bottom lands where the vegetable gardens attested to the wonderful richness of the soil. From the mountain-side the valley seemed a series of colored benches, stepping down, black to gray, and gray to gold, and gold to green with purple tinge, and on to the perfectly ordered, many-hued floor with its innumerable winding, tree-bordered streams glinting in the sunlight.

The extremes of heat and cold never visited Golden Valley. Spokane and the Bend country, just now sweltering in a torrid zone, might as well have been in the Sahara, for all the effect it had on this garden spot of all the Inland Empire. It was hot in the valley, but not unpleasant. In fact, the greatest charm in this secluded vale was its pleasant climate all the year round. No summer cyclones, no winter blizzards, no cloudbursts or bad thunderstorms. It was a country that, once lived in, could never be left.

There were no poor inhabitants in that great area of twenty-five hundred miles; and there were many who were rich. Prosperous little towns dotted the valley floor; and the many smooth, dusty, much-used roads all led to Ruxton, a wealthy and fine city.

Anderson, the rancher, had driven his car to Spokane. Upon his return he had with him a detective, whom he expected to use in the I. W. W. investigations, and a neighbor rancher. They had left Spokane early and had endured almost insupportable dust and heat. A welcome change began as they slid down from the bare desert into the valley; and once across the Copper River, Anderson began to breath freer and to feel he was nearing home.

"God's country!" he said, as he struck the first low swell of rising land, where a cool wind from off the wooded and watered hills greeted his face. Dust there still was, but it seemed a different kind and smelled of apple orchards and alfalfa fields. Here were hard, smooth roads, and Anderson sped his car miles and miles through a country that was a verdant fragrant bower, and across bright, shady streams and by white little hamlets.

At Huntington he dropped his neighbor rancher, and also the detective, Hall, who was to go disguised into the districts overrun by the I. W. W. A further run of forty miles put him on his own property.

Anderson owned a string of farms and ranches extending from the bottomlands to the timberline of the mountains. They represented his life of hard work and fair dealing. Many of these orchard and vegetable lands he had tenant farmers work on shares. The uplands or wheat and grass he operated himself. As he had accumulated property he had changed his place of residence from time to time, at last to build a beautiful and permanent home farther up on the valley slope than any of the others.

It was a modern house, white, with a red roof. Situated upon a high level bench, with the waving gold fields sloping up from it and the green squares of alfalfa and orchards below, it appeared a landmark from all around, and could be plainly seen from Vale, the nearest little town, five miles away.

Anderson had always loved the open, and he wanted a place where he could see the sun rise over the distant valley gateway, and watch it set beyond the bold black range in the west. He could sit on his front porch, wide and shady, and look down over two thousand acres, of his own land. But from the back porch no eye could have encompassed the limit of his broad, swelling slopes of grain and grass.

From the main road he drove up to the right of the house, where, under a dip of wooded slope, clustered barns, sheds, corrals, granaries, engine and machinery houses, a store, and the homes of hired men—a little village in itself.

The sounds he heard were a welcome home—the rush of swift water not twenty yards from where he stopped the car in the big courtyard, the pound of hooves on the barn floor, the shrill whistle of a stallion that saw and recognized him, the drawling laugh of his cowboys and the clink of their spurs as they became aware of his return.

Nash, the suspected driver, was among those who hurried to meet the car.

Anderson's keen, covert glance made note of the driver's worried and anxious face.

"Nash, she'll need a lookin' over," he said, as he uncovered bundles in the back seat and lifted them out.

"All right, sir," replied Nash, eagerly. A note of ended strain was significant in his voice.

"Here, you Jake," cheerily called Anderson to a rawboned, gaunt-faced fellow who wore the garb of a cowboy.

"Boss, I'm powerful glad to see you home," replied Jake, as he received bundle after bundle until he was loaded down. Then he grinned. "Mebbe you want a pack-hoss."

"You're hoss enough for me. Come on," he said, and, waving the other men aside, he turned toward the green, shady hill above which the red and white of the house just showed.

A bridge crossed the rushing stream. Here Jake dropped some of the bundles, and Anderson recovered them. As he straightened up he looked searchingly at the cowboy.

Jake's yellow-gray eyes returned the gaze. And that

exchange showed these two of the same breed and sure of each other.

"Nawthin' come off, boss," he drawled, "but I'm glad you're home."

"Did Nash leave the place?" queried Anderson.

"Twice, at night, an' he was gone long. I didn't foller him because I seen he didn't take no luggage, an' thet boy has some sporty clothes. He was sure comin' back."

"Any sign of his pard—that Glidden?"

"Nope. But there's been more'n one new feller snookin' round."

"Have you heard from any of the boys with the cattle?"

"Yep. Bill Weeks rode down. He said a bunch of I. W. W.'s were campin' above Blue Spring. Thet means they've moved on down to the edge of the timber an' oncomfortable near our wheat. Bill says they're killin' our stock fer meat."

"Hum! . . . How many in the gang?" inquired Anderson, darkly. His early dealings with outlaw rustlers had not left him favorably inclined toward losing a single steer.

"Wal, I reckon we can't say. Mebbe five hundred, countin' all along the valley on this side. Then we hear there's more on the other. . . . Boss, if they git ugly we're goin' to lose stock, wheat, an' mebbe some blood."

"So many as that!" ejaculated the rancher, in amaze.

"They come an' go, an' lately they're most comin'," replied Jake.

"When do we begin cuttin' grain?"

"I reckon tomorrow. Adams didn't want to start till

you got back. It'll be barley an' oats fer a few days, an' then the wheat—if we can git the men."

"An' has Adams hired any?"

"Yes, a matter of twenty or so. They swore they wasn't I. W. W.'s, but Adams says, an' so do I, thet some of them are men who first claimed to our old hands thet they did belong to the I. W. W."

"An' so we've got to take a chance if we're goin' to harvest two thousand acres of wheat?"

"I reckon, boss."

"Any reports from Ruxton way?"

"Wal, yes. But I reckon you'd better git your supper 'fore I tell you, boss."

"Jake, you said nothin' had come off."

"Wal, nawthin' has around here. Come on now, boss. Miss Lenore says I was to keep my mouth shut."

"Jake, who's your boss? Me or Lenore?"

"Wal, you air. But I ain't disobeyin' Miss Lenore."

Anderson walked the rest of the way up the shady path to the house without saying any more to Jake. The beautiful white house stood clear of the grove, bright in the rays of the setting sun. A barking of dogs greeted Anderson, and then the pattering of feet. His daughters appeared on the porch. Kathleen, who was ten, made a dive for him, and Rose, who was fourteen, came flying after her. Both girls were screaming joyously. Their sunny hair danced. Lenore waited for him at the step, and as he mounted the porch, burdened by the three girls, his anxious, sadly smiling wife came out to make perfect the welcome home. No—not perfect, for Anderson's joy held a bitter drop, the absence of his only son!

"Oh, dad, what-all did you fetch me?" cried Kathleen, and she deserted her father for the bundle-laden Jake.

"And me!" echoed Rose.

Even Lenore, in the happiness of her father's return, was not proof against the wonder and promise of those many bundles.

They all went within, through a hall to a great, cozy living room. Mrs. Anderson's very first words, after her welcoming smile, were a half-faltered:

"Any—news of—Jim?"

"Why—yes," replied Anderson, hesitatingly.

Suddenly the three sisters were silent. How closely they resembled one another then—Lenore, a budding woman; Rose, a budding girl; and Kathleen, a rosy, radiant child! Lenore lost a little of her bloom.

"What news, father?" she asked.

"Haven't you heard from him?" returned Anderson.

"Not for a whole week. He wrote the day he reached Spokane. But then he hardly knew anything except that he'd enlisted."

"I'm sure glad Jim didn't wait for the draft," replied the father. "Well, Mother an' girls, Jim was gone when I got to Spokane. All I heard was that he was well when he left for Frisco an' strong for the aviation corps."

"Then he means to—to be an aviator," said Lenore, with quivering lips.

"Sure, if he can get in. An' he's wise. Jim knows engines. He has a knack for machinery. An' nerve! No boy ever had more. He'll make a crack flier."

"But—the danger!" whispered the boy's mother, with a shudder.

"I reckon there'll be a little danger, Mother," replied Anderson, cheerfully. "We've got to take our chance on

Jim. There's one sure bet. If he had stayed home he'd been fightin' I. W. W.'s!"

That trying moment passed. Mrs. Anderson said that she would see to supper being put on the table at once. The younger girls began untying the bundles. Lenore studied her father's face a moment.

"Jake, you run along," she said to the waiting cowboy. "Wait till after supper before you worry father."

"I'll do thet, Miss Lenore," drawled Jake, "an' if he wants worryin' he'll hev to look me up."

"Lass, I'm only tired, not worried," replied Anderson, as Jake shuffled out with jingling spurs.

"Did anything serious happen in Spokane?" she asked, anxiously.

"No. But Spokane men are alive to serious trouble ahead," replied her father. "I spoke to the Chamber of Commerce—sure exploded a bomb in that camp. Then I had conferences with a good many different men. Fact is they ran me pretty hard. Couldn't have slept much, anyhow, in that heat. Lass, this is the place to live! ... I'd rather die here than live in Spokane, in summer."

"Did you see the Governor?"

"Yes, an' he wasn't as anxious about the Golden Valley as the Bend country. He's right, too. We're old Westerners here. We can handle trouble. But they're not Americans up there in the Bend."

"Father, we met one American," said Lenore, dreamily.

"By George! we did! ... An' that reminds me. There was a government official from Washington, come out to Spokane to investigate conditions. I forget his name. He asked to meet me an' he was curious about the Bend—its loyalty to the U. S. I told him all I knew an'

what I thought. An' then he said he was goin' to motor
through that wheat belt an' talk to what Americans he
could find, an' impress upon them that they could do
as much as soldiers to win the war. Wheat—bread—
that's our great gun in this war, Lenore! . . . I knew this,
but I was made pretty blamed sober by that government
man. I told him by all means to go to Palmer an' to have
a talk with young Dorn. I sure gave that boy a good
word. Poor lad! He's true blue. An' to think of him with
that old German devil. Old Dorn has always had a hard
name. An' this war has brought out the German cussedness."

"Father, I'm glad you spoke well of the young man,"
said Lenore, still dreamily.

"Hum! You never told me what you thought," replied her father, with a quick glance of inquiry at her.
Lenore was gazing out of the window, away across the
wheat fields and the range. Anderson watched her a
moment, and then resumed: "If I can get away I'm goin'
to drive up to see Dorn again pretty soon. Do you want
to go?"

Lenore gave a little start, as if the question had
surprised her.

"I—I hardly think so," she replied.

"It's just as well," he said. "That'll be a hard ride.
. . . Guess I'll clean up a little for supper."

Anderson left the room, and, while Kathleen and
Rose gleefully squabbled over the bundles, Lenore continued to gaze dreamily out of the window.

That night Lenore went early to her room, despite
the presence of some young people from a neighboring

village. She locked her door and sat in the dark beside her open window.

An early moon silvered the long slopes of wheat and made the alfalfa squares seem black. A cool, faint, sweet breeze fanned her cheek. She could smell the fragrance of apples, of new-mown hay, and she could hear the low murmur of running water. A hound bayed off somewhere in the fields. There was no other sound. It was a quiet, beautiful, pastoral scene. But somehow it did not comfort Lenore.

She seemed to doubt the sincerity of what she saw there and loved so well. Moon-blanched and serene, lonely and silent, beautiful and promising, the wide acres of "Many Waters," and the silver slopes and dark mountains beyond, did not tell the truth. Way over the dark ranges a hideous war had stretched out a red hand to her country. Her only brother had left his home to fight, and there was no telling if he would ever come back. Evil forces were at work out there in the moonlight. There had come a time for her to be thoughtful.

Her father's asking her to ride to the Bend country had caused some strange little shock of surprise. Lenore had dreamed without thinking. Here in the darkness and silence, watching the crescent moon slowly sink, she did think. And it was to learn that she remembered singularly well the first time she had seen young Dorn, and still more vividly the second time, but the third time seemed both clear and vague. Enough young men had been smitten with Lenore to enable her to gauge the symptoms of these easy-come, easy-go attractions. In fact, they rather repelled her. But she had found Dorn's manner striking, confusing, and unforgettable. And why that should be so interested her intelligence.

It was confusing to discover that she could not lay it to the sympathy she had felt for an American boy in a difficult position, because she had often thought of him long before she had any idea who he was or where he lived.

In the very first place, he had been unforgettable for two reasons—because he had been so struck at sight of her that he had gazed unconsciously, with a glow on his face and a radiance in his eye, as of a young poet spellbound at an inspiration; and because he seemed the physical type of young man she had idealized—a strong, lithe-limbed, blond giant, with a handsome, frank face, clear-cut and smooth, ruddy-cheeked and blue-eyed.

Only after meeting him out there in the desert of wheat had she felt sympathy for him. And now with intelligence and a woman's intuition, barring the old, insidious, dreamy mood, Lenore went over in retrospect all she could remember of that meeting. And the truth made her sharply catch her breath. Dorn had fallen in love with her. Intuition declared that, while her intelligence repudiated it. Stranger than all was the thrill which began somewhere in the unknown depths of her and mounted, to leave her tingling all over. She had told her father that she did not want to ride to the Bend country. But she did want to go! And that thought, flashing up, would not be denied. To want to meet a strange young man again was absolutely a new and irritating discovery for Lenore. It mystified her, because she had not had time to like Dorn. Liking an acquaintance had nothing to do with the fact. And that stunned her.

"Could it be—love at first sight?" she whispered,

incredulously, as she stared out over the shadowing fields.

"For me? Why, how absurd—impossible! ... I—I only remembered him—a big handsome boy with blazing eyes.... And now I'm sorry for him!"

To whisper her amaze and doubt and consternation only augmented the instinctive recurring emotion. She felt something she could not explain. And that something was scarcely owing to this young man's pitiful position between duty to his father and love for his country. It had to do with his blazing eyes; intangible, dreamlike perceptions of him as not real, of vague sweet fancies that retreated before her introspective questioning. What alarmed Lenore was a tendency of her mind to shirk this revealing analysis. Never before had she been afraid to look into herself. But now she was finding unplumbed wells of feeling, secret chambers of dreams into which she had never let the light, strange instinctive activities, more physical than mental. When in her life before had she experienced a nameless palpitation of her heart?

Long she sat there, staring out into the night. And the change in the aspect of the broad spaces, now dark and impenetrable and mysterious, seemed like the change in the knowledge of herself. Once she had flattered herself that she was an inch of crystal water; now she seemed a complex, aloof, and contrary creature, almost on the verge of tumultuous emotions.

She said her prayers that night, a girlish habit resumed since her brother had declared his intention of enlisting in the army. And to that old prayer, which her mother had prayed before her, she added an appeal of her own. Strange that young Dorn's face should flash out of gloom! It was there, and her brother's was fading.

"I wonder—will he and Jim—meet over there—on the battlefield!" she whispered. She hoped they would. Like tigers those boys would fight the Germans. Her heart beat high. Then a cold wind seemed to blow over her. It had a sickening weight. If that icy and somber wind could have been traced to its source, then the mystery of life would have been clear. But that source was the cause of war, as its effect was the horror of women. A hideous and monstrous thing existed out there in the darkness. Lenore passionately loved her brother, and this black thing had taken him away. Why could not women, who suffered most, have some word in the regulation of events? If women could help govern the world there would be no wars.

At last encroaching drowsiness dulled the poignancy of her feelings and she sank to sleep.

CHAPTER
6

*S*INGING of birds at her window awakened Lenore. The dawn streamed in bright and sweetly fragrant. The wheat fields seemed a rosy gold, and all that open slope called to her thrillingly of the beauty of the world and the happiness of youth. It was not possible to be morbid at dawn. "I hear! I hear!" she whispered. "From a thousand slopes far and wide!"

At the breakfast table, when there came opportunity, she looked up serenely and said, "Father, on second thought I will go to the Bend, thank you!"

Anderson laid down his knife and fork and his eyes opened wide in surprise. "Changed your mind!" he exclaimed.

"That's a privilege I have, you know," she replied, calmly.

Mrs. Anderson appeared more anxious than surprised. "Daughter, don't go. That will be a fearful ride."

"Hum! Sure glad to have you, lass," added Anderson, with his keen eyes on her.

"Let me go, too," begged Rose.

Kathleen was solemnly gazing at Lenore, with the wise, penetrating eyes of extreme youth.

"Lenore, I'll bet you've got a new beau up there," she declared.

Lenore flushed scarlet. She was less angry with her little sister than with the incomprehensible fact of a playful word bringing the blood stingingly to her neck and face.

"Kitty, you forget your manners," she said, sharply.

"Kit is fresh. She's an awful child," added Rose, with a superior air.

"I didn't say a thing," cried Kathleen, hotly. "Lenore, if it isn't true, why'd you blush so red?"

"Hush, you silly children!" ordered the mother, reprovingly.

Lenore was glad to finish that meal and to get outdoors. She could smile now at that shrewd and terrible Kitty, but recollection of her father's keen eyes was confusing. Lenore felt there was really nothing to blush for; still, she could scarcely tell her father that upon awakening this morning she had found her mind made up—that only by going to the Bend country could she determine the true state of her feelings. She simply dared not accuse herself of being in unusually radiant spirits because she was going to undertake a long, hard ride into a barren, desert country.

The grave and thoughtful mood of last night had gone with her slumbers. Often Lenore had found problems decided for her while she slept. On this fresh, sweet summer morning, with the sun bright and warm, presaging a hot and glorious day, Lenore wanted to run with the winds, to wade through the alfalfa, to watch with strange and renewed pleasure the waves of shadow as they went over the wheat. All her life she had known and loved the fields of waving gold. But they had never been to her what they had become overnight. Perhaps this was because it had been said that the issue of the great war, the salvation of the world, and its happiness, its hope, depended upon the millions of broad acres of golden grain. Bread was the staff of life. Lenore felt that she was changing and growing. If anything should happen to her brother Jim she would be heiress to thousands of acres of wheat. A pang shot through her heart. She had to drive the cold thought away. And she must learn—must know the bigness of this question. The women of the country would be called upon to help, to do their share.

She ran down through the grove and across the bridge, coming abruptly upon Nash, her father's driver. He had the car out.

"Good morning," he said, with a smile, doffing his cap.

Lenore returned his greeting and asked if her father intended to go anywhere.

"No. I'm taking telegrams to Huntington."

"Telegrams? What's the matter with the phone?" she queried.

"Wire was cut yesterday."

"By I. W. W. men?"

"So your father says. I don't know."

"Something ought to be done to those men," said Lenore, severely.

Nash was a dark-browed, heavy-jawed young man,

with light eyes and hair. He appeared to be intelligent and had some breeding, but his manner when alone with Lenore—he had driven her to town several times—was not the same as when her father was present. Lenore had not bothered her mind about it. But today the look in his eyes was offensive to her.

"Between you and me, Lenore, I've sympathy for those poor devils," he said.

Lenore drew back rather haughtily at this familiar use of her first name. "It doesn't concern me," she said, coldly, and turned away.

"Won't you ride along with me? I'm driving around for the mail," he called after her.

"No," returned Lenore, shortly, and hurried on out of earshot. The impertinence of the fellow!

"Mawnin', Miss Lenore!" drawled a cheery voice. The voice and the jingle of spurs behind her told Lenore of the presence of the best liked of all her father's men.

"Good morning, Jake! Where's my dad?"

"Wal, he's with Adams, an' I wouldn't be Adams for no money," replied the cowboy.

"Neither would I," laughed Lenore.

"Reckon you ain't ridin' this mawnin'. You sure look powerful fine, Miss Lenore, but you can't ride in thet dress."

"Jake, nothing but an airplane would satisfy me today."

"Want to fly, hey? Wal, excuse me from them birds. I seen one, an' thet's enough for me. . . . An', changin' the subject, Miss Lenore, beggin' your pardon—you ain't ridin' in the car much these days."

"No, Jake, I'm not," she replied, and looked at the

cowboy. She would have trusted Jake as she would her brother Jim. And now he looked earnest.

"Wal, I'm sure glad. I heerd Nash call an' ask you to go with him. I seen his eyes when he said it....Sure I know you'd never look at the likes of him. But I want to tell you—he ain't no good. I've been watchin' him. Your dad's orders. He's mixed up with the I. W. W.'s. But thet ain't what I mean. It's—He's—I—"

"Thank you, Jake," replied Lenore, as the cowboy floundered. "I appreciate your thought of me. But you needn't worry."

"I was worryin' a little," he said. "You see, I know men better'n your dad, an' I reckon this Nash would do anythin'."

"What's father keeping him for?"

"Wal, Anderson wants to find out a lot about thet I. W. W., an' he ain't above takin' risks to do it, either."

The stable boys and men Lenore passed all had an eager good morning for her. She often boasted to her father that she could run "Many Waters" as well as he. Sometimes there were difficulties that Lenore had no little part in smoothing over. The barns and corrals were familiar places to her, and she insisted upon petting every horse, in some instances to Jake's manifest concern.

"Some of them hosses are bad," he insisted.

"To be sure they are—when wicked cowboys cuff and kick them," replied Lenore, laughingly.

"Wal, if I'm wicked, I'm a-goin' to war," said Jake, reflectively. "Them Germans bother me."

"But, Jake, you don't come in the draft age, do you?"

"Jest how old do you think I am?"

"Sometimes about fourteen, Jake."

"Much obliged. Wal, the fact is I'm overage, but I'll gamble I can pack a gun an' shoot as straight an' eat as much as any young feller."

"I'll bet so, too, Jake. But I hope you won't go. We absolutely could not run this ranch without you."

"Sure I knew thet. Wal then, I reckon I'll hang around till you're married, Miss Lenore," he drawled.

Again the scarlet mantled Lenore's cheeks.

"Good. We'll have many harvests then, Jake, and many rides," she replied.

"Aw, I don't know—" he began.

But Lenore ran away so that she could hear no more.

"What's the matter with me that people—that Jake should—?" she began, and ended with a hand on each soft, hot cheek. There was something different about her, that seemed certain. And if her eyes were as bright as the day, with its deep blue and white clouds and shining green and golden fields, then anyone might think what he liked and have proof for his tormenting.

"But married! I? Not much. Do I want a husband getting shot?"

The path Lenore trod so lightly led along a great peach and apple orchard where the trees were set far apart and the soil was cultivated, so that not a weed nor a blade of grass showed. The fragrance of fruit in the air, however, did not come from this orchard, for the trees were young and the reddening fruit rare. Down the wide aisles she saw the thick and abundant green of the older orchards.

At length Lenore reached the alfalfa fields, and here among the mounds of newly cut hay that smelled so fresh and sweet she wanted to roll, and she had to run.

Two great wagons with four horses each were being loaded. Lenore knew all the workmen except one. Silas Warner, an old, gray-headed farmer, had been with her father as long as she could remember.

"Whar you goin', lass?" he called, as he halted to wipe his red face with a huge bandana. "It's too hot to run the way you're a-doin'."

"Oh, Silas, it's a grand morning!" she replied.

"Why, so 'tis! Pitchin' hay hyar made me think it was hot," he said, as she tripped on. "Now, lass, don't go up to the wheat fields."

But Lenore heard heedlessly, and she ran on till she came to the uncut alfalfa, which impeded her progress. A wonderful space of green and purple stretched away before her, and into it she waded. It came up to her knees, rich, thick, soft, and redolent of blossom and ripeness. Hard tramping it soon got to be. She grew hot and breathless, and her legs ached from the force expended in making progress through the tangled hay. At last she was almost across the field, far from the cutters, and here she flung herself, to roll and lie flat and gaze up through the deep azure of sky, wonderingly, as if to penetrate its secret. And then she hid her face in the fragrant thickness that seemed to force a whisper from her.

"I wonder—how will I feel—when I see him—again.... Oh, I wonder!"

The sound of the whispered words, the question, the inevitableness of something involuntary, proved traitors to her happy dreams, her assurance, her composure. She tried to burrow under the hay, to hide from that tremendous bright-blue eye, the sky. Suddenly she lay very quiet, feeling the strange glow and throb and race of her blood, sensing the mystery of her body, trying to trace the thrills, to control this queer, tremulous, internal state. But she found she could not think clearly; she could only feel. And she gave up trying. It was sweet to feel.

She rose and went on. Another field lay beyond, a gradual slope, covered with a new growth of alfalfa. It was a light green—a contrast to the rich darkness of that behind her. At the end of this field ran a swift little brook, clear and musical, open to the sky in places, and in others hidden under flowery banks. Birds sang from invisible coverts; a quail sent up clear flutelike notes; and a lark caroled, seemingly out of the sky.

Lenore wet her feet crossing the brook, and, climbing the little knoll above, she sat down upon a stone to dry them in the sun. It had a burn that felt good. No matter how hot the sun ever got there, she liked it. Always there seemed air to breathe and the shade was pleasant.

From this vantage point, a favorite one with Lenore, she could see all the alfalfa fields, the hill crowned by the beautiful white-and-red house, the acres of garden, and the miles of orchards. The grazing and grain fields began behind her.

The brook murmured below her and the birds sang. She heard the bees humming by. The air out here was clear of scent of fruit and hay, and it bore a drier odor, not so sweet. She could see the workmen, first those among the alfalfa, and then the men, and women, too, bending over on the vegetable gardens. Likewise she could see the gleam of peaches, apples, pears, and plums—a colorful and mixed gleam, delightful to the eye.

Wet or dry, it seemed that her feet refused to stay still, and once again she was wandering. A gray, slate-colored field of oats invited her steps, and across this stretch she saw a long yellow slope of barley, where the men were cutting. Beyond waved the golden fields of wheat. Lenore imagined that when she reached them she would not desire to wander farther.

There were two machines cutting on the barley slope, one drawn by eight horses, and the other by twelve. When Lenore had crossed the oat field she discovered a number of strange men lounging in the scant shade of a line of low trees that separated the fields. Here she saw Adams, the foreman; and he espied her at the same moment. He had been sitting down, talking to the men. At once he rose to come toward Lenore.

"Is your father with you?" he asked.

"No; he's too slow for me," replied Lenore. "Who are these men?"

"They're strangers looking for jobs."

"I. W. W. men?" queried Lenore, in lower voice.

"Surely must be," he replied. Adams was not a young, not a robust man, and he seemed to carry a burden of worry. "Your father said he would come right out."

"I hope he doesn't," said Lenore, bluntly. "Father has a way with him, you know."

"Yes, I know. And it's the way we're needing here in the Valley," replied the foreman, significantly.

"Is that the new harvester-thresher father just bought?" asked Lenore, pointing to a huge machine, shining and creeping behind the twelve horses.

"Yes, that's the McCormack and it's a dandy," returned Adams. "With machines like that we can get along without the I. W. W."

"I want a ride on it," declared Lenore, and she ran along to meet the harvester. She waved her hand to the driver, Bill Jones, another old hand, long employed by her father. Bill hauled back on the many-branched reins, and when the horses stopped the clattering, whirring roar of the machine also ceased.

"Howdy, miss! Reckon this 's a regular I. W. W. hold-up."

"Worse than that, Bill," gaily replied Lenore as she mounted the platform where another man sat on a bag of barley. Lenore did not recognize him. He looked rugged and honest, and beamed upon her.

"Watch out fer yer dress," he said, pointing with grimy hand to the dusty wheels and braces so near her.

"Let me drive, Bill?" she asked.

"Wal, now, I wisht I could," he replied, dryly. "You sure can drive, miss. But drivin' ain't all this here job."

"What can't I do? I'll bet you—"

"I never seen a girl thet could throw anythin' straight. Did you?"

"Well, not so very. I forgot how you drove the horses. . . . Go ahead. Don't let me delay the harvest."

Bill called sonorously to his twelve horses, and as they bent and strained and began to bob their heads, the clattering roar filled the air. Also a cloud of dust and thin, flying streams of chaff enveloped Lenore. The high stalks of barley, in wide sheets, fell before the cutter upon an apron, to be carried by feeders into the body of the machine. The straw, denuded of its grain, came out at the rear, to be dropped, while the grain streamed out of a tube on the side next to Lenore, to fall into an open sack. It made a short shift of harvesting.

Lenore liked the even, nodding rhythm of the plodding horses, and the way Bill threw a pebble from a
sack on his seat, to hit this or that horse not keeping
in line or pulling its share. Bill's aim was unerring. He
never hit the wrong horse, which would have been the
case had he used a whip. The grain came out in so tiny
a stream that Lenore wondered how a bag was ever
filled. But she saw presently that even a tiny stream, if
running steadily, soon made bulk. That was proof of the
value of small things, even atoms.

No marvel was it that Bill and his helper were as
grimy as stokers of a furnace. Lenore began to choke
with the fine dust and to feel her eyes smart and to see
it settle on her hands and dress. She then had appreciation of the nature of a ten-hour day for workmen
cutting eighteen acres of barley. How would they ever
cut the two thousand acres of wheat? No wonder many
men were needed. Lenore sympathized with the oper-
ators of that harvester-thresher, but she did not like the
dirt. If she had been a man, though, that labor, hard as
it was, would have appealed to her. Harvesting the grain
was beautiful, whether in the old, slow method of
threshing or with one of these modern man-saving machines.

She jumped off, and the big, ponderous thing, almost gifted with intelligence, it seemed to Lenore, rolled
on with its whirring roar, drawing its cloud of dust, and
leaving behind a litter of straw.

It developed then that Adams had walked along
with the machine, and he now addressed her.

"Will you be staying here till your father comes?"
he asked.

"No, Mr. Adams. Why do you ask?"

"You oughtn't come out here alone or go back alone....All these strange men! Some of them hard customers! You'll excuse me, miss, but this harvest is not like other harvests."

"I'll wait for my father and I'll not go out of sight," replied Lenore. Thanking the foreman for his thoughtfulness, she walked away, and soon she stood at the edge of the first wheat field.

The grain was not yet ripe, but near at hand it was a pale gold. The wind, out of the west, waved and swept the wheat, while the almost imperceptible shadows followed.

A road half overgrown with grass and goldenrod bordered the wheat field, and it wound away down toward the house. Her father appeared mounted on the white horse he always rode. Lenore sat down in the grass to wait for him. Nodding stalks of goldenrod leaned to her face. When looked at closely, how truly gold their color! Yet it was not such a gold as that of the rich blaze of ripe wheat. She was admitting to her consciousness a jealousy of anything comparable to wheat. And suddenly she confessed that her natural love for it had been augmented by a subtle growing sentiment. Not sentiment about the war or the need of the Allies or meaning of the staff of life. She had sensed young Dorn's passion for wheat and it had made a difference to her.

"No use lying to myself!" she soliloquized. "I think of him! ... I can't help it.... I ran out here, wild, restless, unable to reason ... just because I'd decided to see him again—to make sure I—I really didn't care ... How furious—how ridiculous I'll feel—when—when—"

Lenore did not complete her thought, because she was not sure. Nothing could be any truer than the fact that she had no idea how she would feel. She began sensitively to distrust herself. She who had always been so sure of motives, so contented with things as they were, had been struck by an absurd fancy that haunted because it was fiercely repudiated and scorned, that would give her no rest until it was proven false. But suppose it were true!

A succeeding blankness of mind awoke to the clip-clop of hooves and her father's cheery halloo.

Anderson dismounted and, throwing his bridle, he sat down heavily beside her.

"You can ride back home," he said.

Lenore knew she had been reproved for her wandering out there, and she made a motion to rise. His big hand held her down.

"No hurry, now I'm here. Grand day, ain't it? An' I see the barley's goin'. Them sacks look good to me."

Lenore waited with some perturbation. She had a guilty conscience and she feared he meant to quiz her about her sudden change of front regarding the Bend trip. So she could not look up and she could not say a word.

"Jake says that Nash has been tryin' to make up to you. Any sense in what he says?" asked her father, bluntly.

"Why, hardly. Oh, I've noticed Nash is—is rather fresh, as Rose calls it," replied Lenore, somewhat relieved at this unexpected query.

"Yes, he's been makin' eyes at Rose. She told me," replied Anderson.

"Discharge him," said Lenore, forcibly.

"So I ought. But let me tell you, Lenore. I've been hopin' to get Nash dead to rights."

"What more do you want?" she demanded.

"I mean regardin' his relation to the I. W. W.... Listen. Here's the point. Nash has been tracked an' caught in secret talks with prominent men in this country. Men of foreign blood an' mebbe foreign sympathies. We're at the start of big an' bad times in the good old U.S. No one can tell how bad. Well, you know my position in the Golden Valley. I'm looked to. Reckon this I. W. W. has got me a marked man. I'm packin' two guns right now. An' you bet Jake is packin' the same. We don't travel far apart anymore this summer."

Lenore had started shudderingly and her look showed her voiceless fear.

"You needn't tell your mother," he went on, more intimately. "I can trust you an'... To come back to Nash. He an' this Glidden—you remember, one of those men at Dorn's house—they are usin' gold. They must have barrels of it. If I could find out where that gold comes from! Probably they don't know. But I might find out if men here in our own country are hatchin' plots with the I. W. W."

"Plots! What for?" queried Lenore, breathlessly.

"To destroy my wheat, to drive off or bribe the harvest hands, to cripple the crop yield in the Northwest; to draw the militia here; in short, to harass an' weaken an' slow down our government in its preparation against Germany."

"Why, that is terrible!" declared Lenore.

"I've a hunch from Jake—there's a whisper of a plot to put me out of the way," said Anderson, darkly.

"Oh—good Heavens! You don't mean it!" cried Lenore, distractedly.

"Sure I do. But that's no way for Anderson's daughter to take it. Our women have got to fight, too. We've all got to meet these German hired devils with their own weapons. Now, lass, you know you'll get these wheatlands of mine some day. It's in my will. That's because you, like your dad, always loved the wheat. You'd fight, wouldn't you, to save your grain for our soldiers—bread for your own brother Jim—an' for your own land?"

"Fight! Would I?" burst out Lenore, with a passionate little cry.

"Good! Now you're talkin'!" exclaimed her father.

"I'll find out about this Nash—if you'll let me," declared Lenore, as if inspired.

"How? What do you mean, girl?"

"I'll encourage him. I'll make him think I'm a wishy-washy moonstruck girl, smitten with him. All's fair in war!...If he means ill by my father—"

Anderson muttered low under his breath and his big hand snapped hard at the nodding goldenrod.

"For my sake—to help me—you'd encourage Nash—flirt with him a little—find out all you could?"

"Yes, I would!" she cried, deliberately. But she wanted to cover her face with her hands. She trembled slightly, then grew cold, with a sickening disgust at this strange, new, uprising self.

"Wait a minute before you say too much," went on Anderson. "You're my best-beloved child, my Lenore, the lass I've been so proud of all my life. I'd spill blood to avenge an insult to you....But, Lenore, we've entered upon a terrible war. People out here, especially the women, don't realize it yet. But you must realize it. When I said good-bye to Jim, my son, I—I felt I'd never look upon his face again! ... I gave him up. I could have held him back—got exemption for him. But, no, by God! I gave him up—to make safety and happiness and prosperity for—say, your children, an' Rose's an' Kathleen's. ... I'm workin' now for the future. So must every loyal man an' every loyal woman! We love our own country. An' I ask you to see as I see the terrible danger to that country. Think of you an' Rose an' Kathleen bein' treated like those poor Belgian girls. Well, you'd get that an' worse if the Germans won this war. An' the point is, for us to win, every last one of us must fight, sacrifice to that end, an' hang together."

Anderson paused huskily and swallowed hard while he looked away across the fields. Lenore felt herself drawn by an irresistible power. The west wind rustled through the waving wheat. She heard the whir of the threshers. Yet all seemed unreal. Her father's passion had made this place another world.

"So much for that," resumed Anderson. "I'm goin' to do my best. An' I may make blunders. I'll play the game as it's dealt out to me. Lord knows I feel all in the dark. But it's the nature of the effort, the spirit, that'll count. I'm goin' to save most of the wheat on my ranches. An' bein' a Westerner who can see ahead, I know there's goin' to be blood spilled ... I'd give a lot to know who sent this Nash spyin' on me. I'm satisfied now he's an agent, a spy, a plotter for a gang that's marked me. I can't prove it yet, but I feel it. Maybe nothin' worthwhile—worth the trouble—will ever be found out from him. But I don't figure that way. I say play their own game an' take a chance ... If you encouraged Nash you'd probably find out all about him. The worst of it is could you be slick enough? Could a girl as fine an' square an' high-spirited as you ever double-cross a man, even a scoundrel like Nash? I reckon you could, considerin' the motive. Women are wonderful . . . Well, if you can fool him, make him think he's a winner, flatter him till he swells up like a toad, promise to elope with him, be curious, jealous, make him tell where he goes, whom he meets, show his letters, all without ever sufferin' his hand on you, I'll give my consent. I'd think more of you for it. Now the question is, can you do it?"

"Yes," whispered Lenore.

"Good!" exploded Anderson, in a great relief. Then he began to mop his wet face. He arose, showing the weight of heavy guns in his pockets, and he gazed across the wheat fields. "That wheat 'll be ripe in a week. It sure looks fine. . . . Lenore, you ride back home now. Don't let Jake pump you. He's powerful curious. An' I'll go give these I. W. W.'s a first dose of Anderson."

He turned away without looking at her, and he hesitated, bending over to pluck a stem of goldenrod.

"Lass—you're—you're like your mother," he said, unsteadily. "An' she helped me win out durin' my struggle here. You're brave an' you're big."

Lenore wanted to say something, to show her feeling, to make her task seem lighter, but she could not speak.

"We're pards now—with no secrets," he continued, with a different note in his voice. "An' I want you to know that it ain't likely Nash or Glidden will get out of this country alive."

CHAPTER
7

T *HREE* days later, Lenore accompanied her father on the ride to the Bend country. She sat in the back seat of the car with Jake—an arrangement very gratifying to the cowboy, but received with ill-concealed displeasure by the driver, Nash. They had arranged to start at sunrise, and it became manifest that Nash had expected Lenore to sit beside him all during the long ride. It was her father, however, who took the front seat, and behind Nash's back he had slyly winked at Lenore, as if to compliment her on the evident success of their deep plot. Lenore, at the first opportunity that presented, shot Nash a warning glance which was sincere enough. Jake had begun to use keen eyes, and there was no telling what he might do.

The morning was cool, sweet, fresh, with a red sun presaging a hot day. The big car hummed like a droning bee and seemed to cover the miles as if by magic. Lenore sat with face uncovered, enjoying the breeze and the endless colorful scene flashing by, listening to Jake's amusing comments, and trying to keep back thought of what discovery might await her before the end of this day.

Once across the Copper River, they struck the gradual ascent, and here the temperature began to mount and the dust to fly. Lenore drew her veils close and, leaning comfortably back, she resigned herself to wait and to endure.

By the flight of a crow it was about a hundred miles from Anderson's ranch to Palmer; but by the roundabout roads necessary to take the distance was a great deal longer. Lenore was well aware when they got up on the desert, and the time came when she thought she would suffocate. There appeared to be intolerable hours in which no one spoke and only the hum and creak of the machine throbbed in her ears. She could not see through her veils and did not part them until a stop was made at Palmer.

Her father got out, sputtering and gasping, shaking the dust in clouds from his long linen coat. Jake, who always said he lived on dust and heat, averred it was not exactly a regular fine day. Lenore looked out, trying to get a breath of air. Nash busied himself with the hot engine.

The little country town appeared dead, and buried under dust. There was not a person in sight nor a sound to be heard. The sky resembled molten lead, with a blazing center too bright for the gaze of man.

Anderson and Jake went into the little hotel to get some refreshments. Lenore preferred to stay in the car, saying she wanted only a cool drink. The moment the two men were out of sight Nash straightened up to gaze darkly and hungrily at Lenore.

"This's as good a chance as we'll get," he said, in an eager, hurried whisper.

"For what?" asked Lenore, aghast.

"To run off," he replied, huskily.

Lenore had proceeded so cleverly to carry out her scheme that in three days Nash had begun to implore and demand that she elope with him. He had been so much of a fool. But she as yet had found out but little about him. His right name was Ruenke. He was a socialist. He had plenty of money and hinted of mysterious sources for more.

At this Lenore hid her face, and while she fell back in pretended distress, she really wanted to laugh. She had learned something new in these few days, and that was to hate.

"Oh no!" she murmured. "I—I can't think of that—yet."

"But why not?" he demanded, in shrill violence. His gloved hand clenched on the tool he held.

"Mother has been so unhappy—with my brother Jim—off to the war. I—I just couldn't—now. Harry, you must give me time. It's all so—so sudden. Please wait!"

Nash appeared divided between two emotions. Lenore watched him from behind her parted veil. She had been astonished to find out that, side by side with her intense disgust and shame at the part she was playing, there was a strong, keen, passionate interest in it, owing to the fact that, though she could prove little against this man, her woman's intuition had sensed his secret deadly antagonism toward her father. By little significant mannerisms and revelations he had more and more betrayed the German in him. She saw it in his over-bearing conceit, his almost instant assumption that he was her master. At first Lenore feared him, but, as she learned to hate him she lost her fear. She had never been alone with him except under such circumstances as this; and she had decided she would not be.

"Wait?" he was expostulating. "But it's going to get hot for me."

"Oh!...What do you mean?" she begged. "You frighten me."

"Lenore, the I. W. W. will have hard sledding in this wheat country. I belong to that. I told you. But the union is run differently this summer. And I've got work to do—that I don't like, since I fell in love with you. Come, run off with me and I'll give it up."

Lenore trembled at this admission. She appeared to be close upon further discovery.

"Harry, how wildly you talk!" she exclaimed. "I hardly know you. You frighten me with your mysterious talk....Have—a—a little consideration for me."

Nash strode back to lean into the car. Behind his huge goggles his eyes gleamed. His gloved hand closed hard on her arm.

"It is sudden. It's got to be sudden," he said, in fierce undertone. "You must trust me."

"I will. But you must confide in me," she replied, earnestly. "I'm not quite a fool. You're rushing me—too—too—"

Suddenly he released her, threw up his hand, then quickly stepped back to the front of the car. Jake stood in the door of the hotel. He had seen that action of Nash's. Then Anderson appeared, followed by a boy carrying a glass of water for Lenore. They approached the car, Jake sauntering last, with his curious gaze on Nash.

"Go in an' get a bite an' a drink," said Anderson to the driver. "An' hurry."

Nash obeyed. Jake's eyes never left him until he entered the door. Then Jake stepped in beside Lenore.

"Thet water's wet, anyhow," he drawled.

"We'll get a good cold drink at Dorn's," said Anderson. "Lass, how are you makin' it?"

"Fine," she replied, smiling.

"So I seen," significantly added Jake, with a piercing glance at her.

Lenore realized then that she would have to confide in Jake or run the risk of having violence done to Nash. So she nodded wisely at the cowboy and winked mischievously, and, taking advantage of Anderson's entering the car, she whispered in Jake's ear: "I'm finding out things. Tell you—later."

The cowboy looked anything but convinced; and he glanced with narrowed eyes at Nash as that worthy hurried back to the car.

With a lurch and a leap the car left Palmer behind in a cloud of dust. The air was furnace-hot, oppressive, and exceedingly dry. Lenore's lips smarted so that she continually moistened them. On all sides stretched dreary parched wheat fields. Anderson shook his head sadly. Jake said: "Ain't thet too bad? Not half growed, an' sure too late now."

Near at hand Lenore saw the short immature dirty-whitish wheat, and she realized that it was ruined.

"It's been gettin' worse, Jake," remarked Anderson. "Most of this won't be cut at all. An' what is cut won't yield seedlings. I see a yellow patch here an' there on the north slopes, but on the most part the Bend's a failure."

"Father, you remember Dorn's section, that promised so well?" asked Lenore.

"Yes. But it promised only in case of rain. I look for the worst," replied Anderson, regretfully.

"It looks like storm clouds over there," said Lenore, pointing far ahead.

Through the drifting veils of heat, far across the bare, dreamy hills of fallow and the blasted fields of wheat, stood up some huge white columnar clouds, a vivid contrast to the coppery sky.

"By George! there's a thunderhead!" exclaimed Anderson. "Jake, what do you make of that?"

"Looks good to me," replied Jake, who was always hopeful.

Lenore bore the hot wind and the fine, choking dust without covering her face. She wanted to see all the hills and valleys of this desert of wheat. Her heart beat a little faster as, looking across that waste on waste of heroic labor, she realized she was nearing the end of a ride that might be momentous for her. The very aspect of that wide, treeless expanse, with all its overwhelming meaning, seemed to make her a stronger and more thoughtful girl. If those endless wheat fields were indeed ruined, what a pity, what a tragedy! Not only would young Dorn be ruined, but perhaps many other toiling farmers. Somehow Lenore felt no hopeless certainty of ruin for the young man in whom she was interested.

"There, on that slope!" spoke up Anderson, pointing to a field which was yellow in contrast to the surrounding gray field. "There's a half section of fair wheat."

But such tinges of harvest gold were not many in half a dozen miles of dreary hills. Where were the beautiful shadows in the wheat? wondered Lenore. Not a breath of wind appeared to stir across those fields.

As the car neared the top of a hill the road curved into another, and Lenore saw a dusty flash of another car passing on ahead.

Suddenly Jake leaned forward.

"Boss, I seen somethin' throwed out of thet car—into the wheat," he said.

"What?—Mebbe it was a bottle," replied Anderson, peering ahead.

"Nope. Sure wasn't thet. . . . There! I seen it again. Watch, boss!"

Lenore strained her eyes and felt a stir of her pulses. Jake's voice was perturbing. Was it strange that Nash slowed up a little where there was no apparent need? Then Lenore saw a hand flash out of the side of the car ahead and throw a small, glinting object into the wheat.

"There! Seen it again," said Jake.

"I saw! . . . Jake, mark that spot. . . . Nash, slow down," yelled Anderson.

Lenore gathered from the look of her father and the cowboy that something was amiss, but she could not guess what it might be. Nash bent sullenly at his task of driving.

"I reckon about here," said Jake, waving his hand.

"Stop her," ordered Anderson, and as the car came to a halt he got out, followed by Jake.

"Wal, I marked it by thet rock," declared the cowboy.

"So did I," responded Anderson. "Let's get over the

fence an' find what it was they threw in there."

Jake rested a lean hand on a post and vaulted the fence. But Anderson had to climb laboriously and painfully over the barbed-wire obstruction. Lenore marveled at his silence and his persistence. Anderson hated wire fences. Presently he got over, and then he divided his time between searching in the wheat and peering after the strange car that was drawing far away.

Lenore saw Jake pick up something and scrutinize it.

"I'll be doggoned!" he muttered. Then he approached Anderson. "What is thet?"

"Jake, you can lambaste me if I ever saw the likes," replied Anderson. "But it looks bad. Let's rustle after that car."

As Anderson clambered into his seat once more he looked dark and grim.

"Catch that car ahead," he tersely ordered Nash. Whereupon the driver began to go through his usual motions in starting.

"Lenore, what do you make of this?" queried Anderson, turning to show her a small cake of some gray substance, soft and wet to the touch.

"I don't know what it is," replied Lenore, wonderingly. "Do you?"

"No. An' I'd give a lot—Say, Nash, hurry! Overhaul that car!"

Anderson turned to see why his order had not been obeyed. He looked angry. Nash made hurried motions. The car trembled, the machinery began to whir—then came a tremendous buzzing roar, a violent shaking of the car, followed by sharp explosions, and silence.

"You stripped the gears!" shouted Anderson, with the red fading out of his face.

"No; but something's wrong," replied Nash. He got out to examine the engine.

Anderson manifestly controlled strong feeling. Lenore saw Jake's hand go to her father's shoulder. "Boss," he whispered, "we can't ketch thet car now." Anderson resigned himself, averted his face so that he could not see Nash, who was tinkering with the engine. Lenore believed then that Nash had deliberately stalled the engine or disordered something, so as to permit the escape of the strange car ahead. She saw it turn off the long, straight road ahead and disappear to the right. After some minutes' delay Nash resumed his seat and started the car once more.

From the top of the next hill Lenore saw the Dorn farm and home. All the wheat looked parched. She remembered, however, that the section of promising grain lay on the north slope, and therefore out of sight from where she was.

"Looks as bad as any," said Anderson. "Good-bye to my money."

Lenore shut her eyes and thought of herself, her inward state. She seemed calm, and glad to have that first part of the journey almost ended. Her motive in coming was not now the impelling thing that had actuated her.

When next the car slowed down she heard her father say, "Drive in by the house."

Then Lenore, opening her eyes, saw the gate, the trim little orchard with its scant shade, the gray old weather-beaten house which she remembered so well. The big porch looked inviting, as it was shady and held an old rocking chair and a bench with blue cushions. A door stood wide open. No one appeared to be on the premises.

"Nash, blow your horn an' then hunt around for somebody," said Anderson. "Come, get out, Lenore. You must be half dead."

"Oh no. Only half dust and half fire," replied Lenore, laughing, as she stepped out. What a relief to get rid of coat, veils, bonnet, and to sit on a shady porch where a faint breeze blew! Just at that instant she heard a low, distant rumbling. Thunder! It thrilled her. Jake brought her a cold, refreshing drink, and she sent him back after another. She wet her handkerchief and bathed her hot face. It was indeed very comfortable there after that long hot ride.

"Miss Lenore, I seen thet Nash pawin' you," said the cowboy, "an' by Gosh! I couldn't believe my eyes!"

"Not so loud! Jake, the young gentleman imagines I'm in love with him," replied Lenore.

"Wal, I'll remove his imaginin'," declared Jake, coolly.

"Jake, you will do nothing."

"Ahuh! Then you air in love with *him?*"

Lenore was compelled to explain to this loyal cowboy just what the situation meant. Whereupon Jake swore his amaze, and said, "I'm a-goin' to lick him, anyhow, fer thet!" And he caught up the tin cup and shuffled away.

Footsteps and voices sounded on the path, upon which presently appeared Anderson and young Dorn.

"Father's gone to Wheatly," he was saying. "But I'm glad to tell you we'll pay twenty thousand dollars on the debt as soon as we harvest. If it rains we'll pay it all and have thirty thousand left."

"Good! I sure hope it rains. An' that thunder sounds hopeful," responded Anderson.

"It's been hopeful like that for several days, but no rain," said Dorn. And then, espying Lenore, he seemed startled out of his eagerness. He flushed slightly. "I—I didn't see—you had brought your daughter."

He greeted her somewhat bashfully. And Lenore returned the greeting calmly, watching him steadily and waiting for the nameless sensations she had imagined would attend this meeting. But whatever these might be, they did not come to overwhelm her. The gladness of his voice, as he had spoken so eagerly to her father about the debt, had made her feel very kindly toward him. It might have been natural for a young man to resent this dragging debt. But he was fine. She observed, as he sat down, that, once the smile and flush left his face, he seemed somewhat thinner and older than she had pictured him. A shadow lay in his eyes and his lips were sad. He had evidently been working, upon their arrival. He wore overalls, dusty and ragged; his arms, bare to the elbow, were brown and muscular; his thin cotton shirt was wet with sweat and it clung to his powerful shoulders.

Anderson surveyed the young man with friendly glance.

"What's your first name?" he queried, with his blunt frankness.

"Kurt," was the reply.

"Is that American?"

"No. Neither is Dorn. But Kurt Dorn is an American."

"Hum! So I see, an' I'm powerful glad.... An' you've saved the big section of promisin' wheat?"

"Yes. We've been lucky. It's the best and finest wheat father ever raised. If it rains the yield will go sixty bushels to the acre."

"Sixty? Whew!" ejaculated Anderson.

Lenore smiled at these wheat men, and said: "It surely will rain—and likely storm today. I am a prophet who never fails."

"By George! that's true! Lenore has anybody beat when it comes to figurin' the weather," declared Anderson.

Dorn looked at her without speaking, but his smile seemed to say that she could not help being a prophet of good, of hope, of joy.

"Say, Lenore, how many bushels in a section at sixty per acre?" went on Anderson.

"Thirty-eight thousand four hundred," replied Lenore.

"An' what 'll you sell for?" asked Anderson of Dorn.

"Father has sold at two dollars and twenty-five cents a bushel," replied Dorn.

"Good! But he ought to have waited. The government will set a higher price.... How much will that come to, Lenore?"

Dorn's smile, as he watched Lenore do her mental arithmetic, attested to the fact that he already had figured out the sum.

"Eighty-six thousand four hundred dollars," replied Lenore. "Is that right?"

"An' you'll have thirty thousand dollars left after all debts are paid?" inquired Anderson.

"Yes, sir. I can hardly realize it. That's a fortune—

for one section of wheat. But we've had four bad seasons.... Oh, if it only rains today!"

Lenore turned her cheek to the faint west wind. And then she looked long at the slowly spreading clouds, white and beautiful, high up near the skyline, and dark and forbidding down along the horizon.

"I knew a girl who could feel things move when no one else could," said Lenore. "I'm sensitive like that—at least about wind and rain. Right now I can feel rain in the air."

"Then you have brought me luck," said Dorn, earnestly. "Indeed I guess my luck has turned. I hated the idea of going away with that debt unpaid."

"Are you—going away?" asked Lenore, in surprise.

"Yes, rather," he replied, with a short, sardonic laugh. He fumbled in a pocket of his overalls and drew forth a paper which he opened. A flame burned the fairness from his face; his eyes darkened and shone with peculiar intensity of pride. "I was the first man drafted in this Bend country.... My number was the first called!"

"Drafted!" echoed Lenore, and she seemed to be standing on the threshold of an amazing and terrible truth.

"Lass, we forget," said her father, rather thickly.

"Oh, but—why?" cried Lenore. She had voiced the same poignant appeal to her brother Jim. Why need he—why must he go to war? What for? And Jim had called out a bitter curse on the Germans he meant to kill.

"Why?" returned Dorn, with the sad, thoughtful shadow returning to his eyes. "How many times have I asked myself that? ...In one way, I don't know.... I haven't told Father yet! ...It's not for his sake.... But when I think deeply—when I can feel and see—I mean I'm going for my country.... For you and your sisters."

Like a soldier then Lenore received her mortal blow facing him who dealt it, and it was a sudden overwhelming realization of love. No confusion, no embarrassment, no shame attended the agony of that revelation. Outwardly she did not seem to change at all. She felt her father's eyes upon her; but she had no wish to hide the tumult of her heart. The moment made her a woman. Where was the fulfilment of those vague, stingingly sweet, dreamy fancies of love? Where was her maiden reserve, that she so boldly recognized an unsolicited passion? Her eyes met Dorn's steadily, and she felt some vital and compelling spirit pass from her to him. She saw him struggle with what he could not understand. It was his glance that wavered and fell, his hand that trembled, his breast that heaved. She loved him. There had been no beginning. Always he had lived in her dreams. And like her brother he was going to kill and to be killed.

Then Lenore gazed away across the wheat fields. The shadows came waving toward her. A stronger breeze fanned her cheeks. The heavens were darkening and low thunder rolled along the battlements of the great clouds.

"Say, Kurt, what do you make of this?" asked Anderson. Lenore, turning, saw her father hold out the little gray cake that Jake had found in the wheat field.

Young Dorn seized it quickly, felt and smelled and bit it.

"Where'd you get this?" he asked, with excitement.

Anderson related the circumstance of its discovery.

"It's a preparation, mostly phosphorus," replied

Dorn. "When the moisture evaporates it will ignite—set fire to any dry substance. . . . That is a trick of the I. W. W. to burn the wheat fields."

"By all that's—!" swore Anderson, with his jaw bulging. "Jake an' I knew it meant bad. But we didn't know what."

"I've been expecting tricks of all kinds," said Dorn. "I have four men watching the section."

"Good! Say, that car turned off to the right back here some miles. . . . But, worse luck, the I. W. W.'s can work at night."

"We'll watch at night, too," replied Dorn.

Lenore was conscious of anger encroaching upon the melancholy splendor of her emotions, and the change was bitter.

"When the rain comes, won't it counteract the ignition of that phosphorus?" she asked, eagerly, for she knew that rain would come.

"Only for the time being. It'll be just as dry this time tomorrow as it is now."

"Then the wheat's goin' to burn," declared Anderson, grimly. "If that trick had been worked all over this country you're goin' to have worse'n a prairie fire. The job on hand is to save this one section that has a fortune tied up in it."

"Mr. Anderson, that job looks almost hopeless, in the light of this phosphorus trick. What on earth can be done? I've four men. I can't hire any more, because I can't trust these strangers. And how can four men—or five, counting me, watch a square mile of wheat day and night?"

The situation looked hopeless to Lenore and she was sick. What cruel fates toyed with this young farmer!

He seemed to be sinking under this last crowning blow. There in the sky, rolling up and rumbling, was the long-deferred rainstorm that meant freedom from debt, and a fortune besides. But of what avail the rain if it was to rush the wheat to full bursting measure only for the infernal touch of the foreigner?

Anderson, however, was no longer a boy. He had dealt with many and many a trial. Never was he plunged into despair until after the dread crisis had come to pass. His red forehead, frowning and ridged with swelling blood vessels, showed the bent of his mind.

"Oh, it is hard!" said Lenore to Dorn. "I'm so sorry! But don't give up. While there's life there's hope!"

He looked up with tears in his eyes.

"Thank you. . . . I did weaken. You see I've let myself believe too much—for Dad's sake. I don't care about the money for myself. . . . Money! What good will money be to me—now? It's over for me. . . . To get the wheat cut—harvested—that's all I hoped. . . . The army—war—France—I go to be—"

"Hush!" whispered Lenore, and she put a soft hand upon his lips, checking the end of that bitter speech. She felt him start, and the look she met pierced her soul. "Hush! . . . It's going to rain! . . . Father will find some way to save the wheat! . . . And you are coming home—after the war!"

He crushed her hand to his hot lips.

"You make me—ashamed. I won't give—up," he said, brokenly. "And when I'm over—there—in the trenches, I'll think—"

"Dorn, listen to this," rang out Anderson. "We'll fool that I. W. W. gang. . . . It's a-goin' to rain. So far so good. Tomorrow you take this cake of phosphorus an' ride around all over the country. Show it an' tell the farmers their wheat's goin' to burn. An' offer them whose fields are already ruined—that fire can't do no more harm—offer them big money to help you save your section. Half a hundred men could put out a fire if one did start. An' these neighbors of yours, some of them will jump at a chance to beat the I. W. W.... Boy, it can be done!"

He ended with a big fist held aloft in triumph.

"See! Didn't I tell you?" murmured Lenore, softly. It touched her deeply to see Dorn respond to hope. His haggard face suddenly warmed and glowed.

"I never thought of that," he burst out, radiantly. "We can save the wheat.... Mr. Anderson, I—I can't thank you enough."

"Don't try," replied the rancher.

"I tell you it will rain," cried Lenore, gaily. "Let's walk out there—watch the storm come across the hills. I love to see the shadows blow over the wheat."

Lenore became aware, as she passed the car, that Nash was glaring at her in no unmistakable manner. She had forgotten all about him. The sight of his jealous face somehow added to her strange exhilaration.

They crossed the road from the house, and, facing the west, had free prospect of the miles of billowy hills and the magnificent ordnance of the storm clouds. The deep, low mutterings of thunder seemed a grand and welcome music. Lenore stole a look at Dorn, to see him, bareheaded, face upturned, entranced. It was only a rainstorm coming! Down in the valley country such storms were frequent at this season, too common for their meaning to be appreciated. Here in the desert of wheat rain was a blessing, life itself.

The creamy-white, rounded edge of the approaching clouds came and coalesced, spread and mushroomed. Under them the body of the storm was purple, lit now and then by a flash of lightning. Long, drifting veils of rain, gray as thin fog, hung suspended between sky and earth.

"Listen!" exclaimed Dorn.

A warm wind, laden with dry scent of wheat, struck Lenore's face and waved her hair. It brought a silken, sweeping rustle, a whispering of the bearded grain. The soft sound thrilled Lenore. It seemed a sweet, hopeful message that waiting had been rewarded, that the drought could be broken. Again, and more beautiful than ever before in her life, she saw the waves of shadow as they came forward over the wheat. Rippling, like breezes over the surface of a golden lake, they came in long, broken lines, moving, following, changing, until the whole wheat field seemed in shadowy motion.

The cloud pageant rolled on above and beyond. Lenore felt a sweet drop of rain splash upon her upturned face. It seemed like a caress. There came a pattering around her. Suddenly rose a damp, faint smell of dust. Beyond the hill showed a gray pall of rain, coming slowly, charged with a low roar. The whisper of the sweeping wheat was swallowed up.

Lenore stood her ground until heavy raindrops fell thick and fast upon her, sinking through her thin waist to thrill her flesh; and then, with a last gay call to those two man lovers of wheat and storms, she ran for the porch.

There they joined her, Anderson puffing and smiling, Dorn still with that rapt look upon his face. The rain swept up and roared on the roof, while all around was streaked gray.

"Boy, there's your thirty-thousand-dollar rain!" shouted Anderson.

But Dorn did not hear. Once he smiled at Lenore as if she were the good fairy who had brought about this miracle. In his look Lenore had deeper realization of him, of nature, and of life. She loved rain, but always, thenceforth, she would reverence it. Fresh, cool fragrance of a renewed soil filled the air. All that dusty gray hue of the earth had vanished, and it was wet and green and bright. Even as she gazed the water seemed to sink in as it fell, a precious relief to thirsty soil. The thunder rolled away eastward and the storm passed. The thin clouds following soon cleared away from the western sky, rain-washed and blue, with a rainbow curving down to bury its exquisite hues in the golden wheat.

CHAPTER

8

*T*HE journey homeward held many incalculable differences from the uncertain doubts and fears that had tormented Lenore on the outward trip.

For a long time she felt the warm, tight clasp of Dorn's hand on hers as he had said good-bye. Very evidently he believed that was to be his last sight of her. Lenore would never forget the gaze that seemed to try to burn her image on his memory forever. She felt that they would meet again. Solemn thoughts revolved in her mind; still, she was not unhappy. She had given much unsought, but the return to her seemed growing every moment that she lived.

The dust had been settled by the rain for many miles; however, beyond Palmer there began to show evidences that the storm had thinned out or sheered off, because the road gradually grew dry again. When dust rose once more Lenore covered her face, although, obsessed as she was by the deep change in herself, neither dust nor heat nor distance affected her greatly. Like the miles the moments sped by. She was aware through closed eyes when darkness fell. Stops were frequent after the Copper River had been crossed, and her father appeared to meet and question many persons in the towns they passed. Most of his questioning pertained to the I. W. W. And even excited whispering by her father and Jake had no power to interest her. It was midnight when they reached "Many Waters" and Lenore became conscious of fatigue.

Nash crowded in front of Jake as she was about to step out, and assisted her. He gave her arm a hard squeeze and fiercely whispered in her ear, "Tomorrow!"

The whisper was trenchant with meaning and thoroughly aroused Lenore. But she gave no sign and moved away.

"I seen strangers sneakin' off in the dark," Jake was whispering to Anderson.

"Keep your eyes peeled," replied Anderson. "I'll take Lenore up to the house an' come back."

It was pitch black up the path through the grove and Lenore had to cling to her father.

"Is there—any danger?" she whispered.

"We're lookin' for anythin'," replied Anderson, slowly.

"Will you be careful?"

"Sure, lass. I'll take no foolish risks. I've got men watchin' the house an' ranch. But I'd better have the cowboys down. There's Jake—he spots some prowlin' coyotes the minute we reach home."

Anderson unlocked and opened the door. The hall

was dark and quiet. He turned on the electric light. Lenore was detaching her veil.

"You look pale," he said, solicitously. "No wonder. That was a ride. But I'm glad we went. I saved Dorn's wheat."

"I'm glad, too, Father. Good night!"

He bade her good-night, and went out, locking the door. Then his rapid footsteps died away. Wearily Lenore climbed the stairs and went to her room.

She was awakened from deep slumber by Kathleen, who pulled and tugged at her.

"Lenorry, I thought you was dead, your eyes were shut so tight," declared the child. "Breakfast is waiting. Did you fetch me anything?"

"Yes, a new sister," replied Lenore, dreamily.

Kathleen's eyes opened wide. "Where?"

Lenore placed a hand over her heart.

"Here."

"Oh, you do look funny.... Get up, Lenorry. Did you hear the shooting last night?"

Instantly Lenore sat up and stared.

"No. Was there any?"

"You bet. But I don't know what it was all about."

Lenore dispelled her dreamy state, and, hurriedly dressing, she went down to breakfast. Her father and Rose were still at the table.

"Hello, big eyes!" was his greeting.

And Rose, not to be outdone, chirped, "Hello, old sleepyhead!"

Lenore's reply lacked her usual spontaneity. And she felt, if she did not explain, the wideness of her eyes. Her father did not look as if anything worried him. It was a way of his, however, not to show stress or worry. Lenore ate in silence until Rose left the dining room, and then she asked her father if there had been shooting.

"Sure," he replied, with a broad smile. "Jake turned his guns loose on them prowlin' men last night. By George! you ought to have heard them run. One plumped into the gate an' went clear over it, to fall like a log. Another fell into the brook an' made more racket than a drownin' horse. But it was so dark we couldn't catch them."

"Jake shot to frighten them?" inquired Lenore.

"Not much. He stung one I. W. W., that's sure. We heard a cry, an' this mornin' we found some blood."

"What do you suppose these—these night visitors wanted?"

"No tellin'. Jake thinks one of them looked an' walked like the man Nash has been meetin'. Anyway, we're not takin' much more chance on Nash. I reckon it's dangerous keepin' him around. I'll have him drive me today—over to Vale, an' then to Huntington. You can go along. That'll be your last chance to pump him. Have you found out anythin'?"

Lenore told what had transpired between her and the driver. Anderson's face turned fiery red.

"That ain't much to help us," he declared, angrily. "But it shows him up. . . . So his real name's Ruenke? Fine American name, I don't think! That man's a spy an' a plotter. An' before he's another day older I'm goin' to corner him. It's a sure go I can't hold Jake in any longer."

To Lenore it was a further indication of her father's temper that when they went down to enter the car he addressed Nash in cool, careless, easy speech. It made

Lenore shiver. She had heard stories of her father's early career among hard men.

Jake was there, dry, caustic, with keen, quiet eyes that any subtle, clever man would have feared. But Nash's thought seemed turned mostly inward.

Lenore took the front seat in the car beside the driver. He showed unconscious response to that action.

"Jake, aren't you coming?" she asked, of the cowboy.

"Wal, I reckon it'll be sure dull fer you without me. Nobody to talk to while your dad fools around. But I can't go. Me an' the boys air a-goin' to hang some I. W. W.'s this mawnin', an' I can't miss thet fun."

Jake drawled his speech and laughed lazily as he ended it. He was just boasting, as usual, but his hawklike eyes were on Nash. And it was certain that Nash turned pale.

Lenore had no reply to make. Her father appeared to lose patience with Jake, but after a moment's hesitation decided not to voice it.

Nash was not a good nor a careful driver under any circumstances, and this morning it was evident he did not have his mind on his business. There were bumps in the orchard road where the irrigation ditches crossed.

"Say, you ought to be drivin' a hay wagon," called Anderson, sarcastically.

At Vale he ordered the car stopped at the post office, and, telling Lenore he might be detained a few moments, he went in. Nash followed, and presently came back with a package of letters. Upon taking his seat in the car he assorted the letters, one of which, a large, thick envelope, manifestly gave him excited gratification. He pocketed them and turned to Lenore.

"Ah! I see you get letters—from a woman," she said, pretending a poison sweetness of jealousy.

"Certainly. I'm not married yet," he replied. "Lenore, last night—"

"You will never be married—to me—while you write to other women. Let me see that letter!...Let me read it—all of them!"

"No, Lenore—not here. And don't speak so loud. Your father will be coming any minute....Lenore, he suspects me. And that cowboy knows things. I can't go back to the ranch."

"Oh, you must come!"

"No. If you love me you've got to run off with me today."

"But why the hurry?" she appealed.

"It's getting hot for me."

"What do you mean by that? Why don't you explain to me? As long as you are so strange, so mysterious, how can I trust you? You ask me to run off with you, yet you don't put confidence in me."

Nash grew pale and earnest, and his hands shook.

"But if I do confide in you, then will you come with me?" he queried, breathlessly.

"I'll not promise. Maybe what you have to tell will prove—you-you don't care for me."

"It'll prove I do," he replied, passionately.

"Then tell me." Lenore realized she could no longer play the part she had assumed. But Nash was so stirred by his own emotions, so carried along in a current, that he did not see the difference in her.

"Listen. I tell you it's getting hot for me," he whispered. "I've been put here—close to Anderson—to find out things and to carry out orders. Lately I've neglected my job because I fell in love with you. He's your father. If I go on with plans—and harm comes to him—I'll never get you. Is that clear?"

"It certainly is," replied Lenore, and she felt a tightness at her throat.

"I'm no member of the I. W. W.," he went on. "Whatever that organization might have been last year, it's gone wild this year.... There are interests that have used the I. W. W. I'm only an agent, and I'm not high up, either. I see what the government will do to the I. W. W. if the Northwest leaves any of it. But just now there're plots against a few big men like your father. He's to be ruined. His crops and ranches destroyed. And he's to be killed. It's because he's so well known and has so much influence that he was marked. I told you the I. W. W. was being used to make trouble. They are being stirred up by agitators, bribed and driven, all for the purpose of making a great disorder in the Northwest."

"Germany!" whispered Lenore.

"I can't say. But men are all over, and these men work in secret. There are American citizens in the Northwest—one right in this valley—who have plotted to ruin your father."

"Do you know who they are?"

"No, I do not."

"You are for Germany, of course?"

"I have been. My people are German. But I was born in the U. S. And if it suits me I will be for America. If you come with me I'll throw up this dirty job, advise Glidden to shift the plot from your father to some other man—"

"So it's Glidden!" exclaimed Lenore.

Nash bit his lip, and for the first time looked at Lenore without thinking of himself. And surprise dawned in his eyes.

"Yes, Glidden. You saw him speak to me up in the Bend, the first time your father went to see Dorn's wheat. Glidden's playing the I. W. W. against itself. He means to drop out of this deal with big money. . . . Now I'll save your father if you'll stick to me."

Lenore could no longer restrain herself. This man was not even big in his wickedness. Lenore divined that his later words held no truth.

"Mr. Ruenke, you are a detestable coward," she said, with quivering scorn. "I let you imagine—Oh! I can't speak it! . . . You—you—"

"God! You fooled me!" he ejaculated, his jaw falling in utter amaze.

"You were contemptibly easy. You'd better jump out of this car and run. My father will shoot you."

"You deceitful—cat!" he cried, haltingly, as anger overcame his astonishment. "I'll—"

Anderson's big bulk loomed up behind Nash. Lenore gasped as she saw her father, for his eyes were upon her and he had recognized events.

"Say, Mister Ruenke, the postmaster says you get letters here under different names," said Anderson, bluntly.

"Yes—I—I—get them—for a friend," stammered the driver, as his face turned white.

"You lyin' German pup! . . . I'll look over them letters!" Anderson's big hand shot out to clutch Nash, holding him powerless, and with the other hand he searched Nash's inside coat pockets, to tear forth a packet of letters. Then Anderson released him and stepped back. "Get out of that car!" he thundered.

Nash made a slow movement, as if to comply, then suddenly he threw on the power. The car jerked forward.

Anderson leaped to get one hand on the car door, the other on Nash. He almost pulled the driver out of his seat. But Nash held on desperately, and the car, gaining momentum, dragged Anderson. He could not get his feet up on the running board, and suddenly he fell.

Lenore screamed and tore frantically at the handle of the door. Nash struck her, jerked her back into the seat. She struggled until the car shot full speed ahead. Then it meant death for her to leap out.

"Sit still, or you'll kill yourself!" shouted Nash, hoarsely.

Lenore fell back, almost fainting, with the swift realization of what had happened.

CHAPTER
9

KURT DORN had indeed no hope of ever seeing Lenore Anderson again, and he suffered a pang that seemed to leave his heart numb, though Anderson's timely visit might turn out as providential as the saving rainstorm. The wheat waved and rustled as if with renewed and bursting life. The exquisite rainbow still shone, a beautiful promise, in the sky. But Dorn could not be happy in that moment.

This day Lenore Anderson had seemed a bewildering fulfillment of the sweetness he had imagined was latent in her. She had meant what was beyond him to understand. She had gently put a hand to his lips, to check the bitter words, and he had dared to kiss her soft fingers. The thrill, the sweetness, the incomprehensible and perhaps imagined response of her pulse would never leave him. He watched the big car until it was out of sight.

The afternoon was only half advanced and there were numberless tasks to do. He decided he could think and plan while he worked. As he was about to turn away he espied another automobile, this one coming from the opposite direction to that Anderson had taken. The sight of it reminded Dorn of the I. W. W. trick of throwing phosphorus cakes into the wheat. He was suspicious of that car. It slowed down in front of the Dorn homestead, turned into the yard, and stopped near where Dorn stood. The dust had caked in layers upon it. Someone hailed him and asked if this was the Dorn farm. Kurt answered in the affirmative, whereupon a tall man, wearing a long linen coat, opened the car door to step out. In the car remained the driver and another man.

"My name is Hall," announced the stranger, with a pleasant manner. "I'm from Washington, D. C. I represent the government and am in the Northwest in the interest of the Conservation Commission. Your name has been recommended to me as one of the progressive young wheat growers of the Bend; particularly that you are an American, located in a country exceedingly important to the United States just now—a country where foreign-born people predominate."

Kurt, somewhat startled and awed, managed to give a courteous greeting to his visitor, and asked him into the house. But Mr. Hall preferred to sit outdoors on the porch. He threw off hat and coat, and, taking an easy-chair, he produced some cigars.

"Will you smoke?" he asked, offering one.

Kurt declined with thanks. He was aware of this man's penetrating, yet kindly scrutiny of him, and he had begun to wonder. This was no ordinary visitor.

"Have you been drafted?" abruptly queried Mr. Hall.

"Yes, sir. Mine was the first number," replied Kurt, with a little pride.

"Do you want exemption?" swiftly came the second query.

It shocked Dorn, then stung him.

"No," he said, forcibly.

"Your father's sympathy is with Germany, I understand."

"Well, sir, I don't know how you understand that, but it's true—to my regret and shame."

"You want to fight?" went on the official.

"I hate the idea of war. But I—I guess I want to fight. Maybe that's because I'm feeling scrappy over these I. W. W. tricks."

"Dorn, the I. W. W. is only one of the many phases of war that we must meet," returned Mr. Hall, and then for a moment he thoughtfully drew upon his cigar.

"Young man, I like your talk. And I'll tell you a secret. My name's not Hall. Never mind my name. For you it's Uncle Sam!"

Whereupon, with a winning and fascinating manner that seemed to Kurt at once intimate and flattering, he began to talk fluently of the meaning of his visit, and of its cardinal importance. The government was looking far ahead, preparing for a tremendous, and perhaps a lengthy, war. The food of the country must be conserved. Wheat was one of the most vital things in the whole world, and the wheat of America was incalculably precious—only the government knew how precious. If the war was short a wheat famine would come afterward; if it was long, the famine would come before the war ended. But it was inevitable. The very outcome of the war itself depended upon wheat.

The government expected a nationwide propaganda by the German interests which would be carried on secretly and boldly, in every conceivable way, to alienate the labor organizations, to bribe or menace the harvesters, to despoil crops, and particularly to put obstacles in the way of the raising and harvesting, the transporting and storing of wheat. It would take an army to protect the nation's grain.

Dorn was earnestly besought by this official to compass his district, to find out who could be depended upon by the United States and who was antagonistic, to impress upon the minds of all his neighbors the exceeding need of greater and more persistent cultivation of wheat.

"I accept. I'll do my best," replied Kurt, grimly. "I'll be going some the next two weeks."

"It's deplorable that most of the wheat in this section is a failure," said the official. "But we must make up for that next year. I see you have one magnificent wheat field. But, fact is, I heard of that long before I got here."

"Yes? Where?" ejaculated Kurt, quick to catch a significance in the other's words.

"I've motored direct from Wheatly. And I'm sorry to say that what I have now to tell you is not pleasant. ...Your father sold this wheat for eighty thousand dollars in cash. The money was seen to be paid over by a mill operator of Spokane...And your father is reported to be suspiciously interested in the I. W. W. men now at Wheatly."

"Oh, that's awful!" exclaimed Kurt, with a groan. "How did you learn that?"

"From American farmers—men that I had been instructed to approach, the same as in your case. The information came quite by accident, however, and through my inquiring about the I. W. W."

"Father has not been rational since the president declared war. He's very old. I've had trouble with him. He might do anything."

"My boy, there are multitudes of irrational men nowadays and the number is growing...I advise you to go at once to Wheatly and bring your father home. It was openly said that he was taking risks with that large sum of money."

"Risks! Why, I can't understand that. The wheat's not harvested yet, let alone hauled to town. And today I learned the I. W. W. are working a trick with cakes of phosphorus, to burn the wheat."

Kurt produced the cake of phosphorus and explained its significance to the curious official.

"Cunning devils! Who but a German would ever have thought of that?" he exclaimed. "German science! To such ends the Germans put their supreme knowledge!"

"I wonder what my father will say about this phosphorus trick. I just wonder. He loves the wheat. His wheat has taken prizes at three world's fairs. Maybe to see our wheat burn would untwist that twist in his brain and make him American."

"I doubt it. Only death changes the state of a real German, physical, moral, and spiritual. Come, ride back to Glencoe with me. I'll drop you there. You can hire a car and make Wheatly before dark."

Kurt ran indoors, thinking hard as he changed clothes. He told the housekeeper to tell Jerry he was called away and would be back next day. Putting money

and a revolver in his pocket, he started out, but hesitated and halted. He happened to think that he was a
poor shot with a revolver and a fine one with a rifle. So
he went back for his rifle, a small high-power, repeating
gun that he could take apart and hide under his coat.
When he reached the porch the official glanced from
the weapon to Kurt's face and said, with a flash of spirit:

"It appears that you are in earnest!"

"I am. Something told me to take this," responded
Kurt, as he dismounted the rifle. "I've already had one
run-in with an I. W. W. I know tough customers when I
see them. These foreigners are the kind I don't want
near me. And if I see one trying to fire the wheat I'll
shoot his leg off."

"I'm inclined to think that Uncle Sam would not
deplore your shooting a little higher...Dorn, you're
fine! You're all I heard you were! Shake hands!"

Kurt tingled all over as he followed the official out
to the car and took the seat given him beside the driver.
"Back to Glencoe," was the order. And then, even if
conversation had been in order, it would scarcely have
been possible. That driver could drive! He had no fear
and he knew his car. Kurt could drive himself, but he
thought that if he had been as good as this fellow he
would have chosen one of two magnificent services for
the army—an ambulance-driver at the front or an airplane scout.

On the way to Glencoe several squads of idling and
marching men were passed, all of whom bore the ear-
marks of the I. W. W. Sight of them made Kurt hug his
gun and wonder at himself. Never had he been a coward,
but neither had he been one to seek a fight. This suave,
distinguished government official, by his own significant

metaphor, Uncle Sam gone abroad to find true hearts, had wrought powerfully upon Kurt's temper. He sensed events. He revolved in mind the need for him to be cool and decisive when facing the circumstances that were sure to arise.

At Glencoe, which was reached so speedily that Kurt could scarcely credit his eyes, the official said: "You'll hear from me. Good-bye and good luck!"

Kurt hired a young man he knew to drive him over to Wheatly. All the way Kurt brooded about his father's strange action. The old man had left home before the rainstorm. How did he know he could guarantee so many bushels of wheat as the selling price indicated? Kurt divined that his father had acted upon one of his strange weather prophecies. For he must have been absolutely sure of rain to save the wheat.

Darkness had settled down when Kurt reached Wheatly and left the car at the railroad station. Wheatly was a fairly good-sized little town. There seemed to be an unusual number of men on the dark streets. Dim lights showed here and there. Kurt passed several times near groups of conversing men, but he did not hear any significant talk.

Most of the stores were open and well filled with men, but to Kurt's sharp eyes there appeared to be much more gossip going on than business. The town was not as slow and quiet as was usual with Bend towns. He listened for war talk, and heard none. Two out of every three men who spoke in his hearing did not use the English language. Kurt went into the office of the first hotel he found. There was no one present. He glanced at an old register lying on the desk. No guests had registered for several days.

Then Kurt went out and accosted a man leaning against a hitching rail.

"What's going on in this town?"

The man stood rather indistinctly in the uncertain light. Kurt, however, made out his eyes and they were regarding him suspiciously.

"Nothin' onusual," was the reply.

"Has harvesting begun in these parts?"

"Some barley cut, but no wheat. Next week, I reckon."

"How's the wheat?"

"Some bad an' some good."

"Is this town a headquarters for the I. W. W.?"

"No. But there's a big camp of I. W. W.'s near here. Reckon you're one of them union fellers?"

"I am not," declared Kurt, bluntly.

"Reckon you sure look like one, with thet gun under your coat."

"Are you going to hire I. W. W. men?" asked Kurt, ignoring the other's observation.

"I'm only a farmhand," was the sullen reply. "An' I tell you I won't join no I. W. W."

Kurt spared himself a moment to give this fellow a few strong proofs of the fact that any farmhand was wise to take such a stand against the labor organization. Leaving the fellow gaping and staring after him, Kurt crossed the street to enter another hotel. It was more pretentious than the first, with a large, well-lighted office. There were loungers at the tables. Kurt walked to the desk. A man leaned upon his elbows. He asked Kurt if he wanted a room. This man, evidently the proprietor, was a German, though he spoke English.

"I'm not sure," replied Kurt. "Will you let me look at the register?"

The man shoved the book around. Kurt did not find the name he sought.

"My father, Chris Dorn, is in town. Can you tell me where I'll find him?"

"So you're young Dorn," replied the other, with instant change to friendliness. "I've heard of you. Yes, the old man is here. He made a big wheat deal today. He's eating his supper."

Kurt stepped to the door indicated, and, looking into the dining room, he at once espied his father's huge head with its shock of gray hair. He appeared to be in earnest colloquy with a man whose bulk matched his own. Kurt hesitated, and finally went back to the desk.

"Who's the big man with my father?" he asked.

"He is a big man, both ways. Don't you know him?" rejoined the proprietor, in a lower voice.

"I'm not sure," answered Kurt. The lowered tone had a significance that decided Kurt to admit nothing.

"That's Neuman from Ruxton, one of the biggest wheat men in Washington."

Kurt repressed a whistle of surprise. Neuman was Anderson's only rival in the great, fertile valley. What were Neuman and Chris Dorn doing with their heads together?

"I thought he was Neuman," replied Kurt, feeling his way. "Is he in on the big deal with Father?"

"Which one?" queried the proprietor, with shrewd eyes, taking Kurt's measure. "You're in on both, of course?"

"Sure. I mean the wheat sale, not the I. W. W. deal," replied Kurt. He hazarded a guess with that mention of the I. W. W. No sooner had the words passed his lips than he divined he was on the track of sinister events.

"Your father sold out to that Spokane miller. No, Neuman is not in on that."

"I was surprised to hear Father had sold the wheat. Was it speculation or guarantee?"

"Old Chris guaranteed sixty bushels. There were friends of his here who advised against it. Did you have rain over there?"

"Fine. The wheat will go over sixty bushels. I'm sorry I couldn't get here sooner."

"When it rained you hurried over to boost the price. Well, it's too late."

"Is Glidden here?" queried Kurt, hazarding another guess.

"Don't talk so loud," warned the proprietor. "Yes, he just got here in a car with two other men. He's upstairs having supper in his room."

"Supper!" Kurt echoed the word, and averted his face to hide the leap of his blood. "That reminds me, I'm hungry."

He went into the big, dimly lighted dining room. There was a shelf on one side as he went in, and here, with his back turned to the room, he laid the disjointed gun and his hat. Several newspapers lying near attracted his eye. Quickly he slipped them under and around the gun, and then took a seat at the nearest table. A buxom German waitress came for his order. He gave it while he gazed around at his grim-faced old father and the burly Neuman, and his ears throbbed to the beat of his blood. His hand trembled on the table. His thoughts flashed almost too swiftly for comprehension. It took a stern effort to gain self-control.

Evil of some nature was afoot. Neuman's presence there was a strange, disturbing fact. Kurt had made two guesses, both alarmingly correct. If he had any more illusions or hopes, he dispelled them. His father had been won over by this arch conspirator of the I. W. W. And, despite his father's close-fistedness where money was concerned, that eighty thousand dollars, or part of it, was in danger.

Kurt wondered how he could get possession of it. If he could he would return it to the bank and wire a warning to the Spokane buyer that the wheat was not safe. He might persuade his father to turn over the amount of the debt to Anderson. While thinking and planning, Kurt kept an eye on his father and rather neglected his supper. Presently, when old Dorn and Neuman rose and left the dining room, Kurt followed them. His father was whispering to the proprietor over the desk, and at Kurt's touch he glared his astonishment.

"You here! What for?" he demanded, gruffly, in German.

"I had to see you," replied Kurt, in English.

"Did it rain?" was the old man's second demand, husky and serious.

"The wheat is made, if we can harvest it," answered Kurt.

The blaze of joy on old Dorn's face gave Kurt a twinge of pain. He hated to dispel it. "Come aside, here, a minute," he whispered, and drew his father over to a corner under a lamp. "I've got bad news. Look at this!" He produced the cake of phosphorus, careful to hide it from other curious eyes there, and with swift, low words he explained its meaning. He expected an outburst of surprise and fury, but he was mistaken.

"I know about that," whispered his father, hoarsely. "There won't be any thrown in my wheat."

"Father! What assurance have you of that?" queried Kurt, astounded.

The old man nodded his gray head wisely. He knew, but he did not speak.

"Do you think these I. W. W. plotters will spare your wheat?" asked Kurt. "You are wrong. They may lie to your face. But they'll betray you. The I. W. W. is backed by—by interests that want to embarrass the government."

"What government?"

"Why, ours—the U.S. government."

"That's not my government. The more it's embarrassed the better it will suit me."

In the stress of the moment Kurt had forgotten his father's bitter and unchangeable hatred.

"But you're—you're stupid," he hissed, passionately. "That government has protected you for fifty years."

Old Dorn growled into his beard. His huge ox-eyes rolled. Kurt realized then finally how implacable and hopeless he was—how utterly German. Then Kurt importuned him to return the eighty thousand dollars to the bank until he was sure the wheat was harvested and hauled to the railroad.

"My wheat won't burn," was old Dorn's stubborn reply.

"Well, then, give me Anderson's thirty thousand. I'll take it to him at once. Our debt will be paid. We'll have it off our minds."

"No hurry about that," replied his father.

"But there is hurry," returned Kurt, in a hot whisper.

"Anderson came to see you today. He wants his money."

"Neuman holds the small end of that debt. I'll pay him. Anderson can wait."

Kurt felt no amaze. He expected anything. But he could scarcely contain his fury. How this old man, his father, whom he had loved—how he had responded to the influences that must destroy him!

"Anderson shall not wait," declared Kurt. "I've got some say in this matter. I've worked like a dog in those wheat fields. I've a right to demand Anderson's money. He needs it. He has a tremendous harvest on his hands."

Old Dorn shook his huge head in somber and gloomy thought. His broad face, his deep eyes, seemed to mask and to hide. It was an expression Kurt had seldom seen there, but had always hated. It seemed so old to Kurt, that alien look, something not born of his time.

"Anderson is a capitalist," said Chris Dorn, deep in his beard. "He seeks control of farmers and wheat in the Northwest. Ranch after ranch he's gained by taking up and foreclosing mortgages. He's against labor. He grinds down the poor. He cheated Neuman out of a hundred thousand bushels of wheat. He bought up my debt. He meant to ruin me. He—"

"You're talking I. W. W. rot," whispered Kurt, shaking with the effort to subdue his feelings. "Anderson is fine, big, square—a developer of the Northwest. Not an enemy! He's our friend. Oh! if only you had an American's eyes, just for a minute!...Father, I want that money for Anderson."

"My son, I run my own business," replied Dorn, sullenly, with a pale fire in his opaque eyes. "You're a wild boy, unfaithful to your blood. You've fallen in love with an American girl....Anderson says he needs money!"...With hard, gloomy face the old man shook his head. "He thinks he'll harvest!" Again that strange shake of finality. "I know what I know....I keep my money....We'll have other rule....I keep my money."

Kurt had vibrated to those most significant words and he stared speechless at his father.

"Go home. Get ready for harvest," suddenly ordered old Dorn, as if he had just awakened to the fact of Kurt's disobedience in lingering here.

"All right, Father," replied Kurt, and, turning on his heel, he strode outdoors.

When he got beyond the light he turned and went back to a position where in the dark he could watch without being seen. His father and the hotel proprietor were again engaged in earnest colloquy. Neuman had disappeared. Kurt saw the huge shadow of a man pass across a drawn blind in a room upstairs. Then he saw smaller shadows, and arms raised in vehement gesticulation. The very shadows were sinister. Men passed in and out of the hotel. Once old Dorn came to the door and peered all around. Kurt observed that there was a dark side entrance to this hotel. Presently Neuman returned to the desk and said something to old Dorn, who shook his head emphatically, and then threw himself into a chair, in a brooding posture that Kurt knew well. He had seen it so often that he knew it had to do with money. His father was refusing demands of some kind. Neuman again left the office, this time with the proprietor. They were absent some little time.

During this period Kurt leaned against a tree, hidden in the shadow, with keen eyes watching and with puzzled, anxious mind. He had determined, in case his father left that office with Neuman, on one of those significant disappearances, to slip into the hotel at the side entrance and go upstairs to listen at the door of the room with the closely drawn blind. Neuman returned soon with the hotel man, and the two of them half led, half dragged old Dorn out into the street. They took the direction toward the railroad. Kurt followed at a safe distance on the opposite side of the street. Soon they passed the stores with lighted windows, then several dark houses, and at length the railroad station. Perhaps they were bound for the train. Kurt heard rumbling in the distance. But they went beyond the station, across the track, and turned to the right.

Kurt was soft-footed and keen-eyed. He just kept the dim shadows in range. They were heading for some freight cars that stood upon a sidetrack. The dark figures disappeared behind them. Then one figure reappeared, coming back. Kurt crouched low. This man passed within a few yards of Kurt and he was whispering to himself. After he was safely out of earshot Kurt stole on stealthily until he reached the end of the freight cars. Here he paused, listening. He thought he heard low voices, but he could not see the men he was following. No doubt they were waiting in the secluded gloom for the other men apparently necessary for that secret conference. Kurt had sensed this event and he had determined to be present. He tried not to conjecture. It was best for him to apply all his faculties to the task of slipping unseen and unheard close to these men who had involved his father in some dark plot.

Not long after Kurt hid himself on the other side of the freight car he heard soft-padded footsteps and subdued voices. Dark shapes appeared to come out of the gloom. They passed him. He distinguished low, guttural voices, speaking German. These men, three in number, were scarcely out of sight when Kurt laid his rifle on the projecting shelf of the freight car and followed them.

Presently he came to deep shadow, where he paused. Low voices drew him on again, then a light made him thrill. Now and then the light appeared to be darkened by moving figures. A dark object loomed up to cut off Kurt's view. It was a pile of railroad ties, and beyond it loomed another. Stealing along these, he soon saw the light again, quite close. By its glow he recognized his father's huge frame, back to him, and the burly Neuman on the other side, and Glidden, whose dark face was working as he talked. These three were sitting, evidently on a flat pile of ties, and the other two men stood behind. Kurt could not make out the meaning of the low voices. Pressing closer to the freight car, he cautiously and noiselessly advanced.

Glidden was importuning with expressive hands and swift, low utterance. His face gleamed dark, hard, strong, intensely strung with corded, quivering muscles, with eyes apparently green orbs of fire. He spoke in German.

Kurt dared not go closer unless he wanted to be discovered, and not yet was he ready for that. He might hear some word to help explain his father's strange, significant intimations about Anderson.

"... must—have—money," Glidden was saying. To Kurt's eyes treachery gleamed in that working face. Neuman bent over to whisper gruffly in Dorn's ear. One of the silent men standing rubbed his hands together. Old Dorn's head was bowed. Then Glidden spoke so low and so swiftly that Kurt could not connect sentences, but with mounting blood he stood transfixed and horrified, to gather meaning from word on word, until he realized Anderson's doom, with other rich men of the Northwest, was sealed—that there were to be burnings of wheat fields and of storehouses and of freight trains—destruction everywhere.

"I give money," said old Dorn, and with heavy movement he drew from inside his coat a large package wrapped in newspaper. He laid it before him in the light and began to unwrap it. Soon there were disclosed two bundles of bills—the eighty thousand dollars.

Kurt thrilled in all his being. His poor father was being misled and robbed. A melancholy flash of comfort came to Kurt! Then at sight of Glidden's hungry eyes and working face and clutching hands Kurt pulled his hat far down, drew his revolver, and leaped forward with a yell, "Hands up!"

He discharged the revolver right in the faces of the stunned plotters, and, snatching up the bundle of money, he leaped over the light, knocking one of the men down, and was gone into the darkness, without having slowed in the least his swift action.

Wheeling round the end of the freight car, he darted back, risking a hard fall in the darkness, and ran along the several cars to the first one, where he grasped his rifle and kept on. He heard his father's roar, like that of a mad bull, and shrill yells from the other men. Kurt laughed grimly. They would never catch him in the dark. While he ran he stuffed the money into his inside coat pockets. Beyond the railroad station he slowed down to catch his breath. His breast was heaving, his pulse hammering, and his skin was streaming. The excitement was the greatest under which he had ever labored.

"Now—what shall—I do?" he panted. A freight train was lumbering toward him and the headlight was almost at the station. The train appeared to be going slowly through without stopping. Kurt hurried on down the track a little farther. Then he waited. He would get on that train and make his way somehow to Ruxton, there to warn Anderson of the plot against his life.

CHAPTER
10

KURT rode to Adrian on that freight, and upon arriving in the yards there he jumped off, only to mount another, headed south. He meant to be traveling while it was dark. No passenger trains ran at night and he wanted to put as much distance between him and Wheatly as possible before daylight.

He had piled into an open boxcar. It was empty, at least of freight, and the floor appeared to have a thin covering of hay. The train, gathering headway, made a rattling, rolling roar. Kurt hesitated about getting up and groping back in the pitch-black corners of the car. He felt that it contained a presence besides his own. And suddenly he was startled by an object blacker than the shadow, that sidled up close to him. Kurt could not keep the cold chills from chasing up and down his back. The object was a man, who reached for Kurt and felt of him with a skinny hand.

"I. W. W.?" he whispered, hoarsely, in Kurt's ear.

"Yes," replied Kurt.

"Was that Adrian where you got on?"

"It sure was," answered Kurt, with grim humor.

"Then you're the feller?"

"Sure," replied Kurt. It was evident that he had embarked upon an adventure.

"When do we stall this freight?"

"Not while we're on it, you can gamble."

Other dark forms sidled out of the gloomy depths of that cavernlike corner and drew close to Kurt. He realized that he had fallen in with I. W. W. men who apparently had taken him for an expected messenger or leader. He was importuned for tobacco, drink, and money, and he judged that his begging companions consisted of an American tramp, an Austrian, a negro, and a German. Fine society to fall into! That eighty thousand dollars became a tremendous burden.

"How many men on this freight?" queried Kurt, thinking he could ask questions better than answer them. And he was told there were about twenty-five, all of whom expected money. At this information Kurt rather closely pressed his hand upon the revolver in his side coat pocket. By asking questions and making judicious replies he passed what he felt was the dark mark in that mixed company of I. W. W. men; and at length, one by one, they melted away to their warmer corners, leaving Kurt by the door. He did not mind the cold. He wanted to be where, at the first indication of a stop, he could jump off the train.

With his hand on his gun and hugging the bulging coat pockets close to him, Kurt settled himself for what he believed would be interminable hours. He strained eyes and ears for a possible attack from the riffraff I. W. W. men hidden there in the car. And that was why, perhaps, that it seemed only a short while until the train bumped and slowed, preparatory to stopping. The instant it was safe Kurt jumped out and stole away in the gloom. A fence obstructed further passage. He peered around to make out that he was in a road. Thereupon he hurried along it until he was out of hearing of the train. There was light in the east, heralding a dawn that Kurt surely would welcome. He sat down to wait, and addressed to his bewildered judgment a query as to whether or not he ought to keep on carrying the burdensome rifle. It was not only heavy, but when daylight came it might attract attention, and his bulging coat would certainly invite curiosity. He was in a predicament; nevertheless, he decided to hang on to the rifle.

He almost fell asleep, waiting there with his back against a fence post. The dawn came, and then the rosy sunrise. And he discovered, not half a mile away, a good-sized town, where he believed he surely could hire an automobile.

Waiting grew to be so tedious that he decided to risk the early hour, and proceeded toward the town. Upon the outskirts he met a farmer boy, who, in reply to a question, said that the town was Connell. Kurt found another early riser in the person of a blacksmith who evidently was a Yankee and proud of it. He owned a car that he was willing to hire out on good security. Kurt satisfied him on that score, and then proceeded to ask how to get across the Copper River and into Golden Valley. The highway followed the railroad from that town to Kahlotus, and there crossed a big trunk-line railroad, to turn south toward the river.

In half an hour, during which time Kurt was enabled to breakfast, the car was ready. It was a large car, rather ancient and the worse for wear, but its owner assured Kurt that it would take him where he wanted to go and he need not be afraid to drive fast. With that inspiring knowledge Kurt started off.

Before ten o'clock Kurt reached Kilo, far across the Copper River, with the Blue Mountains in sight, and from there less confusing directions to follow. He had been lucky. He had passed the wreck of the freight train upon which he had ridden from Adrian; his car had been surrounded by rough men, and only quick wits saved him at least delay; he had been hailed by more than one group of tramping I. W. W. men; and he had passed camps and freight yards where idlers were congregated. And lastly, he had seen, far across the valley, a pall of smoke from forest fire.

He was going to reach "Many Waters" in time to warn Anderson, and that fact gave him strange exultation. When it was assured and he had the eighty thousand dollars deposited in a bank he could feel that his gray, gloomy future would have several happy memories. How would Lenore Anderson feel toward a man who had saved her father? The thought was too rich, too sweet for Kurt to dwell upon.

Before noon Kurt began to climb gradually up off the wonderfully fertile bottomlands where the endless orchards and boundless gardens delighted his eye, and the towns grew fewer and farther between. Kurt halted at Huntington for water, and when he was about ready to start a man rushed out of a store, glanced hurriedly up and down the almost deserted street, and, espying Kurt, ran to him.

"Message over phone! I. W. W.! Hell to pay!" he cried, excitedly.

"What's up? Tell me the message," replied Kurt, calmly.

"It just come—from Vale. Anderson, the big rancher! He phoned to send men out on all roads—to stop his car! His daughter's in it! She's been made off with! I. W. W.'s!"

Kurt's heart leaped. The bursting blood burned through him and receded to leave him cold, tingling. Anything might happen to him this day! He reached inside the seat to grasp the disjointed rifle, and three swift movements seemed to serve to unwrap it and put the pieces together.

"What else did Anderson say?" he asked, sharply.

"That likely the car would head for the hills, where the I. W. W.'s are camped."

"What road from here leads that way?"

"Take the left-hand road at the end of town," replied the man, more calmly. "Ten miles down you'll come to a fork. There's where the I. W. W.'s will turn off to go up into the foothills. Anderson just phoned. You can head off his car if it's on the hill road. But you'll have to drive....Do you know Anderson's car? Don't you want men with you?"

"No time!" called Kurt, as he leaped into the seat and jammed on the power.

"I'll send cars all over," shouted the man, as Kurt whirred away.

Kurt's eyes and hands and feet hurt with the sudden intensity of strain. All his nervous force seemed set upon the one great task of driving and guiding that car at the limit of its speed. Huntington flashed behind, two indistinct streaks of houses. An open road, slightly rising, stretched ahead. The wind pressed so hard that he could scarcely breathe. The car gave forth a humming roar.

Kurt's heart labored, swollen and tight, high in his breast, and his thoughts were swift, tumultuous. An agony of dread battled with a dominating but strange certainty. He felt belief in his luck. Circumstances one by one had led to this drive, and in every one passed by he felt the direction of chance.

He sped by fields of wheat, a wagon that he missed by an inch, some stragglers on the road, and then, far ahead, he saw a signpost of the forks. As he neared it he gradually shut off the power, to stop at the crossroads. There he got out to search for fresh car tracks turning up to the right. There were none. If Anderson's car was coming on that road he would meet it.

Kurt started again, but at reasonable speed, while his eyes were sharp on the road ahead. It was empty. It sloped down for a long way, and made a wide curve to the right, along the base of hilly pastureland, and then again turned. And just as Kurt's keen gaze traveled that far a big automobile rounded the bend, coming fast. He recognized the red color, the shape of the car.

"Anderson's!" he cried, with that same lift of his heart, that bursting gush of blood. "No dream! . . . I see it! . . . And I'll stop it!"

The advantage was all his. He would run along at reasonable speed, choose a narrow place, stop his car so as to obstruct the road, and get out with his rifle.

It seemed a long stretch down that long slope, and his car crept along, while the other gradually closed the gap. Slower and slower Kurt ran, then turned half across the road and stopped. When he stepped out the other car was two hundred yards or more distant. Kurt saw when the driver slackened his speed. There appeared to be only two people in the car, both in front. But Kurt could not be sure of that until it was only fifty yards away.

Then he swung out his rifle and waved for the driver to stop. But he did not stop. Kurt heard a scream. He saw a white face. He saw the driver swing his hand across that white face, dashing it back.

"Halt!" yelled Kurt, at the top of his lungs.

But the driver hunched down and put on the power. The red car leaped. As it flashed by Kurt recognized Nash and Anderson's daughter. She looked terrified. Kurt dared not shoot, for fear of hitting the girl. Nash swerved, took the narrow space left him, smashing the right front wheel of Kurt's car, and got by.

Kurt stepped aside and took a quick shot at the tire of Nash's left hind wheel. He missed. His heart sank and he was like ice as he risked another. The little high-power bullet struck and blew the tire off the wheel. Nash's car lurched, skidded into the bank not thirty yards away.

With a bound Kurt started for it, and he was there when Nash had twisted out of his seat and over the door.

"Far enough! Don't move!" ordered Kurt, presenting the rifle.

Nash was ghastly white, with hunted eyes and open mouth, and his hands shook.

"Oh, it's—Kurt Dorn!" cried a broken voice.

Kurt saw the girl fumble with the door on her side, open it, and stagger out of his sight. Then she reappeared round the car. Bareheaded, disheveled, white as chalk, with burning eyes and bleeding lips, she gazed at Kurt as if to make sure of her deliverance.

"Miss Anderson—if he's harmed you—" broke out Kurt, hoarsely.

"Oh!...Don't kill him!...He hasn't touched me," she replied, wildly.

"But your lips are bleeding."

"Are they?" She put a trembling hand to them. "He—he struck me....That's nothing....But you—you have saved me—from God only knows what!"

"I have? From him?" demanded Kurt. "What is he?"

"He's a German!" returned Lenore, and red burned out of the white of her cheeks. "Secret agent—I. W. W.! ...Plotter against my father's life!...Oh, he knocked father off the car—dragged him!...He ran the car away—with me—forced me back—he struck me!... Oh, if I were a man!"

Nash responded with a passion that made his face drip with sweat and distort into savage fury of defeat and hate.

"You two-faced cat!" he hissed. "You made love to me! You fooled me! You let me—"

"Shut up!" thundered Kurt. "You German dog! I can't murder you, because I'm American. Do you get that? But I'll beat you within an inch of your life!"

As Kurt bent over to lay down the rifle, Nash darted a hand into the seat for weapon of some kind. But Kurt, in a rush, knocked him over the front guard. Nash howled. He scrambled up with bloody mouth. Kurt was on him again.

"Take that!" cried Kurt, low and hard, as he swung his arm. The big fist that had grasped so many plow handles took Nash full on that bloody mouth and laid him flat. "Come on, German! Get out of the trench!"

Like a dog Nash threshed and crawled, scraping his hands in the dirt, to jump up and fling a rock that Kurt ducked by a narrow margin. Nash followed it, swinging wildly, beating at his adversary.

Passion long contained burst in Kurt. He tasted the salt of his own blood where he had bitten his lips. Nash showed as in a red haze. Kurt had to get his hands on this German, and when he did it liberated a strange and terrible joy in him. No weapon would have sufficed. Hardly aware of Nash's blows, Kurt tore at him, swung and choked him, bore him down on the bank, and there beat him into a sodden, bloody-faced heap.

Only then did a cry of distress, seemingly from far off, pierce Kurt's ears. Miss Anderson was pulling at him with frantic hands.

"Oh, don't kill him! Please don't kill him!" she was crying. "Kurt!—for my sake, don't kill him!"

That last poignant appeal brought Kurt to his senses. He let go of Nash. He allowed the girl to lead him back. Panting hard, he tried to draw a deep, full breath.

"Oh, he doesn't move!" whispered Lenore, with wide eyes on Nash.

"Miss Anderson—he's not—even insensible," panted Kurt. "But he's licked—good and hard."

The girl leaned against the side of the car, with a hand buried in her heaving breast. She was recovering. The gray shade left her face. Her eyes, still wide and dark and beginning to glow with softer emotions, were upon Kurt.

"You—you were the one to come," she murmured. "I prayed. I was terribly frightened. Ruenke was taking me—to the I. W. W. camp, up in the hills."

"Ruenke?" queried Kurt.

"Yes, that's his German name."

Kurt awoke to the exigencies of the situation. Searching in the car, he found a leather belt. With this he securely bound Ruenke's hands behind his back, then rolled him down into the road.

"My first German prisoner," said Kurt, half seriously. "Now, Miss Anderson, we must be doing things. We don't want to meet a lot of I. W. W.'s out here. My car is out of commission. I hope yours is not broken."

Kurt got into the car and found, to his satisfaction, that it was not damaged so far as running gear was concerned. After changing the ruined tire he backed down the road and turned to stop near where Ruenke lay. Opening the rear door, Kurt picked him up as if he had been a sack of wheat and threw him into the car. Next he secured the rifle that had been such a burden and had served him so well in the end.

"Get in, Miss Anderson," he said, "and show me where to drive you home."

She got in beside him, making a grimace as she saw Ruenke lying behind her. Kurt started and ran slowly by the damaged car.

"He knocked a wheel off. I'll have to send back."

"Oh, I thought it was all over when we hit!" said the girl.

Kurt experienced a relaxation that was weakening. He could hardly hold the wheel and his mood became one of exaltation.

"Father suspected this Ruenke," went on Lenore. "But he wanted to find out things from him. And I—I undertook—to twist Mr. Germany round my finger. I made a mess of it....He lied. I didn't make love to him.

But I listened to his lovemaking, and arrogant German lovemaking it was! I'm afraid I made eyes at him and let him believe I was smitten....Oh, and all for nothing! I'm ashamed....But he lied!"

Her confidence, at once pathetic and humorous and contemptuous, augmented Kurt's Homeric mood. He understood that she would not even let him, for a moment, have a wrong impression of her.

"It must have been hard," agreed Kurt. "Didn't you find out anything at all?"

"Not much," she replied. Then she put a hand on his sleeve. "Your knuckles are all bloody."

"So they are. I got that punching our German friend."

"Oh, how you did beat him!" she cried. "I had to look. My ire was up, too!...It wasn't very womanly—of me—that I gloried in the sight."

"But you cried out—you pulled me away!" exclaimed Kurt.

"That was because I was afraid you'd kill him," she replied.

Kurt swerved his glance, for an instant, to her face. It was at once flushed and pale, with the deep blue of downcast eyes shadowy through her long lashes, exceedingly sweet and beautiful to Kurt's sight. He bent his glance again to the road ahead. Miss Anderson felt kindly and gratefully toward him, as was, of course, natural. But she was somehow different from what she had seemed upon the other occasions he had seen her. Kurt's heart was full to bursting.

"I might have killed him," he said. "I'm glad—you stopped me. That—that frenzy of mine seemed to be the breaking of a dam. I have been dammed up within.

Something had to break. I've been unhappy for a long time."

"I saw that. What about?" she replied.

"The war, and what it's done to Father. We're estranged. I hate everything German. I loved the farm. My chance in life is gone. The wheat debt—the worry about the I. W. W.—and that's not all."

Again she put a gentle hand on his sleeve and left it there for a moment. The touch thrilled all through Kurt.

"I'm sorry. Your position is sad. But maybe it is not utterly hopeless. You—you'll come back after the war."

"I don't know that I want to come back," he said. "For then—it'd be just as bad—worse....Miss Anderson, it won't hurt to tell you the truth....A year ago— that first time I saw you—I fell in love with you. I think— when I'm away—over in France—I'd like to feel that you know. It can't hurt you. And it'll be sweet to me.... I fought against the—the madness. But fate was against me....I saw you again....And it was all over with me!"

He paused, catching his breath. She was perfectly quiet. He looked on down the winding road. There were dust clouds in the distance.

"I'm afraid I grew bitter and moody," he went on "But the last forty-eight hours have changed me forever. ...I found that my poor old dad had been won over by these unscrupulous German agents of the I. W. W. But I saved his name....I've got the money he took for the wheat we may never harvest. But if we do harvest I can pay all our debt....Then I learned of a plot to ruin your father—to kill him! ...I was on my way to 'Many Waters.' I can warn him....Last of all I have saved you."

The little hand dropped away from his coat sleeve.

A soft, half-smothered cry escaped her. It seemed to him she was about to weep in her exceeding pity.

"Miss Anderson, I—I'd rather not have—you pity me."

"Mr. Dorn, I certainly don't pity you," she replied, with an unexpected, strange tone. It was full. It seemed to ring in his ears.

"I know there never was and never could be any hope for me. I—I—"

"Oh, you know that!" murmured the soft, strange voice.

But Kurt could not trust his ears and he had to make haste to terminate the confession into which his folly and emotion had betrayed him. He scarcely heard her words.

"Yes.... I told you why I wanted you to know.... And now forget that—and when I'm gone—if you think of me ever, let it be about how much better it made me—to have all this good luck—to help your father and to save you!"

The dust cloud down the road came from a string of automobiles, flying along at express speed. Kurt saw them with relief.

"Here come the cars on your trail," he called out. "Your father will be in one of them."

Kurt opened the door of the car and stepped down. He could not help his importance or his pride. Anderson, who came running between two cars that had stopped abreast, was coatless and hatless, covered with dust, pale and fire-eyed.

"Mr. Anderson, your daughter is safe—unharmed," Kurt assured him.

"My girl!" cried the father, huskily, and hurried to where she leaned out of her seat.

"All right, Dad," she cried, as she embraced him. "Only a little shaky yet."

It was affecting for Dorn to see that meeting, and through it to share something of its meaning. Anderson's thick neck swelled and colored, and his utterance was unintelligible. His daughter loosened her arm from round him and turned her face toward Kurt. Then he imagined he saw two blue stars, sweetly, strangely shining upon him.

"Father, it was our friend from the Bend," she said. "He happened along."

Anderson suddenly changed to the cool, smiling man Kurt remembered.

"Howdy, Kurt?" he said, and crushed Kurt's hand. "What'd you do to him?"

Kurt made a motion toward the back of the car. Then Anderson looked over the seats. With that he opened the door and in one powerful haul he drew Ruenke sliding out into the road. Ruenke's bruised and bloody face was uppermost, a rather gruesome sight. Anderson glared down upon him, while men from the other cars crowded around. Ruenke's eyes resembled those of a cornered rat. Anderson's jaw bulged, his big hands clenched.

"Bill, you throw this fellow in your car and land him in jail. I'll make a charge against him," said the rancher.

"Mr. Anderson, I can save some valuable time," interposed Kurt. "I've got to return a car I broke down. And there's my wheat. Will you have one of these men drive me back?"

"Sure. But won't you come home with us?" said Anderson.

"I'd like to. But I must get home," replied Kurt.

"Please let me speak a few words for your ear alone." He drew Anderson aside and briefly told about the eighty thousand dollars; threw back his coat to show the bulging pockets. Then he asked Anderson's advice.

"I'd deposit the money an' wire the Spokane miller," returned the rancher. "I know him. He'll leave the money in the bank till your wheat is safe. Go to the national bank in Kilo. Mention my name."

Then Kurt told Anderson of the plot against his fortunes and his life.

"Neuman! I. W. W.! German intrigue!" growled the rancher. "All in the same class! . . . Dorn, I'm forewarned, an' that's forearmed. I'll beat this outfit at their own game."

They returned to Anderson's car. Kurt reached inside for his rifle.

"Aren't you going home with us?" asked the girl.

"Why, Miss Anderson, I—I'm sorry. I—I'd love to see 'Many Waters,'" floundered Kurt. "But I can't go now. There's no need. I must hurry back to—to my troubles."

"I wanted to tell you something—at home," she returned, shyly.

"Tell me now," said Kurt.

She gave him such a glance as he had never received in his life. Kurt felt himself as wax before those blue eyes. She wanted to thank him. That would be sweet, but would only make his ordeal harder. He steeled himself.

"You won't come?" she asked, and her smile was wistful.

"No—thank you ever so much."

"Will you come to see me before you—you go to war?"

"I'll try."

"But you must promise. You've done so much for me and my father.... I—I want you to come to see me— at my home."

"Then I'll come," he replied.

Anderson clambered into the car beside his daughter and laid his big hands on the wheel.

"Sure he'll come, or we'll go after him," he declared, heartily. "So long, son."

CHAPTER
11

*L*ATE in the forenoon of the next day Kurt Dorn reached home. A hot harvest wind breathed off the wheat fields. It swelled his heart to see the change in the color of that section of Bluestem—the gold had a tinge of rich, ripe brown.

Kurt's father awaited him, a haggard, gloomy-faced man, unkempt and hollow-eyed.

"Was it you who robbed me?" he shouted, hoarsely.

"Yes," replied Kurt. He had caught the eager hope and fear in the old man's tone. Kurt expected that confession would bring on his father's terrible fury, a mood to dread. But old Dorn showed immense relief. He sat down in his relaxation from what must have been intense strain. Kurt saw a weariness, a shade, in the gray lined face that had never been there before.

"What did you do with the money?" asked the old man.

"I banked it in Kilo," replied Kurt. "Then I wired your miller in Spokane....So you're safe if we can harvest the wheat."

Old Dorn nodded thoughtfully. There had come a subtle change in him. Presently he asked Kurt if men had been hired for the harvest.

"No. I've not seen any I would trust," replied Kurt, and then he briefly outlined Anderson's plan to insure a quick and safe harvesting of the grain. Old Dorn objected to this on account of the expense. Kurt argued with him and patiently tried to show him the imperative need of it. Dorn, apparently, was not to be won over; however, he was remarkably mild in comparison with what Kurt had expected.

"Father, do you realize now that the men you were dealing with at Wheatly are dishonest? I mean with you. They would betray you."

Old Dorn had no answer for this. Evidently he had sustained some kind of shock that he was not willing to admit.

"Look here, Father," went on Kurt, in slow earnestness. He spoke in English, because nothing would make him break his word and ever again speak a word of German. And his father was not quick to comprehend English. "Can't you see that the I. W. W. mean to cripple us wheat farmers this harvest?"

"No," replied old Dorn, stubbornly.

"But they do. They don't *want* work. If they accept work it is for a chance to do damage. All this I. W. W. talk about more wages and shorter hours is deceit. They make a bold face of discontent. That is all a lie. The I.W.W. is out to ruin the great wheat fields and the great lumber forests of the Northwest."

"I do not believe that," declared his father, stoutly. "What for?"

Kurt meant to be careful of that subject.

"No matter what for. It does not make any difference what it's for. We've got to meet it to save our wheat....Now won't you believe me? Won't you let me manage the harvest?"

"I will not believe," replied old Dorn, stubbornly. "Not about *my* wheat. I know they mean to destroy. They are against rich men like Anderson. But not me or my wheat!"

"There is where you are wrong. I'll prove it in a very few days. But in that time I can prepare for them and outwit them. Will you let me?"

"Go ahead," replied old Dorn, gruffly.

It was a concession that Kurt was amazed and delighted to gain. And he set about at once to act upon it. He changed his clothes and satisfied his hunger; then, saddling his horse, he started out to visit his farmer neighbors.

The day bade fair to be rich in experience. Jerry, the foreman, was patrolling his long beat up and down the highway. Jerry carried a shotgun and looked like a sentry. The men under him were on the other side of the section of wheat, and the ground was so rolling that they could not be seen from the highway. Jerry was unmistakably glad and relieved to see Kurt.

"Some goin's-on," he declared, with a grin. "Since you left there's been one hundred and sixteen I. W. W. tramps along this here road."

"Have you had any trouble?" inquired Kurt.

"Wal, I reckon it wasn't trouble, but every time I

took a peg at some sneak I sort of broke out sweatin' cold."

"You shot at them?"

"Sure I shot when I seen any loafin' along in the dark. Two of them shot back at me, an' after thet I wasn't particular to aim high....Reckon I'm about dead for sleep."

"I'll relieve you tonight," replied Kurt. "Jerry, doesn't the wheat look great?"

"Wal, I reckon. An' walkin' along here when it's quiet an' no wind blowin', I can just hear the wheat crack. It's gittin' ripe fast, an' sure the biggest crop we ever raised....But I'm tellin' you—when I think how we'll ever harvest it my insides just sinks like lead!"

Kurt then outlined Anderson's plan, which was received by the foreman with eager approval and the assurance that the neighbor farmers would rally to his call.

Kurt found his nearest neighbor, Olsen, cutting a thin, scarcely ripe barley. Olsen was running a new McCormack harvester, and appeared delighted with the machine, but cast down by the grain prospects. He did not intend to cut his wheat at all. It was a dead loss.

"Two sections—twelve hundred an' eighty acres!" he repeated, gloomily. "An' the third bad year! Dorn, I can't pay the interest to my bank."

Olsen's sun-dried and wind-carved visage was as hard and rugged and heroic as this desert that had resisted him for years. Kurt saw under the lines and the bronze all the toil and pain and unquenchable hope that had made Olsen a type of the men who had cultivated this desert of wheat.

"I'll give you five hundred dollars to help me harvest," said Kurt, bluntly, and briefly stated his plan.

Olsen whistled. He complimented Anderson's shrewd sense. He spoke glowingly of that magnificent section of wheat that absolutely must be saved. He promised Kurt every horse and every man on his farm. But he refused the five hundred dollars.

"Oh, say, you'll have to accept it," declared Kurt.

"You've done me good turns," asserted Olsen.

"But nothing like this. Why, this will be a rush job, with all the men and horses and machines and wagons I can get. It'll cost ten—fifteen thousand dollars to harvest that section. Even at that, and paying Anderson, we'll clear twenty thousand or more. Olsen, you've got to take the money."

"All right, if you insist. I'm needin' it bad enough," replied Olsen.

Further conversation with Olsen gleaned the facts that he was the only farmer in their immediate neighborhood who did not have at least a little grain worth harvesting. But the amount was small and would require only slight time. Olsen named farmers that very likely would not take kindly to Dorn's proposition, and had best not be approached. The majority, however, would stand by him, irrespective of the large wage offered, because the issue was one to appeal to the pride of the Bend farmers. Olsen appeared surprisingly well informed upon the tactics of the I. W. W., and predicted that they would cause trouble, but be run out of the country. He made the shrewd observation that when even those farmers who sympathized with Germany discovered that their wheat fields were being menaced by foreign influences and protected by the home government, they would experience a change of heart. Olsen said the war would be a good thing for the United States, because they would win it, and during the winning would learn and suffer and achieve much.

Kurt rode away from Olsen in a more thoughtful frame of mind. How different and interesting the points of view of different men! Olsen had never taken the time to become a naturalized citizen of the United States. There had never been anything to force him to do it. But his understanding of the worth of the United States and his loyalty to it were manifest in his love for his wheatlands. In fact, they were inseparable. Probably there were millions of pioneers, emigrants, aliens, all over the country who were like Olsen, who needed the fire of the crucible to mold them into a unity with Americans. Of such, Americans were molded!

Kurt rode all day, and when, late that night, he got home, weary and sore and choked, he had enlisted the services of thirty-five farmers to help him harvest the now famous section of wheat.

His father had plainly doubted the willingness of these neighbors to abandon their own labors, for the Bend exacted toil for every hour of every season, whether rich or poor in yield. Likewise he was plainly moved by the facts. His seamed and shaded face of gloom had a moment of light.

"They will make short work of this harvest," he said, thoughtfully.

"I should say so," retorted Kurt. "We'll harvest and haul that grain to the railroad in just three days."

"Impossible!" ejaculated Dorn.

"You'll see," declared Kurt. "You'll see who's managing this harvest."

He could not restrain his little outburst of pride. For the moment the great overhanging sense of calamity that for long had haunted him• faded into the background. It did seem sure that they would save this splendid yield of wheat. How much that meant to Kurt—in freedom from debt, in natural love of the fruition of harvest, in the loyalty to his government! He realized how strange and strong was the need in him to prove he was American to the very core of his heart. He did not yet understand that incentive, but he felt it.

After eating dinner Kurt took his rifle and went out to relieve Jerry.

"Only a few more days and nights!" he exclaimed to his foreman. "Then we'll have all the harvesters in the country right in our wheat."

"Wal, a hell of a lot can happen before then," declared Jerry, pessimistically.

Kurt was brought back to realities rather suddenly. But questioning Jerry did not elicit any new or immediate cause for worry. Jerry appeared tired out.

"You go get some sleep," said Kurt.

"All right. Bill's been dividin' this night watch with me. I reckon he'll be out when he wakes up," replied Jerry, and trudged away.

Kurt shouldered his rifle and slowly walked along the road with a strange sense that he was already doing army duty in protecting property which was at once his own and his country's.

The night was dark, cool, and quiet. The heavens were starry bright. A faint breeze brought the tiny crackling of the wheat. From far distant came the bay of a hound. The road stretched away pale and yellow into the gloom. In the silence and loneliness and darkness, in all around him, and far across the dry, whispering fields, there was an invisible presence that had its affinity in him, hovered over him shadowless and immense, and waved in the bursting wheat. It was life. He felt the wheat ripening. He felt it in reawakened tenderness for his old father and in the stir of memory of Lenore Anderson. The past active and important hours had left little room for thought of her.

But now she came back to him, a spirit in keeping with his steps, a shadow under the stars, a picture of sweet, wonderful young womanhood. His whole relation of thought toward her had undergone some marvelous change. The most divine of gifts had been granted him—an opportunity to save her from harm, perhaps from death. He had served her father. How greatly he could not tell, but if measured by the gratitude in her eyes it would have been infinite. He recalled that expression—blue, warm, soft, and indescribably strange with its unuttered hidden meaning. It was all-satisfying for him to realize that she had been compelled to give him a separate and distinct place in her mind. He must stand apart from all others she knew. It had been his fortune to preserve her happiness and the happiness that she must be to sisters and mother, and that some day she would bestow upon some lucky man. They would all owe it to him. And Lenore Anderson knew he loved her.

These things had transformed his relation of thought toward her. He had no regret, no jealousy, no fear. Even the pang of suppressed and overwhelming love had gone with his confession.

But he did remember her presence, her beauty, her intent blue glance, and the faint, dreaming smile of her lips—remembered them with a thrill, and a wave of emotion, and a contraction of his heart. He had promised to see her once more, to afford her the opportunity, no doubt, to thank him, to try to make him see her gratitude. He would go, but he wished it need not be. He asked no more. And seeing her again might change his fullness of joy to something of pain.

So Kurt trod the long road in the darkness and silence, pausing, and checking his dreams now and then, to listen and to watch. He heard no suspicious sounds, nor did he meet anyone. The night was melancholy, with a hint of fall in its cool breath.

Soon he would be walking a beat in one of the training camps, with a bugle call in his ears and the turmoil of thousands of soldiers in the making around him: soon, too, he would be walking the deck of a transport, looking back down the moon-blanched wake of the ship toward home, listening to the mysterious moan of the ocean; and then soon feeling under his feet the soil of a foreign country, with hideous and incomparable war shrieking its shell furies and its man anguish all about him. But no matter how far away he ever got, he knew Lenore Anderson would be with him as she was there on that dim lonely, starlit country road.

And in these long hours of his vigil Kurt Dorn divined a relation between his love for Lenore Anderson and a terrible need that had grown upon him. A need of his heart and his soul! More than he needed her, if even in his wildest dreams he had permitted himself visions of an earthly paradise, he needed to prove to his blood and his spirit that he was actually and truly American. He had no doubt of his intelligence, his reason, his choice. The secret lay hidden in the depths of him, and he knew it came from the springs of the mother who had begotten him. His mother had given him birth, and by every tie he was mostly hers.

Kurt had been in college during the first year of the world war. And his name, his fair hair and complexion, his fluency in German, and his remarkable efficiency in handicrafts had opened him to many a hint, many a veiled sarcasm that had stung him like a poison brand. There was injustice in all this war spirit. It changed the minds of men and women. He had not doubted himself until those terrible scenes with his father, and, though he had reacted to them as an American, he had felt the drawing, burning blood tie. He hated everything German and he knew he was wrong in doing so. He had clear conception in his mind of the difference between the German war motives and means, and those of the other nations.

Kurt's problem was to understand himself. His great fight was with his own soul. His material difficulties and his despairing love had suddenly been transformed, so that they had lent his spirit wings. How many poor boys and girls in America must be helplessly divided between parents and country! How many faithful and blind parents, obedient to the laws of mind and heart, set for all time, must see a favorite son go out to fight against all they had held sacred!

That was all bad enough, but Kurt had more to contend with. No illusions had he of a chastened German spirit, a clarified German mind, an unbrutalized German heart. Kurt knew his father. What would change his father? Nothing but death! Death for himself or death for his only son! Kurt had an incalculable call to prove forever to himself that he was free. He had to spill his own blood to prove himself, or he had to spill that of an enemy. And he preferred that it should be his own. But that did not change a vivid and terrible picture which haunted him at times. He saw a dark, wide, and barren shingle of the world, a desert of desolation made by man, where strange, windy shrieks and thundering booms and awful cries went up in the night, and where drifting palls of smoke made starless sky, and bursts of reddish fires made hell.

Suddenly Kurt's slow pacing along the road was halted, as was the trend of his thought. He was not sure he had heard a sound. But he quivered all over. The night was far advanced now; the wind was almost still; the wheat was smooth and dark as the bosom of a resting sea. Kurt listened. He imagined he heard, far away, the faint roar of an automobile. But it might have been a train on the railroad. Sometimes on still nights he caught sounds like that.

Then a swish in the wheat, a soft thud, very low, unmistakably came to Kurt's ear. He listened, turning his ear to the wind. Presently he heard it again—a sound relating both to wheat and earth. In a hot flash he divined that someone had thrown fairly heavy bodies into the wheat fields. Phosphorus cakes! Kurt held his breath while he peered down the gloomy road, his heart pounding, his hands gripping the rifle. And when he descried a dim form stealthily coming toward him he yelled, "Halt!"

Instantly the form wavered, moved swiftly, with quick pad of footfalls. Kurt shot once—twice—three times—and aimed as best he could to hit. The form either fell or went on out of sight in the gloom. Kurt answered the excited shouts of his men, calling them to come across to him. Then he went cautiously down the road, peering on the the ground for a dark form. But he failed to find it, and presently had to admit that in the dark his aim had been poor. Bill came out to relieve Kurt, and together they went up and down the road for a mile without any glimpse of a skulking form. It was almost daylight when Kurt went home to get a few hours' sleep.

CHAPTER
12

*N*EXT day was one of the rare, blistering-hot days with a furnace wind that roared over the wheat fields. The sky was steely and the sun like copper. It was a day which would bring the wheat to a head.

At breakfast Jerry reported that fresh auto tracks had been made on the road during the night; and that dust and wheat all around the great field showed a fresh tramping.

Kurt believed a deliberate and particular attempt had been made to insure the destruction of the Dorn wheat field. And he ordered all hands out to search for the dangerous little cakes of phosphorous.

It was difficult to find them. The wheat was almost as high as a man's head and very thick. To force a way through it without tramping it down took care and time. Besides, the soil was soft, and the agents who had perpetrated this vile scheme had perfectly matched the color. Kurt almost stepped on one of the cakes before he saw it. His men were very slow in finding any. But Kurt's father seemed to walk fatally right to them, for in a short hundred yards he found three. They caused a profound change in this gloomy man. Not a word did he utter, but he became animated by a tremendous energy.

The search was discouraging. It was like hunting for dynamite bombs that might explode at any moment. All Kurt's dread of calamity returned fourfold. The intense heat of the day, that would ripen the wheat to bursting, would likewise sooner or later ignite the cakes of phosphorus. And when Jerry found a cake far inside the field, away from the road, showing that powerful had been the arm that had thrown it there, and how impossible it would be to make a thorough search, Kurt almost succumbed to discouragement. Still, he kept up a frenzied hunting and inspired the laborers to do likewise.

About ten o'clock an excited shout from Bill drew Kurt's attention, and he ran along the edge of the field. Bill was sweaty and black, yet through it all Kurt believed he saw the man was pale. He pointed with shaking hand toward Olsen's hill.

Kurt vibrated to a shock. He saw a long circular yellow column rising from the hill, slanting away on the strong wind.

"Dust!" he cried, aghast.

"Smoke!" replied Bill, hoarsely.

The catastrophe had fallen. Olsen's wheat was burning. Kurt experienced a profound sensation of sadness. What a pity! The burning of wheat—the destruction of bread—when part of the world was starving! Tears dimmed his eyes as he watched the swelling column of smoke.

Bill was cursing, and Kurt gathered that the farmhand was predicting fires all around. This was inevitable. But it meant no great loss for most of the wheat growers whose yield had failed. For Kurt and his father, if fire got a hold in their wheat, it meant ruin. Kurt's sadness was burned out by a slow and growing rage.

"Bill, go hitch up to the big mower," ordered Kurt. "We'll have to cut all around our field. Bring drinking water and whatever you can lay a hand on . . . anything to fight fire!"

Bill ran thumping away over the clods. Then it happened that Kurt looked toward his father. The old man was standing with his arms aloft, his face turned toward the burning wheat, and he made a tragic figure that wrung Kurt's heart.

Jerry came running up. "Fire! Fire! Olsen's burnin'! Look! By all thet's dirty, them I. W. W.'s hev done it! . . . Kurt, we're in fer hell! Thet wind's blowin' straight this way."

"Jerry, we'll fight till we drop," replied Kurt. "Tell the men and father to keep on searching for phosphorus cakes. . . . Jerry, you keep to the high ground. Watch for fires starting on our land. If you see one yell for us and make for it. Wheat burns slow till it gets started. We can put out fires if we're quick."

"Kurt, there ain't no chance on earth fer us!" yelled Jerry, pale with anger. His big red hands worked. "If fire starts we've got to hev a lot of men. . . . By Gawd! if I ain't mad!"

"Don't quit, Jerry," said Kurt, fiercely. "You never

can tell. It looks hopeless. But we'll never give up. Hustle now!"

Jerry shuffled off as old Dorn came haltingly, as if stunned, toward Kurt. But Kurt did not want to face his father at that moment. He needed to fight to keep up his own courage.

"Never mind that!" yelled Kurt, pointing at Olsen's hill. "Keep looking for those damned pieces of phosphorus!"

With that Kurt dove into the wheat, and, sweeping wide his arms to make a passage, he strode on, his eyes bent piercingly upon the ground close about him. He did not penetrate deeper into the wheat from the road than the distance he estimated a strong arm could send a stone. Almost at once his keen sight was rewarded. He found a cake of phosphorus half buried in the soil. It was dry, hard, and hot either from the sun or its own generating power. That inspired Kurt. He hurried on. Long practice enabled him to slip through the wheat as a barefoot country boy could run through the cornfields. And his passion gave him the eyes of a hunting hawk sweeping down over the grass. To and fro he passed within the limits he had marked, oblivious to time and heat and effort. And covering that part of the wheat-field bordering the road he collected twenty-seven cakes of phosphorus, the last few of which were so hot they burnt his hands.

Then he had to rest. He appeared as wet as if he had been plunged into water; his skin burned, his eyes pained, his breast heaved. Panting and spent, he lay along the edge of the wheat, with closed eyelids and lax muscles.

When he recovered he rose and went back along

the road. The last quarter of the immense wheat field lay upon a slope of a hill, and Kurt had to mount this before he could see the valley. From the summit he saw a sight that caused him to utter a loud exclamation. Many columns of smoke were lifting from the valley, and before him the sky was darkened. Olsen's hill was as if under a cloud. No flames showed anywhere, but in places the line of smoke appeared to be approaching.

"It's a thousand to one against us," he said, bitterly, and looked at his watch. He was amazed to see that three hours had passed since he had given orders to the men. He hurried back to the house. No one was there except the old servant, who was wringing her hands and crying that the house would burn. Throwing the cakes of phosphorus into a watering trough, Kurt ran into the kitchen, snatched a few biscuits, and then made for the fields, eating as he went.

He hurried down a lane that bordered the big wheat field. On this side was fallow ground for half the length of the section, and the other half was ripe barley, dry as tinder, and beyond that, in line with the burning fields, a quarter section of blasted wheat. The men were there. Kurt saw at once that other men with horses and machines were also there. Then he recognized Olsen and two other of his neighbors. As he ran up he was equally astounded and out of breath, so that he could not speak. Old Dorn sat with gray head bowed on his hands.

"Hello!" shouted Olsen. His grimy face broke into a hard smile. "Fires all over! Wheat's burnin' like prairie grass! Them chips of phosphorus are sure from hell! . . . We've come over to help."

"You—did! You left—your fields!" gasped Kurt.

"Sure. They're not much to leave. And we're goin' to save this section of yours or bust tryin'! . . . I sent my son in his car, all over, to hurry men here with horses, machines, wagons."

Kurt was overcome. He could only wring Olsen's hand. Here was an answer to one of his brooding, gloomy queries. Something would be gained, even if the wheat was lost. Kurt had scarcely any hope left.

"What's to be done?" he panted, hoarsely. In this extremity Olsen seemed a tower of strength. This sturdy farmer was of Anderson's breed, even if he was a foreigner. And he had fought fires before.

"If we have time we'll mow a line all around your wheat replied Olsen.

"Reckon we won't have time," interposed Jerry, pointing to a smoke far down in the corner of the stunted wheat. "There's a fire startin'."

"They'll break out all over," said Olsen, and he waved a couple of his men away. One had a scythe and the other a long pole with a wet burlap bag tied on one end. They hurried toward the little cloud of smoke.

"I found a lot of cakes over along the road," declared Kurt, with a grim surety that he had done that well.

"They've surrounded your wheat," returned Olsen. "But if enough men get here we'll save the whole section. . . . Lucky you've got two wells an' that water tank. We'll need all the water we can get. Keep a man pumpin'. Fetch all the bags an' brooms an' scythes. I'll post lookouts along this lane to watch for fires breakin' out in the big field. When they do we've got to run an' cut an' beat them out. . . . It won't be long till most of this section is surrounded by fire."

Thin clouds of smoke were then blowing across the fields and the wind that carried them was laden with an odor of burning wheat. To Kurt it seemed to be the fragrance of baking bread.

"How'd it be to begin harvestin'?" queried Jerry. "Thet wheat's ripe."

"No combines should be risked in there until we're sure the danger's past," replied Olsen. "There! I see more of our neighbors comin' down the road. We're goin' to beat the I. W. W."

That galvanized Kurt into action and he found himself dragging Jerry back to the barns. They hitched a team to a heavy wagon, in record time, and then began to load with whatever was available for fighting fire. They loaded a barrel, and with huge buckets filled it with water. Leaving Jerry to drive, Kurt rushed back to the fields. During his short absence more men, with horses and machines, had arrived; fire had broken out in the stunted wheat, and also, nearer at hand, in the barley. Kurt saw his father laboring like a giant. Olsen was taking charge, directing the men. The sky was obscured now, and all the west was thick with yellow smoke. The south slopes and valley floor were clouding. Only in the east, over the hill, did the air appear clear. Back of Kurt, down across the barley and wheat on the Dorn land, a line of fire was creeping over the hill. This was on the property adjoining Olsen's. Gremniger, the owner, had abandoned his own fields. At the moment he was driving a mower along the edge of the barley, cutting a nine-foot path. Men behind him were stacking the sheaves. The wind was as hot as if from a blast furnace; the air was thick and oppressive; the light of day was growing dim.

Kurt, mounted on the seat of one of the combine threshers, surveyed with rapid and anxious gaze all the points around him, and it lingered over the magnificent sweep of golden wheat. The wheat bowed in waves before the wind, and the silken rustle, heard above the confusion of yelling men, was like a voice whispering to Kurt. Somehow his dread lessened then and other emotions predominated. He saw more and more farmers arrive, in cars, in wagons, with engines and threshers, until the lane was lined with them and men were hurrying everywhere.

Suddenly Kurt espied a slender column of smoke rising above the wheat out in front of him toward the highway. This was the first sign of fire in the great section that so many farmers had come to protect. Yelling for help, he leaped off the seat and ran with all his might toward the spot. Breasting that thick wheat was almost as hard as breasting waves. Jerry came yelling after him, brandishing a crude beater; and both of them reached the fire at once. It was a small circle, burning slowly. Madly Kurt rushed in to tear and stamp as if the little hissing flames were serpents. He burned his hands through his gloves and his feet through his boots. Jerry beat hard, accompanying his blows with profane speech plainly indicating that he felt he was at work on the I. W. W. In short order they put out this little fire. Returning to his post, Kurt watched until he was called to lend a hand down in the stunted wheat.

Fire had crossed and had gotten a hold on Dorn's lower field. Here the wheat was blasted and so burned all the more fiercely. Horses and mowers had to be taken away to the intervening barley field. A weird, smoky, and ruddy darkness enveloped the scene. Dim red fire, in lines and dots and curves, appeared on three sides, growing larger and longer, meeting in some places, criss-crossed by black figures of threshing men belaboring the flames. Kurt came across his father working like a madman. Kurt warned him not to overexert himself, and the father never heard. Now and then his stentorian yell added to the medley of cries and shouts and blows, and the roar of the wind fanning the flames.

Kurt was put to beating fire in the cut wheat. He stood with flames licking at his boots. It was astonishing how tenacious the fire appeared, how it crept along, eating up the mowed wheat. All the men that could be spared there were unable to check it and keep it out of the standing grain. When it reached this line it lifted a blaze, flamed and roared, and burned like wildfire in grass. The men were driven back, threshing and beating, all to no avail. Kurt fell into despair. There was no hope. It seemed like an inferno.

Flaring high, the light showed the black, violently agitated forms of the fighters, and the clouds of yellow smoke, coalescing and drifting, changing to dark and soaring high.

Olsen had sent three mowers abreast down the whole length of the barley field before the fire reached that line. It was a wise move, and if anything could do so it would save the day. The leaping flame, thin and high, and a mile long, curled down the last of the standing wheat and caught the fallen barley. But here its speed was checked. It had to lick a way along the ground.

In desperation, in unabated fury, the little army of farmers and laborers, with no thought of personal gain, with what seemed to Kurt a wonderful and noble spirit, attacked this encroaching line of fire like men whose homes and lives and ideals had been threatened with destruction. Kurt's mind worked as swiftly as his tireless hands. This indeed was being in a front line of battle. The scene was weird, dark, fitful, at times impressive and again unreal. These neighbors of his, many of them aliens, some of them Germans, when put to this vital test, were proving themselves. They had shown little liking for the Dorns, but here was love of wheat, and so, in some way, loyalty to the government that needed it. Here was the answer of the Northwest to the I. W. W. No doubt if the perpetrators of that phosphorus trick could have been laid hold of then, blood would have been shed. Kurt sensed in the fierce energy, in the dark, grimy faces, shining and wet under the light, in the hoarse yell and answering shout, a nameless force that was finding itself and centering on one common cause.

His old father toiled as ten men. That burly giant pushed ever in the lead, and his hoarse call and strenuous action told of more than a mercenary rage to save his wheat.

Fire never got across that swath of cut barley. It was beaten out as if by a thousand men. Shadow and gloom enveloped the fighters as they rested where their last strokes had fallen. Over the hills faint reflection of dying flames lit up the dark clouds of smoke. The battle seemed won.

Then came the thrilling cry: "Fire! Fire!"

One of the outposts came running out of the dark. "Fire! the other side! Fire!" rang out Olsen's yell.

Kurt ran with the gang pell-mell through the dark, up the barley slope, to see a long red line, a high red flare, and lifting clouds of ruddy smoke. Fire in the big wheat field! The sight inflamed him, carried him beyond his powers, and all he knew was that he became the center of a dark and whirling mêlée encircled by living flames that leaped only to be beaten down. Whether that threshing chaos of fire and smoke and wheat was short or long was beyond him to tell but the fire was extinguished to the last spark.

Walking back with the weary crowd, Kurt felt a clearer breeze upon his face. Smoke was not flying so thickly. Over the western hill, through a rift in the clouds, peeped a star. The only other light he saw twinkled far down the lane. It was that of a lantern. Dark forms barred it now and then. Slowly Kurt recovered his breath. The men were talking and tired voices rang with assurance that the fire was beaten.

Someone called Kurt. The voice was Jerry's. It seemed hoarse and strained. Kurt could see the lean form of his man, standing in the light of the lantern. A small dark group of men, silent and somehow impressive, stood off a little in the shadow.

"Here I am, Jerry," called Kurt, stepping forward. Just then Olsen joined Jerry.

"Boy, we've beat the I. W. W.'s, but—but—" he began, and broke off huskily.

"What's the matter?" queried Kurt, and a cold chill shot over him.

Jerry plucked at his sleeve.

"Your old man—your dad—he's overworked hisself," whispered Jerry. "It's tough. . . . Nobody could stop him."

Kurt felt that the fulfillment of his icy, sickening dread had come. Jerry's dark face, even in the uncertain light, was tragic.

"Boy, his heart went back on him—he's dead!" said Olsen, solemnly.

Kurt pushed the kind hands aside. A few steps brought him to where, under the light of the lantern, lay his father, pale and still, with a strange softening of the iron cast of intolerance.

"Dead!" whispered Kurt, in awe and horror. "Father! Oh, he's gone!—without a word—"

Again Jerry plucked at Kurt's sleeve.

"I was with him," said Jerry. "I heard him fall an' groan....I had the light. I bent over, lifted his head.... An' he said, speaking English, 'Tell my son—I was wrong!' ...Then he died. An' thet was all."

Kurt staggered away from the whispering, sympathetic foreman, out into the darkness, where he lifted his face in the thankfulness of a breaking heart.

It had, indeed, taken the approach of death to change his hard old father. "Oh, he meant—that if he had his life to live over again—he would be different!" whispered Kurt. That was the one great word needed to reconcile Kurt to his father.

The night had grown still, except for the murmuring of the men. Smoke veiled the horizon. Kurt felt an intense and terrible loneliness. He was indeed alone in the world. A hard, tight contraction of throat choked back a sob. If only he could have had a word with his father! But no grief, nothing could detract from the splendid truth of his father's last message. In the black hours soon to come Kurt would have that to sustain him.

CHAPTER
13

*T*HE bright sun of morning disclosed that wide, rolling region of the Bend to be a dreary, blackened waste surrounding one great wheat field, rich and mellow and golden.

Kurt Dorn's neighbor, Olsen, in his kind and matter-of-fact way, making obligation seem slight, took charge of Kurt's affairs, and made the necessary and difficult decisions. Nothing must delay the harvesting and transporting of the wheat. The womenfolk arranged for the burial of old Chris Dorn.

Kurt sat and moved about in a gloomy kind of trance for a day and a half, until his father was laid to rest beside his mother, in the little graveyard on the windy hill. After that his mind slowly cleared. He kept to himself the remainder of that day, avoiding the crowd of harvesters camping in the yard and adjacent field; and at sunset he went to a lonely spot on the verge of the valley, where with sad eyes he watched the last rays of sunlight fade over the blackened hills. All these hours had seemed consecrated to his father's memory, to remembered acts of kindness and of love, of the relation that had gone and would never be again. Reproach and remorse had abided with him until that sunset hour, when the load eased off his heart.

Next morning he went out to the wheat field.

What a wonderful harvesting scene greeted Kurt Dorn! Never had its like been seen in the Northwest, nor perhaps in any other place. A huge pall of dust, chaff, and smoke hung over the vast wheat field, and the air seemed charged with a roar. The glaring gold of the wheat field appeared to be crisscrossed everywhere with bobbing black streaks of horses—bays, blacks, whites, and reds; by big, moving painted machines, lifting arms and puffing straw; by immense wagons piled high with sheaves of wheat, lumbering down to the smoking engines and the threshers that sent long streams of dust and chaff over the lifting strawstacks; by wagons following the combines to pick up the plump brown sacks of wheat; and by a string of empty wagons coming in from the road.

Olsen was rushing thirty combine threshers, three engine threshing machines, forty wagon teams, and over a hundred men well known to him. There was a guard around the field. This unprecedented harvest had attracted many spectators from the little towns. They had come in cars and on horseback and on foot. Olsen trusted no man on that field except those he knew.

The wonderful wheat field was cut into a thousand squares and angles and lanes and curves. The big whirring combines passed one another, stopped and waited and turned out of the way, leaving everywhere little patches and cubes of standing wheat, that soon fell before the onslaught of the smaller combines. This scene had no regularity. It was one of confusion; of awkward halts, delays, hurries; of accident. The wind blew clouds of dust and chaff, alternately clearing one space to cloud another. And a strange roar added the last heroic touch to this heroic field. It was indeed the roar of battle—men and horses governing the action of machinery, and all fighting time. For in delay was peril to the wheat.

Once Kurt ran across the tireless and implacable Olsen. He seemed a man of dust and sweat and fury.

"She's half cut an' over twenty thousand bushels gone to the railroad!" he exclaimed. "An' we're speedin' up."

"Olsen, I don't get what's going on," replied Kurt. "All this is like a dream."

"Wake up. You'll be out of debt an' a rich man in three days," added Olsen, and went his way.

In the afternoon Kurt set out to work as he had never worked in his life. There was need of his strong hands in many places, but he could not choose any one labor and stick by it for long. He wanted to do all. It was as if this was not a real and wonderful harvest of his father's greatest wheat yield, but something that embodied all years, all harvests, his father's death, the lifting of the old, hard debt, the days when he had trod the fields barefoot, and this day when, strangely enough, all seemed over for him. Peace dwelt with him, yet no hope. Behind his calm he could have found the old dread, had he cared to look deeply. He loved these

heroic workers of the fields. It had been given to him—
a great task—to be the means of creating a test for
them, his neighbors under a ban of suspicion; and now
he could swear they were as true as the gold of the
waving wheat. More than a harvest was this most strenuous and colorful of all times ever known in the Bend;
it had a significance that uplifted him. It was American.

First Kurt began to load bags of wheat, as they fell
from the whirring combines, into the wagons. For his
powerful arms a full bag, containing two bushels, was
like a toy for a child. With a lift and a heave he threw
a bag into a wagon. They were everywhere, these brown
bags, dotting the stubble field, appearing as if by magic
in the wake of the machines. They rolled off the plat-
forms. This toil, because it was hard and heavy, held
Kurt for an hour, but it could not satisfy his enormous
hunger to make that whole harvest his own. He passed
to pitching sheaves of wheat and then to driving in the
wagons. From that he progressed to a seat on one of
the immense combines, where he drove twenty-four
horses. No driver there was any surer than Kurt of his
aim with the little stones he threw to spur a lagging
horse. Kurt had felt this when, as a boy, he had begged
to be allowed to try his hand; he liked the shifty cloud
of fragrant chaff, now and then blinding and choking
him; and he liked the steady, rhythmic tramp of hoofs
and the roaring whir of the great complicated machine.
It fascinated him to see the wide swath of nodding wheat
tremble and sway and fall, and go sliding up into the
inside of that grinding maw, and come out, straw and
dust and chaff, and a slender stream of gold filling the
bags.

This day Kurt Dorn was gripped by the unknown.

Some far-off instinct of future drove him, set his spiritual need, and made him register with his senses all that was so beautiful and good and heroic in the scene about him.

Strangely, now and then a thought of Lenore Anderson entered his mind and made sudden havoc. It tended to retard action. He trembled and thrilled with a realization that every hour brought closer the meeting he could not avoid. And he discovered that it was whenever this memory recurred that he had to leave off his present task and rush to another. Only thus could he forget her.

The late afternoon found him feeding sheaves of wheat to one of the steam threshers. He stood high upon a platform and pitched sheaves from the wagons upon the sliding track of the ponderous, rattling threshing machine. The engine stood off fifty yards or more, connected by an endless driving belt to the thresher. Here indeed were whistle and roar and whir, and the shout of laborers, and the smell of smoke, sweat, dust, and wheat. Kurt had arms of steel. If they tired he never knew it. He toiled, and he watched the long spout of chaff and straw as it streamed from the thresher to lift, magically, a glistening, ever-glowing stack. And he felt, as a last and cumulative change, his physical effort, and the physical adjuncts of the scene, pass into something spiritual, into his heart and his memory.

The end of that harvest-time came as a surprise to Kurt. Obsessed with his own emotions, he had actually helped to cut the wheat and harvest it; he had seen it go swath by swath, he had watched the huge wagons lumber away and the huge strawstacks rise without realizing that the hours of this wonderful harvest were numbered.

Sight of Olsen coming in from across the field, and the sudden cessation of roar and action, made Kurt aware of the end. It seemed a calamity. But Olsen was smiling through his dust-caked face. About him were relaxation, an air of finality, and a subtle pride.

"We're through," he said. "She tallies thirty-eight thousand, seven hundred an' forty-one bushels. It's too bad the old man couldn't live to hear that."

Olsen gripped Kurt's hand and wrung it.

"Boy, I reckon you ought to take that a little cheer-fuller," he went on. "But—well, it's been a hard time. ... The men are leavin' now. In two hours the last wagons will unload at the railroad. The wheat will all be in the warehouse. An' our worry's ended."

"I—I hope so," responded Kurt. He seemed overcome with the passionate longing to show his gratitude to Olsen. But the words would not flow. "I—I don't know how to thank you . . . . All my life—"

"We beat the I. W. W.," interposed the farmer, heartily. "An' now what'll you do, Dorn?"

"Why, I'll hustle to Kilo, get my money, send you a check for yourself and men, pay off the debt to Anderson, and then—"

But Kurt did not conclude his speech. His last words were thought-provoking.

"It's turned out well," said Olsen, with satisfaction, and, shaking hands again with Kurt, he strode back to his horses.

At last the wide, sloping field was bare, except for the huge strawstacks. A bright procession lumbered down the road, led by the long strings of wagons filled with brown bags. A strange silence had settled down over the farm. The wheat was gone. That waving stretch of gold had fallen to the thresher and the grain had been hauled away. The neighbors had gone, leaving Kurt rich in bushels of wheat, and richer for the hearty farewells and the grips of horny hands. Kurt's heart was full.

It was evening. Kurt had finished his supper. Already he had packed a few things to take with him on the morrow. He went out to the front of the house. Stars were blinking. There was a low hum of insects from the fields. He missed the soft silken rustle of the wheat. And now it seemed he could sit there in the quiet darkness, in that spot which had been made sweet by Lenore Anderson's presence, and think of her, the meeting soon to come. The feeling abiding with him then must have been happiness, because he was not used to it. Without deserving anything, he had asked a great deal of fate, and, lo! it had been given him. All was well that ended well. He realized now the terrible depths of despair into which he had allowed himself to be plunged. He had been weak, wrong, selfish. There was something that guided events.

He needed to teach himself all this, with strong and repeated force, so that when he went to give Lenore Anderson the opportunity to express her gratitude, to see her sweet face again, and to meet the strange, warm glance of her blue eyes, so mysterious and somehow mocking, he could be a man of restraint, of pride, like any American, like any other college man she knew. This was no time for a man to leave a girl bearing a burden of his unsolicited love, haunted, perhaps, by a generous reproach that she might have been a little to blame. He had told her the truth, and so far he had been dignified. Now let him bid her good-bye, leaving no sorrow for her, and, once out of her impelling presence, let come what might come. He could love her then; he could dare what he had never dared; he could surrender himself to the furious, insistent sweetness of a passion that was sheer bliss in its expression. He could imagine kisses on the red lips that were not for him.

A husky shout from somewhere in the rear of the house diverted Kurt's attention. He listened. It came again. His name! It seemed a strange call from out of the troubled past that had just ended. He hurried through the house to the kitchen. The woman stood holding a lamp, staring at Jerry.

Jerry appeared to have sunk against the wall. His face was pallid, with drops of sweat standing out, with distorted, quivering lower jaw. He could not look at Kurt. He could not speak. With shaking hand he pointed toward the back of the house.

Filled with nameless dread, Kurt rushed out. He saw nothing unusual, heard nothing. Rapidly he walked out through the yard, and suddenly he saw a glow in the sky above the barns. Then he ran, so that he could get an unobstructed view of the valley.

The instant he obtained this he halted as if turned to stone. The valley was a place of yellow light. He stared. With the wheat fields all burned, what was the meaning of such a big light? That broad flare had a center, low down on the valley floor. As he gazed a monstrous flame leaped up, lighting colossal pillars of smoke that swirled upward, and showing plainer than in day the big warehouse and lines of freight cars at the railroad station, eight miles distant.

"My God!" gasped Kurt. "The warehouse—my wheat—on fire!"

Clear and unmistakable was the horrible truth. Kurt heard the roar of the sinister flames. Transfixed, he stood there, at first hardly able to see and to comprehend. For miles the valley was as light as at noonday. An awful beauty attended the scene. How lurid and sinister the red heart of that fire! How weird and hellish and impressive of destruction those black, mountain-high clouds of smoke! He saw the freight cars disappear under this fierce blazing and smoking pall. He watched for what seemed endless moments. He saw the changes of that fire, swift and terrible. And only then did Kurt Dorn awaken to the full sense of the calamity.

"All that work—Olsen's sacrifice—and the farmers'—my father's death—all for nothing!" whispered Kurt. "They only waited—those fiends—to fire the warehouse and the cars!"

The catastrophe had fallen. The wheat was burning. He was ruined. His wheatland must go to Anderson. Kurt thought first and most poignantly of the noble farmers who had sacrificed the little in their wheat fields to save the much in his. Never could he repay them.

Then he became occupied with a horrible heat that seemed to have come from the burning warehouse to all his pulses and veins and to his heart and his soul.

This fiendish work, as had been forecast, was the work of the I. W. W. Behind it was Glidden and perhaps behind him was the grasping, black lust of German might. Kurt's loss was no longer abstract or problematical. It was a loss so real and terrible that it confounded him. He shook and gasped and reeled. He wrung his hands and beat his breast while the tumult swayed him, the physical hate at last yielding up its significance. What, then, was his great loss? He could not tell. The thing was mighty, like the sense of terror and loneliness in the black night. Not the loss for his farmer neighbors, so true in his hour of trial! Not the loss of his father, nor the wheat, nor the land, nor his ruined future! But it must be a loss, incalculable and insupportable, to his soul. His great ordeal had been the need, a terrible and incomprehensible need, to kill something intangible in himself. He had meant to do it. And now the need was shifted, subject to a baser instinct. If there was German blood in him, poisoning the very wells of his heart, he could have spilled it, and so, whether living or dead, have repudiated the taint. That was now clear in his consciousness. But a baser spark had ignited all the primitive passion of the forebears he felt burning and driving within him. He felt no noble fire. He longed to live, to have a hundredfold his strength and fury, to be gifted with a genius for time and place and bloody deed, to have the war gods set him a thousand opportunities, to beat with iron mace and cut with sharp bayonet and rend with hard hand—to kill and kill and kill the hideous thing that was German.

CHAPTER
14

KURT rushed back to the house. Encountering Jerry, he ordered him to run and saddle a couple of horses. Then Kurt got his revolver and a box of shells, and, throwing on his coat, he hurried to the barn. Jerry was leading out the horses. It took but short work to saddle them. Jerry was excited and talkative. He asked Kurt many questions, which excited few replies.

When Kurt threw himself into the saddle Jerry yelled, "Which way?"

"Down the trail!" replied Kurt, and was off.

"Aw, we'll break our necks!" came Jerry's yell after him.

Kurt had no fear of the dark. He knew that trail almost as well by night as by day. His horse was a mettlesome colt that had not been worked during the harvest, and he plunged down the dim, winding trail as if, indeed, to verify Jerry's fears. Presently the thin, pale line that was the trail disappeared on the burned wheat-ground. Here Kurt was at fault as to direction, but he did not slacken the pace for that. He heard Jerry pounding along in the rear, trying to catch up. The way the colt jumped ditches and washes and other obstructions proved his keen sight. Kurt let him go. And then the ride became both perilous and thrilling.

Kurt could not see anything on the blackened earth. But he knew from the contour of the hills just about where to expect to reach the fence and the road. And he did not pull the horse too soon. When he found the gate he waited for Jerry, who could be heard calling from the darkness. Kurt answered him.

"Here's the gate!" yelled Kurt, as Jerry came galloping up. "Good road all the way now!"

"Lickity-cut then!" shouted Jerry, to whom the pace had evidently communicated enthusiasm.

The ride then became a race, with Kurt drawing ahead. Kurt could see the road, a broad, pale belt, dividing the blackness on either side; and he urged the colt to a run. The wind cut short Kurt's breath, beat at his ears, and roared about them. Closer and closer drew the red flare of the dying fire, casting long rays of light into Kurt's eyes.

The colt was almost run out when he entered the circle of reddish flare. Kurt saw the glowing ruins of the elevators and a long, fiery line of boxcars burned to the wheels. Men were running and shouting round in front of the little railroad station, and several were on the roof with brooms and buckets. The freight house had burned, and evidently the station itself had been on fire.

Across the wide street of the little village the roof of a cottage was burning. Men were on top of it, beating the shingles. Hoarse yells greeted Kurt as he leaped out of the saddle. He heard screams of frightened women. On the other side of the burned boxcars a long, thin column of sparks rose straight upward. Over the ruins of the elevators hung a pall of heavy smoke. Just then Jerry came galloping up, his lean face red in the glow.

"Thet you, Kurt? Say, the sons of guns are burnin' down the town." He leaped off. "Lemme have your bridle. I'll tie the hosses up. Find out what we can do."

Kurt ran here and there, possessed by impotent rage. The wheat was gone! That fact gave him a hollow, sickening pang. He met farmers he knew. They all threw up their hands at sight of him. Not one could find a voice. Finally he met Olsen. The little wheat farmer was white with passion. He carried a gun.

"Hello, Dorn! Ain't this hell? They got your wheat!" he said, hoarsely.

"Olsen! How'd it happen? Wasn't anybody set to guard the elevators?"

"Yes. But the I. W. W.'s drove all the guards off but Grimm, an' they beat him up bad. Nobody had nerve enough to shoot."

"Olsen, if I run into that Glidden I'll kill him," declared Kurt.

"So will I.... But, Dorn, they're a hard crowd. They're over there on the side, watchin' the fire. A gang of them! Soon as I can get the men together we'll drive them out of town. There'll be a fight, if I don't miss my guess."

"Hurry the men! Have all of them get their guns! Come on!"

"Not yet, Dorn. We're fightin' fire yet. You an' Jerry help all you can."

Indeed, it appeared there was danger of more than one cottage burning. The exceedingly dry weather of the past weeks had made shingles like tinder, and wherever a glowing spark fell on them there straightway was a smoldering fire. Water, a scarce necessity in that region, had been used until all wells and pumps became dry. It was fortunate that most of the roofs of the little village had been constructed of galvanized iron. Beating out blazes and glowing embers with brooms was not effective enough. When it appeared that the one cottage nearest the rain of sparks was sure to go, Kurt thought of the railroad water tank below the station. He led a number of men with buckets to the tank, and they soon drowned out the smoldering places.

Meanwhile the blazes from the boxcars died out, leaving only the dull glow from the red heap that had once been the elevators. However, this gave forth light enough for anyone to be seen a few rods distant. Sparks had ceased to fall, and from that source no further danger need be apprehended. Olsen had been going from man to man, sending those who were not armed home for guns. So it came about that half an hour after Kurt's arrival a score of farmers, villagers, and a few railroaders were collected in a group, listening to the pale-faced Olsen.

"Men, there's only a few of us, an' there's hundreds, mebbe, in thet I. W. W. gang, but we've got to drive them off," he said, doggedly. "There's no tellin' what they'll do if we let them hang around any longer. They know we're weak in numbers. We've got to do some shootin' to scare them away."

Kurt seconded Olsen in ringing voice.

"They've threatened your homes," he said. "They've burned my wheat—ruined me. They were the death of my father.... These are facts I'm telling you. We can't wait for law or for militia. We've got to meet this I. W. W. invasion. They have taken advantage of the war situation. They're backed by German agents. It's now a question of our property. We've got to fight!"

The crowd made noisy and determined response. Most of them had small weapons; a few had shotguns or rifles.

"Come on, men," called Olsen. "I'll do the talkin'. An' if I say shoot, why, you shoot!"

It was necessary to go around the long line of boxcars. Olsen led the way, with Kurt just back of him. The men spoke but little and in whispers. At the left end of the line the darkness was thick enough to make objects indistinct.

Once around the corner, Kurt plainly described a big dark crowd of men whose faces showed red in the glow of the huge pile of embers which was all that remained of the elevators. They did not see Olsen's men.

"Hold on," whispered Olsen. "If we get in a fight here we'll be in a bad place. We've nothin' to hide behind. Let's go off—more to the left—an' come up behind those freightcars on the switches. That'll give us cover an' we'll have the I. W. W.'s in the light."

So he led off to the left, keeping in the shadow, and climbed between several lines of freightcars, all empty, and finally came out behind the I. W. W.'s. Olsen led to within fifty yards of them, and was halted by some observant member of the gang who sat with the others on top of a flatcar.

This man's yell stilled the coarse talk and laughter of the gang.

"What's that?" shouted a cold, clear voice with authority in it.

Kurt thought he recognized the voice, and it caused a bursting, savage sensation in his blood.

"Here's a bunch of farmers with guns!" yelled the man from the flatcar.

Olsen halted his force near one of the detached lines of boxcars, which he probably meant to take advantage of in case of a fight.

"Hey, you I. W. W.'s!" he shouted, with all his might. There was a moment's silence.

"There's no I. W. W.'s here," replied the authoritative voice.

Kurt was sure now that he recognized Glidden's voice. Excitement and anger then gave place to deadly rage.

"Who are you?" yelled Olsen.

"We're tramps watchin' the fire," came the reply.

"You set that fire!"

"No, we didn't."

Kurt motioned Olsen to be silent, as with lifting breast he took an involuntary step forward.

"Glidden, I know you!" he shouted, in hard, quick tones. "I'm Kurt Dorn. I've met you. I know your voice. ... Take your gang—get out of here—or we'll kill you!"

This pregnant speech caused a blank dead silence. Then came a white flash, a sharp report. Kurt heard the thud of a bullet striking someone near him. The man cried out, but did not fall.

"Spread out an' hide!" ordered Olsen. "An' shoot fer keeps!"

The little crowd broke and melted into the shadows behind and under the boxcars. Kurt crawled under a car and between the wheels, from which vantage point he looked out. Glidden's gang were there in the red glow, most of them now standing. The sentry who had given the alarm still sat on top of the flatcar, swinging his legs. His companions, however, had jumped down. Kurt heard men of his own party crawling and whispering behind him, and he saw dim, dark, sprawling forms under the far end of the car.

"Boss, the hayseeds have run off," called the man from the flatcar.

Laughter and jeers greeted this sally.

Kurt concluded it was about time to begin proceedings. Resting his revolver on the side of the wheel behind which he lay, he took steady aim at the sentry, holding low. Kurt was not a good shot with a revolver and the distance appeared to exceed fifty yards. But as luck would have it, when he pulled trigger the sentry let out a loud bawl of terror and pain, and fell off the car to the ground. Flopping and crawling like a crippled chicken, he got out of sight below.

Kurt's shot was a starter for Olsen's men. Four or five of the shotguns boomed at once; then the second barrels were discharged, along with a sharper cracking of small arms. Pandemonium broke loose in Glidden's gang. No doubt, at least, of the effectiveness of the shotguns! A medley of strange, sharp, enraged, and anguished cries burst upon the air, a prelude to a wild stampede. In a few seconds that lighted spot where the I. W. W. had grouped was vacant, and everywhere were fleeing forms, some swift, others slow. So far as Kurt could see, no one had been fatally injured. But many had been hurt, and that fact augured well for Olsen's force.

Presently a shot came from some hidden enemy. It thudded into the wood of the car over Kurt. Someone on his side answered it, and a heavy bullet, striking iron, whined away into the darkness. Then followed flash here and flash there, with accompanying reports and whistles of lead. From behind and under and on top of cars opened up a fire that proved how well armed these so-called laborers were. Their volley completely drowned the desultory firing of Olsen's squad.

Kurt began to wish for one of the shotguns. It was this kind of weapon that saved Olsen's followers. There were a hundred chances to one of missing an I. W. W. with a single bullet, while a shotgun, aimed fairly well, was generally productive of results. Kurt stopped wasting his cartridges. Someone was hurt behind his car and he crawled out to see. A villager named Schmidt had been wounded in the leg, not seriously, but bad enough to disable him. He had been using a double-barreled breech-loading shotgun, and he wore a vest with rows of shells in the pockets across the front. Kurt borrowed gun and ammunition; and with these he hurried back to his covert, grimly sure of himself. At thought of Glidden he became hot all over, and this heat rather grew with the excitement of battle.

With the heavy fowling piece loaded, Kurt peeped forth from behind his protecting wheel and watched keenly for flashes or moving dark figures. The I. W. W. had begun to reserve their fire, to shift their positions, and to spread out, judging from a wider range of the reports. It looked as if they meant to try and surround Olsen's band. It was extraordinary—the assurance and deadly intent of this riffraff gang of tramp labor agitators. In preceding years a crowd of I. W. W. men had been nothing to worry a rancher. Vastly different it seemed now. They acted as if they had the great war back of them.

Kurt crawled out of his hiding place, and stole from car to car, in search of Olsen. At last he found the rancher, in company with several men, peering from behind a car. One of his companions was sitting down and trying to wrap something round his foot.

"Olsen, they're spreading out to surround us," whispered Kurt.

"That's what Bill here just said," replied Olsen, nervously. "If this keeps up we'll be in a tight place. What'll we do, Dorn?"

"We mustn't break and run, of all things," said Kurt. "They'd burn the village. Tell our men to save their shells. . . . If I only could get some cracks at a bunch of them together—with this big shotgun!"

"Say, we've been watchin' that car—the half-size one, there—next the high boxcar," whispered Olsen. "It's full of them. Sometimes we see a dozen shots come from it, all at once."

"Olsen, I've an idea," returned Kurt, excitedly. "You fellows keep shooting—attract their attention. I'll slip below, climb on top of a boxcar, and get a rake-off at that bunch."

"It's risky, Dorn," said Olsen, with hesitation. "But if you could get in a few tellin' shots—start that gang on the run!"

"I'll try it," rejoined Kurt, and forthwith stole off back toward the shadow. It struck him that there was more light than when the attack began. The fire had increased, or perhaps the I. W. W. had started another; at any rate, the light was growing stronger, and likewise the danger greater. As he crossed an open space a bullet whizzed by him, and then another zipped by to strike up the gravel ahead. These were not random shots. Someone was aiming at him. How strange and rage provoking to be shot at deliberately! What a remarkable experience for a young wheat farmer! Raising wheat in the great Northwest had assumed responsibilities. He had to run, and he was the more furious because of that. Another bullet, flying wide, hummed to his left before he gained the shelter of the farthest line of freight cars. Here he hid and watched. The firing appeared to be all behind him, and, thus encouraged, he stole along to the end of the line of cars, and around. A bright blaze greeted his gaze. An isolated car was on fire. Kurt peered forth to make sure of his bearings, and at length found the high derrick by which he had marked the boxcar that he intended to climb.

He could see plainly, and stole up to his objective point, with little risk to himself until he climbed upon the boxcar. He crouched low, almost on hands and knees, and finally gained the long shadow of a shed between the tracks. Then he ran past the derrick to the dark side of the car. He could now plainly see the revolver flashes and could hear the thud and spang of their bullets striking. Drawing a deep breath, Kurt climbed up the iron ladder on the dark side of the car.

He had the same sensation that possessed him when he was crawling to get a potshot at a flock of wild geese. Only this was mightily more exciting. He did not forget the risk. He lay flat and crawled little by little. Every moment he expected to be discovered. Olsen had evidently called more of his men to his side, for they certainly were shooting diligently. Kurt heard a continuous return fire from the car he was risking so much to get a shot at. At length he was within a yard of the end of the car—as far as he needed to go. He rested a moment. He was laboring for breath, sweating freely, on fire with thrills.

His plan was to raise himself on one knee and fire as many double shots as possible. Presently he lifted his head to locate the car. It was half in the bright light, half in the shadow, lengthwise toward him, about sixty or seventy yards distant, and full of men. He dropped his head, tingling all over. It was a disappointment that the car stood so far away. With fine shot he could not seriously injure any of the I. W. W. contingent, but he was grimly sure of the fright and hurt he could inflict. In his quick glance he had seen flashes of their guns, and many red faces, and dark, huddled forms.

Kurt took four shells and set them, end up, on the roof of the car close to him. Then, cocking the gun, he cautiously raised himself to one knee. He discharged both barrels at once. What a boom and what a terrified outburst of yells! Swiftly he broke the gun, reloaded, fired as before, and then again. The last two shots were fired at the men piling frantically over the side of the car, yelling with fear. Kurt had heard the swishing pattering impact of those swarms of small shot. The I. W. W. gang ran pell-mell down the open track, away from Kurt and toward the light. As he reloaded the gun he saw men running from all points to join the gang. With an old blunderbuss of a shotgun he had routed the I. W. W. It meant relief to Olsen's men; but Kurt had yet no satisfaction for the burning of his wheat, for the cruel shock that had killed his father.

"Come on, Olsen!" he yelled, at the top of his lungs. "They're a lot of cowards!"

Then in his wild eagerness he leaped off the car. The long jump landed him jarringly, but he did not fall or lose hold of the gun. Recovering his balance, he broke into a run. Kurt was fast on his feet. Not a young man of his neighborhood nor any of his college-mates could outfoot him in a race. And then these I. W. W. fellows ran like stiff-legged tramps, long unused to such mode of action. And some of them were limping as they ran. Kurt gained upon them. When he got within range he halted short and freed two barrels. A howl followed the report. Some of the fleeing ones fell, but were dragged up and on by companions. Kurt reloaded and, bounding forward like a deer, yelling for Olsen, he ran until he was within range, then stopped to shoot again. Thus he continued until the pursued got away from the circle of light. Kurt saw the gang break up, some running one way and some another. There were sheds and cars and piles of lumber along the track, affording places to hide. Kurt was halted by the discovery that he had no more ammunition. Panting, he stopped short, realizing that he had snapped an empty gun at men either too tired or too furious or too desperate to run any farther.

"He's out of shells!" shouted a low, hard voice that made Kurt leap. He welcomed the rush of dark forms, and, swinging the gun round his head, made ready to brain the first antagonist who neared him. But some one leaped upon him from behind. The onslaught carried him to his knees. Bounding up, he broke the gun stock on the head of his assailant, who went down in a heap. Kurt tried to pull his revolver. It became impossible, owing to strong arms encircling him. Wrestling, he freed himself, only to be staggered by a rush of several men, all pouncing upon him at once. Kurt went down, but, once down, he heaved so powerfully that he threw off the whole crew. Up again, like a cat, he began to fight. Big and strong and swift, with fists like a blacksmith's, Kurt bowled over this assailant and that one. He thought he recognized Glidden in a man who kept out of his reach and who was urging on the others. Kurt lunged at him and finally got his hands on him. That was fatal for Kurt, because in his fury he forgot Glidden's comrades. In one second his big hand wrenched a yell of mortal pain out of Glidden; then a combined attack of the others rendered Kurt powerless. A blow on the head stunned him—made all dark.

CHAPTER

15

*I*T seemed that Kurt did not altogether lose consciousness, for he had vague sensations of being dragged along the ground. Presently the darkness cleared from his mind and he opened his eyes. He lay on his back. Looking up, he saw stars through the thin, broken clouds of smoke. A huge pile of railroad ties loomed up beside him.

He tried to take note of his situation. His hands were tied in front of him, not so securely, he imagined, that he could not work them free. His legs had not been tied. Both his head and shoulder, on the left side, pained him severely. Upon looking around, Kurt presently made out the dark form of a man. He appeared rigid with attention, but that evidently had no relation to Kurt. The man was listening and watching for his comrades. Kurt heard no voices or shots. After a little while, however, he thought he heard distant footsteps on the gravel. He hardly knew what to make of his predicament. If there was only one guard over him, escape did not seem difficult, unless that guard had a gun.

"Hello, you!" he called.

"Hello, yourself," replied the man, jerking up in evident surprise.

"What's your name?" inquired Kurt, amiably.

"Well, it ain't J. J. Hill or Anderson," came the gruff response.

Kurt laughed. "But you would be one of those names if you could, now wouldn't you?" went on Kurt.

"My name is Dennis," gloomily returned the man.

"It certainly is. *That* is the name of all I. W. W.'s," said Kurt.

"Say, are you the fellow who had the shotgun?"

"I sure am," replied Kurt.

"I ought to knock you on the head."

"Why?"

"Because I'll have to eat standing up for a month."

"Yes?" queried Kurt.

"The seat of my pants must have made a good target, for you sure pasted it full of bird shot."

Kurt smothered a laugh. Then he felt the old anger leap up. "Didn't you burn my wheat?"

"Are you that young Dorn?"

"Yes, I am," replied Kurt, hotly.

"Well, I didn't burn one damn straw of your old wheat."

"You didn't! But you're with these men? You're an I. W. W. You've been fighting these farmers here."

"If you want to know, I'm a tramp," said the man, bitterly. "Years ago I was a prosperous oil producer in

Ohio. I had a fine oil field. Along comes a big fellow, tries to buy me out, and, failing that, he shot off dynamite charges into the ground next my oil field.... Choked my wells! Ruined me!...I came west—went to farming. Along comes a corporation, steals my water for irrigation—and my land went back to desert.... So I quit working and trying to be honest. It doesn't pay. The rich men are getting all the richer at the expense of the poor. So now I'm a tramp."

"Friend, that's a hard-luck story," said Kurt. "It sure makes me think.... But I'll tell you what—you don't belong to this I. W. W. outfit, even if you are a tramp."

"Why not?"

"Because you're American! That's why."

"Well, I know I am. But I can be American and travel with a labor union, can't I?"

"No. This I. W. W. is no labor union. It never was. Their very first rule is to abolish capital. They're anarchists. And now they're backed by German money. The I. W. W. is an enemy to America. All this hampering of railroads, destruction of timber and wheat, is an aid to Germany in the war. The United States is at war! My God! man, can't you see it's your own country that must suffer for such deals as this wheat burning tonight?"

"The hell you say!" ejaculated the man, in amaze.

"This Glidden is a German agent—perhaps a spy. He's no labor leader. What does he care for the interests of such men as you?"

"Young man, if you don't shut up you'll give me a hankering to go back to real work."

"I hope I do. Let me give you a hunch. Throw down this I. W. W. outfit. Go to Ruxton and get Anderson of

'Many Waters' ranch to give you a job. Tell him who you are and that I sent you."

"Anderson of 'Many Waters,' hey? Well, maybe it'll surprise you to know that Glidden is operating there, has a lot of men there, and is going there from here."

"No, it doesn't surprise me. I hope he does go there. For if he does he'll get killed."

"Sssssh!" whispered the guard. "Here comes some of the gang."

Kurt heard low voices and soft footfalls. Some dark forms loomed up.

"Bradford, has he come to yet?" queried the brutal voice of Glidden.

"Nope," replied the guard. "I guess he had a hard knock. He's never budged."

"We've got to beat it out of here," said Glidden. "It's long after midnight. There's a freight train down the track. I want all the gang to board it. You run along, Bradford, and catch up with the others."

"What're you going to do with this young fellow?" queried Bradford, curiously.

"That's none of your business," returned Glidden.

"Maybe not. But I reckon I'll ask, anyhow. You want me to join your I. W. W., and I'm asking questions. Labor strikes—standing up for your rights—is one thing, and burning wheat or slugging young farmers is another. Are you going to let this Dorn go?"

Kurt could plainly see the group of five men, Bradford standing over the smaller Glidden, and the others strung and silent in the intensity of the moment.

"I'll cut his throat," hissed Glidden.

Bradford lunged heavily. The blow he struck Glidden was square in the face. Glidden would have had a hard fall but for the obstruction in the shape of his comrades, upon whom he was knocked. They held him up. Glidden sagged inertly, evidently stunned or unconscious. Bradford backed guardedly away out of their reach, then, wheeling, he began to run with heavy, plodding strides.

Glidden's comrades seemed anxiously holding him up, peering at him, but not one spoke. Kurt saw his opportunity. With one strong wrench he freed his hands. feeling in his pocket for his gun, he was disturbed to find that it had been taken. He had no weapon. But he did not hesitate. Bounding up, he rushed like a hurricane upon the unprepared group. He saw Glidden's pale face upheld to the light of the stars, and by it saw that Glidden was recovering. With all his might Kurt swung as he rushed, and the blow he gave the I. W. W. leader far exceeded Bradford's. Glidden was lifted so powerfully against one of his men that they both fell. Then Kurt, striking right and left, beat down the other two, and, leaping over them, he bounded away into the darkness. Shrill piercing yells behind him lent him wings.

But he ran right into another group of I. W. W. men, dozens in number, he thought, and by the light of what appeared to be a fire they saw him as quickly as he saw them. The yells behind were significant enough. Kurt had to turn to run back, and he had to run the gauntlet of the men he had assaulted. They promptly began to shoot at Kurt. The whistle of lead was uncomfortably close. Never had he run so fleetly. When he flashed past the end of a line of cars, into comparative open, he found himself in the light of a new fire. This was a shed perhaps a score of rods or less from the station. Some one was yelling beyond this, and Kurt thought he recognized Jerry's voice, but he did not tarry to make sure. Bullets scattering the gravel ahead of him and singing around his head, and hoarse cries behind, with a heavy-booted tread of pursuers, gave Kurt occasion to hurry. He flew across the freight yard, intending to distance his pursuers, then circle round the station to the village.

Once he looked back. The gang, well spread out, was not far behind him, just coming into the light of the new fire. No one in it could ever catch him, of that Kurt was sure.

Suddenly a powerful puff of air, like a blast of wind, seemed to lift him. At the same instant a dazzling, blinding, yellow blaze illuminated the whole scene. The solid earth seemed to rock under Kurt's flying feet, and then a terrific roar appalled him. He was thrown headlong through the air, and all about him seemed streaks and rays and bursts of fire. He alighted to plow through the dirt until the momentum of force had been expended. Then he lay prone, gasping and choking, almost blind, but sensitive to the rain of gravel and debris, the fearful cries of terrified men, taste of smoke and dust, and the rank smell of exploded gasoline.

Kurt got up to grope his way through the murky darkness. He could escape now. If that explosion had not killed his pursuers it had certainly scared them off. He heard men running and yelling off to the left. A rumble of a train came from below the village. Finally Kurt got clear of the smoke, to find that he had wandered off into one of the fields opposite the station. Here he halted to rest a little and to take cognizance of his condition. It surprised him to find out that he was only bruised, scratched, and sore. He had expected to find himself full of bullets.

"Whew! They blew up the gasoline shed!" he soliloquized. "But some of them miscalculated, for if I don't lose my guess there was a bunch of I. W. W. closer to that gasoline than I was. . . . Some adventure! . . . I got another punch at Glidden. I felt it in my bones that I'd get a crack at him. Oh, for another! . . . And that Bradford! He did make me think. How he slugged Glidden! Good! Good! There's your old American spirit coming out."

Kurt sat down to rest and to listen. He found he needed a rest. The only sound he heard was the rumbling of a train, gradually drawing away. A heavy smoke rose from the freight yard, but there were no longer any blazes or patches of red fire. Perhaps the explosion had smothered all the flames.

It had been a rather strenuous evening, he reflected. A good deal of satisfaction lay in the fact that he had severely punished some of the I. W. W. members, if he had not done away with any of them.

When he thought of Glidden, however, he did not feel any satisfaction. His fury was gone, but in its place was a strong judgment that such men should be made examples. He certainly did not want to run across Glidden again, because if he did he would have blood on his hands.

Kurt's chance meeting with the man Bradford seemed far the most interesting, if not thrilling, incident of the evening. It opened up a new point of view. How many of the men of that motley and ill-governed. I. W. W. had grievances like Bradford's? Perhaps there were many. Kurt tried to remember instances when, in the Northwest wheat country, laborers and farmers had been cheated or deceived by men of large interests. It made him grave to discover that he could recall many such instances. His own father had long nursed a grievance against Anderson. Neuman, his father's friend, had a hard name. And there were many who had profited by the misfortune of others. That, after all, was a condition of life. He took it for granted, then, that all members of the I. W. W. were not vicious or dishonest. He was glad to have this proof. The I. W. W. had been organized by labor agitators, and they were the ones to blame, and their punishment should be severest. Kurt began to see where the war, cruel as it would be, was going to be of immeasurable benefit to the country.

It amazed Kurt, presently, to note that dawn was at hand. He waited awhile longer, wanting to be sure not to meet any lingering members of the I. W. W. It appeared, indeed, that they had all gone.

He crossed the freight yard. A black ruin, still smoldering, lay where the elevators had been. That wonderful wheat yield of his had been destroyed. In the gray dawn it was hard to realize. He felt a lump in his throat. Several tracks were littered with the remains of burned freight cars. When Kurt reached the street he saw men in front of the cottages. Someone hailed him, and then several shouted. They met him halfway. Jerry and Olsen were in the party.

"We was pretty much scared," said Jerry, and his haggard face showed his anxiety.

"Boy, we thought the I. W. W. had made off with you," added Olsen, extending his hand.

"Not much! Where are they?" replied Kurt.

"Gone on a freight train. When Jerry blew up the gasoline shed that fixed the I. W. W."

"Jerry, did you do that?" queried Kurt.

"I reckon."

"Well, you nearly blew me off the map. I was running, just below the shed. When that explosion came I was lifted and thrown a mile. Thought I'd never light!"

"So far as we can tell, nobody was killed," said Olsen. "Some of our fellows have got bullet holes to nurse. But no one is bad hurt."

"That's good. I guess we came out lucky," replied Kurt.

"You must have had some fight, runnin' off that way after the I. W. W.'s. We heard you shootin' an' the I. W. W.'s yellin'. That part was fun. Tell us what happened to you."

So Kurt had to narrate his experiences from the time he stole off with the big shotgun until his friends saw him again. It made rather a long story, which manifestly was of exceeding interest to the villagers.

"Dorn," said one of the men, "you an' Jerry saved this here village from bein' burned."

"We all had a share. I'm sure glad they're gone. Now what damage was done?"

It turned out that there had been little hurt to the property of the villagers. Some freight cars full of barley, loaded and billed by the railroad people, had been burned, and this loss of grain would probably be paid for by the company. The loss of wheat would fall upon Kurt. In the haste of that great harvest and its transportation to the village no provision had been made for loss. The railroad company had not accepted his wheat for transportation, and was not liable.

"Olsen, according to our agreement I owe you fifteen thousand dollars," said Kurt.

"Yes, but forget it," replied Olsen. "You're the loser here."

"I'll pay it," replied Kurt.

"But, boy, you're ruined!" ejaculated the farmer. "You can't pay that big price now. An' we don't expect it."

"Didn't you leave your burning fields to come help us save ours?" queried Kurt.

"Sure. But there wasn't much of mine to burn."

"And so did many of the other men who came to help. I tell you, Olsen, that means a great deal to me. I'll pay my debt or—or—"

"But how can you?" interrupted Olsen, reasonably. "Sometime, when you raise another crop like this year, then you could pay."

"The farm will bring that much more than I owe Anderson."

"You'll give up the farm?" exclaimed Olsen.

"Yes. I'll square myself."

"Dorn, we won't take that money," said the farmer, deliberately.

"You'll have to take it. I'll send you a check soon—perhaps tomorrow."

"Give up your land!" repeated Olsen. "Why, that's unheard of! Land in your family so many years! . . . What will you do?"

"Olsen, I waited for the draft just on account of my father. If it had not been for him I'd have enlisted. Anyway, I'm going to war."

That silenced the little group of grimy-faced men.

"Jerry, get our horses and we'll ride home," said Kurt.

The tall foreman strode off. Kurt sensed something poignant in the feelings of the men, especially Olsen. This matter of the I. W. W. dealing had brought Kurt and his neighbors closer together. And he thought it a good opportunity for a few words about the United States and the war and Germany. So he launched forth into an eloquent expression of some of his convictions. He was still talking when Jerry returned with the horses. At length he broke off, rather abruptly, and, saying good-bye, he mounted.

"Hold on, Kurt," called Olsen, and left the group to lay a hand on the horse and to speak low. "What you said struck me deep. It applies pretty hard to us of the Bend. We've always been farmers, with no thought of country. An' that's because we left our native country to come here. I'm not German an' I've never been for Germany. But many of my neighbors an' friends are Germans. This war never has come close till now. I know Germans in this country. They have left their fatherland an' they are lost to that fatherland!... It may take some time to stir them up, to make them see, but the day will come.... Take my word for it, Dorn, the German-Americans of the Northwest, when it comes to a pinch, will find themselves an' be true to the country they have adopted."

*T*HE sun was up, broad and bright, burning over the darkened wheat fields, when Kurt and Jerry reached home. Kurt had never seen the farm look like that—ugly and black and bare. But the fallow ground, hundreds of acres of it, billowing away to the south, had not suffered any change of color or beauty. To Kurt it seemed to smile at him, to bid him wait for another spring.

And that thought was poignant, for he remembered he must leave at once for "Many Waters."

He found, when he came to wash the blood and dirt from his person, that his bruises were many. There was a lump on his head, and his hands were skinned. After changing his clothes and packing a few things in a valise, along with his papers, he went down to breakfast. Though preoccupied in mind, he gathered that both the old housekeeper and Jerry were surprised and dismayed to see him ready to leave. He had made no mention of his intentions. And it struck him that this, somehow, was going to be hard.

Indeed, when the moment came he found that speech was difficult and his voice not natural.

"Martha—Jerry—I'm going away for good," he said, huskily. "I mean to make over the farm to Mr. Anderson. I'll leave you in charge here—and recommend that you be kept on. Here's your money up to date....I'm going away to the war—and the chances are I'll never come back."

The old housekeeper, who had been like a mother to him for many years, began to cry; and Jerry struggled with a regret that he could not speak.

Abruptly Kurt left them and hurried out of the house. How strange that difficult feelings had arisen—emotions he had never considered at all! But the truth was that he was leaving his home forever. All was explained in that.

First he went to the graves of his father and mother, out on the south slope, where there were always wind and sun. The fire had not desecrated the simple burying ground. There was no grass. But a few trees and bushes kept it from appearing bare.

Kurt sat down in the shade near his mother's grave and looked away across the hills with dim eyes. Something came to him—a subtle assurance that his mother approved of his going to war. Kurt remembered her—slow, quiet, patient, hard-working, dominated by his father.

The slope was hot and still, with only a rustling of leaves in the wind. The air was dry. Kurt missed the sweet fragrance of wheat. What odor there was seemed to be like that of burning weeds. The great, undulating open of the Bend extended on three sides. His parents had spent the best of their lives there and had now been taken to the bosom of the soil they loved. It seemed natural. Many were the last resting places of toilers of the wheat there on those hills. And surely in the long frontier days, and in the ages before, men innumerable had gone back to the earth from which they had sprung. The dwelling places of men were beautiful; it was only life that was sad. In this poignant, revealing hour Kurt could not resist human longings and regrets, though he gained incalculable strength from these two graves on the windy slope. It was not for any man to understand to the uttermost the meaning of life.

When he left he made his way across some of the fallow land and some of the stubble fields that had yielded, alas! so futilely, such abundant harvest. His boyhood days came back to him, when he used to crush down the stubble with his bare feet. Every rod of the way revealed some memory. He went into the barn and climbed into the huge, airy loft. It smelled of straw and years of dust and mice. The swallows darted in and out, twittering. How friendly they were! Year after year they had returned to their nests—the young birds returning to the homes of the old. Home even for birds was a thing of first and vital importance.

It was a very old barn that had not many more useful years to stand. Kurt decided that he would advise that it be strengthened. There were holes in the rough shingling and boards were off the sides. In the corners and on the rafters was an accumulation of grain dust as thick as snow. Mice ran in and out, almost as tame as the swallows. He seemed to be taking leave of them. He recalled that he used to chase and trap mice with all a boy's savage ingenuity. But that boyish instinct, along with so many things so potential then, was gone now.

Best of all he loved the horses. Most of these were old and had given faithful service for many years. Indeed, there was one—Old Badge—that had carried Kurt when he was a boy. Once he and a neighbor boy had gone to the pasture to fetch home the cows. Old Badge was there, and nothing would do but that they ride him. From the fence Kurt mounted to his broad back. Then the neighbor boy, full of the devil, had struck Old Badge with a stick. The horse set off at a gallop for home with Kurt, frantically holding on, bouncing up and down on his back. That had been the ride of Kurt's life. His father had whipped him, too, for the adventure.

How strangely vivid and thought-compelling were these ordinary adjuncts to his life there on the farm! It was only upon giving them up that he discovered their real meaning. The hills of bare fallow and of yellow slope, the old barn with its horses, swallows, mice, and odorous loft, the cows and chickens—these appeared to Kurt, in the illuminating light of farewell, in their true relation to him. For they, and the labor of them, had made him what he was.

Slowly he went back to the old house and climbed the stairs. Only three rooms were there upstairs, and one of these, his mother's, had not been opened for a long time. It seemed just the same as when he used to go to her with his stubbed toes and his troubles. She had died in that room. And now he was a man, going out to fight for his country. How strange! Why? In his mother's room he could not answer that puzzling question. It stung him, and with a last look, a good-bye, and a word of prayer on his lips, he turned to his own little room.

He entered and sat down on the bed. It was small, with the slope of the roof running down so low that he had learned to stoop when close to the wall. There was no ceiling. Bare yellow rafters and dark old shingles showed. He could see light through more than one little hole. The window was small, low, and without glass. How many times he had sat there, leaning out in the hot dusk of summer nights, dreaming dreams that were never to come true. Alas for the hopes and illusions of boyhood! So long as he could remember, this room was most closely associated with his actions and his thoughts. It was a part of him. He almost took it into his confidence as if it were human. Never had he become what he had dared to dream he would, yet, somehow, at that moment he was not ashamed. It struck him then what few belongings he really had. But he had been taught to get along with little.

Living in that room was over for him. He was filled with unutterable sadness. Yet he would not have had it any different. Bigger, and selfless things called to him. He was bidding farewell to his youth and all that it related to. A solemn procession of beautiful memories passed through his mind, born of the nights there in that room of his boyhood, with the wind at the eaves and the rain pattering on the shingles. What strong and vivid pictures! No grief, no pain, no war could rob him of this best heritage from the past.

He got up to go. And then a blinding rush of tears burned his eyes. This room seemed dearer than all the rest of his home. It was hard to leave. His last look was magnified, transformed. "Good-bye!" he whispered, with a swelling constriction in his throat. At the head of the dark old stairway he paused a moment, and then with bowed head he slowly descended.

*A*N August twilight settled softly down over "Many Waters" while Lenore Anderson dreamily gazed from her window out over the darkening fields so tranquil now after the day's harvest toil.

Of late, in thoughtful hours such as this, she had become conscious of strain, of longing. She had fought out a battle with herself, and confessed her love for Kurt Dorn, and, surrendering to the enchantment of that truth, had felt her love grow with every thought of him and every beat of a thrilling pulse. In spite of a longing that amounted to pain and a nameless dread she could not deny, she was happy. And she waited, with a woman's presaging sense of events, for a crisis that was coming.

Presently she heard her father downstairs, his heavy tread and hearty voice. These strenuous harvest days left him little time for his family. And Lenore, having lost herself in her dreams, had not, of late, sought him out in the fields. She was waiting, and, besides, his keen eyes, at once so penetrating and so kind, had confused her. Few secrets had she ever kept from her father.

"Where's Lenore?" she heard him ask, down in the dining room.

"Lenorry's mooning," replied Kathleen, with a giggle.

"Ah-huh! Well, whereabouts is she moonin'?" went on Anderson.

"Why, in her room!" retorted the child. "And you can't get a word out of her with a crowbar."

Anderson's laugh rang out with a jingle of tableware. He was eating his supper. Then Lenore heard her mother and Rose and Kathleen all burst out with news of a letter come that day from Jim, away training to be a soldier. It was Rose who read this letter aloud to her father, and outside of her swift, soft voice the absolute silence attested to the attention of the listeners. Lenore's heart shook as she distinguished a phrase here and there, for Jim's letter had been wonderful for her. He had gained weight! He was getting husky enough to lick his father! He was feeling great! There was not a boy in the outfit who could beat him to a stuffed bag of a German soldier! And he sure could make some job with that old bayonet! So ran Jim's message to the loved ones at home. Then a strange pride replaced the quake in Lenore's heart. Not now would she have had Jim stay home. She had sacrificed him. Something subtler than thought told her she would never see him again. And, oh, how dear he had become!

Then Anderson roared his delight in that letter and banged the table with his fist. The girls excitedly talked in unison. But the mother was significantly silent. Lenore forgot them presently and went back to her dreaming. It was just about dark when her father called.

"Lenore."

"Yes, father," she replied.

"I'm comin' up," he said, and his heavy tread sounded in the hall. It was followed by the swift patter of little feet. "Say, you kids go back. I want to talk to Lenore."

"Daddy," came Kathleen's shrill, guilty whisper, "I was only in fun—about her mooning."

The father laughed again and slowly mounted the stairs. Lenore reflected uneasily that he seldom came to her room. Also, when he was most concerned with trouble he usually sought her.

"Hello! All in the dark?" he said, as he came in. "May I turn on the light?"

Lenore assented, though not quite readily. But Anderson did not turn on the light. He bumped into things on the way to where she was curled up in her window seat, and he dropped wearily into Lenore's big armchair.

"How are you, Daddy?" she inquired.

"Dog tired, but feelin' fine," he replied. "I've got a meetin' at eight an' I need a rest. Reckon I'd like to smoke—an' talk to you—if you don't mind."

"I'd sure rather listen to my dad than anyone," she replied, softly. She knew he had come with news or trouble or need of help. He always began that way. She could measure his mood by the preliminaries before his disclosure. And she fortified herself.

"Wasn't that a great letter from the boy?" began Anderson, as he lit a cigar. By the flash of the match Lenore got a glimpse of his dark and unguarded face. Indeed, she did well to fortify herself.

"Fine! ... He wrote it to me. I laughed. I swelled with pride. It sent my blood racing. It filled me with fight.... Then I sneaked up here to cry."

"Ah-huh!" exclaimed Anderson, with a loud sigh. Then for a moment of silence the end of his cigar alternately paled and glowed. "Lenore, did you get any—any kind of a hunch from Jim's letter?"

"I don't exactly understand what you mean," replied Lenore.

"Did somethin'—strange an' different come to you?" queried Anderson, haltingly, as if words were difficult to express what he meant.

"Why, yes—I had many strange feelings."

"Jim's letter was just like he talks. But to me it said somethin' he never meant an' didn't know.... Jim will never come back!"

"Yes, dad—I divined just that," whispered Lenore.

"Strange about that," mused Anderson, with a pull on a his cigar.

And then followed a silence. Lenore felt how long ago her father had made his sacrifice. There did not seem to be any need for more words about Jim. But there seemed a bigness in the bond of understanding between her and her father. A cause united them, and they were sustained by unfaltering courage. The great thing was the divine spark in the boy who could not have been held back. Lenore gazed out into the darkening shadows. The night was very still, except for the hum of insects, and the cool air felt sweet on her face. The shadows, the silence, the sleeping atmosphere hovering over "Many Waters," seemed charged with a quality of present sadness, of the inexplicable great world moving to its fate.

"Lenore, you haven't been around much lately," resumed Anderson. "Sure you're missed. An' Jake swears a lot more than usual."

"Father, you told me to stay at home," she replied.

"So I did. An' I reckon it's just as well. But when did you ever before mind me?"

"Why, I always obey you," replied Lenore, with her low laugh.

"Ah-huh! Not so I'd notice it....Lenore, have you seen the big clouds of smoke driftin' over 'Many Waters' these last few days?"

"Yes. And I've smelled smoke, too....From forest fire, is it not?"

"There's fire in some of the timber, but the wind's wrong for us to get smoke from the foothills."

"Then where does the smoke come from?" queried Lenore, quickly.

"Some of the Bend wheat country's been burned over."

"Burned! You mean the wheat?"

"Sure."

"Oh! What part of the Bend?"

"I reckon it's what you called young Dorn's desert of wheat."

"Oh, what a pity!...Have you had word?"

"Nothin' but rumors yet. But I'm fearin' the worst an' I'm sorry for our young friend."

A sharp pain shot through Lenore's breast, leaving behind and an ache.

"It will ruin him!" she whispered.

"Aw no, not that bad," declared Anderson, and there was a red streak in the dark where evidently he waved his cigar in quick, decisive action. "It'll only be tough on him an' sort of embarrassin' for me—an' you. That boy's proud. . . . I'll bet he raised hell among them I. W. W.'s, if he got to them." And Anderson chuckled with the delight he always felt in the western appreciation of summary violence justly dealt.

Lenore felt the rising tide of her anger. She was her father's daughter, yet always had been slow to wrath. That was her mother's softness and gentleness tempering the hard spirit of her father. But now her blood ran hot, beating and bursting about her throat and temples. And there was a leap and quiver to her body.

"Dastards! Father, those foreign I. W. W. devils should be shot!" she cried, passionately. "To ruin those poor, heroic farmers! To ruin that—that boy! It's a crime! And, oh, to burn his beautiful field of wheat—with all his hopes! Oh, what shall I call that!"

"Wal, lass, I reckon it'd take stronger speech than any you know," responded Anderson. "An' I'm usin' that same."

Lenore sat there trembling, with hot tears running down her cheeks, with her fists clenched so tight that her nails cut into her palms. Rage only proved to her how impotent she was to avert catastrophe. How bitter and black were some trials! She shrank with a sense of acute pain at thought of the despair there must be in the soul of Kurt Dorn.

"Lenore," began Anderson, slowly—his tone was stronger, vibrant with feeling—"you love this young Dorn!"

A tumultuous shock shifted Lenore's emotions. She quivered as before, but this was a long, shuddering thrill shot over her by that spoken affirmation. What she had whispered shyly and fearfully to herself when alone and hidden—what had seemed a wonderful and forbidden secret—her father had spoken out. Lenore gasped. Her anger fled as it had never been. Even in the dark she hid her face and tried to grasp the wild, whirling thoughts and emotions now storming her. He had not asked. He had affirmed. He knew. She could not deceive him even if she would. And then for a moment she was weak, at the mercy of contending tides.

"Sure I seen he was in love with you," Anderson was saying. "Seen that right off, an' I reckon I'd not thought much of him if he hadn't been....But I wasn't sure of you till the day Dorn saved you from Ruenke an' fetched you back. Then I seen. An' I've been waitin' for you to tell me."

"There's—nothing—to tell," faltered Lenore.

"I reckon there is," he replied. Leaning over, he threw his cigar out of the window and took hold of her.

Lenore had never felt him so impelling. She was not proof against the strong, warm pressure of his hand. She felt in its clasp, as she had when a little girl, a great and sure safety. It drew her irresistibly. She crept into his arms and buried her face on his shoulder, and she had a feeling that if she could not relieve her heart it would burst.

"Oh, D—Dad," she whispered, with a soft, hushed voice that broke tremulously at her lips, "I—I love him! ...I do love him....It's terrible! ...I knew it—that last time you took me to his home—when he said he was going to war....And, oh, now you know!"

Anderson held her tight against his broad breast that lifted her with its great heave. "Ah-huh! Reckon that's some relief. I wasn't so darn sure," said Anderson. "Has he spoken to you?"

"Spoken! What do you mean?"

"Has Dorn told you he loved you?"

Lenore lifted her face. If that confession of hers had been relief to her father it had been more so to her. What had seemed terrible began to feel natural. Still, she was all intense, vibrating, internally convulsed.

"Yes, he has," she replied, shyly. "But such a confession! He told it as if to explain what he thought was boldness on his part. He had fallen in love with me at first sight! ...And then meeting me was too much for him. He wanted me to know. He was going away to war. He asked nothing....He seemed to apologize for—for daring to love me. He asked nothing. And he has absolutely not the slightest idea I care for him."

"Wal, I'll be doggoned!" ejaculated Anderson. "What's the matter with him?"

"Dad, he is proud," replied Lenore, dreamily. "He's had a hard struggle out there in his desert of wheat. They've always been poor. He imagines there's a vast distance between an heiress of 'Many Waters' and a farmer boy. Then, more than all, I think, the war has fixed a morbid trouble in his mind. God knows it must be real enough! A house divided against itself is what he called his home. His father is German. He is American. He worshiped his mother, who was a native of the United States. He has become estranged from his father. I don't know—I'm not sure—but I felt that he was obsessed by a calamity in his German blood. I divined that was the great reason for his eagerness to go to war."

"Wal, Kurt Dorn's not goin' to war," replied her father. "I fixed that all right."

An amazing and rapturous start thrilled over Lenore. "Daddy!" she cried, leaping up in his arms, "what have you done?"

"I got exemption for him, that's what," replied Anderson, with great satisfaction.

"Exemption!" exclaimed Lenore, in bewilderment.

"Don't you remember the government official from Washington? You met him in Spokane. He was out West to inspire the farmers to rise more wheat. There are many young farmers needed a thousand times more on the wheat fields than on the battlefields. An' Kurt Dorn is one of them. That boy will make the biggest sower of wheat in the Northwest. I recommended exemption for Dorn. An' he's exempted an' doesn't know it."

"Doesn't know! He'll *never* accept exemption," declared Lenore.

"Lass, I'm some worried myself," rejoined Anderson. "Reckon you've explained Dorn to me—that somethin' queer about him. . . . But he's sensible. He can be told things. An' he'll see how much more he's needed to raise wheat than to kill Germans."

"But, father—suppose he *wants* to kill Germans?" asked Lenore, earnestly. How strangely she felt things about Dorn that she could not explain.

"Then, by George! it's up to you, my girl," replied her father, grimly. "Understand me. I've no sentiment about Dorn in this matter. One good wheat raiser is worth a dozen soldiers. To win the war—to feed our country after the war—why, only a man like me knows what it'll take! It means millions of bushels of wheat! ...I've sent my own boy. He'll fight with the best or the worst of them. But he'd never been a man to raise wheat. All Jim ever raised is hell. An' his kind is needed now. So let him go to war. But Dorn must be kept home. An' that's up to Lenore Anderson."

"Me!...Oh—how?" cried Lenore, faintly.

"Woman's wiles, daughter," said Anderson, with his frank laugh. "When Dorn comes let me try to show him his duty. The Northwest can't spare young men like him. He'll see that. If he has lost his wheat he'll come down here to make me take the land in payment of the debt. I'll accept it. Then he'll say he's goin' to war, an' then I'll say he ain't....We'll have it out. I'll offer him such a chance here an' in the Bend that he'd have to be crazy to refuse. But if he has got a twist in his mind—if he thinks he's got to go out an' kill Germans—then you'll have to change him."

"But, Dad, how on earth can I do that?" implored Lenore, distracted between hope and joy and fear.

"You're a woman now. An' women are in this war up to their eyes. You'll be doin' more to keep him home than if you let him go. He's moony about you. You can make him stay. An' it's your future—your happiness.... Child, no Anderson ever loves twice."

"I cannot throw myself into his arms," whispered Lenore, very low.

"Reckon I didn't mean you to," returned Anderson, gruffly.

"Then—if—if he does not ask me to—to marry him—how can I—"

"Lenore, no man on earth could resist you if you just let yourself be sweet—as sweet as you are sometimes. Dorn could never leave you!"

"I'm not so sure of that, Daddy," she murmured.

"Then take my word for it," he replied, and he got up from the chair, though still holding her. "I'll have to go now.... But I've shown my hand to you. Your happiness is more to me than anythin' else in this world. You love that boy. He loves you. An' I never met a finer lad! Wal, here's the point. He need be no slacker to stay home. He can do more good here. Then outside of bein' a wheat man for his army an' his country he can be one for me. I'm growin' old, my lass!... Here's the biggest ranch in Washington to look after, an' I want Kurt Dorn to look after it.... Now, Lenore, do we understand each other?"

She put her arms around his neck. "Dear old Daddy, you're the wonderfulest father any girl ever had! I would do my best—I would obey even if I did not love Kurt Dorn.... To hear you speak so of him—oh, it's sweet! It—chokes me!... Now, good night.... Hurry, before I—"

She kissed him and gently pushed him out of the room. Then before the sound of his slow footfalls had quite passed out of hearing she lay prone upon her bed, her face buried in the pillow, her hands clutching the coverlet, utterly surrendered to a breaking storm of emotion. Terrible indeed had come that presaged crisis of her life. Love of her wild brother Jim, gone to atone forever for the errors of his youth; love of her father, confessing at last the sad fear that haunted him; love

of Dorn, that stalwart clear-eyed lad who set his face
so bravely toward a hopeless, tragic fate—these were
the burden of the flood of her passion, and all they
involved, rushing her from girlhood into womanhood,
calling to her with imperious desires, with deathless
loyalty.

18

*A*FTER Lenore's paroxysm of emotion had subsided and she lay quietly in the dark, she became aware of soft, hurried footfalls passing along the path below her window. At first she paid no particular heed to them, but at length the steady steps became so different in number, and so regular in passing every few moments, that she was interested to go to her window and look out. Watching there awhile, she saw a number of men, whispering and talking low, come from the road, pass under her window, and disappear down the path into the grove. Then no more came. Lenore feared at first these strange visitors might be prowling I. W. W. men. She concluded, however, that they were neighbors and farmhands, come for secret conference with her father.

Important events were pending, and her father had not taken her into his confidence! It must be, then, something that he did not wish her to know. Only a week ago, when the I. W. W. menace had begun to be serious, she had asked him how he intended to meet it, and particularly how he would take sure measures to protect himself. Anderson had laughed down her fears, and Lenore, absorbed in her own tumult, had been easily satisfied. But now, with her curiosity there returned a twofold dread.

She put on a cloak and went downstairs. The hour was still early. She heard the girls with her mother in the sitting room. As Lenore slipped out she encountered Jake. He appeared to loom right out of the darkness and he startled her.

"Howdy, Miss Lenore!" he said. "Where might you be goin'?"

"Jake, I'm curious about the men I heard passing by my window," she replied. Then she observed that Jake had a rifle under his arm, and she added, "What are you doing with that gun?"

"Wal, I've sort of gone back to packin' a Winchester," replied Jake.

Lenore missed his smile, ever ready for her. Jake looked somber.

"You're on guard!" she exclaimed.

"I reckon. There's four of us boys round the house. You're not goin' off thet step, Miss Lenore."

"Oh, ah-huh!" replied Lenore, imitating her father, and bantering Jake, more for the fun of it than from any intention of disobeying him. "Who's going to keep me from it?"

"I am. Boss's orders, Miss Lenore. I'm doggone sorry. But you sure oughtn't to be outdoors this far," replied Jake.

"Look here, my cowboy dictator. I'm going to see where those men went," said Lenore, and forthwith she stepped down to the path.

Then Jake deliberately leaned his rifle against a post and, laying hold of her with no gentle hands, he swung her in one motion back upon the porch. The broad light streaming out of the open door showed that, whatever his force meant, it had paled his face to exercise it.

"Why, Jake—to handle me that way!" cried Lenore, in pretended reproach. She meant to frighten or coax the truth out of him. "You hurt me!"

"I'm beggin' your pardon if I was rough," said Jake. "Fact is, I'm a little upset an' I mean bizness."

Whereupon Lenore stepped back to close the door, and then, in the shadow, she returned to Jake and whispered: "I was only in fun. I would not think of disobeying you. But you can trust me. I'll not tell, and I'll worry less if I know what's what . . . Jake, is father in danger?"

"I reckon. But the best we could do was to make him stand fer a guard. There's four of us cowpunchers with him all day, an' at night he's surrounded by guards. There ain't much chance of his gittin' hurt. So you needn't worry about thet."

"Who are these men I heard passing? Where are they from?"

"Farmers, ranchers, cowboys, from all over this side of the river."

"There must have been a lot of them," said Lenore, curiously.

"Reckon you never heerd the quarter of what's come to attend Anderson's meetin'."

"What for? Tell me, Jake."

The cowboy hesitated. Lenore heard his big hand slap round the rifle stock.

"We've orders not to tell thet," he replied.

"But, Jake, you can tell *me*. You always tell me secrets. I'll not breathe it."

Jake came closer to her, and his tall head reached to a level with hers, where she stood on the porch. Lenore saw his dark, set face, his gleaming eyes.

"Wal, it's jest this here," he whispered, hoarsely. "Your dad has organized vigilantes, like he belonged to in the early days. . . . An' it's the vigilantes thet will attend to this I. W. W. outfit."

Those were thrilling words to Jake, as was attested by his emotion, and they surely made Lenore's knees knock together. She had heard many stories from her father of that famous old vigilante band, secret, making the law where there was no law.

"Oh, I might have expected that of Dad!" she murmured.

"Wal, it's sure the trick out here. An' your father's the man to deal it. There'll be doggoned little wheat burned in this valley, you can gamble on thet."

"I'm glad. I hate the very thought. . . . Jake, you know about Mr. Dorn's misfortune?"

"No, I ain't heerd about him. But I knowed the Bend was burnin' over, an' of course I reckoned Dorn would lose his wheat. Fact is, he had the only wheat up there worth savin'. . . . Wal, these I. W. W.'s an' their German bosses hev put it all over the early days when rustlin' cattle, holdin' up stage-coaches, an' jest plain cussedness was stylish."

"Jake, I'd rather have lived back in the early days," mused Lenore.

"Me too, though I ain't no youngster," he replied. "Reckon you'd better go in now, Miss Lenore.... Don't you worry none or lose any sleep."

Lenore bade the cowboy good-night and went to the sitting room. Her mother sat preoccupied, with sad and thoughtful face. Rose was writing many pages to Jim. Kathleen sat at the table, surreptitiously eating while she was pretending to read.

"My, but you look funny, Lenorry!" she cried.

"Why don't you laugh, then?" retorted Lenore.

"You're white. Your eyes are big and purple. You look like a starved cannibal.... If that's what it's like to be in love—excuse me—I'll never fall for any man!"

"You ought to be in bed. Mother, I recommend the baby of the family be sent upstairs."

"Yes, child, it's long past your bedtime," said Mrs. Anderson.

"Aw, no!" wailed Kathleen.

"Yes," ordered her mother.

"But you'd never thought of it—if Lenorry hadn't said so," replied Kathleen.

"You should obey Lenore," reprovingly said Mrs. Anderson.

"What? *Me!* Mind her!" burst out Kathleen, hotly, as she got up to go. "Well, I guess not!" Kathleen backed to the door and opened it. Then making a frightful face at Lenore, most expressive of ridicule and revenge, she darted upstairs.

"My dear, will you write to your brother?" inquired Mrs. Anderson.

"Yes," replied Lenore. "I'll send mine with Rose's."

Mrs. Anderson bade the girls good-night and left

the room. After that nothing was heard for a while except the scratching of pens.

It was late when Lenore retired, yet she found sleep elusive. The evening had made subtle, indefinable changes in her. She went over in mind all that had been said to her and which she felt, with the result that one thing remained to torment and perplex and thrill her—to keep Kurt Dorn from going to war.

Next day Lenore did not go out to the harvest fields. She expected Dorn might arrive at any time, and she wanted to be there when he came. Yet she dreaded the meeting. She had to keep her hands active that day, so in some measure to control her mind. A thousand times she felt herself on the verge of thrilling and flushing. Her fancy and imagination seemed wonderfully active. The day was more than usually golden, crowned with an azure blue, like the blue of the Pacific. She worked in her room, helped her mother, took up her knitting, and sewed upon a dress, and even lent a hand in the kitchen. But action could not wholly dull the song in her heart. She felt unutterably young, as if life had just opened, with haunting, limitless, beautiful possibilities. Never had the harvest-time been so sweet.

Anderson came in early from the fields that day. He looked like a farmhand, with his sweaty shirt, his dusty coat, his begrimed face. And when he kissed Lenore he left a great smear on her cheek.

"That's a harvest kiss, my lass," he said, with his big laugh. "Best of the whole year!"

"It sure is, Dad," she replied. "But I'll wait till you wash your face before I return it. How's the harvest going?"

"We had trouble today," he said.

"What happened?"

"Nothin' much, but it was annoyin'. We had some machines crippled, an' it took most of the day to fix them.... We've got a couple of hundred hands at work. Some of them are I. W. W.'s that's sure. But they all swear they are not an' we have no way to prove it. An' we couldn't catch them at their tricks.... All the same, we've got half your big wheat field cut. A thousand acres, Lenore!... Some of the wheat'll go forty bushels to the acre, but mostly under that."

"Better than last harvest," Lenore replied, gladly. "We are lucky.... Father, did you hear any news from the Bend?"

"Sure did," he replied, and patted her head. "They sent me a message up from Vale.... Young Dorn wired from Kilo he'd be here today."

"Today!" echoed Lenore, and her heart showed a tendency to act strangely.

"Yep. He'll be here soon," said Anderson, cheerfully. "Tell your mother. Mebbe he'll come for supper. An' have a room ready for him."

"Yes, father," replied Lenore.

"Wal, if Dorn sees you as you look now—sleeves rolled up, apron on, flour on your nose—a regular farmer girl—an' sure huggable, as Jake says—you won't have no trouble winnin' him."

"How you talk!" exclaimed Lenore, with burning cheeks. She ran to her room and made haste to change her dress.

But Dorn did not arrive in time for supper. Eight o'clock came without his appearing, after which, with keen disappointment, Lenore gave up expecting him that night. She was in her father's study, helping him with the harvest notes and figures, when Jake knocked and entered.

"Dorn's here," he announced.

"Good. Fetch him in," replied Anderson.

"Father, I—I'd rather go," whispered Lenore.

"You stay right along by your dad," was his reply, "an' be a real Anderson."

When Lenore heard Dorn's step in the hall the fluttering ceased in her heart and she grew calm. How glad she would be to see him! It had been the suspense of waiting that had played havoc with her feelings.

Then Dorn entered with Jake. The cowboy set down a bag and went out. He seemed strange to Lenore and very handsome in his gray flannel suit.

As he stepped forward in greeting Lenore saw how white he was, how tragic his eyes. There had come a subtle change in his face. It hurt her.

"Miss Anderson, I'm glad to see you," he said, and a flash of red stained his white cheeks. "How are you?"

"Very well, thank you," she replied, offering her hand. "I'm glad to see you."

They shook hands, while Anderson boomed out: "Hello, son! I sure am glad to welcome you to 'Many Waters.'"

No doubt as to the rancher's warm and hearty greeting! It warmed some of the coldness out of Dorn's face.

"Thank you. It's good to come—yet it's—it's hard."

Lenore saw his throat swell. His voice seemed low and full of emotion.

"Bad news to tell," said Anderson. "Wal, forget it. ...Have you had supper?"

"Yes. At Huntington. I'd have been here sooner, but we punctured a tire. My driver said the I. W. W. was breaking bottles on the roads."

"I. W. W. Now where'd I ever hear that name?" asked Anderson, quizzically. "Bustin' bottles, hey? Wal, they'll be bustin' their heads presently.... down, Dorn. You look fine, only you're sure pale."

"I lost my father," said Dorn.

"What! Your old man? Dead? ... Aw, that's tough!"

Lenore felt an almost uncontrollable impulse to go to Dorn. "Oh, I'm sorry!" she said.

"That is a surprise," went on Anderson, rather huskily. "My Lord! But it's only round the corner for every man.... Come on, tell us all about it, an' the rest of the bad news.... Get it over. Then, mebbe Lenore an' me—"

But Anderson did not conclude his last sentence.

Dorn's face began to work as he began to talk, and his eyes were dark and deep, burning with gloom.

"Bad news it is, indeed.... Mr. Anderson, the I. W. W. marked us.... You'll remember your suggestion about getting my neighbors to harvest our wheat in a rush. I went all over, and almost all of them came. We had been finding phosphorus everywhere. Then, on the hot day, fires broke out all around. My neighbors left their own burning fields to save ours. We fought fire. We fought fire all around us, late into the night.... My father had grown furious, maddened at the discovery of how he had been betrayed by Glidden. You remember the—the plot, in which some way my father was involved. He would not believe the I. W. W. meant to burn *his* wheat. And when the fires broke out he worked like a madman....It killed him!...I was not with him when he died. But Jerry, our foreman was....And my father's last words were, 'Tell my son I was wrong.'...Thank God he sent me that message! I think in that he confessed the iniquity of the Germans....Well, my neighbor, Olsen, managed the harvest. He sure rushed it. I'd have given a good deal for you and Miss Anderson to have seen all those big combines at work on one field. It was great. We harvested over thirty-eight thousand bushels and got all the wheat safely to the elevators at the station....And that night the I. W. W. burned the elevators!"

Anderson's face turned purple. He appeared about to explode. There was a deep rumbling within his throat that Lenore knew to be profanity restrained on account of her presence. As for her own feelings, they were a strange mixture of sadness for Dorn and pride in her father's fury, and something unutterably sweet in the revelation about to be made to this unfortunate boy. But she could not speak a word just then, and it appeared that her father was in the same state.

Evidently the telling of his story had relieved Dorn. The strain relaxed in his white face and it lost a little of its stern fixity. He got up and, opening his bag, he took out some papers.

"Mr. Anderson, I'd like to settle all this right now," he said. "I want it off my mind."

"Go ahead, son, an' settle," replied Anderson, thickly. He heaved a big sigh and then sat down, fumbling for a match to light his cigar. When he got it lighted he drew in a big breath and with it manifestly a great draught of consoling smoke.

"I want to make over the—the land—in fact, all

the property—to you—to settle mortgage and interest," went on Dorn, earnestly, and then paused.

"All right. I expected that," returned Anderson, as he emitted a cloud of smoke.

"The only thing is—" here Dorn hesitated, evidently with difficult speech—"the property is worth more than the debt."

"Sure. I know," said Anderson, encouragingly.

"I promised our neighbors big money to harvest our wheat. You remember you told me to offer it. Well, they left their own wheat and barley fields to burn, and they saved ours. And then they harvested it and hauled it to the railroad.... I owe Andrew Olsen fifteen thousand dollars for himself and the men who worked with him.... If I could pay that—I'd—almost be happy.... Do you think my property is worth that much more than the debt?"

"I think it is—just about," replied Anderson. "We'll mail the money to Olsen.... Lenore, write out a check to Andrew Olsen for fifteen thousand."

Lenore's hand trembled as she did as her father directed. It was the most poorly written check she had ever drawn. Her heart seemed too big for her breast just then. How cool and calm her father was! Never had she loved him quite so well as then. When she looked up from her task it was to see a change in Kurt Dorn that suddenly dimmed her eyes.

"There, send this to Olsen," said Anderson. "We'll run into town in a day or so an' file the papers."

Lenore had to turn her gaze away from Dorn. She heard him in broken, husky accents try to express his gratitude.

"Ah-huh! Sure—sure!" interrupted Anderson, has-

tily. "Now listen to me. Things ain't so bad as they look.
...For instance, we're goin' to fool the I. W. W. down
here in the valley."

"How can you? There are so many," returned Dorn.

"You'll see. We're just waitin' a chance."

"I saw hundreds of I. W. W. men between here and
Kilo."

"Can you tell an I. W. W. from any other farmhand?" asked Anderson.

"Yes, I can," replied Dorn, grimly.

"Wal, I reckon we need you round here powerful
much," said the rancher, dryly. "Dorn, I've got a big
proposition to put up to you."

Lenore, thrilling at her father's words, turned once
more. Dorn appeared more composed.

"Have you?" he inquired, in surprise.

"Sure. But there's no hurry about tellin' you. Suppose we put it off."

"I'd rather hear it now. My stay here must be short.
I—I—You know—"

"Hum! Sure I know....Wal then, it's this: Will you
go in business with me? Want you to work that Bend
wheat farm of yours for me—on half shares....More
particular I want you to take charge of 'Many Waters.'
You see, I'm—not so spry as I used to be. It's a big job,
an' I've a lot of confidence in you. You'll live here, of
course, an' run to an' fro with one of my cars. I've some
land-development schemes—an', to cut it short, there's
a big place waitin' for you in the Northwest."

"Mr. Anderson!" cried Dorn, in a kind of rapturous
amaze. Red burned out the white of his face. "That's
great! It's too great to come true. You're good! ...If I'm
lucky enough to come back from the war—"

"Son, you're not goin' to war!" interposed Anderson.

"What!" exclaimed Dorn, blankly. He stared as if he had not heard aright.

Anderson calmly repeated his assertion. He was smiling; he looked kind; but underneath that showed the will that had made him what he was.

"But I *am!*" flashed the young man, as if he had been misunderstood.

"Listen. You're like all boys—hot-headed an' hasty. Let me talk a little," resumed Anderson. And he began to speak of the future of the Northwest. He painted that in the straight talk of a farmer who knew, but what he predicted seemed like a fairy tale. Then he passed to the needs of the government and the armies, and lastly the people of the nation. All depended upon the farmer! Wheat was indeed the staff of life and of victory! Young Dorn was one of the farmers who could not be spared. Patriotism was a noble thing. Fighting, however, did not alone constitute a duty and loyalty to the nation. This was an economic war, a war of peoples, and the nation that was the best fed would last longest. Adventure and the mistaken romance of war called indeed to all red-blooded young Americans. It was good that they did call. But they should not call the young farmer from his wheat fields.

"But I've been drafted!" Dorn spoke with agitation. He seemed bewildered by Anderson's blunt eloquence. His intelligence evidently accepted the elder man's argument, but something instinctive revolted.

"There's exemption, my boy. Easy in your case," replied Anderson.

"Exemption!" echoed Dorn, and a dark tide of blood

rose to his temples. "I wouldn't—I couldn't ask for that!"

"You don't need to," said the rancher. "Dorn, do you recollect that Washington official who called on you some time ago?"

"Yes," replied Dorn, slowly.

"Did he say anythin' about exemption?"

"No. He asked me if I wanted it, that's all."

"Wal, you had it right then. I took it upon myself to get exemption for you. That government official heartily approved of my recommendin' exemption for you. An' he gave it."

"Anderson! You took—it upon—yourself—" gasped Dorn, slowly rising. If he had been white-faced before, he was ghastly now.

"Sure I did....Good Lord! Dorn, don't imagine I ever questioned your nerve....It's only you're not needed—or rather, you're needed more at home....I let my son Jim go to war. That's enough for one family!"

But Dorn did not grasp the significance of Anderson's reply.

"How dared you? What right had you?" he demanded, passionately.

"No right at all, lad," replied Anderson. "I just recommended it an' the official approved it."

"But I refuse!" cried Dorn, with ringing fury. "I won't accept exemption."

"Talk sense now, even if you are mad," returned Anderson, rising. "I've paid you a high compliment, young man, an' offered you a lot. More 'n you see, I guess....Why won't you accept exemption?"

"I'm going to war!" was the grim, hard reply.

"But you're needed here. You'd be more of a soldier here. You could do more for your country than if you gave a hundred lives. Can't you see that?"

"Yes, I can," assented Dorn, as if forced.

"You're no fool, an' you're a loyal American. Your duty is to stay home an' raise wheat."

"I've a duty to myself," returned Dorn, darkly.

"Son, your fortune stares you right in the face—here. Are you goin' to turn from it?"

"Yes."

"You want to get in that war? You've got to fight?"

"Yes."

"Ah-huh!" Anderson threw up his hands in surrender. "Got to kill some Germans, hey? . . . Why not come out to my harvest fields an' hog-stick a few of them German I. W. W.'s?"

Dorn had no reply for that.

"Wal, I'm doggone sorry," resumed Anderson. "I see it's a tough place for you, though I can't understand. You'll excuse me for mixin' in your affairs. . . . An' now, considerin' other ways I've really helped you, I hope you'll stay at my home for a few days. We all owe you a good deal. My family wants to make up to you. Will you stay?"

"Thank you—yes—for a few days," replied Dorn.

"Good! That'll help some. Mebbe, after runnin' around 'Many Waters' with Le—with the girls—you'll begin to be reasonable. I hope so."

"You think me ungrateful!" exclaimed Dorn, shrinking.

"I don't think nothin'," replied Anderson. "I turn you over to Lenore." He laughed as he pronounced Dorn's utter defeat. And his look at Lenore was equivalent to saying the issue now depended upon her, and that he had absolutely no doubt of its outcome. "Lenore, take him in to meet Mother an' the girls, an' entertain him. I've got work to do."

Lenore felt the blushes in her cheeks and was glad Dorn did not look at her. He seemed locked in somber thought. As she touched him and bade him come he gave a start; then he followed her into the hall. Lenore closed her father's door, and the instant she stood alone with Dorn a wonderful calmness came to her.

"Miss Anderson, I'd rather not—not meet your mother and sisters tonight," said Dorn. "I'm upset. Won't it be all right to wait till tomorrow?"

"Surely. But I think they've gone to bed," replied Lenore, as she glanced into the dark sitting room. "So they have. . . . Come, let us go into the parlor."

Lenore turned on the shaded lights in the beautiful room. How inexplicable was the feeling of being alone with him, yet utterly free of the torment that had possessed her before! She seemed to have divined an almost insurmountable obstacle in Dorn's will. She did not have her father's assurance. It made her tremble to realize her responsibility—that her father's earnest wishes and her future of love or woe depended entirely upon what she said and did. But she felt that indeed she had become a woman. And it would take a woman's wit and charm and love to change this tragic boy.

"Miss—Anderson," he began, brokenly, with restraint let down, "your father—doesn't understand. I've *got* to go. . . . And even if I am spared—I couldn't ever come back. . . . To work for him—all the time in love with you—I couldn't stand it. . . . He's so good. I know I could care for him, too. . . . Oh, I thought I was bitterly resigned—hard—inhuman. But all this makes it—so—so much worse."

He sat down heavily, and, completely unnerved, he covered his face with his hands. His shoulders heaved and short, strangled sobs broke from him.

Lenore had to overcome a rush of tenderness. It was all she could do to keep from dropping to her knees beside him and slipping her arms around his neck. In her agitation she could not decide whether that would be womanly or not; only, she must make no mistakes. A hot, sweet flush went over her when she thought that always as a last resort she could reveal her secret and use her power. What would he do when he discovered she loved him?

"Kurt, I understand," she said, softly, and put a hand on his shoulder. And she stood thus beside him, sadly troubled, vaguely divining that her presence was helpful, until he recovered his composure. As he raised his head and wiped tears from his eyes he made no excuses for his weakness, nor did he show any shame.

"Miss Anderson—" he began.

"Please call me Lenore. I feel so—so stiff when you are formal. My friends call me Lenore," she said.

"You mean—you consider me your friend?" he queried.

"Indeed I do," she replied, smiling.

"I—I'm afraid I misunderstood your asking me to visit you," he said. "I thank you. I'm proud and glad that you call me your friend. It will be splendid to remember—when I am over there."

"I wonder if we could talk of anything except trouble and war," replied Lenore, plaintively. "If we can't, then let's look at the bright side."

"Is there a bright side?" he asked, with his sad smile.

"Every cloud, you know.... For instance, if you go to war—"

"Not if. I *am* going," he interrupted.

"Oh, so you say," returned Lenore, softly. And she felt deep in her the inception of a tremendous feminine antagonism. It stirred along her pulse. "Have your own way, then. But *I* say, *if* you go, think how fine it will be for me to get letters from you at the front—and to write you!"

"You'd like to hear from me? ... You would answer?" he asked, breathlessly.

"Assuredly. And I'll knit socks for you."

"You're—very good," he said, with strong feeling.

Lenore again saw his eyes dim. How strangely sensitive he was! If he exaggerated such a little kindness as she had suggested, if he responded to it with such emotion, what would he do when the great and marvelous truth of her love was flung in his face? The very thought made Lenore weak.

"You'll go to training camp," went on Lenore, "and because of your wonderful physique and your intelligence you will get a commission. Then you'll go to— France." Lenore faltered a little in her imagined prospect. "You'll be in the thick of the great battles. You'll give and take. You'll kill some of those—those—Germans. You'll be wounded and you'll be promoted.... Then the Allies will win. Uncle Sam's grand army will have saved the world....Glorious! ...You'll come back—home to us—to take the place Dad offered you. ...There! that is the bright side."

Indeed, the brightness seemed reflected in Dorn's face.

"I never dreamed you could be like this," he said, wonderingly.

"Like what?"

"I don't know just what I mean. Only you're different from my—my fancies. Not cold or—or proud."

"You're beginning to get acquainted with me, that's all. After you've been here awhile—"

"Please don't make it so hard for me," he interrupted, appealingly. "I can't stay."

"Don't you want to?" she asked.

"Yes. And I will stay a couple of days. But no longer. It'll be hard enough to go then."

"Perhaps I—we'll make it so hard for you that you can't go."

Then he gazed piercingly at her, as if realizing a will opposed to his, a conviction not in sympathy with his.

"You're going to keep this up—this trying to change my mind?"

"I surely am," she replied, both wistfully and willfully.

"Why? I should think you'd respect my sense of duty."

"Your duty is more here than at the front. The government man said so. My father believes it. So do I. . . . You have some other—other thing you think duty."

"I hate Germans!" he burst out, with a dark and terrible flash.

"Who does not?" she flashed back at him, and she rose, feeling as if drawn by a powerful current. She realized then that she must be prepared any moment to be overwhelmed by the inevitable climax of this meeting. But she prayed for a little more time. She fought her emotions.

She saw him tremble. "Lenore, I'd better run off in the night," he said.

Instinctively, with swift, soft violence, she grasped his hands. Perhaps the moment had come. She was not afraid, but the suddenness of her extremity left her witless.

"You would not! ... That would be unkind—not like you at all.... To run off without giving me a chance— without good-bye! ... Promise me you will not."

"I promise," he replied, wearily, as if nonplussed by her attitude. "You said you understood me. But I can't understand you."

She released his hands and turned away. "I promise—that you shall understand—very soon."

"You feel sorry for me. You pity me. You think I'll only be cannon fodder for the Germans. You want to be nice, kind, sweet to me—to send me away with better thoughts.... Isn't that what you think?"

He was impatient, almost angry. His glance blazed at her. All about him, his tragic face, his sadness, his defeat, his struggle to hold on to his manliness and to keep his faith in nobler thoughts—these challenged Lenore's compassion, her love, and her woman's combative spirit to save and to keep her own. She quivered again on the brink of betraying herself. And it was panic alone that held her back.

"Kurt—I think—presently I'll give you the surprise of your life," she replied, and summoned a smile.

How obtuse he was! How blind! Perhaps the stress of his emotion, the terrible sense of his fate, left him no keenness, no outward penetration. He answered her smile, as if she were a child whose determined kindness made him both happy and sad.

"I dare say you will," he replied. "You Andersons are full of surprises....But I wish you would not do any more for me. I am like a dog. The kinder you are to me the more I love you....How dreadful to go away to war—to violence and blood and death—to all that's brutalizing—with my heart and mind full of love for a noble girl like you!—If I come to love you any more I'll not be a man."

To Lenore he looked very much of a man, so tall and lithe and white-faced, with his eyes of fire, his simplicity, and his tragic refusal of all that was for most men the best of life. Whatever his ideal, it was magnificent. Lenore had her chance then, but she was absolutely unable to grasp it. Her blood beat thick and hot. If she could only have been sure of herself! Or was it that she still cared too much for herself? The moment had not come. And in her tumult there was a fleeting fury at Dorn's blindness, at his reverence of her, that he dare not touch her hand. Did he imagine she was stone?

"Let us say good night," she said. "You are worn out. And I am—not just myself. Tomorrow we'll be—good friends....Father will take you to your room."

Dorn pressed the hand she offered, and, saying good-night, he followed her to the hall. Lenore tapped on the door of her father's study, then opened it.

"Good night, Dad. I'm going up," she said. "Will you look after Kurt?"

"Sure. Come in, son," replied her father.

Lenore felt Dorn's strange, intent gaze upon her as she passed him. Lightly she ran upstairs and turned at the top. The hall was bright and Dorn stood full in the light, his face upturned. It still wore the softer expression of those last few moments. Lenore waved her hand, and he smiled. The moment was natural. Youth to youth! Lenore felt it. She marveled that he did not. A sweet devil of willful coquetry possessed her.

"Oh, did you say you wouldn't go?" she softly called.

"I said only good night," he replied.

"If you *don't* go, then you will never be General Dorn, will you? What a pity!"

"I'll go. And then it will be—'Private Dorn—missing. No relatives,'" he replied.

That froze Lenore. Her heart quaked. She gazed down upon him with all her soul in her eyes. She knew it and did not care. But he could not see.

"Good night, Kurt Dorn," she called, and ran to her room.

Composure did not come to her until she was ready for bed, with the light out and in her old seat at the window. Night and silence and starlight always lent Lenore strength. She prayed to them now and to the spirit she knew dwelt beyond them. And then she whispered what her intelligence told her was an unalterable fact— Kurt Dorn could never be changed. But her sympathy and love and passion, all that was womanly emotion, stormed at her intelligence and refused to listen to it.

Nothing short of a great shock would divert Dorn from his tragic headlong rush toward the fate he believed unalterable. Lenore sensed a terrible, sinister earnestness in him. She could not divine its meaning. But it was such a driving passion that no man possessing it and free to the violence of war could ever escape death. Even if by superhuman strife, and the guidance of Providence, he did escape death, he would have lost something as precious as life. If Dorn went to war at all—if he ever reached those blood-red trenches, in the thick of fire and shriek and ferocity—there to express in horrible earnestness what she vaguely felt yet could not define—then so far as she was concerned she imagined that she would not want him to come back.

That was the strength of spirit that breathed out of the night and the silence to her. Dorn would go to war as no ordinary soldier, to obey, to fight, to do his duty; but for some strange, unfathomable obsession of his own. And, therefore, if he went at all he was lost. War, in its inexplicable horror, killed the souls of endless hordes of men. Therefore, if he went at all she, too, was lost to the happiness that might have been hers. She would never love another man. She could never marry. She would never have a child.

So his soul and her happiness were in the balance weighed against a woman's power. It seemed to Lenore that she felt hopelessly unable to carry the issue to victory; and yet, on the other hand, a tumultuous and wonderful sweetness of sensation called to her, insidiously, of the infallible potency of love. What could she do to save Dorn's life and his soul? There was only one answer to that. She would do anything. She must make him love her to the extent that he would have no will to carry out this desperate intent. There was little time to do that. The gradual growth of affection through intimacy and understanding was not possible here. It must come as a flash of lightning. She must bewilder him with the revelation of her love, and then by all its incalculable power hold him there.

It was her father's wish; it would be the salvation of Dorn; it meant all to her. But if to keep him there would make him a slacker, Lenore swore she would die before lifting her lips to his. The government would rather he stayed to raise wheat than go out and fight men. Lenore saw the sanity, the cardinal importance of that, as her father saw it. So from all sides she was justified. And sitting there in the darkness and silence, with the cool wind in her face, she vowed she would be all woman, all sweetness, all love, all passion, all that was feminine and terrible, to keep Dorn from going to war.

CHAPTER
19

*L*ENORE awakened early. The morning seemed golden. Birds were singing at her window. What did that day hold in store for her? She pressed a hand hard on her heart as if to hold it still. But her heart went right on, swift, exultant, throbbing with a fullness that was almost pain.

Early as she awakened, it was, nevertheless, late when she could direct her reluctant steps downstairs. She had welcomed every little suggestion and task to delay the facing of her ordeal.

There was merriment in the sitting room, and Dorn's laugh made her glad. The girls were at him, and her father's pleasant, deep voice chimed in. Evidently there was a controversy as to who should have the society of the guest. They had all been to breakfast. Mrs. Anderson expressed surprise at Lenore's tardiness, and said she had been called twice. Lenore had heard nothing except the birds and the music of her thoughts. She peeped into the sitting room.

"Didn't you bring me anything?" Kathleen was inquiring of Dorn.

Dorn was flushed and smiling. Anderson stood beaming upon them, and Rose appeared to be inclined toward jealousy.

"Why—you see—I didn't even know Lenore had a little sister," Dorn explained.

"Oh!" exclaimed Kathleen, evidently satisfied. "All Lenorry's beaux bring me things. But I believe I'm going to like you best."

Lenore had intended to say good morning. She changed her mind, however, at Kathleen's naive speech, and darted back lest she be seen. She felt the blood hot in her cheeks. That awful, irrepressible Kathleen! If she liked Dorn she would take possession of him. And Kathleen was lovable, irresistible. Lenore had a sudden thought that Kathleen would aid the good cause if she could be enlisted. While Lenore ate her breakfast she listened to the animated conversation in the sitting room. Presently her father came in.

"Hello, Lenore! Did you get up?" he greeted her, cheerily.

"I hardly ever did, it seems....Dad, the day was something to face," she said.

"Ah-huh! It's like getting up to work. Lenore, the biggest duty of life is to hide your troubles....Dorn looks like a human bein' this mornin'. The kids have won him. I reckon he needs that sort of cheer. Let them have him. Then after a while you fetch him out to the wheat field. Lenore, our harvestin' is half done. Every day I've expected some trick or deviltry. But it hasn't come yet."

"Are any of the other ranchers having trouble?" she inquired.

"I hear rumors of bad work. But facts told by ranchers an' men who were here only yesterday make little of the rumors. All that burnin' of wheat an' timber, an' the destruction of machines an' strikin' of farmhands, haven't hit Golden Valley yet. We won't need any militia here, you can bet on that."

"Father, it won't do to be overconfident," she said, earnestly. "You know you are the mark for the I. W. W. sabotage. If you are not careful—any moment—"

Lenore paused with a shudder.

"Lass, I'm just like I was in the old rustlin' days. An' I've surrounded myself with cowboys like Jake an' Bill, an' old hands who pack guns an' keep still, as in the good old western days. We're just waitin' for the I. W. W.'s to break loose."

"Then what?" queried Lenore.

"Wal, we'll chase that outfit so fast it'll be lost in dust," he replied.

"But if you chase them away, it'll only be into another state, where they'll make trouble for other farmers. You don't do any real good."

"My dear, I reckon you've said somethin' strong," he replied, soberly, and went out.

Then Kathleen came bouncing in. Her beautiful eyes were full of mischief and excitement. "Lenorry, your new beau has all the others skinned to a frazzle," she said.

For once Lenore did not scold Kathleen, but drew her close and whispered: "Do you want to please me?

Do you want me to do *everything* for you?"

"I sure do," replied Kathleen, with wonderful eyes.

"Then be nice, sweet, good to him....make him love you....Don't tease him about my other beaux. Think how you can make him like 'Many Waters.'"

"Will you promise—*everything?*" whispered Kathleen, solemnly. Evidently Lenore's promises were rare and reliable.

"Yes. Cross my heart. There! And you must not tell."

Kathleen was a precocious child, with all the potentialities of youth. She could not divine Lenore's motive, but she sensed a new and fascinating mode of conduct for herself. She seemed puzzled a little at Lenore's earnestness.

"It's a bargain," she said, soberly, as if she had accepted no slight gauge.

"Now, Kathleen, take him all over the gardens, the orchards, the corrals and barns," directed Lenore. "Be sure to show him the horses—my horses, especially. Take him round the reservoir—and everywhere except the wheat fields. I want to take him there myself. Besides, father does not want you girls to go out to the harvest."

Kathleen nodded and ran back to the sitting room. Lenore heard them all go out together. Before she finished breakfast her mother came in again.

"Lenore, I like Mr. Dorn," she said, meditatively. "He has an old-fashioned manner that reminds me of my boy friends when I was a girl. I mean he's more courteous and dignified than boys are nowadays. A splendid-looking boy, too. Only his face is so sad. When he smiles he seems another person."

"No wonder he's sad," replied Lenore, and briefly told Kurt Dorn's story.

"Ah!" sighed Mrs. Anderson. "We have fallen upon evil days....Poor boy!...Your father seems much interested in him. And you are too, my daughter?"

"Yes, I am," replied Lenore, softly.

Two hours later she heard Kathleen's gay laughter and pattering feet. Lenore took her wide-brimmed hat and went out on the porch. Dorn was indeed not the same somber young man he had been.

"Good morning, Kurt," said Lenore, extending her hand.

The instant he greeted her she saw that the stiffness, the aloofness had gone from him. Kathleen had made him feel at home. He looked younger. There was color in his face.

"Kathleen, I'll take charge of Mr. Dorn now, if you will allow me that pleasure."

"Lenorry, I sure hate to give him up. We sure had a fine time."

"Did he like 'Many Waters'?"

"Well, if he didn't he's a grand fibber," replied Kathleen. "But he did. You can't fool me. I thought I'd never get him back to the house." Then, as she tripped up the porch steps, she shook a finger at Dorn. "Remember!"

"I'll never forget," said Dorn, and he was as earnest as he was amiable. Then, as she disappeared, he exclaimed to Lenore, "What an adorable little girl!"

"Do you like Kathleen?"

"Like her!" Dorn laughed in a way to make light of such words. "My life has been empty. I see that."

"Come, we'll go out to the wheat fields," said Lenore. "What do you think of 'Many Waters'? This is harvest-time. You see 'Many Waters' at its very best."

"I can hardly tell you," he replied. "All my life I've lived on my barren hills. I seem to have come to another world. 'Many Waters' is such a ranch as I never dreamed of. The orchards, the fruit, the gardens—and everywhere running water! It all smells so fresh and sweet. And then the green and red and purple against the background of blazing gold! . . . 'Many Waters' is verdant and fruitful. The Bend is desert."

"Now that you've been here, do you like it better than your barren hills?" asked Lenore.

Kurt hesitated. "I don't know," he answered, slowly. "But maybe that desert I've lived in accounts for much I lack."

"Would you like to stay at 'Many Waters'—if you weren't going to war?"

"I might prefer 'Many Waters' to any place on earth. It's a paradise. But I would not choose to stay here."

"Why? When you return—you know—my father will need you here. And if anything should happen to him I will have to run the ranch. Then *I* would need you."

Dorn stopped in his tracks and gazed at her as if there were slight misgivings in his mind.

"Lenore, if you owned this ranch would you want me—*me* for your manager?" he asked, bluntly.

"Yes," she replied.

"You would? Knowing I was in love with you?"

"Well, I had forgotten that," she replied, with a little laugh. "It would be rather embarrassing—and funny, wouldn't it?"

"Yes, it would," he said, grimly, and walked on

again. He made a gesture of keen discomfiture. "I knew you hadn't taken me seriously."

"I believed you, but I could not take you *very* seriously," she murmured.

"Why not?" he demanded, as if stung, and his eyes flashed on her.

"Because your declaration was not accompanied by the usual—question—that a girl naturally expects under such circumstances."

"Good Heaven! You say that? ... Lenore Anderson, you think me insincere because I did not ask you to marry me," he asserted, with bitter pathos.

"No. I merely said you were not—*very* serious," she replied. It was fascination to torment him this way, yet it hurt her, too. She was playing on the verge of a precipice, not afraid of a misstep, but glorying in the prospect of a leap into the abyss. Something deep and strange in her bade her make him show her how much he loved her. If she drove him to desperation she would reward him.

"I am going to war," he began, passionately, "to fight for you and your sisters.... I am ruined.... The only noble and holy feeling left to me—that I can have with me in the dark hours—is my love for you. If you do not believe that, I am indeed the most miserable of beggars! Most boys going to the front leave many behind whom they love. I have no one but you.... Don't make me a coward."

"I believe you. Forgive me," she said.

"If I had asked you to marry me—*me*—why, I'd have been a selfish, egotistical fool. You are far above me. And I want you to know I know it.... But even if I had not—had the blood I have—even if I had been prosperous instead of ruined, I'd never have asked you, unless I came back whole from the war."

They had been walking out the lane during this conversation and had come close to the wheat field. The day was hot, but pleasant, the dry wind being laden with harvest odors. The hum of the machines was like the roar in a flour mill.

"If you go to war—and come back whole—?" began Lenore, tantalizingly. She meant to have no mercy upon him. It was incredible how blind he was. Yet how glad that made her. He resembled his desert hills, barren of many little things, but rich in hidden strength, heroic of mold.

"Then just to add one more to the conquests girls love I'll—I'll propose to you," he declared, banteringly.

"Beware, boy! I might accept you," she exclaimed.

His play was short-lived. He could not be gay, even under her influence.

"Please don't jest," he said, frowning. "Can't we talk of something besides love and war?"

"They seem to be popular just now," she replied, audaciously. "Anyway, all's fair—you know."

"No, it is not fair," he returned, low-voiced and earnest. "So once for all let me beg of you, don't jest. Oh, I know you're sweet. You're full of so many wonderful, surprising words and looks. I can't understand you....But I beg of you, don't make me a fool!"

"Well, if you pay such compliments and if I—want them—what then? You are very original, very gallant, Mr. Kurt Dorn, and I—I rather like you."

"I'll get angry with you," he threatened.

"You couldn't....I'm the only girl you're going to

leave behind—and if you got angry I'd never write to you."

It thrilled Lenore and wrung her heart to see how her talk affected him. He was in a torment. He believed she spoke lightly, girlishly, to tease him—that she was only a gay-hearted girl, fancy-free and just a little proud of her conquest over even him.

"I surrender. Say what you like," he said, resignedly. "I'll stand anything—just to get your letters."

"If you go I'll write as often as you want me to," she replied.

With that they emerged upon the harvest field. Machines and engines dotted the golden slope, and wherever they were located stood towering strawstacks. Horses and men and wagons were strung out as far as the eye could see. Long streams of chaff and dust and smoke drifted upward.

"Lenore, there's trouble in the very air," said Dorn. "Look!"

She saw a crowd of men gathering round one of the great combine-harvesters. Someone was yelling.

"Let's stay away from trouble," replied Lenore. "We've enough of our own."

"I'm going over there," declared Dorn. "Perhaps you'd better wait for me—or go back."

"Well! You're the first boy who ever—"

"Come on," he interrupted, with grim humor. "I'd rather enjoy your seeing me break loose—as I will if there's any I. W. W. trickery."

Before they got to the little crowd Lenore both heard and saw her father. He was in a rage and not aware of her presence. Jake and Bill, the cowboys, hovered over him. Anderson strode to and fro, from one

side of the harvester to the other. Lenore did not recognize any of the harvest hands, and even the driver
was new to her. They were not a typical western harvest
crew, that was certain. She did not like their sullen
looks, and Dorn's muttered imprecation, the moment
he neared them, confirmed her own opinion.

Anderson's foreman stood gesticulating, pale and
anxious of face.

"No, I don't hold you responsible," roared the
rancher. "But I want action. . . . I want to know why this
machine's broke down."

"It was in perfect workin' order," declared the foreman. "I don't know why it broke down."

"That's the fourth machine in two days. No accident, I tell you," shouted Anderson. Then he espied Dorn
and waved a grimy hand. "Come here, Dorn," he called,
and stepped out of the group of dusty men. "Somethin'
wrong here. This new harvester's broke down. It's a
McCormack an' new to us. But it has worked great an'
I jest believe it's been tampered with. . . . Do you know
these McCormack harvesters?"

"Yes. They're reliable," replied Dorn.

"Ah-huh! Wal, get your coat off an' see what's been
done to this one."

Dorn took off his coat and was about to throw it
down, when Lenore held out her hand for it.

"Unhitch the horses," said Dorn.

Anderson gave this order, which was complied
with. Then Dorn disappeared around or under the big
machine.

"Lenore, I'll bet he tells us somethin' in a minute,"
said Anderson to her. "These new claptraps are beyond
me. I'm no mechanic."

"Dad, I don't like the looks of your harvest hands," whispered Lenore.

"Wal, this is a sample of the lot I hired. No society for you, my lass!"

"I'm going to stay now," she replied.

Dorn appeared to be raising a racket somewhere out of sight under or inside the huge harvester. Rattling and rasping sounds, creaks and cracks, attested to his strong and impatiently seeking hands.

Presently he appeared. His white shirt had been soiled by dust and grease. There was chaff in his fair hair. In one grimy hand he held a large monkey wrench. What struck Lenore most was the piercing intensity of his gaze as he fixed it upon her father.

"Anderson, I knew right where to find it," he said, in a sharp, hard voice. "This monkey-wrench was thrown upon the platform, carried to the elevator into the thresher. . . . Your machine is torn to pieces inside—out of commission!"

"Ah-huh!"exclaimed Anderson, as if the truth was a great relief.

"Where'd that monkey wrench come from?" asked the foreman, aghast. "It's not ours. I don't buy that kind."

Anderson made a slight, significant motion to the cowboys. They lined up beside him, and, like him, they looked dangerous.

"Come here, Kurt," he said, and then, putting Lenore before him, he moved a few steps aside, out of earshot of the shifty-footed harvest hands. "Say, you called the turn right off, didn't you?"

"Anderson, I've had a hard experience, all in one harvest-time," replied Dorn. "I'll bet you I can find out who threw this wrench into your harvester."

"I don't doubt you, my lad. But how?"

"It had to be thrown by one of these men near the machine. That harvester hasn't run twenty feet from where the trick was done.... Let these men face me. I'll find the guilty one."

"Wait till we get Lenore out of the way," replied Anderson.

"Boss, me an' Bill can answer fer thet outfit as it stands, an' no risks fer nobody," put in Jake, coolly.

Anderson's reply was cut short by a loud explosion. It frightened Lenore. She imagined one of the steam engines had blown up.

"That thresher's on fire," shouted Dorn, pointing toward a big machine that was attached by an endless driving belt to an engine.

The workmen, uttering yells and exclamations, ran toward the scene of the new accident, leaving Anderson, his daughter, and the foreman behind. Smoke was pouring out of the big harvester. The harvest hands ran wildly around, shouting and calling, evidently unable to do anything. The line of wagons full of wheat sheaves broke up; men dragged at the plunging horses. Then flame followed the smoke out of the thresher.

"I've heard of threshers catchin' fire," said Anderson, as if dumfounded, "but I never seen one.... Now how on earth did that happen?"

"Another trick, Anderson," replied Dorn. "Some I. W. W. has stuffed a handful of matches into a wheat sheaf. Or maybe a small bomb!"

"Ah-huh!... Come on, let's go over an' see my money burn up.... Kurt, I'm gettin' some new education these days."

Dorn appeared to be unable to restrain himself. He

hurried on ahead of the others. And Anderson whispered to Lenore, "I'll bet somethin's comin' off!"

This alarmed Lenore, yet it also thrilled her.

The threshing machine burned like a house of cards. Farmhands came running from all over the field. But nothing, manifestly, could be done to save the thresher. Anderson, holding his daughter's arm, calmly watched it burn. There was excitement all around; it had not been communicated, however, to the rancher. He looked thoughtful. The foreman darted among the groups of watchers and his distress was very plain. Dorn had gotten out of sight. Lenore still held his coat and wondered what he was doing. She was thoroughly angry and marveled at her father's composure. The big thresher was reduced to a blazing, smoking hulk in short order.

Dorn came striding up. His face was pale and his mouth set.

"Mr. Anderson, you've got to make a strong stand—and quick," he said, deliberately.

"I reckon. An' I'm ready, if it's the right time," replied the rancher. "But what can we prove?"

"That's proof," declared Dorn, pointing at the ruined thresher. "Do you know all your honest hands?"

"Yes, an' I've got enough to clean up this outfit in no time. We're only waitin'."

"What for?"

"Wal, I reckon for what's just come off."

"Don't let them go any farther....Look at these fellows. Can't you tell the I. W. W.'s from the others?"

"No, I can't unless I count all the new harvest hands I. W. W.'s."

"Everyone you don't know here is in with that

gang," declared Dorn, and he waved a swift hand at the groups. His eyes swept piercingly over, and apparently through, the men nearest at hand.

At this juncture Jake and Bill, with two other cowboys, strode up to Anderson.

"Another accident, boss," said Jake, sarcastically. "Ain't it about time we corralled some of this outfit?"

Anderson did not reply. He had suddenly imitated Lenore, who had become solely bent upon Dorn's look. That indeed was cause for interest. It was directed at a member of the nearest group—a man in rough garb, with slouch hat pulled over his eyes. As Lenore looked she saw this man, suddenly becoming aware of Dorn's scrutiny, hastily turn and walk away.

"Hold on!" called Dorn, his voice a ringing command. It halted every moving person on that part of the field. Then Dorn actually bounded across the intervening space.

"Come on, boys," said Anderson, "get in this. Dorn's spotted someone, an' now that's all we want. . . . Lenore, stick close behind me. Jake, you keep near her."

They moved hastily to back up Dorn, who had already reached the workman he had halted. Anderson took out a whistle and blew such a shrill blast that it deafened Lenore, and must have been heard all over the harvest field. Not improbably that was a signal agreed upon between Anderson and his men. Lenore gathered that all had been in readiness for a concerted movement and that her father believed Dorn's action had brought the climax.

"Haven't I seen you before?" queried Dorn, sharply.

The man shook his head and kept it bent a little, and then he began to edge back nearer to the stragglers, who slowly closed into a group behind him. He seemed nervous, shifty.

"He can't speak English," spoke up one of them, gruffly.

Dorn looked aggressive and stern. Suddenly his hand flashed out to snatch off the slouch hat which hid the fellow's face. Amazingly, a gray wig came with it. This man was not old. He had fair thick hair.

For a moment Dorn gazed at the slouch hat and wig. Then with a fierce action he threw them down and swept a clutching hand for the man. The fellow dodged and, straightening up, he reached for a gun. But Dorn lunged upon him. Then followed a hard grappling sound and a hoarse yell. Something bright glinted in the sun. It made a sweeping circle, belched fire and smoke. The report stunned Lenore. She shut her eyes and clung to her father. She heard cries, a scuffling, sodden blows.

"Jake! Bill!" called Anderson. "Hold on! No gunplay yet! Dorn's makin' hash out of that fellow. . . . But watch the others sharp!"

Then Lenore looked again. Dorn had twisted the man around and was in the act of stripping off the further disguise of beard, disclosing the pale and convulsed face of a comparatively young man.

"*Glidden!*" burst out Dorn. His voice had a terrible ring of furious amaze. His whole body seemed to gather as in a knot and then to spring. The man called Glidden went down before that onslaught, and his gun went flying aside.

Three of Glidden's group started for it. The cowboy Bill leaped forward, a gun in each hand. "Hyar! . . . Back!" he yelled. And then all except the two struggling principals grew rigid.

Lenore's heart was burning in her throat. The movements of Dorn were too swift for her sight. But Glidden she saw handled as if by a giant. Up and down he seemed thrown, with bloody face, flinging arms, while he uttered hoarse bawls. Dorn's form grew more distinct. It plunged and swung in frenzied energy. Lenore heard men running and yells from all around. Her father spread wide his arm before her, so that she had to bend low to see. He shouted a warning. Jake was holding a gun thrust forward.

"Boss, he's goin' to kill Glidden!" said the cowboy, in a low tone.

Anderson's reply was incoherent, but its meaning was plain.

Lenore's lips and tongue almost denied her utterance. "Oh!...Don't let him!"

The crowd behind the wrestling couple swayed back and forth, and men changed places here and there. Bill strode across the space, guns leveled. Evidently this action was due to the threatening movements of several workmen who crouched as if to leap on Dorn as he whirled in his light with Glidden.

"Wal, it's about time!" yelled Anderson, as a number of lean, rangy men, rushing from behind, reached Bill's side, there to present an armed and threatening front.

All eyes now centered on Dorn and Glidden. Lenore, seeing clearly for the first time, suffered a strange, hot paroxysm of emotion never before experienced by her. It left her weak. It seemed to stultify the cry that had been trying to escape her. She wanted to scream that Dorn must not kill the man. Yet there was a ferocity in her that froze the cry. Glidden's coat and blouse were half torn off; blood covered him; he strained and flung himself weakly in that iron clutch. He was beaten and bent back. His tongue hung out, bloody, fluttering with strangled cries. A ghastly face, appalling in its fear of death!

Lenore broke her mute spell of mingled horror and passion.

"For God's sake, don't let Dorn kill him!" she implored.

"Why not?" muttered Anderson. "That's Glidden. He killed Dorn's father—burned his wheat—ruined him!"

"Dad—for *my*—sake!" she cried, brokenly.

"Jake, stop him!" yelled Anderson. "Pull him off!"

As Lenore saw it, with eyes again half failing her, Jake could not separate Dorn from his victim.

"Leggo, Dorn!" he yelled. "You're cheatin' the gallows! . . . Hey, Bill, he's a bull! . . . Help, hyar—quick!"

Lenore did not see the resulting conflict, but she could tell by something that swayed the crowd when Glidden had been freed.

"Hold up this outfit!" yelled Anderson to his men. "Come on, Jake, drag him along." Jake appeared, leading the disheveled and wild-eyed Dorn. "Son, you did my heart good, but there was some around here who didn't want you to spill blood. An' that's well. For I am seein' red. . . . Jake, you take Dorn an' Lenore a piece toward the house, then hurry back."

Then Lenore felt that she had hold of Dorn's arm and she was listening to Jake without understanding a word he said, while she did hear her father's yell of command, "Line up there, you I. W. W.'s!"

Jake walked so swiftly that Lenore had to run to

keep up. Dorn stumbled. He spoke incoherently. He tried to stop. At this Lenore clasped his arm and cried, "Oh, Kurt, come home with me!"

They hurried down the slope. Lenore kept looking back. The crowd appeared bunched now, with little motion. That relieved her. There was no more fighting.

Presently Dorn appeared to go more willingly. He had relaxed. "Let go, Jake," he said. "I'm—all right—now. That arm hurts."

"Wal, you'll excuse me, Dorn, for handlin' you rough....Mebbe you don't remember punchin' me one when I got between you an' Glidden?"

"Did I?...I couldn't see, Jake," said Dorn. His voice was weak and had a spent ring of passion in it. He did not look at Lenore, but kept his face turned toward the cowboy.

"I reckon this's fur enough," rejoined Jake, halting and looking back. "No one comin'. An' there'll be hell to pay out there. You go on to the house with Miss Lenore....Will you?"

"Yes," replied Dorn.

"Rustle along, then....An' you, Miss Lenore, don't you worry none about us."

Lenore nodded and, holding Dorn's arm closely, she walked as fast as she could down the lane.

"I—I kept your coat," she said, "though I never thought of it—till just now."

She was trembling all over, hot and cold by turns, afraid to look up at him, yet immensely proud of him, with a strange, sickening dread. He walked rather dejectedly now, or else bent somewhat from weakness. She stole a quick glance at his face. It was white as a sheet. Suddenly she felt something wet and warm trickle from his arm down into her hand. Blood! She shuddered, but did not lose her hold. After a faintish instant there came a change in her.

"Are you—hurt?" she asked.

"I guess—not. I don't know," he said.

"But the—the blood," she faltered.

He held up his hands. His knuckles were bloody and it was impossible to tell whether from injury to them or not. But his left forearm was badly cut.

"The gun cut me....And he bit me, too," said Dorn. "I'm sorry you were there....What a beastly·spectacle for you!"

"Never mind me," she murmured. "I'm all right *now!*...But, oh!—"

She broke off eloquently.

"Was it you who had the cowboys pull me off him? Jake said, as he broke me loose, 'For Miss Lenore's sake!'"

"It was Dad who sent them. But I begged him to."

"That was Glidden, the I. W. W. agitator and German agent....He—just the same as murdered my father....He burned my wheat—lost my all!"

"Yes, I—I know, Kurt," whispered Lenore.

"I meant to kill him!"

"That was easy to tell....Oh, thank God, you did not!...Come, don't let us stop." She could not face the piercing, gloomy eyes that went through her.

"Why should you care? ...Someone will have to kill Glidden."

"Oh, do not talk so," she implored. "Surely, now you're glad you did not?"

"I don't understand myself. But I'm certainly sorry you were there....There's a beast in men—in me!...I had a gun in my pocket. But do you think I'd have used it? ...I wanted to feel his flesh tear, his bones break, his blood spurt—"

"Kurt!"

"Yes! ...That was the Hun in me!" he declared, in sudden bitter passion.

"Oh, my friend, do not talk so!" she cried. "You make me—Oh, there is *no* Hun in you!"

"Yes, that's what ails me!"

"There is *not!*" she flashed back, roused to passion. "You had been made desperate. You acted as any wronged man! You fought. He tried to kill you. I saw the gun. No one could blame you....I had my own reason for begging Dad to keep you from killing him—a selfish woman's reason! ...But I tell you I was so furious—so wrought up—that if it had been any man but *you*—he should have killed him!"

"Lenore, you're beyond my understanding," replied Dorn, with emotion. "But I thank you—for excusing me—for standing up for me."

"It was nothing ...Oh, how you bleed! ...Doesn't that hurt?"

"I've no pain—no feeling at all—except a sort of dying down in me of what must have been hell."

They reached the house and went in. No one was there, which fact relieved Lenore.

"I'm glad Mother and the girls won't see you," she said, hurriedly. "Go up to your room. I'll bring bandages."

He complied without any comment. Lenore searched for what she needed to treat a wound and ran upstairs. Dorn was sitting on a chair in his room, holding his arm, from which blood dripped to the floor. He smiled at her.

"You would be a pretty Red Cross nurse," he said.

Lenore placed a bowl of water on the floor and, kneeling beside Dorn, took his arm and began to bathe it. He winced. The blood covered her fingers.

"My blood on your hands!" he exclaimed, morbidly. "German blood!"

"Kurt, you're out of your head," retorted Lenore, hotly. "If you dare to say that again I'll—" She broke off.

"What will you do?"

Lenore faltered. What would she do? A revelation must come, sooner or later, and the strain had begun to wear upon her. She was stirred to her depths, and instincts there were leaping. No sweet, gentle, kindly sympathy would avail with this tragic youth. He must be carried by storm. Something of the violence he had shown with Glidden seemed necessary to make him forget himself. All his whole soul must be set in one direction. He could not see that she loved him, when she had looked it, acted it, almost spoken it. His blindness was not to be endured.

"Kurt Dorn, don't dare to—to say that again!"

She ceased bathing his arm, and looked up at him suddenly quite pale.

"I apologize. I am only bitter," he said. "Don't mind what I say.... It's so good of you—to do this."

Then in silence Lenore dressed his wound, and if her heart did beat unwontedly, her fingers were steady and deft. He thanked her, with moody eyes seeing far beyond her.

"When I lie—over there—with—"

"If you go!" she interrupted. He was indeed hopeless. "I advise you to rest a little."

"I'd like to know what becomes of Glidden," he said.

"So should I. That worries me."

"Weren't there a lot of cowboys with guns?"

"So many that there's no need for you to go out—and start another fight."

"I did start it, didn't I?"

"You surely did." She left him then, turning in the doorway to ask him please to be quiet and let the day go by without seeking those excited men again. He smiled, but he did not promise.

For Lenore the time dragged between dread and suspense. From her window she saw a motley crowd pass down the lane to the main road. No harvesters were working. At the noon meal only her mother and the girls were present. Word had come that the I. W. W. men were being driven from "Many Waters." Mrs. Anderson worried, and Lenore's sisters for once were quiet. All afternoon the house was lifeless. No one came or left. Lenore listened to every little sound. It relieved her that Dorn had remained in his room. Her hope was that the threatened trouble had been averted, but something told her that the worst was yet to come.

It was nearly supper time when she heard the men returning. They came in a body, noisy and loitering, as if reluctant to break away from one another. She heard the horses tramp into the barns and the loud voices of drivers.

When she went downstairs she encountered her father. He looked impressive, triumphant! His effort at evasion did not deceive Lenore. But she realized at once that in this instance she could not get any news from him. He said everything was all right and that I. W. W. men were to be deported from Washington. But he did not want any supper, and he had a low-voiced, significant interview with Dorn. Lenore longed to know what was pending. Dorn's voice, when he said at his door, "Anderson, I'll go!" was ringing, hard, and deadly. It frightened Lenore. Go where? What were they going to do? Lenore thought of the vigilantes her father had organized. Then she looked around for Jake, but could not see him.

Supper time was an ordeal. Dorn ate a little; then excusing himself, he went back to his room. Lenore got through the meal somehow, and, going outside, she encountered Jake. The moment she questioned him she knew something extraordinary had taken place or was about to take place. She coaxed and entreated. For once Jake was hard to manage. But the more excuses he made, the more he evaded her, the greater became Lenore's need to know. And at last she wore the cowboy out. He could not resist her tears, which began to flow in spite of her.

"See hyar, Miss Lenore, I reckon you care a heap fer young Dorn—beggin' your pardon?" queried Jake.

"Care for him! . . . Jake, I love him."

"Then take a hunch from me an' keep him home—with you—tonight."

"Does Father want Kurt Dorn to go—wherever he's going?"

"Wal, I should smile! Your dad likes the way Dorn handles I. W. W.'s," replied Jake, significantly.

"Vigilantes!" whispered Lenore.

*L*ENORE waited for Kurt, and stood half con-
cealed behind the curtains. It had dawned upon
her that she had an ordeal at hand. Her heart
palpitated. She heard his quick step on the stairs. She
called before she showed herself.

"Hello! . . . Oh, but you startled me!" he exclaimed.
He had been surprised, too, at the abrupt meeting. Certainly he had not been thinking of her. His pale, determined face attested to stern and excitable thought.

He halted before her.

"Where are you going?" asked Lenore.

"To see your father."

"What about?"

"It's rather important," he replied, with hesitation.

"Will it take long?"

He showed embarrassment. "I—He—We'll be occupied 'most all evening."

"Indeed!...Very well. If you'd rather be—*occupied*—than spend the evening with me!" Lenore turned away, affecting a disdainful and hurt manner.

"Lenore, it's not that," he burst out. "I—I'd rather spend an evening with you than anybody else—or do anything."

"That's very easy to say, Mr. Dorn," she returned, lightly.

"But it's true," he protested.

"Come out of the hall. Father will hear us," she said, and led him into the room. It was not so light in there, but what light there was fell upon his face and left hers in shadow.

"I've made an—an appointment for tonight," he declared, with difficulty.

"Can't you break it?" she asked.

"No. That would lay me open to—to cowardice— perhaps your father's displeasure."

"Kurt Dorn, it's brave to give up some things! And if you go you'll incur *my* displeasure."

"Go!" he ejaculated, staring at her.

"Oh, I know!...And I'm—well, not flattered to see you'd rather go hang I. W. W.'s than stay here with me." Lenore did not feel the assurance and composure with which she spoke. She was struggling with her own feelings. She believed that just as soon as she and Kurt understood each other—faced each other without any dissimulation—then she would feel free and strong. If only she could put the situation on a sincere footing! She must work for that. Her difficulty was with a sense of falsity. There was no time to plan. She must change his mind.

Her words had made him start.

"Then you know?" he asked.

"Of course."

"I'm sorry for that," he replied, soberly, as he brushed a hand up through his wet hair.

"But you will stay home?"

"No," he returned, shortly, and he looked hard.

"Kurt, I don't want *you* mixed up with any lynching-bees," she said, earnestly.

"I'm a citizen of Washington. I'll join the vigilantes. I'm American. I've been ruined by these I. W. W.'s. No man in the West has lost so much! Father—home—land—my great harvest of wheat!...Why shouldn't I go?"

"There's no reason except—*me*," she replied, rather unsteadily.

He drew himself up, with a deep breath, as if fortifying himself. "That's a mighty good reason.... But you will be kinder if you withdraw your objections."

"Can't you conceive of any reason why I—I beg you not to go?"

"I can't," he replied, staring at her. It seemed that every moment he spent in her presence increased her effect upon him. Lenore felt this, and that buoyed up her failing courage.

"Kurt, you've made a very distressing—a terrible and horrible blunder," she said, with a desperation that must have seemed something else to him.

"My heavens! What have I done?" he gasped, his face growing paler. How ready he was to see more catastrophe! It warmed her heart and strengthened her nerve.

The moment had come. Even if she did lose her power of speech she still could show him what his blunder was. Nothing in all her life had ever been a hundredth part as hard as this. Yet, as the words formed, her whole heart seemed to be behind them, forcing them out. If only he did not misunderstand!

Then she looked directly at him and tried to speak. Her first attempt was inarticulate, her second was a whisper, "Didn't you ever—think I—I might care for you?"

It was as if a shock went over him, leaving him trembling. But he did not look as amazed as incredulous. "No, I certainly never did," he said.

"Well—that's your blunder—for I—I do. You—you never—never—asked me."

"You do what—care for me? . . . What on earth do you mean by that?"

Lenore was fighting many emotions now, the one most poignant being a wild desire to escape, which battled with an equally maddening one to hide her face on his breast. Yet she could see how white he had grown—how different. His hands worked convulsively and his eyes pierced her very soul.

"What should a girl mean—telling she cared?"

"I don't know. Girls are beyond me," he replied, stubbornly.

"Indeed that's true. I've felt so far beyond you—I had to come to this."

"Lenore," he burst out, hoarsely, "you talk in riddles! You've been so strange, yet so fine, so sweet! And now you say you care for me! . . . Care? . . . What does that mean? A word can drive me mad. But I never dared to hope. I love you—love you—love you—my God! you're all I've left to love. I—"

"Do you think you've a monopoly on all the love

in the world?" interrupted Lenore, coming to her real
self. His impassioned declaration was all she needed.
Her ordeal was over.

It seemed as if he could not believe his ears or
eyes.

"Monopoly! World!" he echoed. "Of course I don't.
But—"

"Kurt, I love you just as much as—as you love me.
...So there!"

Lenore had time for one look at his face before he
enveloped her. What a relief to hide her own! It was
pressed to his breast very closely. Her eyes shut, and
she felt hot tears under her lids. All before her darkened
sight seemed confusion, whirling chaos. It seemed that
she could not breathe and, strangely, did not need to.
How unutterably happy she felt! That was an age-long
moment—wonderful for her own relief and gladness—
full of changing emotions. Presently Kurt appeared to
be coming to some semblance of rationality. He released her from that crushing embrace, but still kept
an arm around her while he held her off and looked at
her.

"Lenore, will you kiss me?" he whispered.

She could have cried out in sheer delight at the
wonder of that whisper in her ear. It had been she who
had changed the world for Kurt Dorn.

"Yes—presently," she replied, with a tremulous little laugh. "Wait till—I get my breath—"

"I was beside myself—am so yet," he replied, low
voiced as if in awe. "I've been lifted to heaven....It
cannot be true. I believe it, yet I'll not be sure till you
kiss me....You—Lenore Anderson, the girl of my
dreams! Do you love me—is it true?"

"Yes, Kurt, indeed I do—very dearly," she replied, and turned to look up into his face. It was transfigured. Lenore's heart swelled as a deep and profound emotion waved over her.

"Please kiss me—then."

She lifted her face, flushing scarlet. Their lips met. Then with her head upon his shoulder and her hands closely held she answered the thousand and one questions of a bewildered and exalted lover who could not realize the truth. Lenore laughed at him and eloquently furnished proof of her own obsession, and told him how and why and when it all came about.

Not for hours did Kurt come back to actualities. "I forgot about the vigilantes," he exclaimed, suddenly. "It's too late now....How the time has flown!...Oh, Lenore, thought of other things breaks in, alas!"

He kissed her hand and got up. Another change was coming over him. Lenore had long expected the moment when realization would claim his attention. She was prepared.

"Yes, you forgot your appointment with Dad and the vigilantes. You've missed some excitement and violence."

His face had grown white again—grave now and troubled. "May I speak to your father?" he asked.

"Yes," she replied.

"If I come back from the war—well—not crippled—will you promise to marry me?"

"Kurt, I promise now."

That seemed to shake him. "But, Lenore, it is not fair to you. I don't believe a soldier should bind a girl by marriage or engagement before he goes to war. She should be free....I want you to be free."

"That's for you to say," she replied, softly. "But for my part, I don't want to be free—if you go away to war."

"If! . . . I'm going," he said, with a start. "You don't want to be free? Lenore, would you be engaged to me?"

"My dear boy, of course I would . . . It seems I am, doesn't it?" she replied, with one of her deep, low laughs.

He gazed at her, fascinated, worked upon by overwhelming emotions. "Would you marry me—before I go?"

"Yes," she flashed.

He bent and bowed then under the storm. Stumbling to her, almost on his knees, he brokenly expressed his gratitude, his wonder, his passion, and the terrible temptation that he must resist, which she must help him to resist.

"Kurt, I love you. I will see things through your eyes, if I must. I want to be a comfort to you, not a source of sorrow."

"But, Lenore, what comfort can I find? . . . To leave you now is going to be horrible! . . . To part from you now—I don't see how I can."

Then Lenore dared to broach the subject so delicate, so momentous.

"You need not part from me. My father has asked me to try to keep you home. He secured exemption for you. You are more needed here than at the front. You can feed many soldiers. You would be doing your duty—with honor! . . . You would be a soldier. The government is going to draft young men for farm duty. Why not you? There are many good reasons why you would be better than most young men. Because you know wheat. And wheat is to become the most important thing in the world. No one misjudges your loyalty.... And surely you see that the best service to your country is what you can do best."

He sat down beside her, with serious frown and somber eyes. "Lenore, are you asking me not to go to war?"

"Yes, I am," she replied. "I have thought it all over. I've given up my brother. I'd not ask you to stay home if you were needed at the front as much as here. That question I have had out with my conscience.... Kurt, don't think me a silly, sentimental girl. Events of late have made me a woman."

He buried his face in his hands. "That's the most amazing of all—you—Lenore Anderson, my American girl—asking me not to go to war."

"But, dear, it is not so amazing. It's reasonable. Your peculiar point of view makes it look different. I am no weak, timid, lovesick girl afraid to let you go!...I've given you good, honorable, patriotic reasons for your exemption from draft. Can you see that?"

"Yes. I grant all your claims. I know wheat well enough to tell you that if vastly more wheat raising is not done the world will starve. That would hold good for the United States in forty years without war."

"Then if you see my point why are you opposed to it?" she asked.

"Because I am Kurt Dorn," he replied, bitterly.

His tone, his gloom made her shiver. It would take all her intelligence and wit and reason to understand him, and vastly more than that to change him. She thought earnestly. This was to be an ordeal profoundly more difficult than the confession of her love. It was indeed a crisis dwarfing the other she had met. She sensed in him a remarkably strange attitude toward this war, compared with that of her brother or other boys she knew who had gone.

"Because you are Kurt Dorn," she said, thoughtfully. "It's in the name, then.... But I think it a pretty name—a good name. Have I not consented to accept it as mine—for life?"

He could not answer that. Blindly he reached out with a shaking hand, to find hers, to hold it close. Lenore felt the tumult in him. She was shocked. A great tenderness, sweet and motherly, flooded over her.

"Dearest, in this dark hour—that was so bright a little while ago—you must not keep anything from me," she replied. "I will be true to you. I will crush my selfish hopes. I will be your mother ... Tell me why you must go to war because you are Kurt Dorn."

"My father was German. He hated this country— yours and mine. He plotted with the I. W. W. He hated your father and wanted to destroy him.... Before he died he realized his crime. For so I take the few words he spoke to Jerry. But all the same he was a traitor to my country. I bear his name. I have German in me.... And by God I'm going to pay!"

His deep, passionate tones struck into Lenore's heart. She fought with a rising terror. She was beginning to understand him. How helpless she felt—how she prayed for inspiration—for wisdom!

"Pay! ... How?" she asked.

"In the only way possible. I'll see that a Dorn goes to war—who will show his American blood—who will fight and kill—and be killed!"

His passion, then, was more than patriotism. It had its springs in the very core of his being. He had, it seemed, a debt that he must pay. But there was more than this in his grim determination. And Lenore divined that it lay hidden in his bitter reference to his German blood. He hated that—doubted himself because of it. She realized now that to keep him from going to war would be to make him doubt his manhood and eventually to despise himself. No longer could she think of persuading him to stay home. She must forget herself. She knew then that she had the power to keep him and she could use it, but she must not do so. This tragic thing was a matter of his soul. But if he went to war with this bitter obsession, with this wrong motive, this passionate desire to spill blood in him that he hated, he would lose his soul. He must be changed. All her love, all her woman's flashing, subtle thought concentrated on this fact. How strange the choice that had been given her! Not only must she relinquish her hope of keeping him home, but she must perhaps go to desperate ends to send him away with a changed spirit. The moment of decision was agony for her.

"Kurt, this is a terrible hour for both of us," she said, "but, thank Heaven, you have confessed to me. Now I will confess to you."

"Confess? . . . You? . . . What nonsense!" he exclaimed. But in his surprise he lifted his head from his hands to look at her.

"When we came in here my mind was made up to make you stay home. Father begged me to do it, and I had my own selfish motive. It was love. Oh, I do love you, Kurt, more than you can dream of! . . . I justified my resolve. I told you that. But I wanted you. I wanted your love—your presence. I longed for a home with you as husband—master—father to my babies. I dreamed of all. It filled me with terror to think of you going to war. You might be crippled—mangled—murdered....Oh, my dear, I could not bear the thought!...So I meant to overcome you. I had it all planned. I meant to love you— to beg you—to kiss you—to make you stay—"

"Lenore, what are you saying?" he cried, in shocked amaze.

She flung her arms around his neck. "Oh, I could— I could have kept you!" she answered, low voiced and triumphant. "It fills me with joy....Tell me I could have kept you—tell me."

"Yes, I've no power.to resist you. But I might have hated—"

"Hush!...It's all might have...I've risen above myself."

"Lenore, you distress me. A little while ago you bewildered me with your sweetness and love...Now— you look like an angel or a goddess....Oh, to have your face like this—always with me! Yet it distresses me— so terrible in purpose. What are you about to tell me? I see something—"

"Listen," she broke in. "I meant to make you weak. I implore you now to be strong. You must go to war! But with all my heart and soul I beg you to go with a changed spirit....You were about to do a terrible thing. You hated the German in you and meant to kill it by violence. You despised the German blood and you meant to spill it. Like a wild man you would have rushed to fight, to stab and beat, to murder—and you would have left your breast open for a bayonet thrust....Oh, I know it!...Kurt, you are horribly wrong. That is no way to go to war....War is a terrible business, but men don't wage it for motives such as yours. We Americans

all have different strains of blood—English—French—
German. One is as good as another. You are obsessed—
you are out of your head on this German question. You
must kill that idea—kill it with one bayonet thrust of
sense. . . . You must go to war as my soldier—with my
ideal. Your country had called you to help uphold its
honor, its pledged word. You must fight to conquer an
enemy who threatens to destroy freedom. . . . You must
be brave, faithful, merciful, clean—an American soldier!
. . . You are only one of a million. You have no personal
need for war. You are as good, as fine, as noble as any
man—my choice, sir, of all the men in the world! . . . I
am sending you. I am giving you up. . . . Oh, my darling—
you will never know how hard it is! . . . But go! Your life
has been sad. You have lost so much. I feel in my woman's heart what will be—if only you'll change—if you
see God in this as I see. Promise me. Love that which
you hated. Prove for yourself what I believe. Trust me—
promise me. . . . Then—oh, I know God will send you
back to me!"

He fell upon his knees before her to bury his face
in her lap. His whole frame shook. His hands plucked
at her dress. A low sob escaped him.

"Lenore," he whispered, brokenly, "I can't see God
in this—for me! . . . I can't promise!"

CHAPTER
21

*T*HIRTY masked men sat around a long harvest mess table. Two lanterns furnished light enough to show a bare barnlike structure, the rough-garbed plotters, the grim set of hard lips below the half masks, and big hands spread out, ready to draw from the hat that was passing.

The talk was low and serious. No names were spoken. A heavy man, at the head of the table, said: "We thirty, picked men, represent the country. Let each member here write on his slip of paper his choice of punishment for the I. W. W.'s—death or deportation...."

The members of the band bent their masked faces and wrote in a dead silence. A noiseless wind blew through the place. The lanterns flickered; huge shadows moved on the walls. When the papers had been passed back to the leader he read them.

"Deportation," he announced. "So much for the

I. W. W. men....Now for the leader....But before we vote on what to do with Glidden let me read an extract from one of his speeches. This is authentic. It has been furnished by the detective lately active in our interest. Also it has been published. I read it because I want to bring home to you all an issue that goes beyond our own personal fortunes here."

Leaning toward the flickering flare of the lantern, the leader read from a slip of paper: "If the militia are sent out here to hinder the I. W. W. we will make it so damned hot for the government that no troops will be able to go to France....I don't give a damn what this country is fighting for....I am fighting for the rights of labor....American soldiers are Uncle Sam's scabs in disguise."

The deep, impressive voice ended. The leader's huge fist descended upon the table with a crash. He gazed up and down the rows of sinister masked figures. "Have you anything to say?"

"No," replied one.

"Pass the slips," said another.

And then a man, evidently on in years, for his hair was gray and he looked bent, got up. "Neighbors," he began, "I lived here in the early days. For the last few years I've been apologizing for my hometown. I don't want to apologize for it any longer."

He sat down. And a current seemed to wave from him around that dark square of figures. The leader cleared his throat as if he had much to say, but he did not speak. Instead he passed the hat. Each man drew forth a slip of paper and wrote upon it. The action was not slow. Presently the hat returned round the table to the leader. He spilled its contents, and with steady hand picked up the first slip of paper.

"Death!" he read, sonorously, and laid it down to pick up another. Again he spoke that grim word. The third brought forth the same, and likewise the next, and all, until the verdict had been called out thirty times.

"At daylight we'll meet," boomed out that heavy voice. "Instruct Glidden's guards to make a show of resistance.... We'll hang Glidden to the railroad bridge. Then each of you get your gangs together. Round up all the I. W. W.'s. Drive them to the railroad yard. There we'll put them aboard a railroad train of empty cars. And that train will pass under the bridge where Glidden will be hanging.... We'll escort them out of the country."

That August dawn was gray and cool, with gold and pink beginning to break over the dark eastern ranges. The town had not yet awakened. It slept unaware of the stealthy forms passing down the gray road and of the distant hum of motorcars and trot of hoofs.

Glidden's place of confinement was a square warehouse, near the edge of town. Before the improvised jail guards paced up and down, strangely alert.

Daylight had just cleared away the gray when a crowd of masked men appeared as if by magic and bore down upon the guards. There was an apparent desperate resistance, but, significantly, no cries or shots. The guards were overpowered and bound.

The door of the jail yielded to heavy blows of an ax. In the corner of a dim, bare room groveled Glidden, bound so that he had little use of his body. But he was terribly awake. When six men entered he asked, hoarsely: "What're you—after? . . . What—you mean?"

They jerked him erect. They cut the bonds from his legs. They dragged him out into the light of breaking day.

When he saw the masked and armed force he cried: "My God! ... What'll you—do with me?"

Ghastly, working, sweating, his face betrayed his terror.

"You're to be hanged by the neck," spoke a heavy, solemn voice.

The man would have collapsed but for the strong hands that upheld him.

"What—for?" he gasped.

"For I. W. W. crimes—for treason—for speeches no American can stand in days like these." Then this deep-voiced man read to Glidden words of his own.

"Do you recognize that?"

Glidden saw how he had spoken his own doom. "Yes, I said that," he had nerve left to say. "But—I insist on arrest—trial—justice! ... I'm no criminal.... I've big interests behind me.... You'll suffer—"

A loop of a lasso, slung over his head and jerked tight, choked off his intelligible utterance. But as the silent, ruthless men dragged him away he gave vent to terrible, half-strangled cries.

The sun rose red over the fertile valley—over the harvest fields and the pastures and the orchards, and over the many towns that appeared lost in the green and gold luxuriance.

In the harvest districts west of the river all the towns were visited by swift-flying motorcars that halted long enough for a warning to be shouted to the citizens, "Keep off the streets!"

Simultaneously armed forces of men, on foot and

on horseback, too numerous to count, appeared in the roads and the harvest fields.

They accosted every man they met. If he were recognized or gave proof of an honest identity he was allowed to go; otherwise he was marched along under arrest. These armed forces were thorough in their search, and in the country districts they had an especial interest in likely camping places, and around old barns and straw stacks. In the towns they searched every corner that was big enough to hide a man.

So it happened that many motley groups of men were driven toward the railroad line, where they were held until a freight train of empty cattle cars came along. This train halted long enough to have the I. W. W. contingent driven aboard, with its special armed guard following, and then it proceeded on to the next station. As stations were many, so were the halts, and news of the train with its strange freight flashed ahead. Crowds lined the railroad tracks. Many boys and men in these crowds carried rifles and pistols which they leveled at the I. W. W. prisoners as the train passed. Jeers and taunts and threats accompanied this presentation of guns.

Before the last station of that wheat district was reached full three hundred members of the I. W. W., or otherwise suspicious characters, were packed into the open cars. At the last stop the number was greatly augmented, and the armed forces were cut down to the few guards who were to see the I. W. W. deported from the country. Here provisions and drinking water were put into the cars. And amid a hurrahing roar of thousands the train with its strange load slowly pulled out.

It did not at once gather headway. The engine whistled a prolonged blast—a signal or warning not lost on many of its passengers.

From the front cars rose shrill cries that alarmed the prisoners in the rear. The reason soon became manifest. Arms pointed and eyes stared at the figure of a man hanging from a rope fastened to the center of a high bridge span under which the engine was about to pass.

The figure swayed in the wind. It turned halfway round, disclosing a ghastly, distorted face, and a huge printed placard on the breast, then it turned back again. Slowly the engine drew one carload after another past the suspended body of the dead man. There were no more cries. All were silent in that slow-moving train. All faces were pale, all eyes transfixed.

The placard on the hanged man's breast bore in glaring red a strange message: *Last warning. 3–7–77.*

The figures were the ones used in the frontier days by vigilantes.

22

A DUSTY motorcar climbed the long road leading up to the Neuman ranch. It was not far from Wade, a small hamlet of the wheat growing section, and the slopes of the hills, bare and yellow with waving grain, bore some semblance to the Bend country. Four men—a driver and three cowboys—were in the automobile.

A big stone gate marked the entrance to Neuman's ranch. Cars and vehicles lined the roadside. Men were passing in and out. Neuman's home was unpretentious, but his barns and granaries and stock houses were built on a large scale.

"Bill, are you goin' in with me after this pard of the Kaiser's?" inquired Jake, leisurely stretching himself as the car halted. He opened the door and stiffly got out. "Gimme a hoss any day fer gittin' places!"

"Jake, my regard fer your rep as Anderson's foreman makes me want to hug the background," replied Bill. "I've done a hell of a lot these last forty-eight hours."

"Wal, I reckon you have, Bill, an' no mistake. . . . But I was figgerin' on you wantin' to see the fun."

"Fun! . . . Jake, it'll be fun enough fer me to sit hyar an' smoke in the shade, an' watch fer you to come a-runnin' from thet big German devil. . . . Pard, they say he's a bad man!"

"Sure. I know thet. All them Germans is bad."

"If the boss hadn't been so doggone strict about gunplay I'd love to go with you," responded Bill. "But he didn't give me no orders. You're the whole outfit this roundup."

"Bill, you'd have to take orders from me," said Jake, coolly.

"Sure. Thet's why I come with Andy."

The other cowboy, called Andy, manifested uneasiness, and he said: "Aw, now, Jake, you ain't a-goin' to ask me to go in there? . . . An' me hatin' Germans the way I do!"

"Nope. I guess I'll order Bill to go in an' fetch Neuman out," replied Jake, complacently, as he made as if to reenter the car.

Bill collapsed in his seat. "Jake," he expostulated, weakly, "this job was given you because of your rep fer deploomacy. . . . Sure I haven't none of thet . . . An' you, Jake, why you're the smoothest an' slickest talker thet ever come to the Northwest."

Evidently Jake had a vulnerable point. He straightened up with a little swagger. "Wal, you watch me," he said. "I'll fetch the big Dutchman eatin' out of my hand.

...An' say, when we git him in the car an' start back let's scare the daylights out of him."

"Thet'd be powerful fine. But how?"

"You fellers take a hunch from me," replied Jake. And he strode off up the lane toward the ranch house.

Jake had been commissioned to acquaint Neuman with the fact that recent developments demanded his immediate presence at "Many Waters." The cowboy really had a liking for the job, though he pretended not to.

Neuman had not yet begun harvesting. There were signs to Jake's experienced eye that the harvest hands were expected this very day. Jake fancied he knew why the rancher had put off his harvesting. And also he knew that the extra force of harvest hands would not appear. He was regarded with curiosity by the women members of the Neuman household, and rather enjoyed it. There were several comely girls in evidence. Jake did not look a typical Northwest foreman and laborer. Booted and spurred, with his gun swinging visibly, and his big sombrero and gaudy scarf, he looked exactly what he was, a cowman of the open ranges.

His inquiries elicited the fact that Neuman was out in the fields, waiting for the harvest hands.

"Wal, if he's expectin' thet outfit of I. W. W.'s he'll never harvest," said Jake, "for some of them is hanging! an' the rest run out of the country."

Jake did not wait to see the effect of his news. He strode back toward the fields, and with the eye of a farmer he appraised the barns and corrals, and the fields beyond. Neuman raised much wheat, and enough alfalfa to feed his stock. His place was large and valuable, but not comparable to "Many Waters."

Out in the wheat fields were engines with steam already up, with combines and threshers and wagons waiting for the word to start. Jake enjoyed the keen curiosity roused by his approach. Neuman strode out from a group of waiting men. He was huge of build, ruddy-faced and bearded, with deep-set eyes.

"Are you Neuman?" inquired Jake.

"That's me," gruffly came the reply.

"I'm Anderson's foreman. I've been sent over to tell you thet you're wanted pretty bad at 'Many Waters.'"

The man stared incredulously. "What?...Who wants me?"

"Anderson. An' I reckon there's more—though I ain't informed."

Neuman rumbled a curse. Amaze dominated him.

"Anderson!...Well, I don't want to see him," he replied.

"I reckon you don't," was the cowboy's cool reply.

The rancher looked him up and down. However familiar his type was to Anderson, it was strange to Neuman. The cowboy breathed a potential force. The least significant thing about his appearance was that swinging gun. He seemed cool and easy, with hard, keen eyes. Neuman's face took a shade off color.

"But I'm going to harvest today," he said. "I'm late. I've a hundred hands coming."

"Nope. You haven't none comin'," asserted Jake.

"What!" ejaculated Neuman.

"Reckon it's near ten o'clock," said the cowboy. "We run over here powerful fast."

"Yes, it's near ten," bellowed Neuman, on the verge of a rage.... "I haven't harvest hands coming!...What's this talk?"

"Wal, about nine-thirty I seen all your damned I. W. W.'s except what was shot an' hanged, loaded in a cattle car an' started out of the country."

A blow could not have hit harder than the cowboy's biting speech. Astonishment and fear shook Neuman before he recovered control of himself.

"If it's true, what's that to me?" he bluffed, in hoarse accents.

"Neuman, I didn't come to answer questions," said the cowboy, curtly. "My boss jest sent me fer you, an' if you bucked on comin', then I was to say it was your only chance to avoid publicity an' bein' run out of the country."

Neuman was livid of face now and shaking all over his huge frame.

"Anderson threatens me!" he shouted. "Anderson suspicions me!...*Gott in Himmel!*...Me he always cheated! An' now he insults—"

"Say, it ain't healthy to talk like thet about my boss," interrupted Jake, forcibly. "An' we're wastin' time. If you don't go with me we'll be comin' back—the whole outfit of us!...Anderson means you're to face his man!"

"What man?"

"Dorn. Young Dorn, son of old Chris Dorn of the Bend....Dorn has some things to tell you thet you won't want made public....Anderson's givin' you a square deal. If it wasn't fer thet I'd sling my gun on you!...Do you git my hunch?"

The name of Dorn made a slack figure of the aggressive Neuman.

"All right—I go," he said, gruffly, and without a word to his men he started off.

Jake followed him. Neuman made a short cut to

the gate, thus avoiding a meeting with any of his family. At the road, however, some men observed him and called in surprise, but he waved them back.

"Bill, you an' Andy collect yourself an' give Mr. Neuman a seat," said Jake, as he opened the door to allow the farmer to enter.

The two cowboys gave Neuman the whole of the back seat, and they occupied the smaller side seats. Jake took his place beside the driver.

"Burn her up!" was his order.

The speed of the car made conversation impossible until the limits of a town necessitated slowing down. Then the cowboys talked. For all the attention they paid to Neuman, he might as well not have been present. Before long the driver turned into a road that followed a railroad track for several miles and then crossed it to enter a good-sized town. The streets were crowded with people and the car had to be driven slowly. At this juncture Jake suggested:

"Let's go down by the bridge."

"Sure," agreed his allies.

Then the driver turned down a still more peopled street that sloped a little and evidently overlooked the railroad tracks. Presently they came in sight of a railroad bridge, around which there appeared to be an excited yet awestruck throng. All faces were turned up toward the swaying form of a man hanging by a rope tied to the high span of the bridge.

"Wal, Glidden's hangin' there yet," remarked Jake, cheerfully.

With a violent start Neuman looked out to see the ghastly placarded figure, and then he sank slowly back in his seat. The cowboys apparently took no notice of him. They seemed to have forgotten his presence.

"Funny they'd cut all the other I. W. W.'s down an' leave Glidden hangin' there," observed Bill.

"Them vigilantes sure did it up brown," added Andy. "I was dyin' to join the band. But they didn't ask me."

"Nor me," replied Jake, regretfully. "An' I can't understand why, onless it was they was afeared I couldn't keep a secret."

"Who is them vigilantes, anyhow?" asked Bill, curiously.

"Wal, I reckon nobody knows. But I seen a thousand armed men this mornin'. They sure looked bad. You ought to have seen them poke the I. W. W.'s with cocked guns."

"Was anyone shot?" queried Andy.

"Not in the daytime. Nobody killed by this Citizens' Protective League, as they call themselves. They just rounded up all the suspicious men an' herded them on to thet cattle train an' carried them off. It was at night when the vigilantes worked—masked an' secret an' sure bloody. Jest like the old vigilante days! . . . An' you can gamble they ain't through yet."

"Uncle Sam won't need to send any soldiers here."

"Wal, I should smile not. Thet'd be a disgrace to the Northwest. It was a bad time fer the I. W. W. to try any tricks on us."

Jake shook his lean head and his jaw bulged. He might have been haranguing, cowboy like, for the benefit of the man they feigned not to notice, but it was plain, nevertheless, that he was angry.

"What gits me wuss 'n them I. W. W.'s is the skunks thet give Uncle Sam the double-cross," said Andy, with dark face. "I'll stand fer any man an' respect him if he's aboveboard an' makes his fight in the open. But them coyotes thet live off the land an' pretend to be American when they ain't—they make me pisen mad."

"I heerd the vigilantes has marked men like thet," observed Bill.

"I'll give you a hunch, fellers," replied Jake, grimly. "By Gawd! the West won't stand fer traitors!"

All the way to "Many Waters," where it was possible to talk and be heard, the cowboys continued in like strain. And not until the driver halted the car before Anderson's door did they manifest any awareness of Neuman.

"Git out an' come in," said Jake to the pallid, sweating rancher.

He led Neuman into the hall and knocked upon Anderson's study door. It was opened by Dorn.

"Wal, hyar we are," announced Jake, and his very nonchalance attested to pride.

Anderson was standing beside his desk. He started, and his hand flashed back significantly as he sighted his rival and enemy.

"No gunplay, boss, was your orders," said Jake. "An' Neuman ain't packin' no gun."

It was plain that Anderson made a great effort at restraint. But he failed. And perhaps the realization that he could not kill this man liberated his passion. Then the two big ranchers faced each other—Neuman livid and shaking, Anderson black as a thundercloud.

"Neuman, you hatched up a plot with Glidden to kill me," said Anderson, bitterly.

Neuman, in hoarse, brief answer, denied it.

"Sure! Deny it. What do we care? ...We've got you,

Neuman," burst out Anderson, his heavy voice ringing with passion. "But it's not your low-down plot thet's riled me. There's been a good many men who've tried to do away with me. I've outplayed you in many a deal. So your personal hate for me doesn't count. I'm sore— an' you an' me can't live in the same place, because you're a damned traitor. You've lived here for twenty years. You've grown rich off the country. An' you'd sell us to your rotten Germany. What I think of you for that I'm goin' to tell you."

Anderson paused to take a deep breath. Then he began to curse Neuman. All the rough years of his frontier life, as well as the quieter ones of his ranching days, found expression in the swift, thunderous roll of his terrible scorn. Every vile name that had ever been used by cowboy, outlaw, gambler, leaped to Anderson's stinging tongue. All the keen, hard epithets common to the modern day he flung into Neuman's face. And he ended with a profanity that was as individual in character as its delivery was intense.

"I'm callin' you for my own relief," he concluded, "an' not that I expect to get under your hide."

Then he paused. He wiped the beaded drops from his forehead, and he coughed and shook himself. His big fists unclosed. Passion gave place to dignity.

"Neuman, it's a pity you an' men like you can't see the truth. That's the mystery to me—why anyone who had spent half a lifetime an' prospered here in our happy an' beautiful country could ever hate it. I never will understand that. But I do understand that America will never harbor such men for long. You have your reasons, I reckon. An' no doubt you think you're justified. That's the tragedy. You run off from hard-ruled Germany. You

will not live there of your own choice. You succeed here
an' live here in peace an' plenty....An', by God! you
take up with a lot of foreign riffraff an' double-cross the
people you owe so much!...What's wrong with your
mind? ...Think it over....An' that's the last word I have
for you."

Anderson, turning to his desk, took up a cigar and
lighted it. He was calm again. There was really sadness
where his face had shown only fury. Then he addressed
Dorn.

"Kurt, it's up to you now," he said. "As my super-
intendent an' someday partner, what you'll say goes
with me....I don't know what bein' square would mean
in relation to this man."

Anderson sat down heavily in his desk chair and
his face became obscured in cigar smoke.

"Neuman, do you recognize me?" asked Dorn, with
his flashing eyes on the rancher.

"No," replied Neuman.

"I'm Chris Dorn's son. My father died a few days
ago. He overtaxed his heart fighting fire in the wheat.
...Fire set by I. W. W. men.- Glidden's men!...They
burned our wheat. Ruined us!"

Neuman showed shock at the news, at the sudden
death of an old friend, but he did not express himself
in words.

"Do you deny implication in Glidden's plot to kill
Anderson?" demanded Dorn.

"Yes," replied Neuman.

"Well, you're a liar!" retorted Dorn. "I saw you with
Glidden and my father. I followed you at Wheatly—out
along the railroad tracks. I slipped up and heard the

plot. It was I who snatched the money from my father."

Neuman's nerve was gone, but with his stupid and stubborn process of thought he still denied, stuttering incoherently.

"Glidden has been hanged," went on Dorn. "A vigilante band has been organized here in the valley. Men of your known sympathy will not be safe, irrespective of your plot against Anderson. But as to that, publicity alone will be enough to ruin you.... Americans of the West will not tolerate traitors.... Now the question you've got to decide is this. Will you take the risks or will you sell out and leave the country?"

"I'll sell out," replied Neuman.

"What price do you put on your ranch as it stands?"

"One hundred thousand dollars."

Dorn turned to Anderson and asked, "Is it worth that much?"

"No. Seventy-five thousand would be a big price," replied the rancher.

"Neuman, we will give you seventy-five thousand for your holdings. Do you accept?"

"I have no choice," replied Neuman, sullenly.

"Choice!" exclaimed Dorn. "Yes, you have. And you're not being cheated. I've stated facts. You are done in this valley. You're ruined *now!* And Glidden's fate stares you in the face.... Will you sell and leave the country?"

"Yes," came the deep reply, wrenched from a stubborn breast.

"Go draw up your deeds, then notify us," said Dorn, with finality.

Jake opened the door. Stolidly and slowly Neuman went out, precisely as he had entered, like a huge man in conflict with unintelligible thoughts.

"Send him home in the car," called Anderson.

CHAPTER

23

*F*OR two fleeting days Lenore Anderson was happy when she forgot, miserable when she remembered. Then the third morning dawned.

At the breakfast table her father had said, cheerily, to Dorn: "Better take off your coat an' come out to the fields. We've got some job to harvest that wheat with only half force. . . . But, by George! my trouble's over."

Dorn looked suddenly blank, as if Anderson's cheery words had recalled him to the realities of life. He made an incoherent excuse and left the table.

"Ah-huh!" Anderson's characteristic exclamation might have meant little or much. "Lenore, what ails the boy?"

"Nothing that I know of. He has been as—as happy as I am," she replied.

"Then it's all settled?"

"Father, I—I—"

Kathleen's high, shrill, gleeful voice cut in: "Sure it's settled! Look at Lenorry blush!"

Lenore indeed felt the blood stinging face and neck. Nevertheless, she laughed.

"Come into my room," said Anderson.

She followed him there, and as he closed the door she answered his questioning look by running into his arms and hiding her face.

"Wal, I'll be doggoned!" the rancher ejaculated, with emotion. He held her and patted her shoulder with his big hand. "Tell me, Lenore."

"There's little to tell," she replied, softly. "I love him—and he loves me so—so well that I've been madly happy—in spite of—of—"

"Is that all?" asked Anderson, dubiously.

"Is not that enough?"

"But Dorn's lovin' you so well doesn't say he'll not go to war."

And it was then that forgotten bitterness returned to poison Lenore's cup of joy.

"Ah!" ... she whispered.

"Good Lord! Lenore, you don't mean you an' Dorn have been alone all the time these few days—an' you haven't settled that war question?" queried Anderson, in amaze.

"Yes.... How strange! ... But since—well, since something happened—we—we forgot," she replied, dreamily.

"Wal, go back to it," said Anderson, forcibly. "I want Dorn to help me.... Why, he's a wonder! ... He's saved the situation for us here in the valley. Every rancher I know is praisin' him high. An' he sure treated Neuman square. An' here I am with three big wheat ranches on my hands! . . . Lenore, you've got to keep him home."

"Dad! . . . I—I could not!" replied Lenore. She was strangely realizing an indefinable change in herself. "I can't try to keep him from going to war. I never thought of that since—since we confessed our love. . . . But it's made some difference. . . . It'll kill me, I think, to let him go—but I'd die before I'd ask him to stay home."

"Ah-huh!" sighed Anderson, and, releasing her, he began to pace the room. "I don't begin to understand you, girl. But I respect your feelin's. It's a hell of a muddle! . . . I'd forgotten the war myself while chasin' off them I. W. W.'s. . . . But this war has *got* to be reckoned with! . . . Send Dorn to me!"

Lenore found Dorn playing with Kathleen. These two had become as brother and sister.

"Kurt, Dad wants to see you," said Lenore seriously.

Dorn looked startled, and the light of fun on his face changed to a sober concern.

"You told him?"

"Yes, Kurt, I told him what little I had to tell."

He gave her a strange glance and then slowly went toward her father's study. Lenore made a futile attempt to be patient. She heard her father's deep voice, full and earnest, and she heard Dorn's quick, passionate response. She wondered what this interview meant. Anderson was not one to give up easily. He had set his heart upon holding this capable young man in the great interests of the wheat business. Lenore could not understand why she was not praying that he be successful. But she was not. It was inexplicable and puzzling—this change in her—this end of her selfishness. Yet she shrank in terror from an impinging sacrifice. She thrust the thought from her with passionate physical gesture and with stern effort of will.

Dorn was closeted with her father for over an hour. When he came out he was white, but apparently composed. Lenore had never seen his eyes so piercing as when they rested upon her.

"Whew!" he exclaimed, and wiped his face. "Your father has my poor old dad—what does Kathleen say?—skinned to a frazzle!"

"What did he say?" asked Lenore, anxiously.

"A lot—and just as if I didn't know it all better than he knows," replied Dorn, sadly. "The importance of wheat; his three ranches and nobody to run them; his growing years; my future and a great opportunity as one of the big wheat men of the Northwest; the present need of the government; his only son gone to war, which was enough for his family....And then he spoke of you—heiress to 'Many Waters'—what a splendid, noble girl you were—like your mother! What a shame to ruin your happiness—your future!...He said you'd make the sweetest of wives—the truest of mothers!...Oh, my God!"

Lenore turned away her face, shocked to her heart by his tragic passion. Dorn was silent for what seemed a long time.

"And—then he cussed me—hard—as no doubt I deserved," added Dorn.

"But—what did you say?" she whispered.

"I said a lot, too," replied Dorn, remorsefully.

"Did—did you—?" began Lenore, and broke off, unable to finish.

"I arrived—to where I am now—pretty dizzy," he responded, with a smile that was both radiant and sorrowful. He took her hands and held them close. "Lenore! ...if I come home from the war—still with my arms and legs—whole—will you marry me?"

"Only come home *alive,* and no matter what you lose, yes!—yes!" she whispered, brokenly.

"But it's a conditional proposal, Lenore," he insisted. "You must never marry half a man."

"I will marry *you!*" she cried, passionately.

It seemed to her that she loved him all the more, every moment, even though he made it so hard for her. Then through blurred, dim eyes she saw him take something from his pocket and felt him put a ring on her finger.

"It fits! Isn't that lucky," he said, softly. "My mother's ring, Lenore...."

He kissed her hand.

Kathleen was standing near them, open-eyed and open-mouthed, in an ecstasy of realization.

"Kathleen, your sister has promised to marry me—when I come from the war," said Dorn to the child.

She squealed with delight, and, manifestly surrendering to a long-considered temptation, she threw her arms around his neck and hugged him close.

"It's perfectly grand!" she cried. "But what a chump you are for going at all—when you could marry Lenorry!"

That was Kathleen's point of view, and it must have coincided somewhat with Mr. Anderson's.

"Kathleen, you wouldn't have me be a slacker?" asked Dorn, gently.

"No. But we let Jim go," was her argument.

Dorn kissed her, then turned to Lenore. "Let's go out to the fields."

*   *   *

It was not a long walk to the alfalfa, but by the time she got there Lenore's impending woe was as if it had never been. Dorn seemed strangely gay and unusually demonstrative; apparently he forgot the war cloud in the joy of the hour. That they were walking in the open seemed not to matter to him.

"Kurt, someone will see you," Lenore remonstrated.

"You're more beautiful than ever today," he said, by way of answer, and tried to block her way.

Lenore dodged and ran. She was fleet, and eluded him down the lane, across the cut field, to a huge square stack of baled alfalfa. But he caught her just as she got behind its welcome covert. Lenore was far less afraid of him than of laughing eyes. Breathless, she backed up against the stack.

"You're—a—cannibal!" she panted. But she did not make much resistance.

"You're—a goddess!" he replied.

"Me! . . . Of what?"

"Why, of 'Many Waters'! . . . Goddess of wheat! . . . The sweet, waving wheat, rich and golden—the very spirit of life!"

"If anybody sees you—mauling me—this way—I'll not seem a goddess to him. . . . My hair is down—my waist—Oh, Kurt!"

Yet it did not very much matter how she looked or what happened. Beyond all was the assurance of her dearness to him. Suddenly she darted away from him again. Her heart swelled, her spirit soared, her feet were buoyant and swift. She ran into the uncut alfalfa. It was thick and high, tangling round her feet. Here her progress was retarded. Dorn caught up with her. His strong hands on her shoulders felt masterful, and the sweet terror they inspired made her struggle to get away.

"You shall—not—hold me!" she cried.

"But I will. You must be taught—not to run," he said, and wrapped her tightly in his arms.

"Now surrender your kisses meekly!"

"I—surrender!...But, Kurt, someone will see.... Dear, we'll go back—or—somewhere—"

"Who can see us here but the birds?" he said, and the strong hands held her fast. "You will kiss me—enough—right now—even if the whole world—looked on!" he said, ringingly. "Lenore, my soul!...Lenore, I love you!"

He would not be denied. And if she had any desire to deny him it was lost in the moment. She clasped his neck and gave him kiss for kiss.

But her surrender made him think of her. She felt his effort to let her go.

Lenore's heart felt too big for her breast. It hurt. She clung to his hand and they walked on across the field and across a brook, up the slope to one of Lenore's favorite seats. And there she wanted to rest. She smoothed her hair and brushed her dress, aware of how he watched her, with his heart in his eyes.

Had there ever in all the years of the life of the earth been so perfect a day? How dazzling the sun! What heavenly blue the sky! And all beneath so gold, so green! A lark caroled over Lenore's head and a quail whistled in the brush below. The brook babbled and gurgled and murmured along, happy under the open sky. And a soft breeze brought the low roar of the harvest fields and the scent of wheat and dust and straw.

Life seemed so stingingly full, so poignant, so immeasurably worth living, so blessed with beauty and richness and fruitfulness.

"Lenore, your eyes are windows—and I can see into your soul. I can read—and first I'm uplifted and then I'm sad."

It was he who talked and she who listened. This glorious day would be her strength when the—Ah! but she would not complete a single bitter thought.

She led him away, up the slope, across the barley field, now cut and harvested, to the great, swelling golden spaces of wheat. Far below, the engines and harvesters were humming. Here the wheat waved and rustled in the wind. It was as high as Lenore's head.

"It's fine wheat," observed Dorn. "But the wheat of my desert hills was richer, more golden, and higher than this."

"No regrets today!" murmured Lenore, leaning to him.

There was magic in those words—the same enchantment that made the hours fly. She led him, at will, here and there along the rustling-bordered lanes. From afar they watched the busy harvest scene, with eyes that lingered long on a great, glittering combine with its thirty-two horses plodding along.

"I can drive them. Thirty-two horses!" she asserted, proudly.

"No!"

"Yes. Will you come? I will show you."

"It is a temptation," he said, with a sigh. "But there are eyes there. They would break the spell."

"Who's talking about eyes now?" she cried.

They spent the remainder of that day on the windy

wheat slope, high up, alone, with the beauty and richness of "Many Waters" beneath them. And when the
sun sent its last ruddy and gold rays over the western
hills, and the weary harvesters plodded homeward, Lenore still lingered, loath to break the spell. For on the
way home, she divined, he would tell her he was soon
to leave.

Sunset and evening star! Their beauty and serenity
pervaded Lenore's soul. Surely there was a life somewhere else, beyond in that infinite space. And the defeat
of earthly dreams was endurable.

They walked back down the wheat lanes hand in
hand, as dusk shadowed the valley; and when they
reached the house he told her gently that he must go.

"But—you will stay tonight?" she whispered.

"No. It's all arranged," he replied, thickly. "They're
to drive me over—my train's due at eight.... I've kept
it—till the last few minutes."

They went in together.

"We're too late for dinner," said Lenore, but she
was not thinking of that, and she paused with head bent.
"I—I want to say good-bye to you—here." She pointed
to the dim, curtained entrance of the living room.

"I'd like that, too," he replied. "I'll go up and get
my bag. Wait."

Lenore slowly stepped to that shadowed spot beyond the curtains where she had told her love to Dorn;
and there she stood, praying and fighting for strength
to let him go, for power to conceal her pain. The one
great thing she could do was to show him that she would
not stand in the way of his duty to himself. She realized
then that if he had told her sooner, if he were going to
remain one more hour at "Many Waters" she would

break down and beseech him not to leave her.

She saw him come downstairs with his small hand-bag, which he set down. His face was white. His eyes burned. But her woman's love made her divine that this was not a shock to his soul, as it was to hers, but stimulation—a man's strange spiritual accounting to his fellowmen.

He went first into the dining room, and Lenore heard her mother's and sisters' voices in reply to his. Presently he came out to enter her father's study. Lenore listened, but heard no sound there. Outside, a motorcar creaked and hummed by the window, to stop by the side porch. Then the door of her father's study opened and closed, and Dorn came to where she was standing.

Lenore did precisely as she had done a few nights before, when she had changed the world for him. But, following her kiss, there was a terrible instant when, with her arms around his neck, she went blind at the realization of loss. She held to him with a savage intensity of possession. It was like giving up life. She knew then, as never before, that she had the power to keep him at her side. But a thought saved her from exerting it—the thought that she could not make him less than other men—and so she conquered.

"Lenore, I want you to think always—how you loved me," he said.

"Loved you? Oh, my boy! It seems your lot has been hard. You've toiled—you've lost all—and now . . ."

"Listen," he interrupted, and she had never heard his voice like that. "The thousands of boys who go to fight regard it a duty. For our country! . . . I had that, but more. . . . My father was German . . . and he was a traitor.

The horror for me is that I hate what is German in *me*. . . . I will have to kill that. But you've helped me. . . . I know I'm American. I'll do my duty, whatever it is. I would have gone to war only a beast with my soul killed before I ever got there. . . . With no hope—no possibility of return! . . . But you love me! . . . Can't you see—how great the difference?"

Lenore understood and felt it in his happiness. "Yes, Kurt, I know. . . . Thank God, I've helped you. . . . I want you to go. I'll pray always. I believe you will come back to me. . . . Life could not be so utterly cruel . . ." She broke off.

"Life can't rob me now—nor death," he cried, in exaltation. "I have your love. Your face will always be with me—as now—lovely and brave! . . . Not a tear! . . . And only that sweet smile like an angel's! . . . Oh, Lenore, what a girl you are!"

"Say good-bye—and go," she faltered. Another moment would see her weaken.

"Yes, I must hurry." His voice was a whisper—almost gone. He drew a deep breath. "Lenore—my promised wife—my star for all the black nights—God bless you—keep you! . . . Good-bye!"

She spent all her strength in her embrace, all her soul in the passion of her farewell kiss. Then she stood alone, tottering, sinking. The swift steps, now heavy and uneven, passed out of the hall—the door closed—the motorcar creaked and rolled away—the droning hum ceased.

For a moment of despairing shock, before the storm broke, Lenore blindly wavered there, unable to move from the spot that had seen the beginning and the end of her brief hour of love. Then she summoned strength to drag herself to her room, to lock her door.

Alone! In the merciful darkness and silence and loneliness!...She need not lie nor play false nor fool herself here. She had let him go! Inconceivable and monstrous truth! For what?...It was not now with her, that deceiving spirit which had made her brave. But she was a woman. She fell upon her knees beside her bed, shuddering.

That moment was the beginning of her sacrifice, the sacrifice she shared in common now with thousands of other women. Before she had pitied; now she suffered. And all that was sweet, loving, noble, and motherly— all that was womanly—rose to meet the stretch of gray future, with its endless suspense and torturing fear, its face of courage for the light of day, its despair for the lonely night, and its vague faith in the lessons of life, its possible and sustaining and eternal hope of God.

CHAPTER
24

CAMP——, *October—.*

***D**EAR SISTER LENORE,* —It's been long since I wrote you. I'm sorry, dear. But—I haven't just been in shape to write. Have been transferred to a training camp not far from New York. I don't like it. The air is raw, penetrating, different from our high mountain air in the West. So many gray, gloomy days! And wet—why you never saw a rain in Washington! Fine bunch of boys, though. We get up in the morning at 4:30. Sweep the streets of the camp! I'm glad to get up and sweep, for I'm near frozen long before daylight. Yesterday I peeled potatoes till my hands were cramped. Nine million spuds, I guess! I'm wearing citizen's clothes—too thin, by gosh!—and sleeping in a tent, on a canvas cot, with one blanket. Wouldn't care a—(scoose me, sis)—I wouldn't mind if I had a real gun, and some real fighting to look forward to. Some life, I don't think! But I meant to tell you why I'm here.

You remember how I always took to cowboys. Well, I got chummy with a big cowpuncher from Montana. His name was Andersen. Isn't that queer? His name same as mine except for the last e where I have o. He's a Swede or Norwegian. True-blue American? Well, I should smile. Like all cowboys! He's six feet four, broad as a door, with a flat head of an Indian, and a huge, bulging chin. Not real handsome, but say! he's one of the finest fellows that ever lived. We call him Montana.

There were a lot of roughnecks in our outfit, and right away I got in bad. You know I never was much on holding my temper. Anyway, I got licked powerful fine, as Dad would say, and I'd been all beaten up but for Montana. That made us two fast friends, and sure some enemies, you bet.

We had the tough luck to run into six of the roughnecks, just outside of the little town, where they'd been drinking. I never heard the name of one of that outfit. We weren't acquainted at all. Strange how they changed my soldier career, right at the start! This day, when we met them, they got fresh, and of course I had to start something. I soaked that roughneck, sis, and don't you forget it. Well, it was a fight, sure. I got laid out—not knocked out, for I could see—but I wasn't any help to pard Montana. It looked as if he didn't need any. The roughnecks jumped him. Then, one after another, he piled them up in the road. Just a swing—and down went each one—cold. But the fellow I hit came to and, grabbing up a pick handle, with all his might he soaked Montana over the head. What an awful crack! Montana went down, and there was blood everywhere.

They took Montana to the hospital, sewed up his head. It wasn't long before he seemed all right again, but he told me sometimes he felt queer. Then they put us on a troop train, with boys from California and all over, and we came East. I haven't seen any of those other Western boys, though, since we got here.

One day, without any warning, Montana keeled over, down and out. Paralysis! They took him to a hospital in New York. No hope, the doctors said, and he was getting worse all the time. But some New York surgeon advised operation, anyway. So they opened that healed-over place in his head, where the pick-handle hit—and what do you think they found? A splinter off that pick handle, stuck two inches under his skull, in his brain! They took it out. Every day they expected Montana to die. But he didn't. But he *will* die. I went over to see him. He's unconscious part of the time—crazy the rest. No part of his right side moves! It broke me all up. Why couldn't that soak he got have been on the Kaiser's head?

I tell you, Lenore, a fellow has his eye teeth cut in this getting ready to go to war. It makes me sick. I enlisted to fight, not to be chased into a climate that doesn't agree with me—not to sweep roads and juggle a wooden gun. There are a lot of things, but say! I've got to cut out that kind of talk.

I feel almost as far away from you all as if I were in China. But I'm nearer France! I hope you're well and standing pat, Lenore. Remember, you're Dad's white hope. I was the black sheep, you know. Tell him I don't regard my transfer as a disgrace. The officers didn't and he needn't. Give my love to Mother and the girls. Tell

them not to worry. Maybe the war will be over before—
I'll write you often now, so cheer up.

Your loving brother,

JIM

CAMP——, *October*—

MY DEAREST LENORE,—If my writing is not very leg-
ible it is because my hand shakes when I begin this
sweet and sacred privilege of writing to my promised
wife. My other letter was short, and this is the second
in the weeks since I left you. What an endless time! You
must understand and forgive me for not writing oftener
and for not giving you definite address.

I did not want to be in a western regiment, for
reasons hard to understand. I enlisted in New York, and
am trying hard to get into the Rainbow Division, with
some hope of success. There is nothing to me in being
a member of a crack regiment, but it seems that this
one will see action first of all American units. I don't
want to be an officer, either.

How will it be possible for me to write you as I
want to—letters that will be free of the plague of myself—letters that you can treasure if I never come back?
Sleeping and waking, I never forget the wonderful truth
of your love for me. It did not seem real when I was
with you, but, now that we are separated, I know that
it is real. Mostly my mind contains only two things—
this constant memory of you, and that other terrible
thing of which I will not speak. All else that I think or
do seems to be mechanical.

The work, the training, is not difficult for me, though
so many boys find it desperately hard. You know I followed a plow, and that is real toil. Right now I see the

brown fallow hills and the great squares of gold. But visions or thoughts of home are rare. That is well, for they hurt like a stab. I cannot think now of a single thing connected with my training here that I want to tell you. Yet some things I must tell. For instance, we have different instructors, and naturally some are more forcible than others. We have one at whom the boys laugh. He tickles them. They like him. But he is an ordeal for me. The reason is that in our first bayonet practice, when we rushed and thrust a stuffed bag, he made us yell, *"Goddamn you, German—die!"* I don't imagine this to be general practice in army exercises, but the fact is he started us that way. I can't forget. When I begin to charge with a bayonet those words leap silently, but terribly, to my lips. Think of this as reality, Lenore—a sad and incomprehensible truth in 1917. All in me that is spiritual, reasonable, all that was once hopeful, revolts at this actuality and its meaning. But there is another side, that dark one, which revels in anticipation. It is the caveman in me, hiding by night, waiting with a bludgeon to slay. I am beginning to be struck by the gradual change in my comrades. I fancied that I alone had suffered a retrogression. I have a deep consciousness of baseness that is going to keep me aloof from them. I seem to be alone with my own soul. Yet I seem to be abnormally keen to impressions. I feel what is going on in the soldiers' minds, and it shocks me, sets me wondering, forces me to doubt myself. I keep saying it must be my peculiar way of looking at things.

Lenore, I remember your appeal to me. Shall I ever forget your sweet face—your sad eyes when you bade me hope in God?—I am trying, but I do not see God yet. Perhaps that is because of my morbidness—my limitations. Perhaps I will face him over there, when I go down into the Valley of the Shadow. One thing, however, I do begin to see is that there is a divinity in men. Slowly something divine is revealing itself to me. To give up work, property, friends, sister, mother, home, sweetheart, to sacrifice all and go out to fight for country, for honor—that indeed is divine. It is beautiful. It inspires a man and lifts his head. But, alas! if he is a thinking man, when he comes in contact with the actual physical preparation for war, he finds that the divinity was the hour of his sacrifice and that, to become a good soldier, he must change, forget, grow hard, strong, merciless, brutal, humorous, and callous, all of which is to say base. I see boys who are tenderhearted, who love life, who were born sufferers, who cannot inflict pain! How many silent cries of protest, of wonder, of agony, must go up in the night over this camp! The sum of them would be monstrous. The sound of them, if voiced, would be a clarion blast to the world. It is sacrifice that is divine, and not the making of an efficient soldier.

I shall write you endlessly. The action of writing relieves me. I feel less burdened now. Sometimes I cannot bear the burden of all this unintelligible consciousness. My mind is not large enough. Sometimes I feel that I am going to be every soldier and every enemy— each one in his strife or his drifting or his agony or his death. But despite that feeling I seem alone in a horde. I make no friends. I have no way to pass my leisure but writing. I can hardly read at all. When off duty the boys amuse themselves in a hundred ways—going to town, the theaters, and movies; chasing the girls (especially that, to judge by their talk); play; boxing; games; and I am sorry to add, many of them gamble and drink. But I cannot do any of these things. I cannot forget what I am here for. I cannot forget that I am training to kill men. Never do I forget that soon I will face death. What a terrible, strange, vague thrill that sends shivering over me! Amusement and forgetfulness are past for Kurt Dorn. I am concerned with my soul. I am fighting that black passion which makes of me a sleepless watcher and thinker.

If this war only lets me live long enough to understand its meaning! Perhaps that meaning will be the meaning of life, in which case I am longing for the unattainable. But underneath it all must be a colossal movement of evolution, of spiritual growth—or of retrogression. Who knows? When I ask myself what I am going to fight for, I answer—for my country, as a patriot—for my hate, as an individual. My time is almost up. I go on duty. The rain is roaring on the thin roof. How it rains in this East! Whole days and nights it pours. I cannot help but think of my desert hills, always so barren and yellow, with the dust clouds whirling. One day of this rain, useless and wasted here, would have saved the Bend crop of wheat. Nature is almost as inscrutable as God.

Lenore, good-bye for this time. Think of me, but not as lonely or unhappy or uncomfortable out there in the cold, raw, black, wet night. I will be neither. Someone—a spirit—will keep beside me as I step the beat. I have put unhappiness behind me. And no rain or mud or chill will ever faze me.

Yours with love,

KURT DORN.

CAMP——, *October——.*

DEAR SISTER LENORE,—After that little letter of yours I could do nothing more than look up another pin like the one I sent Kathleen. I enclose it. Hope you will wear it.

I'm very curious to see what your package contains. It hasn't arrived yet. All the mail comes late. That makes the boys sore.

The weather hasn't been so wet lately as when I last wrote, but it's colder. Believe me these tents are not steam heated! But we grin and try to look happy. It's not the most cheerful thing to hear the old call in the morning and tumble out in the cold gray dawn. Say! I've got two blankets now. *Two!* Just time for mess, then we hike down the road. I'm in for artillery now, I guess. The air service really fascinated me, but you can't have what you want in this business.

Saturday.—This letter will be in sections. No use sending you a little dab of news now and then. I'll write when I can, and mail when the letter assumes real proportions. Your package arrived and I was delighted. I think I slept better last night on your little pillow than any night since we were called out. My pillow before was your sleeveless jersey.

It's after three A.M. and I'm on guard—that is, battery guard, and I have to be up from midnight to reveille, not on a post, but in my tent, so that if any of my men (I'm a corporal now), whom I relieve every two hours, get into trouble they can call me. Noncoms go on guard once in six days, so about every sixth night I get along with no sleep.

We have been ordered to do away with all personal property except shaving outfit and absolutely necessary articles. We can't keep a footlocker, trunk, valise, or even an ordinary soapbox in our tents. Everything must be put in one barrack bag, a canvas sack just like a laundry bag.

Thank the girls for the silk handkerchief and candy they sent. I sure have the sweetest sisters of any boy I know. I never appreciated them when I had them. I'm learning bitter truths these days. And tell Mother I'll write her soon. Thank her for the pajamas and the napkins. Tell her I'm sorry a soldier has no use for either.

This morning I did my washing of the past two weeks, and I was so busy that I didn't hear the bugle blow, and thereby got on the "black book." Which means that I won't get any time off soon.

Before I forget, Lenore, let me tell you that I've taken ten thousand dollars' life insurance from the government, in your favor as beneficiary. This costs me only about six and a half dollars per month, and in case of my death—Well, I'm a soldier, now. Please tell Rose I've taken a fifty-dollar Liberty Bond of the new issue for her. This I'm paying at the rate of five dollars per month and it will be delivered to her at the end of ten months. Both of these, of course, I'm paying out of my government pay as a soldier. The money Dad sent me I spent like water, lent to the boys, threw away. Tell him not to send me any more. Tell him the time has come for Jim Anderson to make good. I've a rich dad and he's the best dad any harum-scarum boy ever had. I'm going to prove more than one thing this trip.

We hear so many rumors, and none of them ever come true. One of them is funny—that we have so many rich men with political influence in our regiment that we will never get to France! Isn't that the limit? But it's funny because, if we have rich men, I'd like to see them. Still, there are thirty thousand soldiers here, and in my neck of the woods such rumors are laughed and cussed at. We hear also that we're going to be ordered South. I wish that would come true. It's so cold and drab and muddy and monotonous.

My friend Montana fooled everybody. He didn't die. He seems to be hanging on. Lately he recovered consciousness. Told me he had no feeling on his left side, except sometimes his hand itched, you know, like prickly needles. But Montana will never be any good again. That fine big cowboy! He's been one grand soldier. It sickens me sometimes to think of the difference between what thrilled me about this war game and what we get. Maybe, though—There goes my call. I must close. Love to all.

JIM.

NEW YORK CITY, *October*—.

DEAREST LENORE,—It seems about time that I had a letter from you. I'm sure letters are on the way, but they do not come quickly. The boys complain of the mail service. Isn't it strange that there is not a soul to write me except you? Jeff, my farmhand, will write me whenever I write him, which I haven't done yet.

I'm on duty here in New York at an armory bazaar. It's certainly the irony of fate. Why did the officer pick on me, I'd like to know? But I've never complained of an order so far, and I'm standing it. Several of us—and they chose the husky boys—have been sent over here, for absolutely no purpose that I can see except to exhibit ourselves in uniform. It's a woman's bazaar, to raise money for war-relief work and so on. The hall is almost as large as that field back of your house, and every night it is packed with people, mostly young. My comrades are having fun out of it, but I feel like a fish out of water.

Just the same, Lenore, I'm learning more every day. If I was not so disgusted I'd think this was a wonderful opportunity. As it is, I regard it only as an experience over which I have no control and that interests me in spite of myself. New York is an awful place—endless, narrow, torn-up streets crowded with hurrying throngs, taxicabs, cars, and full of noise and dust. I am always choked for air. And these streets reek. Where do the people come from and where are they going? They look wild, as if they had to go somewhere, but did not know where that was. I've no time or inclination to see New York, though under happier circumstances I think I'd like to.

People in the East seem strange to me. Still, as I never mingled with many people in the West, I cannot say truly whether eastern people are different from western people. But I think so. Anyway, while I was in Spokane, Portland, San Francisco, and Los Angeles I did not think people were greatly concerned about the war. Denver people appeared not to realize there was a war. But here in New York everything is war. You can't escape it. You see that war will soon obsess rich and poor, alien and neutral and belligerent, pacifist and militarist. Since I wrote you last I've tried to read the newspapers sent to us. It's hard to tell you which makes me the sicker—the prattle of the pacifist or the mathematics of the military experts. Both miss the spirit of men. Neither has any soul. I think the German minds must all be mathematical.

But I want to write about the women and girls I see, here in New York, in the camps and towns, on the trains, everywhere. Lenore, the war has thrown them off their balance. I have seen and studied at close hand women of all classes. Believe me, as the boys say, I have thought more than twice whether or not I would tell you the stark truth. But somehow I am impelled to. I have an overwhelming conviction that all American girls and mothers should know what the truth is. They will never be told, Lenore, and most would never believe if they were told. And that is one thing wrong with people.

I believe every soldier, from the time he enlists until the war is ended, should be kept away from women. This is a sweeping statement and you must take into account the mind of him who makes it. But I am not leaping at conclusions. The soldier boys have terrible peril facing them long before they get to the trenches. Not all, or nearly all, the soldiers are going to be vitally affected by the rottenness of great cities or by the mushroom hotbeds of vice springing up near the camps. These evils exist and are being opposed by military and government, by police and Y. M. C. A., and good influence of good people. But they will never wholly stamp it out.

Nor do I want to say much about the society women who are "rushing" the officers. There may be one here and there with her heart in the right place, but with most of them it must be, first, this something about war that has unbalanced women; and secondly, a fad, a novelty, a new sentimental stunt, a fashion set by some leader. Likewise I want to say but little about the horde of common, street-chasing, rattle-brained women and girls who lie in wait for soldiers at every corner, so to speak. All these, to be sure, may be unconsciously actuated by motives that do not appear on the surface; and if this be true, their actions are less bold, less raw than they look.

What I want to dwell upon is my impression of something strange, unbalanced, incomprehensible, about the frank conduct of so many well-educated, refined, and good women I see; and about the eagerness, restlessness, the singular response of nice girls to situations that are not natural.

Tonight a handsome, stylishly gowned woman of about thirty came up to me with a radiant smile and a strange brightness in her eyes. There were five hundred couples dancing on the floor, and the music and sound of sliding feet made it difficult to hear her. She said: "You handsome soldier boy! Come dance with me?" I replied politely that I did not dance. Then she took hold of me and said, "I'll teach you." I saw a wedding ring on the hand she laid on my arm. Then I looked straight at her, "Madam, very soon I'll be learning the dance of death over in France, and my mind's concerned with that." She grew red with anger. She seemed amazed. And she snapped, "Well, you *are* a queer soldier!" Later I watched her flirting and dancing with an officer.

Overtures and advances innumerable have been made to me, ranging from the assured possession-taking onslaught like this woman's to the slight, subtle something, felt more than seen, of a more complex nature. And, Lenore, I blush to tell you this, but I've been mobbed by girls. They have a thousand ways of letting a soldier *know!* I could not begin to tell them. But I do not actually realize what it is that is conveyed, that I know; and I am positive the very large majority of soldiers *misunderstand*. At night I listen to the talks of my comrades, and, well—if the girls only heard! Many times I go out of hearing, and when I cannot do that I refuse to hear.

Lenore, I am talking about nice girls now. I am merciless. There are many girls like you—they seem like you, though none so pretty. I mean, you know, there are certain manners and distinctions that at once mark a really nice girl. For a month I've been thrown here and there, so that it seems I've seen as many girls as soldiers. I have been sent to different entertainments given for soldiers. At one place a woman got up and invited the girls to ask the boys to dance. At another a crowd of girls were lined up wearing different ribbons, and the boys marched along until each one found the girl wearing a ribbon to match the one he wore. That was his partner. It was interesting to see the eager, mischievous, brooding eyes of these girls as they watched and waited. Just as interesting was it to see this boy's face when he found his partner was ugly, and that boy swell with pride when he found he had picked a "winner." It was all adventure for both boys and girls. But I saw more than that in it. Whenever I could not avoid meeting a girl I tried to be agreeable and to talk about war, and soldiers, and what was going on. I did not dance, of course, and I imagine more than one girl found me a "queer soldier."

It always has touched me, though, to see and feel the sweetness, graciousness, sympathy, kindness, and that other indefinable something, in the girls I have met. How they made me think of you, Lenore! No doubt about their hearts, their loyalty, their Americanism. Every soldier who goes to France can fight for some girl! They make you feel that. I believe I have gone deeper than most soldiers in considering what I will call war-relation of the sexes. If it is normal, then underneath it all is a tremendous inscrutable design of nature or God. If that be true, actually true, then war must be inevitable and right! How horrible! My thoughts confound me sometimes. Anyway, the point I want to make is this: I heard an officer tell an irate father, whose two daughters had been insulted by soldiers: "My dear sir, it is regrettable. These men will be punished. But they are not greatly to blame, because so many girls throw themselves at their heads. Your daughters did not, of course, but they should not have come here." That illustrates the fixed idea of the military, all through the ranks—*Women throw themselves at soldiers!* It is true that they do. But the idea is false, nevertheless, because the mass of girls are misunderstood.

Misunderstood!—I can tell you why. Surely the mass of American girls are nice, fine, sweet, wholesome. They are young. The news of war liberates something in them that we can find no name for. But it must be noble. A soldier! The very name, from childhood, is one to make a girl thrill. What then the actual thing, the uniform, invested somehow with chivalry and courage, the clean-cut athletic young man, somber and fascinating with his intent eyes, his serious brow, or his devil-may-care gallantry, the compelling presence of him that breathes of his sacrifice, of his near departure to privation, to squalid, comfortless trenches, to the fire and hell of war, to blood and agony and death—in a word to fight, fight,

fight for women!...So through this beautiful emotion women lose their balance and many are misunderstood. Those who would not and could not be bold are susceptible to advances that in an ordinary time would not affect them. War invests a soldier with a glamour. Love at first sight, flirtations, rash intimacies, quick engagements, immediate marriages. The soldier who is soon going away to fight and perhaps to die strikes hard at the very heart of a girl. Either she is not her real self then, or else she is suddenly transported to a womanhood that is instinctive, elemental, universal for the future. She feels what she does not know. She surrenders because there is an imperative call to the depths of her nature. She sacrifices because she is the inspirator of the soldier, the reward for his loss, the savior of the race. If women are the spoils of barbarous conquerors, they are also the sinews, the strength, the soul of defenders.

And so, however you look at it, war means for women sacrifice, disillusion, heartbreak, agony, doom. I feel that so powerfully that I am overcome; I am sick at the gaiety and playing; I am full of fear, wonder, admiration, and hopeless pity for them.

No man can tell what is going on in the souls of soldiers while noble women are offering love and tenderness, throwing themselves upon the altar of war, hoping blindly to send their great spirits marching to the front. Perhaps the man who lives through the war will feel the change in his soul if he cannot tell it. Day by day I think I see a change in my comrades. As they grow physically stronger they seem to grow spiritually lesser. But maybe that is only my idea. I see evidences of fear, anger, sullenness, moodiness, shame. I see a growing indifference to fatigue, toil, pain. As these boys harden physically they harden mentally. Always, 'way off there is the war, and that seems closely related to the near duty here—what it takes to make a man. These fellows will measure men differently after this experience with sacrifice, obedience, labor, and pain. In that they will become great. But I do not think these things stimulate a man's mind. Changes are going on in me, some of which I am unable to define. For instance, physically I am much bigger and stronger than I was. I weigh one hundred and eighty pounds! As for my mind, something is always tugging at it. I feel that it grows tired. It wants to forget. In spite of my will, all of these keen desires of mine to know everything lag and fail often, and I catch myself drifting. I see and feel and hear without thinking. I am only an animal then. At these times sight of blood, or a fight, or a plunging horse, or a broken leg—and these sights are common—affects me little until I am quickened and think about the meaning of it all. At such moments I have a revulsion of feeling. With memory comes a revolt, and so on, until I am the distressed, inquisitive, and morbid person I am now. I shudder at what war will make me. Actual contact with earth, exploding guns, fighting comrades, striking foes, will make brutes of us all. It is wrong to shed another man's blood. If life was meant for that why do we have progress? I cannot reconcile a God with all this horror. I have misgivings about my mind. If I feel so acutely here in safety and comfort, what shall I feel over there in peril and agony? I fear I shall laugh at death. Oh, Lenore consider that! To laugh in the ghastly face of death! If I yield utterly to a fiendish joy of bloody combat, then my mind will fail, and that in itself would be evidence of God.

I do not read over my letters to you. I just write. Forgive me if they are not happier. Every hour I think of you. At night I see your face in the shadow of the tent wall. And I love you unutterably. Faithfully,

KURT DORN.

CAMP——, *November*——.

DEAR SISTER,—It's bad news I've got for you this time. Something bids me tell you, though up to now I've kept unpleasant facts to myself.

The weather has knocked me out. My cold came back, got worse and worse. Three days ago I had a chill that lasted for fifteen minutes. I shook like a leaf. It left me, and then I got a terrible pain in my side. But I didn't give in, which I feel now was a mistake. I stayed up till I dropped.

I'm here in the hospital. It's a long shed with three stoves, and a lot of beds with other sick boys. My bed is far away from a stove. The pain is bad yet, but duller, and I've fever. I'm pretty sick, honey. Tell Mother and Dad, but not the girls. Give my love to all. And don't worry. It'll all come right in the end. This beastly climate's to blame.

Later,—It's night now. I was interrupted. I'll write a few more lines. Hope you can read them. It's late and the wind is moaning outside. It's so cold and dismal. The fellow in the bed next to me is out of his head. Poor devil! He broke his knee, and they put off the operation—too busy! So few doctors and so many patients! And now he'll lose his leg. He's talking about home. Oh, Lenore! *Home!* I never knew what home was—till now.

I'm worse tonight. But I'm always bad at night. Only, tonight I feel strange. There's a weight on my chest, besides the pain. That moan of wind makes me feel so lonely. There's no one here—and I'm so cold. I've thought a lot about you girls and Mother and Dad. Tell Dad I made good.

JIM.

*J*IM'S last letter was not taken seriously by the other members of the Anderson family. The father shook his head dubiously. "That ain't like Jim," but made no other comment. Mrs. Anderson sighed. The young sisters were not given to worry. Lenore, however, was haunted by an unwritten meaning in her brother's letter.

Weeks before, she had written to Dorn and told him to hunt up Jim. No reply had yet come from Dorn. Every day augmented her uneasiness, until it was dreadful to look for letters that did not come. All this fortified her, however, to expect calamity. Like a bolt out of the clear sky it came in shape of a telegram from Camp—saying that Jim was dying.

The shock prostrated the mother. Jim had been her favorite. Mr. Anderson left at once for the East. Lenore had the care of her mother and the management of

"Many Waters" on her hands, which duties kept her mercifully occupied. Mrs. Anderson, however, after a day, rallied surprisingly. Lenore sensed in her mother the strength of the spirit that sacrificed to a noble and universal cause. It seemed to be Mrs. Anderson's conviction that Jim had been shot, or injured by accident in gun training, or at least by a horse. Lenore did not share her mother's idea and was reluctant to dispel it. On the evening of the fifth day after Mr. Anderson's departure a message came, saying that he had arrived too late to see Jim alive. Mrs. Anderson bore the news bravely, though she weakened perceptibly.

The family waited then for further news. None came. Day after day passed. Then one evening, while Lenore strolled in the gloaming, Kathleen came running to burst out with the announcement of their father's arrival. He had telephoned from Vale for a car to meet him.

Not long after that, Lenore, who had gone to her room, heard the return of the car and recognized her father's voice. She ran down in time to see him being embraced by the girls, and her mother leaning with bowed head on his shoulder.

"Yes, I fetched Jim—back," he said, steadily, but very low. "It's all arranged....An' we'll bury him tomorrow."

"Oh—Dad!" cried Lenore.

"Hello, my girl!" he replied, and kissed her. "I'm sorry to tell you I couldn't locate Kurt Dorn....That New York—an' that trainin' camp!"

He held up his hands in utter futility of expression. Lenore's quick eyes noted his face had grown thin and haggard, and she made sure with a pang that his hair was whiter.

"I'm sure glad to be home," he said, with a heavy expulsion of breath. "I want to clean up an' have a bite to eat."

Lenore was so disappointed at failing to hear from Dorn that she did not think how singular it was her father did not tell more about Jim. Later he seemed more like himself, and told them simply that Jim had contracted pneumonia and died without any message for his folk at home. This prostrated Mrs. Anderson again.

Later Lenore sought her father in his room. He could not conceal from her that he had something heartrending on his mind. Then there was more than tragedy in his expression. Lenore felt a leap of fear at what seemed her father's hidden anger. She appealed to him—importuned him. Plainer it came to her that he wanted to relieve himself of a burden. Then doubling her persuasions, she finally got him to talk.

"Lenore, it's not been so long ago that right here in this room Jim begged me to let him enlist. He wasn't of age. But would I let him go—to fight for the honor of our country—for the future safety of our home? ... We all felt the boy's eagerness, his fire, his patriotism. Wayward as he's been, we suddenly were proud of him. We let him go. We gave him up. He was a part of our flesh an' blood—sent by us Andersons—to do our share."

Anderson paused in his halting speech, and swallowed hard. His white face twitched strangely and his brow was clammy. Lenore saw that his piercing gaze looked far beyond her for the instant that he broke down.

"Jim was a born fighter," the father resumed. "He wasn't vicious. He just had a leanin' to help anybody. As a lad he fought for his little pards—always on the right side—an' he always fought fair.... This opportunity to train for a soldier made a man of him. He'd have made his mark in the war. Strong an' game an' fierce, he'd...he'd...Well, he's dead—he's *dead!*...Four months after enlistment he's dead....An' he never had a rifle in his hands! He never had his hands on a machine gun or a piece of artillery!...He never had a uniform! He never had an overcoat! He never ..."

Then Mr. Anderson's voice shook so that he had to stop to gain control. Lenore was horrified. She felt a burning stir within her.

"Lemme get this—out," choked Anderson, his face now livid, his veins bulging. "I'm drove to tell it. I was near all day locatin' Jim's company. Found the tent where he'd lived. It was cold, damp, muddy. Jim's messmates spoke high of him. Called him a prince!...They all owed him money. He'd done many a good turn for them. He had only a thin blanket, an' he caught cold. All the boys had colds. One night he gave that blanket to a boy sicker than he was. Next day he got worse.... There was miles an' miles of them tents. I like to never found the hospital where they'd sent Jim. An' then it was six o'clock in the mornin'—a raw, bleak day that'd freeze one of us to the marrow. I had trouble gettin' in. But a soldier went with me an'—an' ..."

Anderson's voice went to a whisper, and he looked pityingly at Lenore.

"That hospital was a barn. No doctors! Too early.

... The nurses weren't in sight. I met one later, an', poor girl! she looked ready to drop herself! ... We found Jim in one of the little rooms. No heat! It was winter there. ... Only a bed! ... Jim lay on the floor, dead! He'd fallen or pitched off the bed. He had on only his underclothes that he had on—when he—left home. ... He was stiff—an' must have—been dead—a good while."

Lenore held out her trembling hands. "Dead—Jim dead—like that!" she faltered.

"Yes. He got pneumonia," replied Anderson, hoarsely. "The camp was full of it."

"But—my God! Were not the—the poor boys taken care of?" implored Lenore, faintly.

"It's a terrible time. All was done that *could* be done!"

"Then—it was all—for nothing?"

"All! All! Our boy an' many like him—the best blood of our country—Western blood—dead because ... because ..."

Anderson's voice failed him.

"Oh, Jim! Oh, my brother! ... Dead like a poor neglected dog! Jim—who enlisted to fight—for—"

Lenore broke down then and hurried away to her room.

With great difficulty Mrs. Anderson was revived, and it became manifest that the prop upon which she had leaned had been slipped from under her. The spirit which had made her strong to endure the death of her boy failed when the sordid bald truth of a miserable and horrible waste of life gave the lie to the splendid fighting chance Jim had dreamed of.

When Anderson realized that she was fading daily he exhausted himself in long expositions of the illness and injury and death common to armies in the making. More deaths came from these causes than from war. It was the elision of the weaker element—the survival of the fittest; and some, indeed very many, mothers must lose their sons that way. The government was sound at the core, he claimed; and his own rage was at the few incompetents and profiteers. These must be weeded out—a process that was going on. The gigantic task of a government to draft and prepare a great army and navy was something beyond the grasp of ordinary minds. Anderson talked about what he had seen and heard, proving the wonderful stride already made. But all that he said now made no impression upon Mrs. Anderson. She had made her supreme sacrifice for a certain end, and that was as much as the boy's fiery ambition to fight as it was her duty, common with other mothers, to furnish a man at the front. What a hopeless, awful sacrifice! She sank under it.

Those were trying days for Lenore, just succeeding her father's return; and she had little time to think of herself. When the mail came, day after day, without a letter from Dorn, she felt the pang in her breast grow heavier. Intimations crowded upon her of impending troubles that would make the present ones seem light.

It was not long until the mother was laid to rest beside the son.

When that day ended, Lenore and her father faced each other in her room, where he had always been wont to come for sympathy. They gazed at each other, with hard, dry eyes. Stark-naked truth—grim reality—the nature of this catastrophe—the consciousness of war— dawned for each in the look of the other. Brutal shock and then this second exceeding bitter woe awakened their minds to the futility of individual life.

"Lenore—it's over!" he said, huskily, as he sank into a chair. "Like a nightmare!...What have I got to live for?"

"You have us girls," replied Lenore. "And if you did not have us there would be many others for you to live for....Dad, can't you see—*now?*"

"I reckon. But I'm growin' old an' mebbe I've quit."

"No, Dad, you'll never quit. Suppose all we Americans quit. That'd mean a German victory. Never! Never! Never!"

"By God! you're right!" he ejaculated, with the trembling strain of his face suddenly fixing. Blood and life shot into his eyes. He got up heavily and began to stride to and fro before her. "You see clearer than me. You always did, Lenore."

"I'm beginning to see, but I can't tell you," replied Lenore, closing her eyes. Indeed, there seemed a colossal vision before her, veiled and strange. "Whatever happens, we *cannot* break. It's because of the war. We have our tasks—greater now than ever we believed could be thrust upon us. Yours to show men what you are made of! To raise wheat as never before in your life! Mine to show my sisters and my friends—all the women—what their duty is. We must sacrifice, work, prepare, and fight for the future."

"I reckon," he nodded, solemnly. "Loss of mother an' Jim changes this damned war. Whatever's in my power to do must go on. So someone can take it up when I—"

"That's the great conception, Dad," added Lenore, earnestly. "We are tragically awakened. We've been surprised—terribly struck in the dark. Something monstrous and horrible!...I can feel the menace in it for all—over every family in this broad land."

"Lenore, you said once that Jim—Now, how'd you know it was all over for him?"

"A woman's heart, Dad. When I said good-bye to Jim I knew it was good-bye forever."

"Did you feel that way about Kurt Dorn?"

"No. He will come back to me. I dream it. It's in my spirit—my instinct of life, my flesh-and-blood life of the future—it's in my belief in God. Kurt Dorn's ordeal will be worse than death for him. But I believe as I pray— that he will come home alive."

"Then, after all, you do hope," said her father. "Lenore, when I was down East, I seen what women were doin'. The bad women are good an' the good women are great. I think women have more to do with war than men, even if they do stay home. It must be because women are mothers....Lenore, you've bucked me up. I'll go at things now. The need of wheat next year will be beyond calculation. I'll buy ten thousand acres of that wheatland round old Chris Dorn's farm. An' my shot at the Germans will be wheat. I'll raise a million bushels!"

Next morning in the mail was a long, thick envelope addressed to Lenore in handwriting that shook her heart and made her fly to the seclusion of her room.

NEW YORK CITY, *November*—.

DEAREST,—When you receive this I will be in France.

*　　　　*　　　　*

Then Lenore sustained a strange shock. The beloved handwriting faded, the thick sheets of paper fell; and all about her seemed dark and whirling, as the sudden joy and excitement stirred by the letter changed to sickening pain.

"*France!* He's in France!" she whispered. "Oh, Kurt!" A storm of love and terror burst over her. It had the onset and the advantage of a bewildering surprise. It laid low, for the moment, her fortifications of sacrifice, strength, and resolve. She had been forced into womanhood, and her fear, her agony, were all the keener for the intelligence and spirit that had repudiated selfish love. Kurt Dorn was in France in the land of the trenches! Strife possessed her and had a moment of raw, bitter triumph. She bit her lips and clenched her fists, to restrain the impulse to rush madly around the room, to scream out her fear and hate. With forcing her thoughts, with hard return to old well-learned arguments, there came back the nobler emotions. But when she took up the letter again, with trembling hands, her heart fluttered high and sick, and she saw the words through blurred eyes.

. . . I'll give the letter to an ensign, who has promised to mail it the moment he gets back to New York.

Lenore, your letter telling me about Jim was held up in the mail. But thank goodness, I got it in time. I'd already been transferred, and expected orders any day to go on board the transport, where I am writing now. I'd have written you, or at least telegraphed you, yesterday, after seeing Jim, if I had not expected to see him again today. But this morning we were marched on board and I cannot even get this letter off to you.

Lenore, your brother is a very sick boy. I lost some hours finding him. They did not want to let me see him. But I implored—said that I was engaged to his sister—and finally I got in. The nurse was very sympathetic. But I didn't care for the doctors in charge. They seemed hard, hurried, brusque. But they have their troubles. The hospital was a long barracks, and it was full of cripples.

The nurse took me into a small, bare room, too damp and cold for a sick man, and I said so. She just looked at me.

Jim looks like you more than any other of the Andersons. I recognized that at the same moment I saw how very sick he was. They had told me outside that he had a bad case of pneumonia. He was awake, perfectly conscious, and he stared at me with eyes that set my heart going.

"Hello, Jim!" I said, and offered my hand, as I sat down on the bed. He was too weak to shake hands.

"Who're you?" he asked. He couldn't speak very well. When I told him my name and that I was his sister's fiancé his face changed so he did not look like the same person. It was beautiful. Oh, it showed how homesick he was! Then I talked a blue streak about you, about the girls, about "Many Waters"—how I lost my wheat, and everything. He was intensely interested, and when I got through he whispered that he guessed Lenore had picked a "winner." What do you think of that? He was curious about me, and asked me questions till the nurse made him stop. I was never so glad about anything as I was about the happiness it evidently gave him to meet me and hear from home. I promised to come next day if we did not sail. Then he showed what I must call despair. He must have been passionately eager to get to France. The nurse dragged me out. Jim called weakly after me: "Good-bye, Kurt. Stick some Germans for me!" I'll never forget his tone nor his look. . . . Lenore, he doesn't expect to get over to France.

I questioned the nurse, and she shook her head doubtfully. She looked sad. She said Jim had been the lion of his regiment. I questioned a doctor, and he was annoyed. He put me off with a sharp statement that Jim was not in danger. But I think he is. I hope and pray he recovers.

Thursday.

We sailed yesterday. It was a wonderful experience, leaving Hoboken. Our transport and the dock looked as if they had a huge swarm of yellow bees hanging over everything. The bees were soldiers. The most profound emotion I ever had—except the one when you told me you loved me—came over me as the big boat swung free of the dock—of the good old U. S., of home. I wanted to jump off and swim through the eddying green water to the piles and hide in them till the boat had gone. As we backed out, pulled up tugs, and got started down the river, my thrills increased, until we passed the Statue of Liberty—and then I couldn't tell how I felt. One thing, I could not see very well. . . . I gazed beyond the colossal statue that France gave to the U. S.—way across the water and the ships and the docks toward the West that I was leaving. Feeling like mine then only comes once to a man in his life. First I seemed to see all the vast space, the farms, valleys, woods, deserts, rivers, and mountains between me and my golden wheat hills. Then I saw my home, and it was as if I had a magnificent photograph before my very eyes. A sudden rush of tears blinded me. Such a storm of sweetness, regret, memory! Then at last you—*you* as you stood before me last, the very loveliest girl in all the world. My heart almost burst, and in the wild, sick pain of the moment I had a strange, comforting flash of thought that a man who could leave you must be impelled by something great in store for him. I feel that. I told you once. To laugh at death! That is what I shall do. But perhaps that is not the great experience which will come to me.

I saw the sun set in the sea, way back toward the western horizon, where the thin, dark line that was land disappeared in the red glow. The wind blows hard. The water is rough, dark gray, and cold. I like the taste of the spray. Our boat rolls heavily and many boys are already sick. I do not imagine the motion will affect me. It is stuffy below deck. I'll spend what time I can above, where I can see and feel. It was dark just now when I came below. And as I looked out into the windy darkness and strife I was struck by the strangeness of the sea and how it seemed to be like my soul. For a long time I have been looking in my soul, and I find such ceaseless strife, such dark, unlit depths, such chaos. These thoughts and emotions, always with me, keep me from getting close to my comrades. No, not me, but it keeps them away from me. I think they regard me strangely. They all talk of submarines. They are afraid. Some will lose sleep at night. But I never think of a submarine when I gaze out over the tumbling black waters. What I think of, what I am going after, what I need seems far, far away. Always! I am no closer now than when I was at your home. So it has not to do with distance. And

Lenore, maybe it has not to do with trenches or Germans.

Wednesday.

It grows harder to get a chance to write and harder for me to express myself. When I could write I have to work or am on duty; when I have a little leisure I am somehow clamped. This old chugging boat beats the waves hour after hour, all day and all night. I can feel the vibration when I'm asleep. Many things happen that would interest you, just the duty and play of the soldiers, for that matter, and the stories I hear going from lip to lip, and the accidents. Oh! so much happens. But all these rush out of my mind the moment I sit down to write. There is something at work in me as vast and heaving as the ocean.

At first I had a fear, a dislike of the ocean. But that is gone. It is indescribable to stand on the open deck at night as we are driving on and on and on—to look up at the grand, silent stars, that know, that understand, yet are somehow merciless—to look out across the starlit, moving sea. Its ceaseless movement at first distressed me; now I feel that it is perpetually moving to try to become still. To seek a level! To find itself! To quiet down to peace! But that will never be. And I think if the ocean is not like the human heart, then what is it like?

This voyage will be good for me. The hard, incessant objective life, the physical life of a soldier, somehow comes to a halt on board ship. And every hour now is immeasurable for me. Whatever the mystery of life, of death, of what drives me, of why I cannot help fight the demon in me, of this thing called war—the certainty is that these dark, strange nights on the sea have given me a hope and faith that the truth is not utterly unattainable.

Sunday.

We're in the danger zone now, with destroyers around us and a cruiser ahead. I am all eyes and ears. I lose sleep at night from thinking so hard. The ship doctor stopped me the other day—studied my face. Then he said: "You're too intense. You think too hard. ...Are you afraid?" And I laughed in his face. "Absolutely no!" I told him. "Then forget—and mix with the boys. Play—cut up—fight—do anything but *think!*" That doctor is a good chap, but he doesn't figure Kurt Dorn if he imagines the Germans can kill me by making me think.

We're nearing France now, and the very air is charged. An airplane came out to meet us—welcome us, I guess, and it flew low. The soldiers went wild. I never had such a thrill. That air game would just suit me, if I were fitted for it. But I'm no mechanic. Besides, I'm too big and heavy. My place will be in the front line with a bayonet. Strange how a bayonet fascinates me!

They say we can't write home anything about the war. I'll write you something, whenever I can. Don't be unhappy if you do not hear often—or if my letters cease to come. My heart and my mind are full of you. Whatever comes to me—the training over here—the going to the trenches—the fighting—I shall be safe if only I can remember you.

With love,   KURT.

Lenore carried that letter in her bosom when she went out to walk in the fields, to go over the old ground she and Kurt had trod hand in hand. From the stone seat above the brook she watched the sunset. All was still except the murmur of the running water, and somehow she could not long bear that. As the light began to shade on the slopes, she faced them, feeling, as always, a strength come to her from their familiar lines. Twilight found her high above the ranch, and absolutely alone. She would have this lonely hour, and then, all her mind and energy must go to what she knew was imperative duty. She would work to the limit of her endurance.

It was an autumn twilight, with a cool wind, gray sky, and sad, barren slopes. The fertile valley seemed half obscured in melancholy haze, and over toward the dim hills beyond night had already fallen. No stars, no moon, no afterglow of sunset illumined the grayness that in this hour seemed prophetic of Lenore's future.

"'Safe!' he said. 'I shall be safe if only I can remember you,'" she whispered to herself, wonderingly. "What did he mean?"

Pondering the thought, she divined it had to do with Dorn's singular spiritual mood. He had gone to lend his body as so much physical brawn, so much weight, to a concerted movement of men, but his mind was apart from a harmony with that. Lenore felt that whatever had been the sacrifice made by Kurt Dorn, it had been passed with his decision to go to war. What she prayed for then was something of his spirit.

Slowly, in the gathering darkness, she descended the long slope. The approaching night seemed sad, with autumn song of insects. All about her breathed faith, from the black hills above, the gray slopes below, from the shadowy void, from the murmuring of insect life in the grass. The rugged fallow ground under her feet seemed to her to be a symbol of faith—faith that winter would come and pass—the spring sun and rain would burst the seeds of wheat—and another summer would see the golden fields of waving grain. If she did not live to see them, they would be there just the same; and so life and nature had faith in its promise. That strange whisper was to Lenore the whisper of God.

CHAPTER
26

*T*HROUGH the pale obscurity of a French night, cool, raw, moist, with a hint of spring in its freshness, a line of soldiers plodded along, the lonely, melancholy lanes. Wan starlight showed in the rifts between the clouds. Neither dark nor light, the midnight hour had its unreality in this line of marching men; and its reality in the dim, vague hedges, its spectral posts, its barren fields.

Rain had ceased to fall, but a fine, cold, penetrating mist filled the air. The ground was muddy in places, slippery in others; and here and there it held pools of water ankle-deep. The stride of the marching men appeared short and dragging, without swing or rhythm. It was weary, yet full of the latent power of youth, of unused vitality. Stern, clean-cut, youthful faces were set northward, unchanging in the shadowy, pale gleams of the night. These faces lifted intensely whenever a strange, muffled, deep-toned roar rolled out of the murky north. The night looked stormy, but that rumble was not thunder. Fifty miles northward, beyond that black and mysterious horizon, great guns were booming war.

Sometimes, as the breeze failed, the night was silent except for the slow, sloppy tramp of the marching soldiers. Then the low voices were hushed. When the wind freshened again it brought at intervals those deep, significant detonations which, as the hours passed, seemed to grow heavier and more thunderous.

At length a faint gray light appeared along the eastern sky, and gradually grew stronger. The dawn of another day was close at hand. It broke as if reluctantly, cold and gray and sunless.

The detachment of United States troops halted for camp outside of the French village of A——.

Kurt Dorn was at mess with his squad.

The months in France had flown away on wings of training and absorbing and waiting. Dorn had changed incalculably. But all he realized of it was that he weighed one hundred and ninety pounds and that he seemed to have lived a hundred swift lives. All that he saw and felt became part of him. His comrades had been won to him as friends by virtue of his ever-ready helping hand, by his devotion to training, by his close-lipped acceptance of all the toils and knocks and pains common to the making of a soldier. The squad lived together as one large family of brothers. Dorn's comrades had at first tormented him with his German name; they had made fun of his abstraction and his letter writing; they had misunderstood his aloofness. But the ridicule died away, and now, in the presaged nature of events, his comrades, all governed by the physical life of the soldier, took him for a man.

Perhaps it might have been chance, or it might have been true of all the American squads, but the fact was that Dorn's squad was a strangely assorted set of young men. Perhaps that might have been Dorn's conviction from coming to live long with them. They were a part of the New York Division of the——th, all supposed to be New York men. As a matter of fact, this was not true. Dorn was a native of Washington. Sanborn was a thick-set, sturdy fellow with the clear brown tan and clear brown eyes of the Californian. Brewer was from South Carolina, a lean, lanky southerner, with deep-set dark eyes. Dixon hailed from Massachusetts, from a fighting family, and from Harvard, where he had been a noted athlete. He was a big, lithe, handsome boy, red-faced and curly-haired. Purcell was a New Yorker, of rich family, highly connected, and his easy, clean, fine ways, with the elegance of his person, his blond distinction, made him stand out from his khaki-clad comrades, though he was clad identically with them. Rogers claimed the Bronx to be his home and he was proud of it. He was little, almost undersized, but a knot of muscle, a keen-faced youth with Irish blood in him. These particular soldiers of the squad were closest to Dorn.

Corporal Bob Owens came swinging in to throw his sombrero down.

"What's the orders, Bob?" someone inquired.

"We're going to rest here," he replied.

The news was taken impatiently by several and agreeably by the majority. They were all travel-stained and worn. Dorn did not comment on the news, but the fact was that he hated the French villages. They were so old, so dirty, so obsolete, so different from what he had been accustomed to. But he loved the pastoral French countryside, so calm and picturesque. He reflected that soon he would see the devastation wrought by the Huns.

"Any news from the front?" asked Dixon.

"I should smile," replied the corporal, grimly.

"Well, open up, you clam!"

Owens thereupon told swiftly and forcibly what he had heard. More advance of the Germans—it was familiar news. But somehow it was taken differently here within sound of the guns. Dorn studied his comrades, wondering if their sensations were similar to his. He expressed nothing of what he felt, but all the others had something to say. Hard, cool, fiery, violent speech that differed as those who uttered it differed, yet its predominant note rang fight.

"Just heard a funny story," said Owens, presently.

"Spring it," somebody replied.

"This comes from Berlin, so they say. According to rumor, the Kaiser and the Crown Prince seldom talk to each other. They happened to meet the other day. And the Crown Prince said: 'Say, pop, what got us into this war?'

"The Emperor replied, 'My son, I was deluded.'

"'Oh, sire, impossible!' exclaimed the Prince. 'How could it be?'

"'Well, some years ago I was visited by a grinning son-of-a-gun from New York—no other than the great T. R. I took him around. He was most interested in my troops. After he had inspected them, and particularly the Imperial Guard, he slapped me on the back and shouted, "Bill, you could lick the world!"...And, my son, I fell for it!'"

This story fetched a roar from every soldier present except Dorn. An absence of mirth in him had been noted before.

"Dorn, can't you laugh!" protested Dixon.

"Sure I can—when I hear something funny," replied Dorn.

His comrades gazed hopelessly at him.

"My Lawd! boy, thet was shore funny," drawled Brewer with his lazy southern manner.

"Kurt, you're not human," said Owens, sadly. "That's why they call you Demon Dorn."

All the boys in the squad had nicknames. In Dorn's case several had been applied by irrepressible comrades before one stuck. The first one received a poor reception from Kurt. The second happened to be a great blunder for the soldier who invented it. He was not in Dorn's squad, but he knew Dorn pretty well, and in a moment of devilry he had coined for Dorn the name, "Kaiser Dorn." Dorn's reaction to this appellation was discomfiting and painful for the soldier. As he lay flat on the ground, where Dorn had knocked him, he had struggled with a natural rage, quickly to overcome it. He showed the right kind of spirit. He got up. "Dorn, I apologize. I was only in fun. But some fun is about as funny as death." On the way out he suggested a more felicitous name—Demon Dorn. Somehow the boys took to that. It fitted many of Dorn's violent actions in training, especially the way he made a bayonet charge. Dorn objected strenuously. But the name stuck. No comrade or soldier ever again made a hint of Dorn's German name or blood.

"Fellows, if a funny story can't make Dorn laugh, he's absolutely a dead one," said Owens.

"Spring a new one, quick," spoke up someone. "Gee! it's great to laugh.... Why, I've not heard from home for a month!"

"Dorn, will you beat it so I can spring this one?" queried Owens.

"Sure," replied Dorn, amiably, as he started away. "I suppose you think me one of these I-dare-you-to-make-me-laugh sort of chaps."

"Forget her, Dorn—come out of it!" chirped up Rogers.

To Dorn's regret, he believed that he failed his comrades in one way, and he was always trying to make up for it. Part of the training of a soldier was the ever-present need and duty of cheerfulness. Every member of the squad had his secret, his own personal memory, his inner consciousness that he strove to keep hidden. Long ago Dorn had divined that this or that comrade was looking toward the bright side, or pretending there was one. They all played their parts. Like men they faced this incomprehensible duty, this tremendous separation, this dark and looming future, as if it was only hard work that must be done in good spirit. But Dorn, despite all his will, was mostly silent, aloof, brooding, locked up in his eternal strife of mind and soul. He could not help it. Notwithstanding all he saw and divined of the sacrifice and pain of his comrades, he knew that his ordeal was infinitely harder. It was natural that they hoped for the best. He had no hope.

"Boys," said Owens, "there's a squad of Blue Devils camped over here in an old barn. Just back from the front. Someone said there wasn't a man in it who hadn't had a dozen wounds, and some twice that many. We must see that bunch. Bravest soldiers of the whole war! They've been through the three years—at Verdun—on the Marne—and now this awful Flanders drive. It's up to us to see them."

News like this thrilled Dorn. During all the months he had been in France the deeds and valor of these German-named Blue Devils had come to him, here and there and everywhere. Dorn remembered all he heard, and believed it, too, though some of the charges and some of the burdens attributed to these famed soldiers seemed unbelievable. His opportunity had now come. With the moving up to the front he would meet reality; and all within him, the keen, strange eagerness, the curiosity that perplexed, the unintelligible longing, the heat and burn of passion, quickened and intensified.

Not until late in the afternoon, however, did off duty present an opportunity for him to go into the village. It looked the same as the other villages he had visited, and the inhabitants, old men, old women and children, all had the somber eyes, the strained, hungry faces, the oppressed look he had become accustomed to see. But sad as were these inhabitants of a village near the front, there was never in any one of them any absence of welcome to the Americans. Indeed, in most people he met there was a quick flashing of intense joy and gratitude. The Americans had come across the sea to fight beside the French. That was the import, tremendous and beautiful.

Dorn met Dixon and Rogers on the main street of the little village. They had been to see the Blue Devils.

"Better stay away from them," advised Dixon, dubiously.

"No!...Why?" ejaculated Dorn.

Dixon shook his head. "Greatest bunch I ever looked at. But I think they resented our presence. Pat and I were talking about them. It's strange, Dorn, but I believe these Blue Devils that have saved France and England, and perhaps America, too, don't like our being here."

"Impossible!" replied Dorn.

"Go and see for yourself," put in Rogers. "I believe we all ought to look them over."

Thoughtfully Dorn strode on in the direction indicated, and presently he arrived at the end of the village, where in an old orchard he found a low, rambling, dilapidated barn, before which clusters of soldiers in blue lounged around smoking fires. As he drew closer he saw that most of them seemed fixed in gloomy abstraction. A few were employed at some task of hand, and several bent over the pots on the fires. Dorn's sweeping gaze took in the whole scene, and his first quick, strange impression was that these soldiers resembled ghouls who had lived in dark holes of mud.

Kurt meant to make the most of his opportunity. To him, in his peculiar need, this meeting would be of greater significance than all else that had happened to him in France. The nearest soldier sat on a flattened pile of straw around which the ground was muddy. At first glance Kurt took him to be an African, so dark were face and eyes. No one heeded Kurt's approach. The moment was poignant to Kurt. He spoke French fairly well, so that it was emotion rather than lack of fluency which made his utterance somewhat unintelligible. The soldier raised his head. His face seemed a black flash—

his eyes piercingly black, staring, deep, full of terrible shadow. They did not appear to see in Kurt the man, but only the trim, clean United States army uniform. Kurt repeated his address, this time more clearly.

The Frenchman replied gruffly, and bent again over the faded worn coat he was scraping with a knife. Then Kurt noticed two things—the man's great, hollow, spare frame and the torn shirt, stained many colors, one of which was dark red. His hands resembled both those of a mason, with the horny callous inside, and those of a saltwater fisherman, with bludgy fingers and barked knuckles that never healed.

Dorn had to choose his words slowly, because of unfamiliarity with French, but he was deliberate, too, because he wanted to say the right thing. His eagerness made the Frenchman glance up again. But while Dorn talked of the long waits, the long marches, the arrival at this place, the satisfaction at nearing the front, his listener gave no sign that he heard. But he did hear, and so did several of his comrades.

"We're coming strong," he went on, his voice thrilling. "A million of us this year! We're untrained. We'll have to split up among English and French troops and learn how from you. But we've come—and we'll fight!"

Then the Frenchman put on his coat. That showed him to be an officer. He wore medals. The dark glance he then flashed over Dorn was different from his first. It gave Dorn both a twinge of shame and a thrill of pride. It took in Dorn's characteristic Teutonic blond features, and likewise an officer's swift appreciation of an extraordinarily splendid physique.

"You've German blood," he said.

"Yes. But I'm American," replied Dorn, simply, and

he met that soul-searching black gaze with all his intense and fearless spirit. Dorn felt that never in his life had he been subjected to such a test of his manhood, of his truth.

"My name's Huon," said the officer, and he extended one of the huge deformed hands.

"Mine's Dorn," replied Kurt, meeting that hand with his own.

Whereupon the Frenchman spoke rapidly to the comrade nearest him, so rapidly that all Kurt could make of what he said was that here was an American soldier with a new idea. They drew closer, and it became manifest that the interesting idea was Kurt's news about the American army. It was news here, and carefully pondered by these Frenchmen, as slowly one by one they questioned him. They doubted, but Dorn convinced them. They seemed to like his talk and his looks. Dorn's quick faculties grasped the simplicity of these soldiers. After three terrible years of unprecedented warfare, during which they had performed the impossible, they did not want a fresh army to come along and steal their glory by administering a final blow to a tottering enemy. Gazing into those strange, seared faces, beginning to see behind the iron mask, Dorn learned the one thing a soldier lives, fights, and dies for—glory.

Kurt Dorn was soon made welcome. He was made to exhaust his knowledge of French. He was studied by eyes that had gleamed in the face of death. His hand was wrung by hands that had dealt death. How terribly he felt that! And presently, when his excitement and emotion had subsided to the extent that he could really see what he looked at, then came the reward of reality, with all its incalculable meaning expressed to him in the gleaming bayonets, in the worn accoutrements, in the greatcoats like clapboards of mud, in the hands that were claws, in the feet that hobbled, in the strange, wonderful significance of bodily presence, standing there as proof of valor, of man's limitless endurance. In the faces, ah! there Dorn read the history that made him shudder and lifted him beyond himself. For there in those still, dark faces, of boys grown old in three years, shone the terror of war and the spirit that had resisted it.

Dorn, in his intensity, in the overemotion of his self-centered passion, so terribly driven to prove to himself something vague yet all-powerful, illusive yet imperious, divined what these Blue Devil soldiers had been through. His mind was more than telepathic. Almost it seemed that souls were bared to him. These soldiers, quiet, intent, made up a grim group of men. They seemed slow, thoughtful, plodding, wrapped and steeped in calm. But Dorn penetrated all this, and established the relation between it and the nameless and dreadful significance of their weapons and medals and uniforms and stripes, and the magnificent vitality that was now all but spent.

Dorn might have resembled a curious, adventure-loving boy, to judge from his handling of rifles and the way he slipped a strong hand along the gleaming bayonet blades. But he was more than the curious youth: he had begun to grasp a strange, intangible something for which he had no name. Something that must be attainable for him! Something that, for an hour or a moment, would make him a fighter not to be slighted by these supermen!

Whatever his youth or his impelling spirit of manhood, the fact was that he inspired many of these veterans of the bloody years to Homeric narratives of the siege of Verdun, of the retreat toward Paris, of the victory of the Marne, and lastly of the Kaiser's battle, this last and most awful offensive of the resourceful and frightful foe.

Brunelle told how he was the last survivor of a squad at Verdun who had been ordered to hold a breach made in a front stone wall along the outposts. How they had faced a bombardment of heavy guns—a whistling, shrieking, thundering roar, pierced by the higher explosion of a bursting shell—smoke and sulphur and gas—the crumbling of walls and downward fling of shrapnel. How the lives of soldiers were as lives of gnats hurled by wind and burned by flame. Death had a manifold and horrible diversity. A soldier's head, with ghastly face and conscious eyes, momentarily poised in the air while the body rode away invisibly with an exploding shell! He told of men blown up, shot through and riddled and brained and disemboweled, while their comrades, grim and unalterable, standing in a stream of blood, lived through the rain of shells, the smashing of walls, lived to fight like madmen the detachment following the bombardment, and to kill them every one.

Mathie told of the great retreat—how men who had fought for days, who were unbeaten and unafraid, had obeyed an order they hated and could not understand, and had marched day and night, day and night, eating as they toiled on, sleeping while they marched, on and on, bloody-footed, desperate, and terrible, filled with burning thirst and the agony of ceaseless motion, on with dragging legs and laboring breasts and red-hazed eyes, on and onward, unquenchable, with the spirit of France.

Sergeant Delorme spoke of the sudden fierce about-face at the Marne, of the irresistible onslaught of men whose homes had been invaded, whose children had been murdered, whose women had been enslaved, of a ruthless fighting, swift and deadly, and lastly of a bayonet charge by his own division, running down upon superior numbers, engaging them in hand-to-hand conflict, malignant and fatal, routing them over a field of blood and death.

"Monsieur Dorn, do you know the French use of a bayonet?" asked Delorme.

"No," replied Dorn.

"*Allons!* I will show you," he said, taking up two rifles and handing one to Dorn. "Come. It is so—and so—a trick. The Boches can't face cold steel....An, monsieur, you have the supple wrists of a juggler! You have the arms of a giant! You have the eyes of a duelist! You will be one grand spitter of German pigs!"

Dorn felt the blanching of his face, the tingling of his nerves, the tightening of his muscles. A cold and terrible meaning laid hold of him even in the instant when he trembled before this flaming-eyed French veteran who complimented him while he instructed. How easily, Dorn thought, could this soldier slip the bright bayonet over his guard and pierce him from breast to back! How horrible the proximity of that sinister blade, with its glint, its turn, its edge, so potently expressive of its history! Even as Dorn crossed bayonets with this inspired Frenchman he heard a soldier comrade say that Delorme had let daylight through fourteen Boches in that memorable victory of the Marne.

"You are very big and strong and quick, monsieur," said the officer Huon, simply. "In bayonet work you will be a killer of Boches."

In their talk and practice and help, in their intent to encourage the young American soldier, these Blue Devils one and all dealt in frank and inevitable terms of death. That was their meaning in life. It was immeasurably horrible for Dorn, because it seemed a realization of his imagined visions. He felt like a child among old savages of a war tribe. Yet he was fascinated by this close-up suggestion of man to man in battle, of German to American, of materialist to idealist, and beyond all control was the bursting surge of his blood. The exercises he had gone through, the trick he had acquired, somehow had strange power to liberate his emotion.

The officer Huon spoke English, and upon his words Dorn hung spellbound.

"You Americans have the fine dash, the nerve. You will perform wonders. But you don't realize what this war is. You will perish of sheer curiosity to see or eagerness to fight. But these are the least of the horrors of this war.

"Actual fighting is to me a relief, a forgetfulness, an excitement, and is so with many of my comrades. We have survived wounds, starvation, shell shock, poison gas and fire, the diseases of war, the awful toil of the trenches. And each and every one of us who has served long bears in his mind the particular horror that haunts him. I have known veterans to go mad at the screaming of shells. I have seen good soldiers stand up on a trench, inviting the fire that would end suspense.

For a man who hopes to escape alive this war is indeed the ninth circle of hell.

"My own particular horrors are mud, water, and cold. I have lived in dark, cold mud-holes so long that my mind concerning them is not right. I know it the moment I come out to rest. Rest! Do you know that we cannot rest? The comfort of this dirty old barn, of these fires, of this bare ground, is so great that we cannot rest, we cannot sleep, we cannot do anything. When I think of the past winter I do not remember injury and agony for myself, or the maimed and mangled bodies of my comrades. I remember only the horrible cold, the endless ages of waiting, the hopeless misery of the dug-outs, foul, black ratholes that we had to crawl into through sticky mud and filthy water. Mud, water, and cold, with the stench of the dead clogging your nostrils! That to me is war!...*Les Misérables!* You Americans will never know that, thank God. For it could not be endured by men who did not belong to this soil. After all, the filthy water is half blood and the mud is part of the dead of our people."

Huon talked on and on, with the eloquence of a Frenchman who relieves himself of a burden. He told of trenches dug in a swamp, lived in and fought in, and then used for the graves of the dead, trenches that had to be lived in again months afterward. The rotting dead were everywhere. When they were covered the rain would come to wash away the earth, exposing them again. That was the strange refrain of this soldier's moody lament—the rain that fell, the mud that forever held him rooted fast in the tracks of his despair. He told of night and storm, of a weary squad of men, lying flat, trying to dig in under cover of rain and darkness, of the hell of cannonade over and around them. He told of hours that blasted men's souls, of death that was a blessing, of escape that was torture beyond the endurance of humans. Crowning that night of horrors piled on horrors, when he had seen a dozen men buried alive in mud lifted by a monster shell, when he had seen a refuge deep underground opened and devastated by a like projectile, came a cloudburst that flooded the trenches and the fields, drowning soldiers whose injuries and mud-laden garments impeded their movements, and rendering escape for the others an infernal labor and a hideous wretchedness, unutterable and insupportable.

Round the camp fires the Blue Devils stood or lay, trying to rest. But the habit of the trenches was upon them. Dorn gazed at each and every soldier, so like in strange resemblance, so different in physical characteristics; and the sad, profound, and terrifying knowledge came to him of what they must have in their minds. He realized that all he needed was to suffer and fight and live through some little part of the war they had endured and then some truth would burst upon him. It was there in the restless steps, in the prone forms, in the sunken, glaring eyes. What soldiers, what men, what giants! Three and a half years of unnamable and indescribable fury of action and strife of thought! Not dead, nor stolid like oxen, were these soldiers of France. They had a simplicity that seemed appalling. We have given all; we have stood in the way, borne the brunt, saved you—this was flung at Dorn, not out of their thought, but from their presence. The fact that they were there were enough. He needed only to find these bravest of brave warriors real, alive, throbbing men.

Dorn lingered there, loath to leave. The great lesson of his life held vague connection in some way with this squad of French privates. But he could not pierce the veil. This meeting came as a climax to four months of momentous meetings with the best and the riffraff of many nations. Dorn had studied, talked, listened, and learned. He who had as yet given nothing, fought no enemy, saved no comrade or refugee or child in all this whirlpool of battling millions, felt a profound sense of his littleness, his ignorance. He who had imagined himself unfortunate had been blind, sick, self-centered. Here were soldiers to whom comfort and rest were the sweetest blessings upon the earth, and they could not grasp them. No more could they grasp them than could the gaping civilians and the distinguished travelers grasp what these grand hulks of veteran soldiers had done. Once a group of civilians halted near the soldiers. An officer was their escort. He tried to hurry them on, but failed. Delorme edged away into the gloomy, damp barn rather than meet such visitors. Some of his comrades followed suit. Ferier, the incomparable of the Blue Devils, the wearer of all the French medals and the bearer of twenty-five wounds received in battle—he sneaked away, afraid and humble and sullen, to hide himself from the curious. That action of Ferier's was a revelation to Dorn. He felt a sting of shame. There were two classes of people in relation to this war—those who went to fight and those who stayed behind. What had Delorme or Mathie or Ferier to do with the world of selfish, comfortable, well-fed men? Dorn heard a million voices of France crying out the bitter truth—that if these war-bowed veterans ever returned alive to their homes it would be with hopes and hearts and faiths burned out, with hands forever lost to their old use, with bodies that the war had robbed.

Dorn Bade his new-made friends adieu, and in the darkening twilight he hurried toward his own camp.

"If I could go back home now, honorably and well, I would never do it," he muttered. "I couldn't bear to live knowing what I know now—unless I had laughed at this death, and risked it—and dealt it!"

He was full of gladness, of exultation, in contemplation of the wonderful gift the hours had brought him. More than any men of history or present, he honored these soldiers the Germans feared. Like an Indian, Dorn respected brawn, courage, fortitude, silence, aloofness.

"There was a divinity in those soldiers," he soliloquized. "I felt it in their complete ignorance of their greatness. Yet they had pride, jealousy. Oh, the mystery of it all! ... When my day comes I'll last one short and terrible hour. I would never make a soldier like one of them. No American could. They are Frenchmen whose homes have been despoiled."

In the tent of his comrades that night Dorn reverted from old habit, and with a passionate eloquence he told all he had seen and heard, and much that he had felt. His influence on these young men, long established, but subtle and unconscious, became in that hour a tangible fact. He stirred them. He felt them thoughtful and sad, and yet more unflinching, stronger and keener for the inevitable day.

CHAPTER
27

*T*HE monstrous possibility that had consumed Kurt Dorn for many months at last became an event—he had arrived on the battlefront in France.

All afternoon the company of United States troops had marched from far back of the line, resting, as darkness came on, at a camp of reserves, and then going on. Artillery fire had been desultory during this march; the big guns that had rolled their thunder miles and miles were now silent. But an immense activity and a horde of soldiers back of the lines brought strange leaden oppression to Kurt Dorn's heart.

The last slow travel of his squad over dark, barren space and through deep, narrow, winding lanes in the ground had been a nightmare ending to the long journey. France had not yet become clear to him; he was a stranger in a strange land; in spite of his tremendous interest and excitement, all seemed abstract matters of his feeling, the plague of himself made actuality the substance of dreams. That last day, the cumulation of months of training and travel, had been one in which he had observed, heard, talked and felt in a nervous and fevered excitement. But now he imagined he could not remember any of it. His poignant experience with the Blue Devils had been a reality he could never forget, but now this blackness of subterranean cavern, this damp, sickening odor of earth, this presence of men, the strange, muffled sounds—all these were unreal. How had he come here? His mind labored with a burden strangely like that on his chest. A different, utterly unfamiliar emotion seemed rising over him. Maybe that was because he was very tired and very sleepy. Sometime that night he must go on duty. He ought to sleep. It was impossible. He could not close his eyes. An effort to attend to what he was actually doing disclosed the fact that he was listening with all his strength. For what? He could not answer then. He heard the distant, muffled sounds, and low voices nearer, and thuds and footfalls. His comrades were near him; he heard their breathing; he felt their presence. They were strained and intense; like him, they were locked up in their own prison of emotions.

Always heretofore, on nights that he lay sleepless, Dorn had thought of the two things dearest on earth to him—Lenore Anderson and the golden wheat hills of his home. This night he called up Lenore's image. It hung there in the blackness, a dim, pale phantom of her sweet face, her beautiful eyes, her sad lips, and then it vanished. Not at all could he call up a vision of his beloved wheat fields. So the suspicion that something was wrong with his mind became a certainty. It angered him, quickened his sensitiveness, even while he despaired. He ground his teeth and clenched his fists and swore to realize his presence there, and to rise to the occasion as had been his vaunted ambition.

Suddenly he felt something slimy and hairy against his wrist—then a stinging bite. A rat! A trench rat that lived on flesh! He flung his arm violently and beat upon the soft earth. The incident of surprise and disgust helped Dorn at least in one way. His mind had been set upon a strange and supreme condition of his being there, of an emotion about to overcome him. The bite of a rat, drawing blood, made a literal fact of his being a soldier, in a dugout at the front waiting in the blackness for his call to go on guard. This incident proved to Dorn his limitations, and that he was too terribly concerned with his feelings ever to last long as a soldier. But he could not help himself. His pulse, his heart, his brain, all seemed to beat, beat, beat with a nameless passion.

Was he losing his nerve—was he afraid? His denial did not reassure him. He understood that patriotism and passion were emotions, and that the realities of a soldier's life were not.

Dorn forced himself to think of realities, hoping thus to get a grasp upon his vanishing courage. And memory helped him. Not so many days, weeks, months back he had been a different man. At Bordeaux, when his squad first set foot upon French soil! That was a splendid reality. How he had thrilled at the welcome of the French sailors!

Then he thought of the strenuous round of army duties, of training tasks, of traveling in cold boxcars, of

endless marches, of camps and villages, of drills and
billets. Never to be forgotten was that morning, now
seemingly long ago, when an officer had ordered the
battalion to pack. "We are going to the front!" he announced. Magic words! What excitement, what whoop-
ing, what bragging and joy among the boys, what hurry
and bustle and remarkable efficiency! That had been a
reality of actual experience, but the meaning of it, the
terrible significance, had been beyond the mind of any
American.

"I'm here—at the front—now," whispered Dorn to
himself. "A few rods away are Germans!" ... Inconceivable—no reality at all! He went on with his swift account
of things, with his mind ever sharpening, with that
strange, mounting emotion flooding to the full, ready to
burst its barriers. When he and his comrades had
watched their transport trains move away—when they
had stood waiting for their own trains—had the idea
of actual conflict yet dawned upon them? Dorn had to
answer no. He remembered that he had made few
friends among the inhabitants of towns and villages
where he had stayed. What leisure time he got had been
given to a seeking out of sailors, soldiers, and men of
all races, with whom he found himself in remarkable
contact. The ends of the world brought together by one
war! How could his memory ever hold all that had come
to him? But it did. Passion liberated it. He saw now that
his eye was a lens, his mind a sponge, his heart a gulf.

Out of the hundreds of thousands of American
troops in France, what honor it was to be in the chosen
battalion to go to the front! Dorn lived only with his
squad, but he felt the envy of the whole army. What
luck! To be chosen from so many—to go out and see

the game through quickly! He began to consider that differently now. The luck might be with the soldiers left behind. Always, underneath Dorn's perplexity and pondering, under his intelligence and spirit at their best, had been a something deeply personal, something of the internal of him, a selfish instinct. It was the nature of man—self-preservation. Like a tempest swept over Dorn the most significant ordeal and lesson of his experience in France—that wonderful reality when he met the Blue Devils and they took him in. However long he lived, his life must necessarily be transformed from contact with those great men.

The night march over the unending roads, through the gloom and the spectral starlight, with the dull rumblings of cannon shocking his heart—that Dorn lived over, finding strangely a minutest detail of observation and a singular veracity of feeling fixed in his memory.

Afternoon of that very day, at the reserve camp somewhere back there, had brought an officer's address to the soldiers, a strong and emphatic appeal as well as order—to obey, to do one's duty, to take no chances, to be eternally vigilant, to believe that every man had advantage on his side, even in war, if he were not a fool or a daredevil. Dorn had absorbed the speech, remembered every word, but it all seemed futile now. Then had come the impressive inspection of equipment, a careful examination of gas masks, rifles, knapsacks. After that the order to march!

Dorn imagined that he had remembered little, but he had remembered all. Perhaps the sense of strange unreality was only the twist in his mind. Yet he did not know where he was—what part of France—how far north or south on the front line—in what sector. Could not that account for the sense of feeling lost?

Nevertheless, he was there at the end of all this incomprehensible journey. He became possessed by an irresistible desire to hurry. Once more Dorn attempted to control the far-flinging of his thoughts—to come down to earth. The earth was there under his hand, soft, sticky, moldy, smelling vilely. He dug his fingers into it, until the feel of something like a bone made him jerk them out. Perhaps he had felt a stone. A tiny, creeping, chilly shudder went up his back. Then he remembered, he felt, he saw his little attic room, in the old home back among the wheat hills of the Northwest. Six thousand miles away! He would never see that room again. What unaccountable vagary of memory had ever recalled it to him? It faded out of his mind.

Some of his comrades whispered; now and then one rolled over; none snored, for none of them slept. Dorn felt more aloof from them than ever. How isolated each one was, locked in his own trouble! Every one of them, like himself, had a lonely soul. Perhaps they were facing it. He could not conceive of a careless, thoughtless, emotionless attitude toward this first night in the frontline trench.

Dorn gradually grew more acutely sensitive to the many faint, rustling, whispering sounds in and near the dugout.

A soldier came stooping into the opaque square of the dugout door. His rifle, striking the framework, gave out a metallic clink. This fellow expelled a sudden heavy breath as if throwing off an oppression.

"Is that you, Sanborn?" This whisper Dorn recognized as Dixon's. It was full of suppressed excitement.

"Yes."

"Guess it's my turn next. How—how does it go?"

Sanborn's laugh had an odd little quaver. "Why, so far as I know, I guess it's all right. Damn queer, though. I wish we'd got here in daytime....But maybe that wouldn't help."

"Humph!...Pretty quiet out there?"

"So Bob says, but what's he know—more than us? I heard guns up the line, and rifle fire not so far off."

"Can you see any—"

"Not a damn thing—yet everything," interrupted Sanborn, enigmatically.

"Dixon!" called Owens, low and quickly, from the darkness.

Dixon did not reply. His sudden hard breathing, the brushing of his garments against the door, then swift, soft steps dying away attested to the fact of his going.

Dorn tried to compose himself to rest, if not to sleep. He heard Sanborn sit down, and then apparently stay very still for some time. All of a sudden he whispered to himself. Dorn distinguished the word "hell."

"What's ailin' you, pard?" drawled Brewer.

Sanborn growled under his breath, and when someone else in the dugout quizzed him curiously he burst out: "I'll bet you galoots the state of California against a dill pickle that when your turn comes you'll be sick in your gizzards!"

"We'll take our medicine," came in the soft, quiet voice of Purcell.

No more was said. The men all pretended to fall asleep, each ashamed to let his comrade think he was concerned.

A short, dull, heavy rumble seemed to burst the outer stillness. For a moment the dugout was silent as a tomb. No one breathed. Then came a jar of the earth, a creaking of shaken timbers. Someone gasped involuntarily. Another whispered:

"By God! the real thing!"

Dorn wondered how far away that jarring shell had alighted. Not so far! It was the first he had ever heard explode near him. Roaring of cannon, exploding of shell—this had been a source of everyday talk among his comrades. But the jar, the tremble of the earth, had a dreadful significance. Another rumble, another jar, not so heavy or so near this time, and then a few sharply connected reports, clamped Dorn as in a cold vise. Machine-gun shots! Many thousand machine-gun shots had he heard, but none with the life and the spite and the spang of these. Did he imagine the difference? Cold as he felt, he began to sweat, and continually, as he wiped the palms of his hands, they grew wet again. A queer sensation of light-headedness and weakness seemed to possess him. The roots of his willpower seemed numb. Nevertheless, all the more revolving and all-embracing seemed his mind.

The officer in his speech a few hours back had said the sector to which the battalion had been assigned was alive. By this he meant that active bombardment, machine-gun fire, hand-grenade throwing, and gas shelling, or attack in force might come any time, and certainly must come as soon as the Germans suspected the presence of an American force opposite them.

That was the stunning reality to Dorn—the actual existence of the Huns a few rods distant. But realization of them had not brought him to the verge of panic. He would not flinch at confronting the whole German army. Nor did he imagine he put a great price upon his life.

Nor did he have any abnormal dread of pain. Nor had the well-remembered teachings of the Bible troubled his spirit. Was he going to be a coward because of some incalculable thing in him or force operating against him? Already he sat there, shivering and sweating, with the load on his breast growing laborsome, with all his sensorial being absolutely at keenest edge.

Rapid footfalls halted his heart beats. They came from above, outside the dugout, from the trench.

"Dorn, come out!" called the corporal.

Dorn's response was instant. But he was as blind as if he had no eyes, and he had to feel his way to climb out. The indistinct, blurred form of the corporal seemed half merged in the pale gloom of the trench. A cool wind whipped at Dorn's hot face. Surcharged with emotion, the nature of which he feared, Dorn followed the corporal, stumbling and sliding over the wet boards, knocking bits of earth from the walls, feeling a sick, icy gripe in his bowels. Some strange light flared up—died away. Another rumble, distinct, heavy, and vibrating! To his left somewhere the earth received a shock. Dorn felt a wave of air that was not wind.

The corporal led the way past motionless men peering out over the top of the wall, and on to a widening, where an abutment of filled bags loomed up darkly. Here the corporal cautiously climbed up breaks in the wall and stooped behind the fortification. Dorn followed. His legs did not feel natural. Something was lost out of them. Then he saw the little figure of Rogers beside him. Dorn's turn meant Rogers's relief. How pale against the night appeared the face of Rogers! As he peered under his helmet at Dorn a low whining passed in the air overhead. Rogers started slightly. A thump sounded out there, interrupting the corporal, who had begun to speak. He repeated his order to Dorn, bending a little to peer into his face. Dorn tried to open his lips to say he did not understand, but his lips were mute. Then the corporal led Rogers away.

That moment alone, out in the open, with the strange, windy pall of night—all enveloping, with the flares, like sheet lightning, along the horizon, with a rumble here and a roar there, with whistling fiends riding the blackness above, with a series of popping, impelling reports seemingly close in front—that drove home to Kurt Dorn a cruel and present and unescapable reality.

At that instant, like bitter fate, shot up a rocket, or a star flare of calcium light, bursting to expose all underneath in pitiless radiance. With a gasp that was a sob, Dorn shrank flat against the wall, staring into the fading circle, feeling a creep of paralysis. He must be seen. He expected the sharp, biting series of a machinegun or the bursting of a bomb. But nothing happened, except that the flare died away. It had come from behind his own lines. Control of his muscles had almost returned when a heavy boom came from the German side. Miles away, perhaps, but close! That boom meant a great shell speeding on its hideous mission. It would pass over him. He listened. The wind came from that side. It was cold; it smelled of burned powder; it carried sounds he was beginning to appreciate—shots, rumbles, spats, and thuds, whistles of varying degree, all isolated sounds. Then he caught a strange, low moaning. It rose. It was coming fast. It became an o-o-o-O-O-O! Nearer and nearer! It took on a singing whistle. It was passing—no—falling! . . . A mighty blow was delivered to the earth—a jar—a splitting shock to windy darkness; a wave of heavy air was flung afar—and then came the soft, heavy thumping of falling earth.

That shell had exploded close to the place where Dorn stood. It terrified him. It reduced him to a palpitating, stricken wretch, utterly unable to cope with the terror. It was not what he had expected. What were words, anyhow? By words alone he had understood this shell thing. Death was only a word, too. But to be blown to atoms! It came every moment to some poor devil; it might come to him. But that was not fighting. Somewhere off in the blackness a huge iron monster belched this hell out upon defenseless men. Revolting and inconceivable truth!

It was Dorn's ordeal that his mentality robbed this hour of novelty and of adventure, that while his natural, physical fear incited panic and nausea and a horrible, convulsive internal retching, his highly organized, exquisitely sensitive mind, more like a woman's in its capacity for emotion, must suffer through imagining the infinite agonies that he might really escape. Every shell then must blow him to bits; every agony of every soldier must be his.

But he knew what his duty was, and as soon as he could move he began to edge along the short beat. Once at the end he drew a deep and shuddering breath, and, fighting all his involuntary instincts, he peered over the top. An invisible thing whipped close over his head. It did not whistle; it cut. Out in front of him was only thick, pale gloom, with spectral forms, leading away to the horizon, where flares, like sheet lightning of a summer night's storm, ran along showing smoke and bold, ragged outlines. Then he went to the other end to peer over there. His eyes were keen, and through long years of habit at home, going about at night without light, he could see distinctly where ordinary sight would meet only a blank wall. The flat ground immediately before him was bare of living or moving objects. That was his duty as sentinel here—to make sure of no surprise patrol from the enemy lines. It helped Dorn to realize that he could accomplish this duty even though he was in a torment.

That space before him was empty, but it was charged with current. Wind, shadow, gloom, smoke, electricity, death, spirit—whatever that current was, Dorn felt it. He was more afraid of that than the occasional bullets which zipped across. Sometimes shots from his own squad rang out up and down the line. Off somewhat to the north a machine gun on the Allies' side spoke now and then spitefully. Way back a big gun boomed. Dorn listened to the whine of shells from his own side with a far different sense than that with which he heard shells whine from the enemy. How natural and yet how unreasonable! Shells from the other side came over to destroy him; shells from his side went back to save him. But both were shot to kill! Was he, the unknown and shrinking novice of a soldier, any better than an unknown and shrinking soldier far across there in the darkness? What was equality? But these were Germans! That thing so often said—so beaten into his brain—did not convince out here in the face of death.

Four o'clock! With the gray light came a gradually increasing number of shells. Most of them struck far back. A few, to right and left, dropped near the front line. The dawn broke—such a dawn as he never dreamed of—smoky and raw, with thunder spreading to a circle all around the horizon.

He was relieved. On his way in he passed Purcell at the nearest post. The elegant New Yorker bore himself with outward calm. But in the gray dawn he looked haggard and drawn. Older! That flashed through Dorn's mind. A single night had contained years, more than years. Others of the squad had subtly changed. Dixon gave him a penetrating look, as if he wore a mask, under which was a face of betrayal, of contrast to that soldier bearing, of youth that was gone forever.

CHAPTER

28

THE squad of men to which Dorn belonged had to be on the lookout continually for an attack that was inevitable. The Germans were feeling out the line, probably to verify spy news of the United States troops taking over a sector. They had not, however, made sure of this fact.

The gas shells came over regularly, making life for the men a kind of suffocation most of the time. And the great shells that blew enormous holes in front and in back of their position never allowed a relaxation from strain. Drawn and haggard grew the faces that had been so clean-cut and brown and fresh.

One evening at mess, when the sector appeared quiet enough to permit of rest, Rogers was talking to some comrades before the door of the dugout.

"It sure got my goat, that little promenade of ours

last night over into No Man's Land," he said. "We had orders to slip out and halt a German patrol that was supposed to be stealing over to our line. We crawled on our bellies, looking and listening every minute. If that isn't the limit! My heart was in my mouth. I couldn't breathe. And for the first moments, if I'd run into a Hun, I'd had no more strength than a rabbit. But all seemed clear. It was not a bright night—sort of opaque and gloomy—shadows everywhere. There wasn't any patrol coming. But Corporal Owens thought he heard men farther on working with wire. We crawled some more. And we must have got pretty close to the enemy lines— in fact, we had—when up shot one of those damned calcium flares. We all burrowed into the ground. I was paralyzed. It got as light as noon—strange greenish-white flare. It magnified. Flat as I lay, I saw the German embankments not fifty yards away. I made sure we were goners. Slowly the light burned out. Then that machine gun you all heard began to rattle. Something queer about the way every shot of a machine gun bites the air. We heard the bullets, low down, right over us. Say, boys, I'd almost rather be hit and have it done with! . . . We began to crawl back. I wanted to run. We all wanted to. But Owens is a nervy guy and he kept whispering. Another machine gun cut loose, and bullets rained over us. Like hail they hit somewhere ahead, scattering the gravel. We'd almost reached our line when Smith jumped up and ran. He said afterward that he just couldn't help himself. The suspense was awful. I know. I've been a clerk in a bank! Get that? And there I was under a hail of Hun lead, without being able to under-stand why, or feel that any time had passed since giving up my job to go to war. Queer how I saw my old desk!

...Well, that's how Smith got his. I heard the bullets spat him, sort of thick and soft....Ugh!...Owens and I dragged him along, and finally into the trench. He had a bullet through his shoulder and leg. Guess he'll live, all right....Boys, take this from me. Nobody can *tell* you what a machine gun is like. A rifle, now, is not so much. You get shot at, and you know the man must reload and aim. That takes time. But a machine gun! Whew! It's a comb—a fine-toothed comb—and you're the louse it's after! You hear that steady rattle, and then you hear bullets everywhere. Think of a man against a machine gun! It's not a square deal."

Dixon was one of the listeners. He laughed.

"Rogers, I'd like to have been with you. Next time I'll volunteer. You had action—a run for your money. That's what I enlisted for. Standing still—doing nothing but wait—that drives me half mad. My years of football have made action necessary. Otherwise I go stale in mind and body....Last night, before you went on that scouting trip, I had been on duty two hours. Near midnight. The shelling had died down. All became quiet. No flares—no flashes anywhere. There was a luminous kind of glow in the sky—moonlight through thin clouds. I had to listen and watch. But I couldn't keep back my thoughts. There I was, a soldier, facing No Man's Land, across whose dark space were the Huns we have come to regard as devils in brutality, yet less than men....And I thought of home. No man knows what home really is until he stands that lonely midnight guard. A shipwrecked sailor appreciates the comforts he once had; a desert wanderer, lost and starving, remembers the food he once wasted; a volunteer soldier, facing death in the darkness, thinks of his home! It is a hell of a feeling! . . . And, thinking of home, I remembered my girl. I've been gone four months—have been at the front seven days (or is it seven years?) and last night in the darkness she came to me. Oh yes! she was there! She seemed reproachful, as she was when she coaxed me not to enlist. My girl was not one of the kind who sends her lover to war and swears she will die an old maid unless he returns. Mine begged me to stay home, or at least wait for the draft. But I wasn't built that way. I enlisted. And last night I felt the bitterness of a soldier's fate. All this beautiful stuff is bunk! . . . My girl is a peach. She had many admirers, two in particular that made me run my best down the stretch. One is club-footed. He couldn't fight. The other is all yellow. Him she liked best. He had her fooled, the damned slacker. . . . I wish I could believe I'd get safe back home, with a few Huns to my credit—the Croix de Guerre—and an officer's uniform. That would be great. How I could show up those fellows! . . . But I'll get killed—as sure as God made little apples I'll get killed—and she will marry one of the men who would not fight!"

It was about the middle of a clear morning, still cold, but the sun was shining. Guns were speaking intermittently. Those soldiers who were off duty had their gas masks in their hands. All were gazing intently upward.

Dorn sat a little apart from them. He, too, looked skyward, and he was so absorbed that he did not hear the occasional rumble of a distant gun. He was watching the airmen at work—the most wonderful and famous feature of the war. It absolutely enthralled Dorn. As a boy he had loved to watch the soaring of the golden eagles, and once he had seen a great wide-winged condor, swooping along a mountain crest. How he had envied them the freedom of the heights—the loneliness of the unscalable crags—the companionship of the clouds! Here he gazed and marveled at the man-eagles of the air.

German planes had ventured over the lines, flying high, and English planes had swept up to intercept them. One was rising then not far away, climbing fast, like a fish hawk with prey in its claws. Its color, its framework, its propeller, and its aviator showed distinctly against the sky. The buzzing, high-pitched drone of its motor floated down.

The other airplanes, far above, had lost their semblance to mechanical man-driven machines. They were now the eagles of the air. They were rising, circling, diving in maneuvers that Dorn knew meant pursuit. But he could not understand these movements. To him the air battle looked as it must have looked to an Indian. Birds of prey in combat! Dorn recalled verses he had learned as a boy, written by a poet who sang of future wars in the air. What he prophesied had come true. Was there not a sage now who could pierce the veil of the future and sing of such a thing as sacred human life? Dorn had his doubts. Poets and dreamers appeared not to be the men who could halt materialism. Strangely then, as Dorn gazed bitterly up at these fierce fliers who fought in the heavens, he remembered the story of the three wise men and of Bethlehem. Was it only a story? Where on this sunny spring morning was Christ, and the love of man for man?

At that moment one of the forward airplanes, which was drifting back over the enemy lines, lost its singular grace of slow, sweeping movement. It poised in the air. It changed shape. It pitched as if from wave to wave of wind. A faint puff of smoke showed. Tiny specks, visible to Dorn's powerful eyes, seemed to detach themselves and fall, to be followed by the plane itself in sheer downward descent.

Dorn leaped to his feet. What a thrilling and terrible sight! His comrades stood bareheaded, red faces uplifted, open-mouthed and wild with excitement, not daring to disobey orders and yell at the top of their lungs. Dorn felt, strong above the softened wonder and thought of a moment back, a tingling, pulsating wave of gushing blood go over him. Like his comrades, he began to wave his arms and stamp and bite his tongue.

Swiftly the doomed plane swept down out of sight. Gone! At that instant something which had seemed like a bird must have become a broken mass. The other planes drifted eastward.

Dorn gasped, and broke the spell on him. He was hot and wet with sweat, quivering with a frenzy. How many thousand soldiers of the Allies had seen that downward flight of the Boche? Dorn pitied the destroyed airman, hated himself, and had all the fury of savage joy that had been in his comrades.

Dorn, relieved from guard and firing post, rushed back to the dugout. He needed the dark of that dungeon. He crawled in and, searching out the remotest, blackest corner, hidden from all human eyes, and especially his own, he lay there clammy and wet all over, with an icy, sickening rend, like a wound, in the pit of his stomach. He shut his eyes, but that did not shut out what he saw. "*So help me God!*" he whispered to himself. . . . Six endless months had gone to the preparation of a deed that had taken one second! That transformed him! His life on earth, his spirit in the beyond, could never be now what they might have been. And he sobbed through grinding teeth as he felt the disintegrating, agonizing, irremediable forces at work on body, mind, and soul.

He had blown out the brains of his first German.

Fires of hell, in two long lines, bordering a barren, ghastly, hazy strip of land, burst forth from the earth. From holes where men hid poured thunder of guns and stream of smoke and screeching of iron. That worthless strip of land, barring deadly foes, shook as with repeated earthquakes. Huge spouts of black and yellow earth lifted, fountainlike, to the dull, heavy bursts of shells. Pound and jar, whistle and whine, long, broken rumble, and the rattling concatenation of quick shots like metallic cries, exploding hailstorm of iron in the air, a desert over which thousands of puffs of smoke shot up and swelled and drifted, the sliding crash far away, the sibilant hiss swift overhead. Boom! Weeeee— eeeeoooo! from the east. Boom! Weeeee—eeeeoooo! from the west.

At sunset there was no letup. The night was all the more hideous. Along the horizon flashed up the hot sheets of lightning that were not of a summer storm. Angry, lurid, red, these upflung blazes and flames illumined the murky sky, showing in the fitful and flickering intervals wagons driving toward the front, and patrols of soldiers running toward some point, and great upheavals of earth spread high.

This heavy cannonading died away in the middle of the night until an hour before dawn, when it began again with redoubled fury and lasted until daybreak.

Dawn came reluctantly, Dorn thought. He was glad. It meant a charge. Another night of that hellish shrieking and bursting of shells would kill his mind, if not his body. He stood on guard at a fighting post. Corporal Owens lay at his feet, wounded slightly. He would not retire. As the cannons ceased he went to sleep. Rogers stood close on one side, Dixon on the other. The squad had lived through that awful night. Soldiers were bringing food and drink to them. All appeared grimly gay.

Dorn was not gay. But he knew this was the day he would laugh in the teeth of death. A slumbrous, slow heat burned deep in him, like a covered fire, fierce and hot at heart, awaiting the wind. Watching there, he did not voluntarily move a muscle, yet all his body twitched like that of the trained athlete, strained to leap into the great race of his life.

An officer came hurrying through. The talking hushed. Men on guard, backs to the trench, never moved their eyes from the forbidden land in front. The officer spoke. Look for a charge! Reserves were close behind. He gave his orders and passed on.

Then an Allied gun opened up with a boom. The shell moaned on over. Dorn saw where it burst, sending smoke and earth aloft. That must have been a signal for a bombardment of the enemy all along this sector, for big and little guns began to thunder and crack.

The spectacle before Dorn's hard, keen eyes was one that he thought wonderful. Far across No Man's Land, which sloped somewhat at that point in the plain, he saw movement of troops and guns. His eyes were telescopic. Over there the ground appeared grassy in places, with green ridges rising, and patches of brush and straggling trees standing out clearly. Faint, gray-colored squads of soldiers passed in sight with helmets flashing in the sun; guns were being hauled forward; mounted horsemen dashed here and there, vanishing and reappearing; and all through that wide area of color and action shot up live black spouts of earth crowned in white smoke that hung in the air after the earth fell back. They were beautiful, these shell bursts. Round balls of white smoke magically appeared in the air, to spread and drift; long, yellow columns or streaks rose here, and there leaped up a fan-shaped, dirty cloud, savage and sinister; sometimes several shells burst close together, dashing the upflung sheets of earth together and blending their smoke; at intervals a huge, creamy-yellow explosion, like a geyser, rose aloft to spread and mushroom, then to detach itself from the heavier body it had upheaved, and float away, white and graceful, on the wind.

Sinister beauty! Dorn soon lost sight of that. There came a gnawing at his vitals. The far scene of action could not hold his gaze. That dark, uneven, hummocky break in the earth, which was a goodly number of rods distant, yet now seemed close, drew a startling attention. Dorn felt his eyes widen and pop. Spots and dots, shiny, illusive, bobbed along that break, behind the mounds, beyond the farther banks. A yell as from one lusty throat ran along the line of which Dorn's squad held the center. Dorn's sight had a piercing intensity. All was hard under his grip—his rifle, the boards and bags against which he leaned. Corporal Owens rose beside him, bareheaded, to call low and fiercely to his men.

The gray dots and shiny spots leaped up magically and appallingly into men. German soldiers! Boches!

Huns on a charge! They were many, but wide apart. They charged, running low.

Machine-gun rattle, rifle fire, and strangled shouts blended along the line. From the charging Huns seemed to come a sound that was neither battle cry nor yell nor chant, yet all of them together. The gray advancing line thinned at points opposite the machine guns, but it was coming fast.

Dorn cursed his hard, fumbling hands, which seemed so eager and fierce that they stiffened. They burned, too, from their grip on the hot rifle. Shot after shot he fired, missing. He could not hit a field full of Huns. He dropped shells, fumbled with them at the breech, loaded wildly, aimed at random, pulled convulsively. His brain was on fire. He had no anger, no fear, only a great and futile eagerness. Yell and crack filled his ears. The gray, stolid, unalterable Huns must be driven back. Dorn loaded, crushed his rifle steady, pointed low at a great gray bulk, and fired. That Hun pitched down out of the gray advancing line. The sight almost overcame Dorn. Dizzy, with blurred eyes, he leaned over his gun. His abdomen and breast heaved, and he strangled over his gorge. Almost he fainted. But violence beside him somehow, great heaps of dust and gravel flung over him, hoarse, wild yells in his ears, roused him. The boches were on the line! He leaped up. Through the dust he saw charging gray forms, thick and heavy. They plunged, as if actuated by one will. Bulky blond men, ashen of face, with eyes of blue fire and brutal mouths set grim—Huns!

Up out of the shallow trench sprang comrades on each side of Dorn. No rats to be cornered in a hole! Dorn seemed drawn by powerful hauling chains. He did not need to climb! Four big Germans appeared simultaneously upon the embankment of bags. They were shooting. One swung aloft an arm and closed fist. He yelled like a demon. He was a bomb thrower. On the instant a bullet hit Dorn, tearing at the side of his head, stinging excruciatingly, knocking him down, flooding his face with blood. The shock, like a weight, held him down, but he was not dazed. A body, khaki-clad, rolled down beside him, convulsively flopped against him. He bounded erect, his ears filled with a hoarse and clicking din, his heart strangely lifting in his breast.

Only one German now stood upon the embankment of bags and he was the threatening bomb thrower. The others were down—gray forms wrestling with brown. Dixon was lunging at the bomb thrower, and, reaching him with the bayonet, ran him through the belly. He toppled over with an awful cry and fell hard on the other side of the wall of loaded bags. The bomb exploded. In the streaky burst Dixon seemed to charge in bulk—to be flung aside like a leaf by a gale.

Little Rogers had engaged an enemy who towered over him. They feinted, swung, and cracked their guns together, then locked bayonets. Another German striding from behind stabbed Rogers in the back. He writhed off the bloody bayonet, falling toward Dorn, showing a white face that changed as he fell, with quiver of torture and dying eyes.

That dormant inhibited self of Dorn suddenly was no more. Fast as a flash he was upon the murdering Hun. Bayonet and rifle barrel lunged through him, and so terrible was the thrust that the German was thrown back as if at a blow from a battering ram. Dorn whirled the bloody bayonet, and it crashed to the ground the rifle of the other German. Dorn saw not the visage of the foe—only the thick-set body, and this he ripped open in one mighty slash. The German's life spilled out horribly.

Dorn leaped over the bloody mass. Owens lay next, wide-eyed, alive, but stricken. Purcell fought with clubbed rifle, backing away from several foes. Brewer was being beaten down. Gray forms closing in! Dorn saw leveled small guns, flashes of red, the impact of lead striking him. But he heard no shots. The roar in his ears was the filling of a gulf. Out of that gulf pierced his laugh. Gray forms—guns—bullets—bayonets— death—he laughed at them. His moment had come. Here he would pay. His immense and terrible joy bridged the ages between the past and this moment when he leaped light and swift, like a huge cat, upon them. They fired and they hit, but Dorn sprang on, tigerishly, with his loud and nameless laugh. Bayonets thrust at him were straws. These enemies gave way, appalled. With sweep and lunge he killed one and split a second's skull before the first had fallen. A third he lifted and upset and gored, like a bull, in one single stroke. The fourth and last of that group, screaming his terror and fury, ran in close to get beyond that sweeping blade. He fired as he ran. Dorn tripped him heavily, and he had scarcely struck the ground when that steel transfixed his bulging throat.

Brewer was down, but Purcell had been reinforced. Soldiers in brown came on the run, shooting, yelling, brandishing. They closed in on the Germans, and Dorn ran into that mêlée to make one thrust at each gray form he encountered.

Shriller yells along the line—American yells—the

enemy there had given ground! Dorn heard. He saw the gray line waver. He saw reserves running to aid his squad. The Germans would be beaten back. There was whirling blackness in his head through which he seemed to see. The laugh broke hoarse and harsh from his throat. Dust and blood choked him.

Another gray form blocked his leaping way. Dorn saw only low down, the gray arms reaching with bright, unstained blade. His own bloody bayonet clashed against it, locked, and felt the helplessness of the arms that wielded it. An instant of pause—a heaving, breathless instinct of impending exhaustion—a moment when the petrific mace of primitive man stayed at the return of the human—then with bloody foam on his lips Dorn spent his madness.

A supple twist—the French trick—and Dorn's powerful lunge, with all his ponderous weight, drove his bayonet through the enemy's lungs.

"*Ka—ma—rad!*" came the strange, strangling cry.

A weight sagged down on Dorn's rifle. He did not pull out the bayonet, but as it lowered with the burden of the body his eyes, fixed at one height, suddenly had brought into their range the face of his foe.

A boy—dying on his bayonet! Then came a resurrection of Kurt Dorn's soul. He looked at what must be his last deed as a soldier. His mind halted. He saw only the ghastly face, the eyes in which he expected to see hate, but saw only love of life, suddenly reborn, suddenly surprised at death.

"God save you, German! I'd give my life for yours!"

Too late! Dorn watched the youth's last clutching of empty fingers, the last look of consciousness at his conqueror, the last quiver. The youth died and slid back off the rigid bayonet. War of men!

A heavy thud sounded to the left of Dorn. A bursting flash hid the face of his German victim. A terrific wind, sharp and hard as nails, lifted Dorn into roaring blackness....

"*MANY WATERS*" shone white and green under the bright May sunshine. Seen from the height of slope, the winding brooks looked like silver bands across a vast belt of rainy green and purple that bordered the broad river in the bottomlands. A summer haze filled the air, and hints of gold on the waving wheat slopes presaged an early and bountiful harvest.

It was warm up there on the slope where Lenore Anderson watched and brooded. The breeze brought fragrant smell of fresh-cut alfalfa and the rustling song of the wheat. The stately house gleamed white down on the terraced green knoll; horses and cattle grazed in the pasture; workmen moved like snails in the brown gardens; a motorcar crept along the road far below, with its trail of rising dust.

Two miles of soft green wheat-slope lay between

Lenore and her home. She had needed the loneliness and silence and memory of a place she had not visited for many months. Winter had passed. Summer had come with its birds and flowers. The wheatfields were again waving, beautiful, luxuriant. But life was not as it had been for Lenore Anderson.

Kurt Dorn, private, mortally wounded!—So had read the brief and terrible line in a Spokane newspaper, publishing an Associated Press dispatch of Pershing's casualty list. No more! That had been the only news of Kurt Dorn for a long time. A month had dragged by, of doubt, of hope, of slow despairing.

Up to the time of that fatal announcement Lenore had scarcely noted the fleeting of the days. With all her spirit and energy she had thrown herself into the organizing of the women of the valley to work for the interests of the war. She had made herself a leader who spared no effort, no sacrifice, no expense in what she considered her duty. Conservation of food, intensive farm production, knitting for soldiers, Liberty Loans and Red Cross—these she had studied and mastered, to the end that the women of the great valley had accomplished work which won national honor. It had been excitement, joy, and a strange fulfillment for her. But after the shock caused by the fatal news about Dorn she had lost interest, though she had worked on harder than ever.

Just a night ago her father had gazed at her and then told her to come to his office. She did so. And there he said: "You're workin' too hard. You've got to quit."

"Oh no, Dad. I'm only tired tonight," she had replied. "Let me go on. I've planned so—"

"No!" he said, banging his desk. "You'll run yourself down."

"But, Father, these are wartimes. Could I do less— could I think of—"

"You've done wonders. You've been the life of this work. Someone else can carry it on now. You'd kill yourself. An' this war has cost the Andersons enough."

"Should we count the cost?" she asked.

Anderson had sworn. "No, we shouldn't. But I'm not goin' to lose my girl. Do you get that hunch? . . . I've bought bonds by the bushel. I've given thousands to your relief societies. I gave up my son Jim—an' that cost us mother. . . . I'm raisin' a million bushels of wheat this year that the government can have. An' I'm starvin' to death because I don't get what I used to eat. . . . Then this last blow—Dorn!—that fine young wheat-man, the best—Aw! Lenore . . ."

"But, Dad, is—isn't there any—any hope?"

Anderson was silent.

"Dad," she had pleaded, "if he were really dead— buried—oh! wouldn't I feel it?"

"You've overworked yourself. Now you've got to rest," her father had replied, huskily.

"But, Dad . . ."

"I said no. . . . I've a heap of pride in what you've done. An' I sure think you're the best Anderson of the lot. That's all. Now kiss me an' go to bed."

That explained how Lenore came to be alone, high up on the vast wheat-slope, watching and feeling, with no more work to do. The slow climb there had proved to her how much she needed rest. But work even under strain or pain would have been preferable to endless hours to think, to remember, to fight despair.

Mortally wounded! She whispered the tragic phrase. When? Where? How had her lover been mortally wounded? That meant death. But no other word had come and no spiritual realization of death abided in her soul. It seemed impossible for Lenore to accept things as her father and friends did. Nevertheless, equally impossible was it not to be influenced by their practical minds. Because of her nervousness, of her overstrain, she had lost a good deal of her mental poise; and she divined that the only help for that was certainty of Dorn's fate. She could bear the shock if only she could know positively. And leaning her face in her hands, with the warm wind blowing her hair and bringing the rustle of the wheat, she prayed for divination.

No answer! Absolutely no mystic consciousness of death—of an end to her love here on the earth! Instead of that breathed a strong physical presence of life all about her, in the swelling, waving slopes of wheat, in the beautiful butterflies, in the singing birds low down and the soaring eagles high above—life beating and surging in her heart, her veins, unquenchable and indomitable. It gave the lie to her morbidness. But it seemed only a physical state. How could she find any tangible hold on realities?

She lifted her face to the lonely sky, and her hands pressed to her breast where the deep ache throbbed heavily.

"It's not that I can't give him up," she whispered, as if impelled to speak. "I *can*. I *have* given him up. It's this torture of suspense. Oh, not to *know!* . . . But if that newspaper had claimed him one of the killed, I'd not believe."

So Lenore trusted more to the mystic whisper of

her woman's soul than to all the unproven outward things. Still trust as she might, the voice of the world dinned in her ears, and between the two she was on the rack. Loss of Jim—loss of her mother—what unfilled gulfs in her heart! She was one who loved only few, but these deeply. Today when they were gone was different from yesterday when they were here—different because memory recalled actual words, deeds, kisses of loved ones whose life was ended. Utterly futile was it for Lenore to try to think of Dorn in that way. She saw his stalwart form down through the summer haze, coming with his springy stride through the wheat. Yet—the words—mortally wounded! They had burned into her thoughts so that when she closed her eyes she saw them, darkly red, against the blindness of sight. Pain was a sluggish stream with source high in her breast, and it moved with her unquickened blood. If Dorn were really dead, what would become of her? Selfish question for a girl whose lover had died for his country! She would work, she would be worthy of him, she would never pine, she would live to remember. But, ah! the difference to her! Never for her who had so loved the open, the silken rustle of the wheat and the waving shadows, the green-and-gold slopes, the birds of the air and the beasts of the field, the voice of child and the sweetness of life—never again would these be the same to her, if Dorn were gone forever.

That ache in her heart had communicated itself to all her being. It filled her mind and her body. Tears stung her eyes, and again they were dry when tears would have soothed. Just as any other girl she wept, and then she burned with fever. A longing she had only faintly known, a physical thing which she had resisted, had become real, insistent, beating. Through love and loss she was to be denied a heritage common to all women. A weariness dragged at her. Noble spirit was not a natural thing. It must be intelligence seeing the higher. But to be human was to love life, to hate death, to faint under loss, to throb and pant with heavy sighs, to lie sleepless in the long dark night, to shrink with unutterable sadness at the wan light of dawn, to follow duty with a laggard sense, to feel the slow ebb of vitality and not to care, to suffer with a breaking heart.

Sunset hour reminded Lenore that she must not linger there on the slope. So, following the grass-grown lane between the sections of wheat, she wended a reluctant way homeward. Twilight was falling when she reached the yard. The cooling air was full of a fragrance of flowers freshly watered. Kathleen appeared on the path, evidently waiting for her. The girl was growing tall. Lenore remembered with a pang that her full mind had left little time for her to be a mother to this sister. Kathleen came running, excited and wide-eyed.

"Lenore, I thought you'd never come," she said. "I know something. Only Dad told me not to tell you."

"Then don't," replied Lenore, with a little start.

"But I'd never keep it," burst out Kathleen, breathlessly. "Dad's going to New York."

Lenore's heart contracted. She did not know how she felt. Somehow it was momentous news.

"New York! What for?" she asked.

"He says it's about wheat. But he can't fool me. He told me not to mention it to you."

The girl was keen. She wanted to prepare Lenore, yet did not mean to confide her own suppositions. Lenore checked a rush of curiosity. They went into the house. Lenore hurried to change her outing clothes and boots, and then went down to supper. Rose sat at table, but her father had not yet come in. Lenore called him. He answered, and presently came tramping into the dining room, blustering and cheerful. Not for many months had Lenore given her father such close scrutiny as she did then. He was not natural, and he baffled her. A fleeting, vague hope that she had denied lodgment in her mind seemed to have indeed been wild and unfounded. But the very fact that her father was for once unfathomable made this situation remarkable. All through the meal Lenore trembled, and she had to force herself to eat.

"Lenore, I'd like to see you," said her father, at last, as he laid down his napkin and rose. Almost he convinced her then that nothing was amiss or different, and he would have done so if he had not been too clever, too natural. She rose to follow, catching Kathleen's whisper:

"Don't let him put it over on you, now!"

Anderson lighted a big cigar, as always after supper, but to Lenore's delicate sensitiveness he seemed to be too long about it.

"Lenore, I'm takin' a run to New York—leave tonight at eight—an' I want you to sort of manage while I'm gone. Here's some jobs I want the men to do—all noted down here—an' you'll answer letters, phone calls, an' all that. Not much work, you know, but you'll have to hang around. Somethin' important might turn up."

"Yes, Dad. I'll be glad to," she replied. "Why—why this sudden trip?"

Anderson turned away a little and ran his hand over the papers on his desk. Did she only imagine that his hand shook a little?

"Wheat deals, I reckon—mostly," he said. "An' mebbe I'll run over to Washington."

He turned then, puffing at his cigar, and calmly met her direct gaze. If there were really more than he claimed in his going, he certainly did not intend to tell her. Lenore tried to still her mounting emotion. These days she seemed all imagination. Then she turned away her face.

"Will you try to find out if Kurt Dorn died of his wound—and all about him?" she asked, steadily, but very low.

"Lenore, I sure will!" he exclaimed, with explosive emphasis. No doubt the sincerity of that reply was an immense relief to Anderson. "Once in New York, I can pull wires, if need be. I absolutely promise you I'll find out—what—all you want to know."

Lenore bade him good-bye and went to her room, where calmness deserted her for a while. Upon recovering, she found that the time set for her father's departure had passed. Strangely, then the oppression that had weighed upon her so heavily eased and lifted. The moment seemed one beyond her understanding. She attributed her relief, however, to the fact that her father would soon end her suspense in regard to Kurt Dorn.

In the succeeding days Lenore regained her old strength and buoyancy, and something of a control over the despondency which at times had made life misery.

A golden day of sunlight and azure blue of sky ushered in the month of June. "Many Waters" was a world of verdant green. Lenore had all she could do to keep from flying to the slopes. But as every day now brought nearer the possibility of word from her father, she stayed at home. The next morning about nine o'clock, while she was at her father's desk, the telephone bell rang. It did that many times every morning, but this ring seemed to electrify Lenore. She answered the call hurriedly.

"Hello, Lenore, my girl! How are you?" came rolling on the wire.

"Dad! Dad! Is it—you?" cried Lenore, wildly.

"Sure is. Just got here. Are you an' the girls O.K.?"

"We're well—fine. Oh, Dad . . ."

"You needn't send the car. I'll hire one."

"Yes—yes—but, Dad—Oh, tell me . . ."

"Wait! I'll be there in five minutes."

She heard him slam up the receiver, and she leaned there, palpitating, with the queer, vacant sounds of the telephone filling her ear.

"Five minutes!" Lenore whispered. In five more minutes she would know. They seemed an eternity. Suddenly a flood of emotion and thought threatened to overwhelm her. Leaving the office, she hurried forth to find her sisters, and not until she had looked everywhere did she remember that they were visiting a girlfriend. After this her motions seemed ceaseless; she could not stand or sit still, and she was continually going to the porch to look down the shady lane. At last a car appeared, coming fast. Then she ran indoors quite aimlessly and out again. But when she recognized her father all her outward fears and tremblings vanished. The broad, brown flash of his face was reality. He got out of the car lightly for so heavy a man, and, taking his valise, he dismissed the chauffeur. His smile was one of gladness, and his greeting a hearty roar.

Lenore met him at the porch steps, seeing in him, feeling as she embraced him, that he radiated a strange triumph and finality.

"Say, girl, you look somethin' like your old self," he said, holding her by the shoulders. "Fine! But you're a woman now.... Where are the kids?"

"They're away," replied Lenore.

"How you stare!" laughed Anderson, as with arm round her he led her in. "Anythin' queer about your dad's handsome mug?"

His jocular tone did not hide his deep earnestness. Never had Lenore felt him so forceful. His ruggedness seemed to steady her nerves that again began to fly. Anderson took her into his office, closed the door, threw down his valise.

"Great to be home!" he exploded, with heavy breath.

Lenore felt her face blanch; and that intense quiver within her suddenly stilled.

"Tell me—quick!" she whispered.

He faced her with flashing eyes, and all about him changed. "You're an Anderson! You can stand shock?"

"Any—any shock but suspense."

"I lied about the wheat deal—about my trip to New York. I got news of Dorn. I was afraid to tell you."

"Yes?"

"Dorn is alive," went on Anderson.

Lenore's hands went out in mute eloquence.

"He was all shot up. He can't live," hurried Anderson, hoarsely. "But he's alive—he'll live to see you."

"Oh! I knew, I *knew!*" whispered Lenore clasping her hands. "Oh, thank God!"

"Lenore, steady now. You're gettin' shaky. Brace there, my girl! ...Dorn's alive. I've brought him home. He's here."

"*Here!*" screamed Lenore.

"Yes. They'll have him here in half an hour."

Lenore fell into her father's arms, blind and deaf to all outward things. The light of day failed. But her consciousness did not fade. Before it seemed a glorious radiance that was the truth lost for the moment, blindly groping in whirling darkness. When she did feel herself again it was as a weak, dizzy, palpitating child, unable to stand. Her father, in alarm, and probable anger with himself, was coaxing and swearing in one breath. Then suddenly the joy that had shocked Lenore almost into collapse forced out the weakness with amazing strength. She blazed. She radiated. She burst into utterance too swift to understand.

"Hold on there, girl!" interrupted Anderson. You've got the bit in your teeth.... Listen, will you? Let me talk. Well—well, there now.... Sure, it's all right, Lenore. You made me break it sudden-like.... Listen. There's all summer to talk. Just now you want to get a few details. Get 'em straight.... Dorn is on the way here. They put his stretcher—we've been packin' him on one—into a motortruck. There's a nurse come with me—a man nurse. We'd better put Dorn in mother's room. That's the biggest an' airiest. You hurry an' open up the windows an' fix the bed.... An' don't go out of your head with joy. It's sure more'n we ever hoped for to see him alive, to get him home. But he's done for, poor boy! He can't live.... An' he's in such shape that I don't want you to see him when they fetch him in. Savvy, girl! You'll stay in your room till we call you. An' now rustle."

Lenore paced and crouched and lay in her room, waiting, listening with an intensity that hurt. When a slow procession of men, low-voiced and soft-footed, carried Kurt Dorn into the house and upstairs Lenore trembled with a storm of emotion. All her former agitation, love, agony, and suspense, compared to what she felt then, was as nothing. Not the joy of his being alive, not the terror of his expected death, had so charged her heart as did this awful curiosity to see him, to realize him.

At last a step—a knock—her father's voice: "Lenore—come!"

Her ordeal of waiting was over. All else she could withstand. That moment ended her weakness. Her blood leaped with the irresistible, revivifying current of her spirit. Unlocking the door, Lenore stepped out. Her father stood there with traces of extreme worry fading from his tired face. At sight of her they totally vanished.

"Good! You've got nerve. You can see him now alone. He's unconscious. But he's not been greatly weakened by the trip. His vitality is wonderful. He comes to once in a while. Sometimes he's rational. Mostly, though, he's out of his head. An' his left arm is gone."

Anderson said all this rapidly and low while they walked down the hall toward the end room which had not been used since Mrs. Anderson's death. The door was ajar. Lenore smelled strong, pungent odors of antiseptics.

Anderson knocked softly.

"Come out, you men, an' let my girl see him," he called.

Doctor Lowell, the village practitioner Lenore had known for years, tiptoed out, important and excited.

"Lenore, it's too bad," he said, kindly, and he shook his head.

Another man glided out with the movements of a woman. He was not young. His aspect was pale, serious.

"Lenore, this is Mr. Jarvis, the nurse.... Now—go in, an' don't forget what I said."

She closed the door and leaned back against it, conscious of the supreme moment of her life. Dorn's face, strange yet easily recognizable, appeared against the white background of the bed. That moment was supreme because it showed him there alive, justifying the spiritual faith which had persisted in her soul. If she had ever, in moments of distraction, doubted God, she could never doubt again.

The large room had been bright, with white curtains softly blowing inward from the open windows. As she crept forward, not sure on her feet, all seemed to blur, so that when she leaned over the still face to kiss it she could not see clearly. Her lips quivered with that kiss and with her sob of thankfulness.

"My soldier!"

She prayed then, with her head beside his on the pillow, and through that prayer and the strange stillness of her lover she received a subtle shock. Sweet it was to touch him as she bent with eyes hidden. Terrible it would be to look—to see how the war had wrecked him. She tried to linger there, all tremulous, all gratitude, all woman and mother. But an incalculable force lifted her up from her knees.

"Ah!" she gasped, as she saw him with cleared sight. A knife blade was at her heart. Kurt Dorn lay before her gaze—a man, and not the boy she had sacrificed to war—a man by a larger frame, and by older features, and by a change difficult to grasp.

These features seemed a mask, transparent, unable to hide a beautiful, sad, stern, and ruthless face beneath, which in turn slowly gave to her startled gaze sloping lines of pain and shades of gloom, and the pale, set muscles of forced manhood, and the faint hectic flush of fever and disorder and derangement. A livid, angry scar, smooth, yet scarcely healed, ran from his left temple back as far as she could see. That established his identity as a wounded soldier brought home from the war. Otherwise to Lenore his face might have been that of an immortal suddenly doomed with the curse of humanity, dying in agony. She had expected to see Dorn bronzed, haggard, gaunt, starved, bearded and rough-skinned, bruised and battered, blinded and mutilated, with gray in his fair hair. But she found none of these. Her throbbing heart sickened and froze at the nameless history recorded in his face. Was it beyond her to understand what had been his bitter experience? Would she never suffer his ordeal? Never! That was certain. An insupportable sadness pervaded her soul. It was not his life she thought of, but the youth, the nobility, the splendor of him that war had destroyed. No intuition, no divination, no power so penetrating as a woman's love! By that piercing light she saw the transformed man. He knew. He had found out all of physical life. His hate had gone with his blood. Deeds—deeds of terror had left their imprint upon his brow, in the shadows under his eyes, that resembled blank walls potent with invisible meaning. Lenore shuddered through all her soul as she read the merciless record of the murder he had dealt, of the strong and passionate duty that had driven him, of the eternal remorse. But she did not see or feel that he had found God; and, stricken as he seemed; she could not believe he was near to death.

This last confounding thought held her transfixed and thrilling, gazing down at Dorn, until her father entered to break the spell and lead her away.

*I*T was night. Lenore should have been asleep, but she sat up in the dark by the window. Underneath on the porch, her father, with his men as audience, talked like a torrent. And Lenore, hearing what otherwise would never have gotten to her ears, found listening irresistible. Slow, dragging footsteps and the clinking of spurs attested to the approach of cowboys.

"Howdy, boys! Sit down an' be partic'lar quiet. Here's some smokes. I'm wound up an' gotta go off or bust," Anderson said. "Well, as I was sayin' we folks don't know there's a war, from all outward sign here in the Northwest. But in that New York town I just come from—God Almighty! what goin's-on! Boys, I never knew before how grand it was to be American. New York's got the people, the money, an' it's the outgoin' an' incomin' place of all pertainin' to this war. The Lib-

erty Loan drive was on. The streets were crowded.
Bands an' parades, grand-opera stars singin' on the corners, famous actors sellin' bonds, flags an' ribbons an'
banners everywhere, an' every third man you bumped
into wearin' some kind of uniform! An' the women were
runnin' wild, like a stampede of two-year-olds....I rode
down Fifth Avenue on one of them high-topped buses
with seats on. Talk about your old stagecoach—why,
these 'buses had 'em beat a mile! I've rode some in my
day, but this was the ride of my life. I couldn't hear
myself think. Music at full blast, roar of traffic, voices
like whisperin' without end, flash of red an' white an'
blue, shine of a thousand automobiles down that wonderful street that's like a canyon! An' up overhead a
huge cigar-shaped balloon, an' then an airplane sailin'
swift an' buzzin' like a bee. Then was the first airships
I ever seen. No wonder—Jim wanted to—"

Anderson's voice broke a little at this juncture and
he paused. All was still except the murmur of the running water and the song of the insects. Presently Anderson cleared his throat and resumed:

"I saw five hundred Australian soldiers just arrived
in New York by way of Panama. Lean, wiry boys like
Arizona cowboys. Looked good to me! You ought to
have heard the cheerin'. Roar an' roar, everywhere they
marched along. I saw United States sailors, marines,
soldiers, airmen, English officers, an' Scotch soldiers.
Them last sure got my eye. Funny plaid skirts they
wore—an' they had bare legs. Three I saw walked lame.
An' all had medals. Someone said the Germans called
these Scotch 'Ladies from hell.'...When I heard that I
had to ask questions, an' I learned these queer-lookin'
half-women-dressed fellows were simply hell with cold

steel. An' after I heard that I looked again an' wondered why I hadn't seen it. I ought to know men!...Then I saw the outfit of Blue Devil Frenchmen that was sent over to help stimulate the Liberty Loan. An' when I seen them I took off my hat. I've knowed a heap of tough men an' bad men an' handy men an' fightin' men in my day, but I reckoned I'd never seen the like of the Blue Devils. I can't tell you why, boys. Blue Devils is another German name for a regiment of French soldiers. They had it on the Scotchmen. Any western man, just to look at them, would think of Wild Bill an' Billy the Kid an' Geronimo an' Custer, an' see that mebbe the whole four mixed in one might have made a Blue Devil.

"My young friend Dorn, that's dyin' upstairs, now—he had a name given him. 'Pears that this war-time is like the old days when we used to hit on right pert names for everybody....Demon Dorn they called him, an' he got that handle before he ever reached France. The boys of his outfit gave it to him because of the way he run wild with a bayonet. I don't want my girl Lenore ever to know that.

"A soldier named Owens told me a lot. He was the corporal of Dorn's outfit, a sort of foreman, I reckon. Anyway, he saw Dorn every day of the months they were in the service, an' the shell that done Dorn made a cripple of Owens. This fellow Owens said Dorn had not got so close to his bunk mates until they reached France. Then he begun to have influence over them. Owens didn't know how he did it—in fact, never knew it at all until the outfit got to the front, somewhere in northern France, in the first line. They were days in the first line, close up to the Germans, watchin' an' sneakin' all the time, shootin' an' dodgin', but they never had but one real fight.

"That was when one mornin' the Germans came pilin' over on a charge, far outnumberin' our boys. Then it happened. Lord! I wish I could remember how Owens told that scrap! Boys, you never heard about a real scrap. It takes war like this to make men fighters.... Listen, now, an' I'll tell you some of the things that come off durin' this German charge. I'll tell them just as they come to mind. There was a boy named Griggs who ran the German barrage—an' that's a gauntlet—seven times to fetch ammunition to his pards. Another boy, on the same errand, was twice blown off the road by explodin' shells, an' then went back. Owens told of two of his company who rushed a bunch of Germans, killed eight of them, an' captured their machine gun. Before that German charge a big shell came over an' kicked up a hill of mud. Next day the Americans found their sentinel buried in mud, dead at his post, with his bayonet presented.

"Owens was shot just as he jumped up with his pards to meet the chargin' Germans. He fell an' dragged himself against a wall of bags, where he lay watchin' the fight. An' it so happened that he faced Dorn's squad, which was attacked by three times their number. He saw Dorn shot—go down, an' thought he was done—but no! Dorn came up with one side of his face all blood. Dixon, a college football man, rushed a German who was about to throw a bomb. Dixon got him, an' got the bomb, too, when it went off. Little Rogers, an Irish boy, mixed it with three Germans, an' killed one before he was bayoneted in the back. Then Dorn, like the demon they'd named him, went on the stampede. He had a

different way with a bayonet, so Owens claimed. An'
Dorn was heavy, powerful, an' fast. He lifted an' slung
those two Germans, one after another, quick as that!—
like you'd toss a couple of wheat sheafs with your pitch-
fork, an' he sent them rollin,' with blood squirtin' all
over. An' then four more Germans were shootin' at him.
Right into their teeth Dorn run—laughin' wild an' terrible, Owens said, an' the Germans couldn't stop that
flashin' bayonet. Dorn ripped them all open, an' before
they'd stopped floppin' he was on the bunch that'd killed
Brewer an' were makin' it hard for his other pards....
Whew!—Owens told it all as if it'd took lots of time,
but that fight was like lightnin' an' I can't remember
how it was. Only Demon Dorn laid out nine Germans
before they retreated. *Nine!* Owens seen him do it, like
a mad bull loose. Then the shell came over that put
Dorn out, an' Owens, too.

"Well, Dorn had a mangled arm an' many wounds.
They amputated his arm in France, patched him up, an'
sent him back to New York with a lot of other wounded
soldiers. They expected him to die long ago. But he
hangs on. He's full of lead now. What a hell of a lot of
killin' some men take!... My boy Jim would have been
like that!

"So there, boys, you have a little bit of American
fightin' come home to you, straight an' true. I say that's
American. I've seen that in a hundred men. An' that's
what the Germans have roused. Well, it was a bad day
for them when they figgered everythin' on paper, had
it all cut an' dried, but failed to see the spirit of men!"

Lenore tore herself away from the window so that
she could not hear any more, and in the darkness of
her room she began to pace to and fro, beginning to

undress for bed, shaking in some kind of a frenzy, scarcely knowing what she was about, until sundry knocks from furniture and the falling over a chair awakened her to the fact that she was in a tumult.

"What—*am* I—doing?" she panted, in bewilderment, reaching out in the dark to turn on the light.

Like awakening from a nightmare, she saw the bright light flash up. It changed her feeling. Who was this person whose image stood reflected in the mirror? Lenore's recognition of herself almost stunned her. What had happened? She saw that her hair fell wildly over her bare shoulders; her face shone white, with red spots in her cheeks; her eyes seemed balls of fire; her lips had a passionate, savage curl; her breast, bare and heaving, showed a throbbing, tumultuous heart. And as she realized how she looked, it struck her that she felt an inexplicable passion. She felt intense as steel, hot as fire, quivering with the pulsation of rapid blood, a victim to irrepressible thrills that rushed over her from the very soles of her feet to the roots of her hair. Something glorious, terrible, and furious possessed her. When she understood what it was she turned out the light and fell upon the bed, where, as the storm slowly subsided, she thought and wondered and sorrowed, and whispered to herself.

The tale of Dorn's tragedy had stirred to the depths the primitive, hidden, and unplumbed in the unknown nature of her. Just now she had looked at herself, at her two selves—the white-skinned and fair-haired girl that civilization had produced—and the blazing, panting, savage woman of the bygone ages. She could not escape from either. The story of Demon Dorn's terrible fight had retrograded her, for the moment, to the female of the species, more savage and dangerous than the male. No use to lie! She had gloried in his prowess. He was her man, gone out with club, to beat down the brutes that would steal her from him.

"Alas! What are we? What am I?" she whispered. "Do I know myself? What could I not have done a moment ago?"

She had that primitive thing in her, and, though she shuddered to realize it, she had no regret. Life was life. That Dorn had laid low so many enemies was grand to her, and righteous, since these enemies were as cavemen come for prey. Even now the terrible thrills chased over her. Demon Dorn! What a man! She had known just what he would do—and how his spiritual life would go under. The woman of her gloried in his fight and the soul of her sickened at its significance. No hope for any man or any woman except in God!

These men, these boys, like her father and Jake, like Dorn and his comrades—how simple, natural, inevitable, elemental they were! They loved a fight. They might hate it, too, but they loved it most. Life of men was all strife, and the greatness in them came out in war. War searched out the best and the worst in men. What were wounds, blood, mangled flesh, agony, and death to men—to those who went out for liberation of something unproven in themselves? Life was only a breath. The secret must lie in the beyond, for men could not act that way for nothing. Some hidden purpose through the ages!

Anderson had summoned a great physician, a specialist of world renown. Lenore, of course, had not been present when the learned doctor examined Kurt Dorn, but she was in her father's study when the report was made. To Lenore this little man seemed all intellect, all science, all electric current.

He stated that Dorn had upward of twenty-five wounds, some of them serious, most trivial, and all of them combined not necessarily fatal. Many soldiers with worse wounds had totally recovered. Dorn's vitality and strength had been so remarkable that great loss of blood and almost complete lack of nourishment had not brought about the present grave condition.

"He will die, and that is best for him," said the specialist. "His case is not extraordinary. I saw many like it in France during the first year of war when I was there. But I will say that he must have been both physically and mentally above the average before he went to fight. My examination extended through periods of his unconsciousness and aberration. Once, for a little time, he came to, apparently sane. The nurse said he had noticed several periods of this rationality during the last forty-eight hours. But these, and the prolonged vitality, do not offer any hope.

"An emotion of exceeding intensity and duration has produced lesions in the kinetic organs. Some passion has immeasurably activated his brain, destroying brain cells which might not be replaced. If he happened to live he might be permanently impaired. He might be neurasthenic, melancholic, insane at times, or even grow permanently so.... It is very sad. He appears to have been a fine young man. But he will die, and that really is best for him."

Thus the man of science summed up the biological case of Kurt Dorn. When he had gone Anderson wore the distressed look of one who must abandon his last hope. He did not understand, though he was forced to believe. He swore characteristically at the luck, and then at the great specialist.

"I've known Indian medicine men who could give that doctor cards an' spades," he exploded, with gruff finality.

Lenore understood her father perfectly and imagined she understood the celebrated scientist. The former was just human and the latter was simply knowledge. Neither had that which caused her to go out alone into the dark night and look up beyond the slow-rising slope to the stars. These men, particularly the scientist, lacked something. He possessed all the wonderful knowledge of body and brain, of the metabolism and chemistry of the organs, but he knew nothing of the source of life. Lenore accorded science its place in progress, but she hated its elimination of the soul. Stronger than ever, strength to endure and to trust pervaded her spirit. The dark night encompassing her, the vast, lonely heave of wheat-slope, the dim sky with its steady stars—these were voices as well as tangible things of the universe, and she was in mysterious harmony with them. "Lift thine eyes to the hills from whence cometh thy help!"

The day following the specialist's visit Dorn surprised the family doctor, the nurse, Anderson, and all except Lenore by awakening to a spell of consciousness which seemed to lift, for the time at least, the shadow of death.

Kathleen was the first to burst in upon Lenore with the wonderful news. Lenore could only gasp her intense eagerness and sit trembling, hands over her heart, while the child babbled.

"I listened, and I peeped in," was Kathleen's re-iterated statement. "Kurt was awake. He spoke, too, but very soft. Say, he knows he's at 'Many Waters.' I heard him say, 'Lenore'.... Oh, I'm so happy, Lenore—that before he dies he'll know you—talk to you."

"Hush, child!" whispered Lenore. "Kurt's not going to die."

"But they all say so. That funny little doctor yes-terday—he made me tired—but he said so. I heard him as Dad put him into the car."

"Yes, Kathie, I heard him, too, but I do not believe," replied Lenore, dreamily.

"Kurt doesn't look so—so sick," went on Kathleen. "Only—only I don't know what—different, I guess. I'm crazy to go in—to see him. Lenore, will they ever let me?"

Their father's abrupt entrance interrupted the con-versation. He was pale, forceful, as when issues were at stake but were undecided.

"Kathie, go out," he said.

Lenore rose to face him.

"My girl—Dorn's come to—an' he's asked for you. I was for lettin' him see you. But Lowell an' Jarvis say no—not yet.... Now he might die any minute. Seems to me he ought to see you. It's right. An' if you say so—"

"Yes," replied Lenore.

"By Heaven! he shall see you, then," said Anderson, breathing hard. "I'm justified even—even if it ..." He did not finish his significant speech, but left her abruptly.

Presently Lenore was summoned. When she left her room she was in the throes of uncontrolled agitation, and all down the long hallway she fought herself. At the half-open door she paused to lean against the wall. There she had the will to still her nerves, to acquire serenity; and she prayed for wisdom to make her presence and her words of infinite good to Dorn in this crisis.

She was not aware of when she moved—how she ever got to Dorn's beside. But seemingly detached from her real self, serene, with emotions locked, she was there looking down upon him.

"Lenore!" he said, with far-off voice that just reached her. Gladness shone from his shadowy eyes.

"Welcome home—my soldier boy!" she replied. Then she bent to kiss his cheek and to lay hers beside it.

"I never—hoped—to see you—again," he went on.

"Oh, but I knew!" murmured Lenore, lifting her head. His right hand, brown, bare, and rough, lay outside the coverlet upon his breast. It was weakly reaching for her. Lenore took it in both hers, while she gazed steadily down into his eyes. She seemed to see then how he was comparing the image he had limned upon his memory with her face.

"Changed—you're older—more beautiful—yet the same," he said. "It seems—long ago."

"Yes, long ago. Indeed I am older. But—all's well that ends well. You are back."

"Lenore, haven't you—been told—I can't live?"

"Yes, but it's untrue," she replied, and felt that she might have been life itself speaking.

"Dear, something's gone—from me. Something vital gone—with the shell that—took my arm."

"*No!*" she smiled down upon him. All the conviction

of her soul and faith she projected into that single word and serene smile—all that was love and woman in her opposing death. A subtle, indefinable change came over Dorn.

"Lenore—I paid—for my father," he whispered. "I killed Huns! . . . I spilled the—blood in me—I hated! . . But all was wrong—wrong!"

"Yes, but you could not help that," she said, piercingly. "Blame can never rest upon you. You were only an—American soldier . . . Oh, I know! You were magnificent. . . . But your duty that way is done. A higher duty awaits you."

His eyes questioned sadly and wonderingly.

"You must be the great sower of wheat."

"Sower of wheat?" he whispered, and a light quickened in that questioning gaze.

"There will be starving millions after this war. Wheat is the staff of life. You *must* get well. . . . Listen!"

She hesitated, and sank to her knees beside the bed. "Kurt, the day you're able to sit up I'll marry you. Then I'll take you home—to your wheat hills."

For a second Lenore saw him transformed with her spirit, her faith, her love, and it was that for which she had prayed. She had carried him beyond hopelessness, beyond incredulity. Some guidance had divinely prompted her. And when his mute rapture suddenly vanished, when he lost consciousness and a pale gloom and shade fell upon his face, she had no fear.

In her own room she unleashed the strange bonds on her feelings and suffered their recurrent surge and strife, until relief and calmness returned to her. Then came a flashing uplift of soul, a great and beautiful exaltation. Lenore felt that she had been gifted with incalculable power. She had pierced Dorn's fatalistic consciousness with the truth and glory of possible life, as opposed to the dark and evil morbidity of war. She saw for herself the wonderful and terrible stairs of sand which women had been climbing all the ages, and must climb on to the heights of solid rock, of equality, of salvation for the human race. She saw woman, the primitive, the female of the species, but she saw her also as the mother of the species, made to save as well as perpetuate, learning from the agony of childbirth and child care the meaning of Him who said, "Thou shalt not kill!" Tremendous would be the final resistance of woman to the brutality of man. Women were to be the saviors of humanity. It seemed so simple and natural that it could not be otherwise. Lenore realized, with a singular conception of the splendor of its truth, that when most women had found themselves, their mission in life, as she had found hers, then would come an end to violence, to greed, to hate, to war, to the black and hideous imperfection of mankind.

With all her intellect and passion Lenore opposed the theory of the scientist and biologists. If they proved that strife and fight were necessary to the development of man, that without violence and bloodshed and endless contention the race would deteriorate, then she would say that it would be better to deteriorate and to die. Women all would declare against that, and in fact would never believe. She would never believe with her heart, but if her intellect was forced to recognize certain theories, then she must find a way to reconcile life to the inscrutable designs of nature. The theory that continual strife was the very life of plants, birds, beasts, and men seemed verified by every reaction of the present; but if these things were fixed materialistic rules of the existence of animated forms upon the earth, what then was God, what was the driving force in Kurt Dorn that made war duty some kind of murder which overthrew his mind, what was the love in her heart of all living things, and the nameless sublime faith in her soul?

"If we poor creatures *must* fight," said Lenore, and she meant this for a prayer, "let the women fight eternally against violence, and let the men forever fight their destructive instincts!"

From that hour the condition of Kurt Dorn changed for the better. Doctor Lowell admitted that Lenore had been the one medicine which might defeat the death that all except she had believed inevitable.

Lenore was permitted to see him a few minutes every day, for which fleeting interval she must endure the endless hours. But she discovered that only when he was rational and free from pain would they let her go in. What Dorn's condition was all the rest of the time she could not guess. But she began to get inklings that it was very bad.

"Dad, I'm going to insist on staying with Kurt as— as long as I want," asserted Lenore, when she had made up her mind.

This worried Anderson, and he appeared at a loss for words.

"I told Kurt I'd marry him the very day he could sit up," continued Lenore.

"By George! that accounts," exclaimed her father. "He's been tryin' to sit up, an' we've had hell with him."

"Dad, he will get well. And all the sooner if I can be with him more. He loves me. I feel I'm the only thing that counteracts—the—the madness in his mind—the death in his soul."

Anderson made one of his violent gestures. "I believe you. That hits me with a bang. It takes a woman! ...Lenore, what's your idea?"

"I want to—to marry him," murmured Lenore. "To nurse him—to take him home to his wheat fields."

"You shall have your way," replied Anderson, beginning to pace the floor. "It can't do any harm. It might save him. An' anyway, you'll be his wife—if only for ... By George! we'll do it. You never gave me a wrong hunch in your life ... but, girl, it'll be hard for you to see him when—when he has the spells."

"Spells!" echoed Lenore.

"Yes. You've been told that he raves. But you didn't know how. Why, it gets even my nerve! It fascinated me, but once was enough. I couldn't stand to see his face when his Huns come back to him."

"His Huns!" ejaculated Lenore, shuddering. "What do you mean?"

"Those Huns he killed come back to him. He fights them. You see him go through strange motions, an' it's as if his left arm wasn't gone. He uses his right arm—an the motions he makes are the ones he made when he killed the Huns with his bayonet. It's terrible to watch him—the look on his face! ...I heard at the hospital in New York that in France they photographed him when he had one of the spells.... I'd hate to have you see him then. But maybe after Doctor Lowell explains it, you'll understand."

"Poor boy! How terrible for him to live it all over! But when he gets well—he has his wheat hills and me to fill his mind—those spells will fade."

"Maybe—maybe. I hope so. Lord knows it's all beyond me. But you're goin' to have your way."

Doctor Lowell explained to Lenore that Dorn, like all mentally deranged soldiers, dreamed when he was asleep, and raved when he was out of his mind, of only one thing—the foe. In his nightmares Dorn had to be held forcibly. The doctor said that the remarkable and hopeful indication about Dorn's condition was a gradual daily gain in strength and a decline in the duration and violence of his bad spells.

This assurance made Lenore happy. She began to relieve the worn-out nurse during the day, and she prepared herself for the first ordeal of actual experience of Dorn's peculiar madness. But Dorn watched her many hours and would not or could not sleep while she was there; and the tenth day of his stay at "Many Waters" passed without her seeing what she dreaded. Meanwhile he grew perceptibly better.

The afternoon came when Anderson brought a minister. Then a few moments sufficed to make Lenore Dorn's wife.

CHAPTER
31

*T*HE remarkable happened. Scarcely had the minister left when Kurt Dorn's smiling wonder and happiness sustained a break, as sharp and cold and terrible as if nature had transformed him from man to beast.

His face became like that of a gorilla. Struggling up, he swept his right arm over and outward with singular twisting energy. A bayonet thrust! And for him his left arm was still intact! A savage, unintelligible battle cry, yet unmistakably German, escaped his lips.

Lenore stood one instant petrified. Her father, grinding his teeth, attempted to lead her away. But as Dorn was about to pitch off the bed, Lenore, with piercing cry, ran to catch him and force him back. There she held him, subdued his struggles, and kept calling with that intensity of power and spirit which must have penetrated even his delirium. Whatever influence she exerted, it quieted him, changed his savage face, until he relaxed and lay back passive and pale. It was possible to tell exactly when his reason returned, for it showed in the gaze he fixed upon Lenore.

"I had—one—of my fits!" he said, huskily.

"Oh—I don't know what it was," replied Lenore, with quavering voice. Her strength began to leave her now. Her arms that had held him so firmly began to slip away.

"Son, you had a bad spell," interposed Anderson, with his heavy breathing. "First one she's seen."

"Lenore, I laid out my Huns again," said Dorn, with a tragic smile. "Lately I could tell when—they were coming back."

"Did you know just now?" queried Lenore.

"I think so. I wasn't really out of my head. I've known when I did that. It's a strange feeling—thought— memory . . . and action drives it away. Then I seem always to *want* to—kill my Huns all over again."

Lenore gazed at him with mournful and passionate tenderness. "Do you remember that we were just married?" she asked.

"My wife!" he whispered.

"Husband! . . . I knew you were coming home to me. . . . I knew you would not die. . . . I know you will get well."

"I begin to feel that, too. Then—maybe the black spells will go away."

"They must or—or you'll lose me," faltered Lenore. "If you go on killing your Huns—over and over—it'll be I who will die."

She carried with her to her room a haunting sense of Dorn's reception of her last speech. Some tremendous impression it made on him, but whether of fear or domination or resolve, or all combined, she could not tell. She had weakened in mention of the return of his phantoms. But neither Dorn nor her father ever guessed that, once in her room, she collapsed from sheer feminine horror at the prospect of seeing Dorn change from a man to a gorilla, and to repeat the savage orgy of remurdering his Huns. That was too much for Lenore. She who had been invincible in faith, who could stand any tests of endurance and pain, was not proof against a spectacle of Dorn's strange counterfeit presentment of the actual and terrible killing he had performed with a bayonet.

For days after that she was under a strain which she realized would break her if it was not relieved. It appeared to be solely her fear of Dorn's derangement. She was with him almost all the daylight hours, attending him, watching him sleep, talking a little to him now and then, seeing with joy his gradual improvement, feeling each day the slow lifting of the shadow over him, and yet every minute of every hour she waited in dread for the return of Dorn's madness. It did not come. If it recurred at night she never was told. Then after a week a more pronounced change for the better in Dorn's condition marked a lessening of the strain upon Lenore. A little later it was deemed safe to dismiss the nurse. Lenore dreaded the first night vigil. She lay upon a couch in Dorn's room and never closed her eyes. But he slept, and his slumber appeared sound at times, and then restless, given over to dreams. He talked incoherently, and moaned; and once appeared to be drifting into a nightmare, when Lenore awakened him. Next day he sat up and said he was hungry. Thereafter Lenore began to lose her dread.

*   *   *

"Well, son, let's talk wheat," said Anderson, cheerily, one beautiful June morning, as he entered Dorn's room.

"Wheat!" sighed Dorn, with a pathetic glance at his empty sleeve. "How can I ever do a man's work again in the fields?"

Lenore smiled bravely at him. "You will sow more wheat than ever, and harvest more, too."

"I should smile," corroborated Anderson.

"But how? I've only one arm," said Dorn.

"Kurt, you hug me better with that one arm than you ever did with two arms," replied Lenore, in sublime assurance.

"Son, you lose that argument," roared Anderson. "Me an' Lenore stand pat. You'll sow more an' better wheat than ever—than any other man in the Northwest. Get my hunch?...Well, I'll tell you later....Now see here, let me declare myself about you. I seen it worries you more an' more, now you're gettin' well. You miss that good arm, an' you feel the pain of bullets that still lodge somewhere's in you, an' you think you'll be a cripple always. Look things in the face square. Sure, compared to what you once was, you'll be a cripple. But Kurt Dorn weighin' one hundred an' ninety let loose on a bunch of Huns was some man! My Gawd!...Forget that, an' forget that you'll never chop a cord of wood again in a day. Look at facts like me an' Lenore. We gave you up. An' here you're with us, comin' along fine, an' you'll be able to do hard work some day, if you're crazy about it. Just think how good that is for Lenore, an' me, too....Now listen to this." Anderson unfolded a newspaper and began to read:

"Continued improvement, with favorable weather conditions, in the winter-wheat states and encouraging messages from the Northwest warrant an increase of crop estimates made two weeks ago and based mainly upon the government's report. In all probability the yield from winter fields will slightly exceed 600,000,000 bushels. Increase of acreage in the spring states is unexpectedly large. For example, Minnesota's Food Administrator says the addition in his state is 40 per cent instead of the early estimate of 20 percent. Throughout the spring area the plants have a good start and are in excellent condition. It may be that the yield will rise to 300,000,000 bushels, making a total of about 900,000,000. From such a crop 280,000,000 could be exported in normal times, and by conservation the surplus can easily be enlarged to 350,000,000 or even 400,000,000. In Canada also estimates of acreage increase have been too low. It was said that the addition in Alberta was 20 percent., but recent reports make it 40 percent. Canada may harvest a crop of 300,000,000 bushels, or nearly 70,000,000 more than last year's. Our allies in Europe can safely rely upon the shipment of 500,000,000 bushels from the United States and Canada.

"After the coming harvest there will be an ample supply of wheat for the foes of Germany at ports which can easily be reached. In addition, the large surplus stocks in Australia and Argentina will be available when ships can be spared for such service. And the ships are coming from the builders. For more than a year to come there will be wheat enough for our war partners, the Belgians, and the northern European neutral countries with which we have trade agreements."

Lenore eagerly watched her husband's face in plea-surable anticipation, yet with some anxiety. Wheat had been a subject little touched upon and the war had never been mentioned.

"Great!" he exclaimed, with a glow in his cheeks. "I've been wanting to ask.... Wheat for the Allies and neutrals—for more than a year!... Anderson, the United States will feed and save the world!"

"I reckon. Son, we're sendin' thousands of soldiers a day now—ships are buildin' fast—airplanes comin' like a swarm of bees—money for the government to burn—an' every American gettin' mad.... Dorn, the Germans don't know they're ruined!... What do you say?"

Dorn looked very strange. "Lenore, help me stand up," he asked, with strong tremor in his voice.

"Oh, Kurt, you're not able yet," appealed Lenore.

"Help me. I want *you* to do it."

Lenore complied, wondering and frightened, yet fascinated, too. She helped him off the bed and steadied him on his feet. Then she felt him release himself so he stood free.

"What do I say? Anderson, I say this. I killed Ger-mans who had grown up with a training and a passion for war. I've been a farmer. I did not want to fight. Duty and hate forced me. The Germans I met fell before me. I was shell shot, shocked, gassed, and bayoneted. I took twenty-five wounds, and then it was a shell that downed me. I saw my comrades kill and kill before they fell. That is American. Our enemies are driven, blinded, stolid, brutal, obsessed, and desperate. They are Ger-man. They lack—not strength nor efficiency nor cour-age—but soul."

White and spent, Dorn then leaned upon Lenore and got back upon his bed. His passion had thrilled her. Anderson responded with an excitement he plainly endeavored to conceal.

"I get your hunch," he said. "If I needed any assurance, you've given it to me. To hell with the Germans! Let's don't talk about them anymore....An' to come back to our job. Wheat! Son, I've plans that'll raise your hair. We'll harvest a bumper crop at 'Many Waters' in July. An' we'll sow two thousand acres of winter wheat. So much for 'Many Waters'—I got mad this summer. I blowed myself. I bought about all the farms around yours up in the Bend country. Big harvest of spring wheat comin'. You'll superintend that harvest, an' I'll look after ours here....An' you'll sow ten thousand acres of fallow on your own rich hills—this fall. Do you get that? Ten thousand acres!"

"Anderson!" gasped Dorn.

"Yes, Anderson," mimicked the rancher. "My blood's up. But I'd never have felt so good about it if you hadn't come back. The land's not all paid for, but it's ours. We'll meet our notes. I've been up there twice this spring. You'd never know a few hills had burned over last harvest. Olsen, an' your other neighbors, or most of them, will work the land on half shares. You'll be boss. An' sure you'll be well for fall sowin'. That'll make you the biggest sower of wheat in the Northwest."

"My sower of wheat!" murmured Lenore, seeing his rapt face through tears.

"Dreams are coming true," he said, softly. "Lenore, just after I saw you the second time—and fell so in love with you—I had vain dreams of you. But even my wildest never pictured you as the wife of a wheat farmer. I never dreamed you loved wheat."

"But, ah, I do!" replied Lenore. "Why, when I was born Dad bought 'Many Waters' and sowed the slopes in wheat. I remember how he used to take me up to the fields all green or golden. I've grown up with wheat. I'd never want to live anywhere away from it. Oh, you must listen to me someday while I tell you what I know—about the history and romance of wheat."

"Begin," said Dorn, with a light of pride and love and wonder in his gaze.

"Leave that for some other time," interposed Anderson. "Son, would it surprise you if I'd tell you that I've switched a little in my ideas about the I. W. W.?"

"No," replied Dorn.

"Well, things happen. What made me think hard was the way that government man got results from the I. W. W. in the lumber country. You see, the government had to have an immense amount of timber for ships, an' spruce for airplanes. Had to have it quick. An' all the lumbermen an' loggers were I. W. W.—or most of them. Anyhow, all the strikin' lumbermen last summer belonged to the I. W. W. These fellows believed that under the capitalistic order of labor the workers an' their employers had nothin' in common, an' the government was hand an' glove with capital. Now this government official went up there an' convinced the I. W. W. that the best interests of the two were identical. An' he got the work out of them, an' the government got the lumber. He dealt with them fairly. Those who were on the level he paid high an' considered their wants. Those who were crooked he punished accordin' to their offense. An' the innocent didn't have to suffer with the guilty.

"That deal showed me how many of the I. W. W. could be handled. An' we've got to reckon with the I. W. W. Most all the farmhands in the country belong to it. This summer I'll give the square harvesters what they want, an' that's a big comedown for me. But I won't stand any monkey bizness from soreheaded disorganizers. If men want to work they shall have work at big pay. You will follow out this plan up in the Bend country. We'll meet this labor union halfway. After the war there may come trouble between labor an' capital. It begins to seem plain to me that men who work hard ought to share somethin' of the profits. If that doesn't settle the trouble, then we'll know we're up against an outfit with socialist an' anarchist leaders. Time enough then to resort to measures I regret we practiced last summer."

"Anderson, you're fine—you're as big as the hills!" burst out Dorn. "But you know there was bad blood here last summer. Did you ever get proof that German money backed the I. W. W. to strike and embarrass our government?"

"No. But I believe so, or else the I. W. W. leaders took advantage of a critical time. I'm bound to say that now thousands of I. W. W. laborers are loyal to the United States, an' that made me switch."

"I'll deal with them the same way," responded Dorn, with fervor.

Then Lenore interrupted their discussion, and, pleading that Dorn was quite worn-out from excitement and exertion, she got her father to leave the room.

* * *

The following several days Lenore devoted to the happy and busy task of packing what she wanted to take to Dorn's home. She had set the date, but had reserved the pleasure of telling him. Anderson had agreed to her plan and decided to accompany them.

"I'll take the girls," he said. "It'll be a fine ride for them. We'll stay in the village overnight an' come back home next day....Lenore, it strikes me sudden-like, your leavin'....What will become of me?"

All at once he showed the ravages of pain and loss that the last year had added to his life of struggle. Lenore embraced him and felt her heart full.

"Dad, I'm not leaving you," she protested. "He'll get well up there—find his balance sooner among those desert wheat hills. We will divide our time between the two places. Remember, you can run up there any day. Your interests are there now. Dad, don't think of it as separation. Kurt has come into our family—and we're just going to be away some of the time."

Thus she won back a smile to the worn face.

"We've all got a weak spot," he said, musingly. "Mine is here—an' it's a fear of growin' old an' bein' left alone. That's selfish. Life is a queer mixture. Sometimes I think it's all selfish. But I've lived, an' I reckon I've no more to ask for."

Lenore could not help being sad in the midst of her increasing happiness. Joy to some brought to others only gloom! Life was sunshine and storm—youth and age.

This morning she found Kathleen entertaining Dorn. This was the second time the child had been permitted to see him, and the immense novelty had not yet worn off. Kathleen was a hero-worshiper. If she had been devoted to Dorn before his absence, she now manifested symptoms of complete idolatry. Lenore had forbidden her to question Dorn about anything in regard to the war. Kathleen never broke her promises, but it was plain that Dorn had read the mute, anguished wonder and flame in her eyes when they rested upon his empty sleeve, and evidently had told her things. Kathleen was white, wide-eyed, and beautiful then, with all a child's imagination stirred.

"I've been telling Kathie how I lost my arm," explained Dorn.

"I hate Germans! I hate war!" cried Kathleen, passionately.

"My dear, hate them always," said Dorn.

When Kathleen had gone Lenore asked Dorn if he thought it was right to tell the child always to hate Germans.

"Right!" exclaimed Dorn, with a queer laugh. Every day now he showed signs of stronger personality. "Lenore, what I went through has confused my sense of right and wrong. Someday perhaps it will all come clear. But, Lenore, all my life, if I live to be ninety, I shall hate Germans."

"Oh, Kurt, it's too soon for you to—to be less narrow, less passionate," replied Lenore, with hesitation. "I understand. The day will come when you'll not condemn a people because of a form of government—of military class."

"It will never come," asserted Dorn, positively. "Lenore, people in our country do not understand. They are too far away from realities. But I was six months in France. I've seen the ruined villages, thousands of refugees—and I've met the Huns at the front. I *know* I've seen the realities. In regard to this war I can only feel. You've got to go over there and see for yourself before you realize. You *can* understand this—that but for you and your power over me I'd be a worn-out, emotionally *burnt*-out man. But through you I seem to be reborn. Still, I shall hate Germans all my life, and in the after-life, whatever that may be. I could give you a thousand reasons. One ought to suffice. You've read, of course, about that regiment of Frenchmen called Blue Devils. I met some of them—got friendly with them. They are great—beyond words to tell! One of them told me that when his regiment drove the Huns out of his own village he had found his mother disemboweled, his wife vio-lated and murdered, his sister left a maimed thing to become the mother of a Hun, his daughter carried off, and his little son crippled for life!...These are cold facts. As long as I live I will never forget the face of that Frenchman when he told me. Had he cause to hate the Huns? Have I? ...I saw all that in the faces of those Huns who would have killed me if they could."

Lenore covered her face with her hands. "Oh—horrible! ... Is there nothing—no hope—only ...?" She faltered and broke down.

"Lenore, because there's hate does not prove there's nothing left.... Listen. The last fight I had was with a boy. I didn't know it when we met. I was rushing, head down, bayonet low. I saw only his body, his blade that clashed with mine. To me his weapon felt like a toy in the hands of a child. I swept it aside—and lunged. He screamed '*Kamarad!*' before the blade reached him. Too late! I ran him through. Then I looked. A boy of nineteen! He never ought to have been forced to meet me. It was murder. I saw him die on my bayonet. I saw him slide off it and stretch out....I did not hate *him* then. I'd have given my life for his. I hated what he represented....That moment was the end of me as a soldier. If I had not been in range of the exploding shell that downed me I would have dropped my rifle and have stood strengthless before the next Hun....So you see, though I killed then, and though I hate now, there's something—something strange and inexplicable."

"That something is the divine in you. It is God!... Oh, believe it, my husband!" cried Lenore.

Dorn somberly shook his head. "God! I did not find God out there. I cannot see God's hand in this infernal war."

"But *I* can. What called you so resistlessly? What made you go?"

"You know. The debt I thought I ought to pay. And duty to my country."

"Then when the debt was paid, the duty fulfilled— when you stood stricken at sight of that poor boy dying on your bayonet—what happened in your soul?"

"I don't know. But I saw the wrong of war. The wrong to him—the wrong to me! I thought of no one else. Certainly not of God!"

"If you had stayed your bayonet—if you had spared that boy, as you would have done had you seen or heard him in time—what would that have been?"

"Pity, maybe, or scorn to slay a weaker foe."

"No, no, no—I can't accept that," replied Lenore, passionately. "Can't you see beyond the physical?"

"I see only that men will fight and that war will come again. Out there I learned the nature of men."

"If there's divinity in you there's divinity in every man. That will oppose war—end it eventually. Men are not taught right. Education and religion will bring peace on earth, goodwill to man."

"No, they will not. They never have done so. We have educated men and religious men. Yet war comes despite them. The truth is that life is a fight. Civilization is only skin-deep. Underneath man is still a savage. He is a savage still because he wants the same he had to have when he lived in primitive state. War isn't necessary to show how every man fights for food, clothing, shelter. Today it's called competition in business. Look at your father. He has fought and beaten men like Neuman. Look at the wheat farmers in my country. Look at the I. W. W. They all fight. Look at the children. They fight even at their games. Their play is a make-believe battle or escaping or funeral or capture. It must be then that some kind of strife was implanted in the first humans and that it is necessary to life."

"Survival of the fittest!" exclaimed Lenore, in earnest bitterness. "Kurt, we have changed. You are facing realities and I am facing the infinite. You represent the physical, and I the spiritual. We must grow into harmony with each other. We can't ever hope to learn the unattainable truth of life. There is something beyond us—something infinite which I believe is God. My soul finds it in you.... The first effects of the war upon you have been trouble, sacrifice, pain, and horror. You have come out of it impaired physically and with mind still clouded. These will pass, and therefore I beg of you don't grow fixed in absolute acceptance of the facts of evolution and materialism. They cannot be denied, I grant. I see that they are realities. But also I see beyond them. There is some great purpose running through the ages. In our day the Germans have risen, and in the eyes of most of

the world their brutal force tends to halt civilization
and kill idealism. But that's only apparent—only tem-
porary. We shall come out of this dark time better, finer,
wiser. The history of the world is a proof of a slow
growth and perfection. It will never be attained. But is
not the growth a beautiful and divine thing? Does it not
oppose a hopeless prospect? ... Life is inscrutable.
When I think—only think without faith—all seems so
futile. The poet says we are here as on a darkling plain,
swept by confused alarms of struggle and flight, where
ignorant armies clash by night. ... Trust me, my husband! There is something in woman—the instinct of
creation—the mother—that feels what cannot be expressed. It is the hope of the world."

"The mother!" burst out Dorn. "I think of that—in
you. ... Suppose I have a son, and war comes in his day.
Suppose he is killed, as I killed that poor boy! ... How,
then, could I reconcile that with this—this something
you feel so beautifully? This strange sense of God! This
faith in a great purpose of the ages!"

Lenore trembled in the exquisite pain of the faith
which she prayed was beginning to illumine Dorn's dark
and tragic soul.

"If we are blessed with a son—and if he must go
to war—to kill and be killed—you will reconcile that
with God because our son shall have been taught what
you should have been taught—what must be taught to
all the sons of the future."

"What will—that be?" queried Dorn.

"The meaning of life—the truth of immortality,"
replied Lenore. "We live on—we improve. That is
enough for faith."

"How will that prevent war?"

"It will prevent it—in the years to come. Mothers will take good care that children from babyhood shall learn the *consequences* of fight—of war. Boys will learn that if the meaning of war to them is the wonder of charge and thunder of cannon and medals of distinction, to their mothers the meaning is loss and agony. They will learn the terrible difference between your fury and eagerness to lunge with bayonet and your horror of achievement when the disemboweled victims lie before you. The glory of a statue to the great general means countless and nameless graves of forgotten soldiers. The joy of the conquering army contrasts terribly with the pain and poverty and unquenchable hate of the conquered."

"I see what you mean," rejoined Dorn. "Such teaching of children would change the men of the future. It would mean peace for the generations to come. But as for my boy—it would make him a poor soldier. He would not be a fighter. He would fall easy victim to the son of the father who had not taught this beautiful meaning of life and terror of war. I'd want my son to be a man."

"That teaching—would make him—all the more a man," said Lenore, beginning to feel faint.

"But not in the sense of muscle, strength, courage, endurance. I'd rather there never was peace than have my son inferior to another man's."

"My hope for the future is that *all* men will come to teach their sons the wrong of violence."

"Lenore, never will that day come," replied Dorn.

She saw in him the inevitableness of the masculine attitude; the difference between man and woman; the preponderance of blood and energy over the higher motives. She felt a weak little woman arrayed against the whole of mankind. But she could not despair. Unquenchable as the sun was this fire within her.

"But it *might* come?" she insisted, gently, but with inflexible spirit.

"Yes, it might—if men change!"

"You have changed."

"Yes. I don't know myself."

"If we do have a boy, will you let me teach him what I think is right?" Lenore went on, softly.

"Lenore! As if I would not!" he exclaimed. "I try to see your way, but just because I can't I'll never oppose you. Teach *me* if you can!"

She kissed him and knelt beside his bed, grieved to see shadow return to his face, yet thrilling that the way seemed open for her to inspire. But she must never again choose to talk of war, of materialism, of anything calculated to make him look into darkness of his soul, to ponder over the impairment of his mind. She remembered the great specialist speaking of lesions of the organic system, of a loss of brain cells. Her inspiration must be love, charm, care—a healing and building process. She would give herself in all the unutterableness and immeasurableness of her woman's heart. She would order his life so that it would be a fulfillment of his education, of a heritage from his fathers, a passion born in him, a noble work through which surely he could be saved—the cultivation of wheat.

"Do you love me?" she whispered.

"Do I!...Nothing could ever change my love for you."

"I am your wife, you know."

The shadow left his face.

"Are you? Really? Lenore Anderson ..."

"Lenore Dorn. It is a beautiful name now."

"It does sound sweet. But you—my wife? Never will I believe!"

"You will have to—very soon."

"Why?" A light, warm and glad and marveling, shone in his eyes. Indeed, Lenore felt then a break in the strange aloofness of him—in his impersonal, gentle acceptance of her relation to him.

"Tomorrow. I'm going to take you home to your wheat hills."

CHAPTER

32

*L*ENORE told her conception of the history and the romance of wheat to Dorn at this critical time when it was necessary to give a trenchant call to hope and future.

In the beginning man's struggle was for life and the mainstay of life was food. Perhaps the original discoverer of wheat was a meat-eating savage who, in roaming the forests and field, forced by starvation to eat bark and plant and berry, came upon a stalk of grain that chewed with strange satisfaction. Perhaps through that accident he became a sower of wheat.

Who actually were the first sowers of wheat would never be known. They were older than any history, and must have been among the earliest of the human race.

The development of grain produced wheat, and wheat was ground into flour, and flour was baked into bread, and bread had for untold centuries been the sustenance and the staff of life.

Centuries ago an old Chaldean priest tried to ascertain if wheat had ever grown wild. That question never was settled. It was universally believed, however, that wheat had to have the cultivation of man. Nevertheless, the origin of the plant must have been analogous to that of other plants. Wheat growers must necessarily have been people who stayed long in one place. Wandering tribes could not till and sow the fields. The origin of wheat furnished a legendary theme for many races, and mythology contained tales of wheat gods favoring chosen peoples. Ancient China raised wheat twenty-seven centuries before Christ; grains of wheat had been found in prehistoric ruins; the dwellers along the Nile were not blind to the fertility of the valley. In the days of the Pharaohs the old river annually inundated its low banks, enriching the soil of vast areas, where soon a green-and-gold ocean of wheat waved and shone under the hot Egyptian sun. The Arabs, on their weird beasts of burden, rode from the desert wastes down to the land of waters and of plenty. Rebekah, when she came to fill her earthen pitcher at the palm-shaded well, looked out with dusky, dreamy eyes across the golden grain toward the mysterious east. Moses, when he stood in the night, watching his flock on the starlit Arabian waste, felt borne to him on the desert wind a scent of wheat. The Bible said, "He maketh peace in thy borders and filleth thee with the finest of the wheat."

Black-bread days of the Middle Ages, when crude grinding made impure flour, were the days of the oppressed peasant and the rich landowner; dark days of toil and poverty and war, of blight and drought and famine; when common man in his wretchedness and hunger cried out, "Bread or blood!"

But with the spreading of wheat came the dawn of a higher civilization; and the story of wheat down to modern times showed the development of man. Wheat fields of many lands, surrounding homes of prosperous farmers; fruitful toil of happy peoples; the miller and his humming mill!

When wheat crossed the ocean to America it came to strange and wonderful fulfillment of its destiny. America, fresh, vast, and free, with its sturdy pioneers ever spreading the golden grain westward; with the advancing years when railroad lines kept pace with the indomitable wheat sowers; with unprecedented harvests yielding records to each succeeding year; with boundless fields tilled and planted and harvested by machines that were mechanical wonders; with enormous flour mills, humming and whirring, each grinding daily ten thousand barrels of flour, pouring like a white stream from the steel rolls, pure, clean, and sweet, the whitest and finest in the world!

America, the new country, became in 1918 the salvation of starving Belgium, the mainstay of England, the hope of France! Wheat for the world! Wheat—that was to say food, strength, fighting life for the armies opposed to the black, hideous, medieval horde of Huns! America to succor and to save, to sacrifice and to sow, rising out of its peaceful slumber to a mighty wrath, magnificent and unquenchable, throwing its vast resources of soil, its endless streams of wheat, into the gulf of war! It was an exalted destiny for a people. Its truth was a blazing affront in the face of age-old autocracy. Fields and toil and grains of wheat, first and last, the salvation of mankind, the freedom and the food of the world!

Far up the slow-rising bulge of valley slope above the gleaming river two cars climbed leisurely and rolled on over the height into what seemed a bare and lonely land of green.

It was a day in June, filled with a rich, thick, amber light, with a fragrant warm wind blowing out of the west.

At a certain point on this road, where Anderson always felt compelled to halt, he stopped the car this day and awaited the other that contained Lenore and Dorn.

Lenore's joy in the ride was reflected in her face. Dorn rested comfortably beside her, upon an improvised couch. As he lay half propped up by pillows he could see out across the treeless land that he knew. His eyes held a look of the returned soldier who had never expected to see his native land again. Lenore, sensitive to every phase of his feeling, watched him with her heart mounting high.

Anderson got out of his car, followed by Kathleen, who looked glad and mischievous and pretty as a wild rose.

"I just never can get by this place," explained the rancher, as he came and stood so that he could put a hand on Dorn's knee. "Look, son—an' Lenore, don't you miss this."

"Never fear, Dad," replied Lenore. "It was I who first told you to look here."

"Terrible big and bare, but grand!" exclaimed Kathleen.

Lenore looked first at Dorn's face as he gazed away across the length and breadth of land. Could that land mean as much to him as it did before he went to war? Infinitely more, she saw, and rejoiced. Her faith was coming home to her in verities. Then she thrilled at the wide prospect before her.

It was a scene that she knew could not be duplicated in the world. Low, slow-sloping, billowy green hills, bare and smooth with square brown patches, stretched away to what seemed infinite distance. Valleys and hills, with less fallow ground than ever before, significant and striking: lost the meager details of clumps of trees and dots of houses in a green immensity. A million shadows out of the west came waving over the wheat. They were ripples of an ocean of grain. No dust clouds, no bleached roads, no yellow hills today! June, and the desert found its analogy only in the sweep and reach! A thousand hills billowing away toward that blue haze of mountain range where rolled the Oregon. Acreage and mileage seemed insignificant. All was green—green, the fresh and hopeful color, strangely serene and sweet and endless under the azure sky. Beautiful and lonely hills they were, eloquent of toil, expressive with the brown squares in the green, the lowly homes of men, the long lines of roads running every whither, overwhelmingly pregnant with meaning—wheat—wheat—nothing but wheat, a staggering visual manifestation of vital need, of noble promise.

"That—that!" rolled out Anderson, waving his big hand, as if words were useless. "Only a corner of the great old U. S.!...What would the Germans say if they could look out over this? ...What do *you* say, Lenore?"

"Beautiful!" she replied, softly. "Like the rainbow in the sky—God's promise of life!"

"An', Kathie, what do *you* say?" went on Anderson.

"Some wheat fields!" replied Kathleen, with an air of woman's wisdom. "Fetch on your young wheat sowers, Dad, and I'll pick out a husband."

"An' *you,* son?" finished Anderson, as if wistfully, yet heartily playing his last card. He was remembering Jim—the wild but beloved son—the dead soldier. He was fearful for the crowning hope of his years.

"As ye sow—so shall ye reap!" was Dorn's reply, strong and thrilling. And Lenore felt her father's strange, heart-satisfying content.

Twilight crept down around the old home on the hill.

Dorn was alone, leaning at the window. He had just strength to lean there, with uplifted head. Lenore had left him alone, divining his wish. As she left him there came a sudden familiar happening in his brain, like a snap back, and the contending tide of gray forms—the Huns—rushed upon him. He leaned there at the window, but just the same he awaited the shock on the ramparts of the trench. A ferocious and terrible storm of brain, that used to have its reaction in outward violence, now worked inside him, like a hot wind that drove his blood. During the spell he fought out his great fight—again for the thousandth time he rekilled his foes. That storm passed through him without an outward quiver.

His Huns—charged again—bayoneted again—and he felt acute pain in the left arm that was gone. He felt the closing of the hand which was not there. His Huns lay in the shadow, stark and shapeless, with white faces upward—a line of dead foes, remorseless and abhorrent to him, forever damned by his ruthless spirit. He saw the boy slide off his bayonet, beyond recall, murdered by some evil of which Dorn had been the motion. Then the prone, gray forms vanished in the black gulf of Dorn's brain.

"Lenore will never know—how my Huns come back to me," he whispered.

Night with its trains of stars! Softly the darkness unfolded down over the dim hills, lonely, tranquil, sweet. A night bird caroled. The song of insects, very faint and low, came to him like a still, sad music of humanity, from over the hills, far away, in the strife-ridden world. The world of men was there and life was incessant, monstrous, and inconceivable. This old home of his—the old house seemed full of well-remembered sounds of mouse and cricket and leaf against the roof and soft night wind at the eaves—sounds that brought his boyhood back, his bare feet on the stairs, his father's aloofness, his mother's love.

Then clearly floated to him a slow sweeping rustle of the wheat. Breast-high it stood down there, outside his window, a moving body, higher than the gloom. That rustle was a voice of childhood, youth, and manhood, whispering to him, thrilling as never before. It was a growing rustle, different from that when the wheat had matured. It seemed to change and grow in volume, in meaning. The night wind bore it, but life—bursting life was behind it, and behind that seemed to come a driving and a mighty spirit. Beyond the growth of the wheat, beyond its life and perennial gift, was something measureless and obscure, infinite and universal. Suddenly Dorn saw that something as the breath and the blood and the spirit of wheat—and of man. Dust and to dust returned they might be, but this physical form was only the fleeting inscrutable moment on earth, springing up, giving birth to seed, dying out for that ever-increasing purpose which ran through the ages.

A soft footfall sounded on the stairs. Lenore came. She leaned over him and the starlight fell upon her face, sweet, luminous, beautiful. In the sense of her compelling presence, in the tender touch of her hands, in the whisper of woman's love, Dorn felt uplifted high above the dark pale of the present with its war and pain and clouded mind to wheat—to the fertile fields of a golden age to come.